The Path Between Words

Valerie Emerson

Published by Valerie Emerson, 2024.

This is a work of fiction. Similarities to real people, places, or events are entirely coincidental.

THE PATH BETWEEN WORDS

First edition. October 6, 2024.

Copyright © 2024 Valerie Emerson.

ISBN: 979-8227471239

Written by Valerie Emerson.

Chapter 1: Pages of Change

The creaking floorboards beneath my feet sang a familiar tune as I wandered deeper into the aisles of "Whispers of the Past." Dust motes danced in the sunlight streaming through the bay window, illuminating the well-loved spines that lined the shelves. Each book whispered secrets and adventures, stories of distant lands and heartbreak, tales of triumph and despair, yet they felt stifling at that moment. I brushed my fingers over their worn covers, hoping to find inspiration in the textured fabric of their stories, but the thrill that usually accompanied the touch of well-loved pages eluded me. Instead, I felt an ache of longing, a yearning for something beyond the confines of my shop.

Maplewood was a small town, nestled between sprawling hills and winding rivers, where time seemed to pause as the world outside rushed on. Each day bled into the next, punctuated only by the rhythmic toll of the church bells and the gentle hum of the river that snaked along the edge of town. I knew every face that passed by the window, every little quirk and nuance of their lives; Mrs. Thompson, who always wore a lavender hat that matched her lilac garden, or young Billy, who chased after his dreams with a skateboard that had seen better days. Yet, their routines felt like heavy weights, anchoring me in place when my spirit ached to soar.

As I stood there, the faint scent of lavender from Mrs. Thompson's garden wafted through the window, mingling with the crisp smell of parchment and ink. It reminded me of long summer afternoons spent reading under the shade of the old oak tree, where the world felt vast and full of possibility. Those were the moments I cherished most, lost in the pages of novels that transported me to realms where adventure awaited at every turn. But now, the reality of my life seemed to shrink with each passing day, and I could no longer ignore the gnawing sensation that I was meant for something different.

I set the book down and stepped back, surveying the cozy confines of my shop. My beloved bookstore, once a vibrant hub of activity, now felt more like a mausoleum for forgotten dreams. The chairs were slightly askew, remnants of discussions that once flowed freely among avid readers who sought refuge in my little corner of the world. But lately, the laughter had faded, and the only sounds that filled the air were the echoes of my own footsteps.

Perhaps I needed to venture beyond the familiar. The thought sent a thrill through me, igniting a spark of curiosity that had long been dormant. What lay beyond the rolling hills of Maplewood? What stories awaited me outside this cocoon I had spun for myself? I pictured bustling city streets with people rushing about, their lives intermingling like threads in a grand tapestry. The thought was intoxicating, yet it left me feeling vulnerable, as if I were shedding a skin I had worn for too long.

With resolve blooming in my chest, I turned back to my shelves, running my fingers along the spines of travelogues and memoirs, each a reminder of the world's vastness. There was a book on the shelf that had always called to me: a guide to the National Parks of America. I pulled it from its resting place, feeling the weight of its promise. The open roads, the majestic mountains, the wild rivers—all beckoning me to step outside my comfort zone.

As I skimmed through the pages, vivid photographs leaped out at me. Golden canyons and towering redwoods, vast lakes reflecting azure skies—each image pulsed with life, igniting a yearning deep within me. I imagined the air thick with the scent of pine, the sound of leaves rustling in the wind, and the feel of cool water splashing against my skin as I dipped my toes in a mountain stream. I could almost hear the call of the wild, urging me to abandon my fears and embrace the unknown.

In that moment, I made a decision. I would not let the fear of change hold me captive any longer. I would pack a bag, grab my trusty old camera, and set off on an adventure that might just rewrite the narrative of my life. The prospect thrilled me, and for the first time in a long while, I felt truly alive.

The idea of closing the bookstore felt like pulling at the threads of my very being, a choice that would leave a mark on my heart. But I reminded myself that change was often necessary for growth, like pruning a rosebush to encourage new blooms. I could always return to Maplewood, but first, I needed to discover who I was beyond the walls of my shop.

With renewed vigor, I set about preparing for my journey. I found a vibrant backpack, slightly faded but sturdy enough to hold my essentials. I gathered my notebooks, where I'd scribbled thoughts and dreams over the years, and the camera that had captured countless moments in time. Each item felt like a piece of my story, a reminder of the life I had built, yet also a stepping stone toward the new adventures that awaited me.

As the sun dipped below the horizon, casting a warm golden glow across the landscape, I stood by the shop window one last time, looking out at the familiar streets of Maplewood. The gentle hum of the river blended with the laughter of children playing outside, and I felt a bittersweet pang in my chest. But underneath that sorrow, a thrill of anticipation bubbled up.

I closed the door behind me, the familiar jingle of the bell marking the end of one chapter and the beginning of another. The road ahead shimmered with the promise of adventure, and for the first time, I stepped into the unknown with my heart wide open, ready to embrace whatever awaited me.

The next morning arrived with a cascade of sunlight that streamed through my window, bathing my room in a warm golden hue. It was a stark contrast to the fog of uncertainty that had lingered over my thoughts just days before. I could hear the chirping of birds outside, their cheerful songs a far cry from the muted conversations of Maplewood. They were calling me to embrace the day, to step beyond the threshold of comfort and into the vibrant world waiting outside.

I slipped out of bed, anticipation coursing through my veins like a jolt of electricity. Today marked a departure from the familiar rhythm of my life, and I could feel the weight of possibility in the air. As I dressed, I reached for my favorite sundress—an explosion of sunflower yellow, it always made me feel like I was radiating joy, a walking celebration of summer. I twirled in front of the mirror, the fabric swirling around me, and laughed at my own reflection, a small act of defiance against the shadows of doubt that had loomed over me.

With a simple breakfast of toast and the last of my blueberry jam, I packed a small cooler with snacks and a thermos filled with steaming coffee. I threw in a couple of my well-loved travel guides, their spines creased from years of use, as if they too were eager to accompany me on this new adventure. I slung my camera strap across my shoulder, its weight a reassuring presence, a reminder that I would capture not just images but moments that could transform into stories.

Stepping outside, the sun kissed my skin, and a gentle breeze played with my hair. The streets of Maplewood felt different in the morning light, each house glowing with warmth and charm. The white picket fences, the wildflowers bursting forth in a riot of colors—everything seemed to whisper encouragement. I made my way to the outskirts of town, the familiar landscape giving way to the open road, a ribbon of asphalt leading me to the unknown.

As I drove, the trees flanking the road transformed from the familiar maples of my hometown to towering pines, their needles swaying rhythmically in the wind. I cranked up the radio, letting the music spill out and mingle with the wind, the lyrics a backdrop to my thoughts. The countryside unfurled before me like a lush green tapestry, dotted with patches of golden corn and grazing cattle, each scene a postcard of Americana that felt achingly picturesque.

The first stop on my journey was the nearby National Park, an expanse of wilderness I had only glimpsed in photographs. The drive twisted through the hills, revealing breathtaking views that made my heart swell with gratitude. I parked at the visitor center, my excitement bubbling over as I stepped out into the embrace of nature. The air was crisp, laced with the earthy scent of pine and the distant sound of a cascading waterfall.

As I hiked along the winding trails, I felt the burdens of Maplewood slip away with each step. The path beneath my worn hiking boots crunched softly, a rhythmic accompaniment to the symphony of chirping birds and rustling leaves. I was no longer merely a spectator in my own life; I was an explorer, a seeker of stories woven into the fabric of the landscape.

I paused at a clearing, my breath hitching at the sight before me. A breathtaking vista stretched out like a painting—a sweeping view of verdant valleys, layered mountains kissing the horizon, and a sky so blue it felt surreal. I pulled out my camera, eager to capture the moment. I framed the shot, adjusted the settings, and pressed the shutter, freezing the beauty in time. With each click, I felt like I was distilling a piece of my soul, anchoring my newfound freedom into tangible memories.

After wandering the trails for hours, I found a tranquil spot by a bubbling brook. I settled onto a large rock, allowing the cool mist from the water to refresh my spirit. Here, the world felt infinitely expansive, each ripple in the water a reminder of the changes swirling within me. I retrieved my notebook, its pages filled with half-formed thoughts and ideas, and began to write.

The ink flowed from my pen like the brook before me, each word a revelation as I poured out my heart. I wrote about the stifling weight of my old life, about my yearning for adventure, about the joy of stepping into the unknown. With each sentence, I felt the chains of predictability break, replaced by a sense of empowerment that resonated through my very core.

As the sun began its descent, painting the sky in shades of pink and orange, I reluctantly tore myself away from my idyllic spot. The promise of new beginnings filled the air, and I could almost hear the whispers of the stories waiting to be written. I returned to my car, feeling lighter, as if I had shed the layers of uncertainty that had weighed me down for far too long.

The drive back was a blur of twilight hues and the fading light of day. I couldn't stop smiling, a giddy realization blooming within me. This journey was not just about escaping the predictability of Maplewood; it was about finding pieces of myself I had long neglected. With every mile, I understood that my life didn't have to be confined to the walls of my bookstore. There were stories to chase, moments to capture, and a world brimming with possibilities waiting for me.

As I pulled back into town, the familiar streets felt different, alive with a new vibrancy that had been absent just the day before. I envisioned returning to "Whispers of the Past" with fresh energy, each book a portal to new adventures and every customer a potential friend, a kindred spirit seeking solace in the stories I cherished.

Tonight, the horizon sparkled with the promise of tomorrow. As I parked my car and stepped onto the pavement, I felt a pulse of excitement in my veins. I was ready to embrace whatever came next, armed with my camera, my notebook, and a heart open to the world. The future awaited, and I intended to meet it head-on, every step an exploration of the narrative yet to unfold.

With the sun setting behind the trees, casting long shadows that danced across the pavement, I made my way back to "Whispers of the Past." The familiar jingle of the doorbell greeted me as I stepped inside, yet today it felt like a portal, not just into my bookstore but into a realm where stories could leap off the pages and into my life. Each book around me had the power to transport me somewhere extraordinary, and as I surveyed the dimly lit shelves, I sensed that they held the keys to countless adventures, just waiting for someone daring enough to unlock them.

That evening, I began a new ritual: before closing the shop, I would choose a book at random, a way to expand my horizons and perhaps discover the world beyond my little town. As the last customers trickled out, I felt a thrill of anticipation as I reached for a slim volume hidden behind larger tomes. The cover was unassuming, but the title—The Road Less Traveled—spoke to me, as if it had been waiting all along for me to notice. I took it home, the words a promise of change echoing in my mind as I poured over its pages.

Sitting in my favorite reading nook—a plush armchair that had cradled many a late-night story—I delved into the author's exploration of choices, consequences, and the beauty of stepping into the unknown. Each sentence felt like a gentle nudge, pushing me further down the path of self-discovery I had just begun to tread. It spoke of courage, urging readers to break free from societal expectations and embrace the uncertainty of change. With every word, my resolve to embark on my own journey solidified.

The next morning dawned bright and fresh, a canvas of blue stretching overhead. I rose early, the excitement coursing through me like the rich coffee I brewed to awaken my senses. Today, I would map out a course for my adventure, inspired by the very words that had illuminated my path. I spread a large map across my kitchen table, its edges curling with age, and traced routes that spiraled out from Maplewood toward the vastness of the United States. Each line symbolized a potential adventure, a whisper of distant landscapes and stories yet untold.

My heart raced at the thought of driving along the Pacific Coast Highway, the ocean glimmering alongside me, or exploring the wild expanse of Yellowstone, where bison roamed and geysers erupted in majestic displays. There were also cities to discover, bustling metropolises bursting with culture and stories, each waiting for someone with an open heart to experience them. I grinned, envisioning myself as an intrepid explorer, armed with nothing but my notebook, camera, and a thirst for discovery.

With a sense of purpose, I penned a rough itinerary on a yellow legal pad. I would start with a drive to the mountains of Colorado, immersing myself in the crisp air and the grandeur of the Rockies. The thought of scaling trails and soaking in breathtaking vistas filled me with exhilaration. I imagined standing atop a mountain peak, my heart soaring as high as the eagles gliding overhead, the world spread out beneath me like a patchwork quilt stitched together with rivers and valleys.

Once the plan was set, I felt an unfamiliar urgency to pack my belongings. I spent the afternoon gathering everything I might need for my journey: hiking boots that had seen their fair share of trails, a sturdy tent, and a backpack filled with essentials. I also rummaged through the corners of my shop for old journals and art supplies, knowing that documenting my adventures would be just as vital as experiencing them. Each item added to my excitement, transforming the mundane into the extraordinary, as if I were packing the essence of possibility itself.

As the sun dipped low, casting a warm glow over Maplewood, I took one last stroll through town. The comforting sights—the bakery with its warm pastries, the old general store with its creaky wooden floors—were etched into my heart. They were the anchors of my past, but I was ready to set sail into the great unknown. Each step echoed with the laughter of friends and the whispers of memories, a bittersweet farewell that filled me with nostalgia and determination.

That night, sleep came slowly, my mind racing with dreams of adventure. I envisioned sunrises over mountain ranges, laughter shared with strangers who would become friends, and stories I would weave into the fabric of my life. I felt a profound sense of gratitude for the life I had led thus far, but also a thrilling recognition that the best was yet to come.

When morning broke, I packed the final items into my car, ensuring my camera was perched within easy reach. With my heart pounding in sync with the rev of the engine, I pulled out of my driveway, the familiar streets fading in the rearview mirror. The world ahead was uncharted territory, and as I drove, the landscape shifted from the gentle rolling hills of Maplewood to the grandeur of towering pines and rugged mountains.

The road wound like a river, carving its path through valleys and over hills, each bend revealing new vistas that took my breath away. I turned up the music, letting the rhythm drown out the worries that had once clouded my mind. The melodies of familiar songs filled the car, their lyrics resonating with my spirit as I embraced the freedom of the open road.

Stopping at a scenic overlook, I stepped out of the car, inhaling the crisp mountain air deeply, as if to capture the essence of this moment within my lungs. The view spread out before me, an expansive canvas painted with shades of green and blue, punctuated by the jagged peaks of the Rockies standing tall against the skyline. I fumbled for my camera, my fingers trembling with excitement as I framed the shot. With each click, I captured not just the scenery, but the joy of being alive in that moment—an affirmation of my choice to chase adventure.

Continuing along the winding roads, I found myself enveloped in the beauty of nature, each stop a reminder of the richness of life that lay beyond the borders of my small town. I explored charming mountain towns filled with local artisans, sampled artisanal cheeses and fresh pastries, and exchanged stories with fellow travelers, each encounter adding layers to my experience.

One night, I stumbled upon a local festival in a quaint village nestled among the mountains. The air was alive with laughter, the scent of roasted chestnuts wafting through the crowd, and the sound of live music drew me in. I joined a circle of dancers, letting the rhythm guide my movements as joy surged through me. For the first time in ages, I felt truly connected to the world, my heart beating in time with the laughter and music surrounding me.

Days turned into weeks as I journeyed from one breathtaking location to another, each experience a thread weaving its way into the tapestry of my life. I hiked through the awe-inspiring landscapes of national parks, slept under the stars, and stood in awe of nature's grandeur. Each sunrise brought new adventures, and each sunset was a gentle reminder of how far I had come. I captured moments not just with my camera but within the depths of my soul, embracing the essence of freedom and discovery that lay at my fingertips.

As I navigated through this vibrant world, I began to discover pieces of myself I had long forgotten, the joy of spontaneity, the thrill of new connections, and the exhilarating feeling of being alive. Maplewood had been my home, but now I was carving out my own path, one story at a time. The journey was far from over; it was merely the beginning of a new chapter, one that promised endless possibilities and adventures waiting to unfold.

Chapter 2: Unlikely Encounters

The storm was relentless, a cacophony of raindrops that transformed the world outside into a blurring watercolor painting, each splash erasing the sharp edges of reality. The quaint bookstore, nestled on a corner of Elm Street, had always felt like my sanctuary, a refuge filled with the musky scent of old paper and freshly brewed coffee. On days like this, the cozy atmosphere was thick with the warmth of familiarity; each title lined up on the shelves held its own stories, waiting to be discovered by eager readers. I had just turned the "Open" sign to "Closed," relishing the stillness that enveloped the space, when the tempest outside intensified, rattling the windows as if urging me to leave my cocoon.

But then came the crash—a sound so jarring that it cut through the comforting drumming of the rain. I jumped, my heart racing, and instinctively moved toward the door. As I swung it open, the deluge rushed in, carrying with it a gust of wind that tugged at my hair and clothes, turning me into an unintended participant in this chaotic dance of nature. And there, standing just beyond the threshold, was the source of the ruckus.

Ethan. The name felt oddly fitting, like a forgotten piece of a jigsaw puzzle finally slotting into place. He was an unkempt whirlwind of soaked denim and an indigo hoodie that clung to him like a second skin. Water dripped from his hair, which was tousled in a way that suggested he had recently lost a battle with a particularly rambunctious wind. His blue eyes sparkled, reflecting the stormy sky but holding a glimmer of mischief beneath the surface. I couldn't help but notice the way his grin broke through the rain-soaked chaos, a beacon of light amidst the gloom.

"I'm so sorry!" he exclaimed, his voice rising above the sound of the storm. He glanced back at the chaos he'd created on my doorstep—what was left of a battered umbrella that seemed to have surrendered to the elements. "It was a good umbrella until it decided to betray me."

For a moment, I simply stood there, trying to piece together the bizarre tableau. Here was this disheveled stranger, dripping wet and looking entirely unfazed by his predicament. It was as if the storm had nudged him right into my life, a twist of fate that was both unexpected and oddly welcome. I could have easily shut the door and resumed my solitude, but something held me there, rooted in place by an invisible thread of curiosity.

"Looks like it put up quite a fight," I said, my voice teasing, allowing a small smile to creep onto my lips. "You might need a new battle plan."

Ethan laughed, the sound warm and genuine, breaking the tension that hung in the air. "I suppose I'll have to upgrade to something more weather-resistant. Any suggestions?"

"Well," I replied, stepping aside and gesturing for him to enter, "I could offer you a warm drink while you consider your options. Coffee or tea?"

"Coffee sounds perfect, especially if it comes with a side of shelter from this crazy storm," he said, stepping inside, shaking off droplets like a puppy newly emerged from a bath.

As he stepped into my cozy refuge, the scent of books and coffee wrapped around him like an embrace. I busied myself at the counter, preparing a steaming cup while I sneaked glances at my unexpected guest. His energy seemed to infuse the space with a vibrancy that contrasted sharply with the dreary weather outside.

"So, do you always get caught in storms while trying to rescue rogue umbrellas?" I asked, trying to keep the conversation light.

"Only on days that end in 'Y'," he replied, feigning seriousness. "In truth, I was on my way to meet a friend, but it looks like fate had other plans. Maybe it's a sign I needed a little adventure." He leaned back against the counter, a playful grin returning to his face. "Or at least a good cup of coffee."

I handed him the steaming mug, our fingers brushing briefly, sending a jolt of warmth up my arm. There was something about the way he held my gaze, as if he was genuinely interested in everything I had to say, that made me feel both seen and valued. We fell into easy conversation, sharing stories of childhood adventures, favorite books, and peculiar encounters with city pigeons. With every laugh, every shared anecdote, I felt that initial flutter in my chest grow into something more substantial, a sensation I hadn't felt in ages.

As the rain continued its relentless patter against the roof, the storm became a backdrop to our unfolding connection. It was as if the world outside had faded away, leaving just the two of us in this little sanctuary. Time slipped through our fingers like the grains of sand in an hourglass, each moment punctuated by laughter and an unspoken understanding that neither of us fully grasped yet.

But with each sip of coffee, I began to wonder if perhaps this was the spark I had been longing for. The thought flitted through my mind like a whisper, a soft plea that echoed in the warm glow of the bookstore. Was it possible that this stranger, who had stumbled into my life drenched and disheveled, might be the catalyst for the change I had secretly yearned for?

The storm raged on outside, but inside, the air hummed with potential. As our conversation wove its way through the labyrinth of our lives, I felt an undeniable pull toward him, an urge to uncover the layers hidden beneath that boyish charm and carefree laughter. And in that moment, amidst the storm and the scent of coffee, I knew I was ready to embrace whatever adventure fate had in store for me.

The following days, the storm clouds slowly cleared, both in the sky and in my heart. The sunlight streamed through the windows of the bookstore, casting a warm glow on the shelves filled with forgotten stories. Yet, despite the brilliance of the day, my mind wandered back to that unexpected encounter with Ethan. It was strange how one fleeting moment could unravel the tapestry of a mundane routine, threading it with colors vibrant and unforeseen. Each time the bell above the door jingled, I found myself glancing up, half-hoping to see him again, half-wondering if he was merely a figment of my imagination conjured up by a dreary storm.

Days turned into weeks, and life resumed its familiar rhythm. I immersed myself in the world of words, shelving new arrivals and guiding customers toward their next great adventure. Yet, each time I recommended a novel, I felt an inexplicable longing for that same thrill of connection I had experienced with Ethan. The book spines, once an endless source of solace, seemed to mock my heart's longing for something more. The whirr of the ceiling fan above hummed a tune of complacency that rang hollow against the vibrant memories of that rainy day.

Then, on a particularly unremarkable Thursday, as I was arranging a display of summer reads, the bell chimed once more. My heart quickened, but it was only Mrs. Dalrymple, an elderly woman who frequented the store, her face alight with curiosity and a hint of mischief. She shuffled toward me, her scarf trailing behind like a banner announcing her presence. "Dear, do you ever get bored in here?" she asked, her eyes sparkling with amusement.

"Boredom is a luxury I can hardly afford," I replied with a wry smile, adjusting a particularly stubborn book that refused to sit straight. "Besides, the characters in these stories are far more interesting than my own life."

"Oh, but that's where you're mistaken!" she exclaimed, leaning closer as if to share a delicious secret. "Life is filled with stories just waiting to be written. You just have to look for them." With a wink, she added, "Or sometimes, let them come to you."

Her words lingered in the air long after she had left, a gentle reminder that stories don't always lie within the pages of a book.

The universe, it seemed, was not done spinning the threads of my narrative just yet. That evening, as I closed the store and stepped into the dusky twilight, I made a decision: I would be open to new possibilities, however unlikely they might be. I would step outside my comfort zone and seek the stories that lay just beyond the edge of familiarity.

As I wandered through the neighborhood, the scent of rain-dampened earth filled the air, and the soft glow of street lamps illuminated my path. I found myself at the local café, a cozy nook known for its eclectic décor and the best coffee in town. I stepped inside, the warmth enveloping me like a soft embrace, and made my way to the counter. The barista, a cheerful woman with an impressive collection of tattoos, greeted me with a smile.

"Just a coffee today?" she asked, her voice bubbling with enthusiasm.

"Make it a double," I replied, grinning back at her, feeling emboldened by the notion of breaking free from routine. As I waited for my drink, I turned to survey the room. It was a delightful chaos of mismatched furniture and art, with patrons scattered around, each absorbed in their own world. But my gaze fell upon a familiar figure in the far corner—a mop of unruly hair, those bright blue eyes, and that same infectious grin.

Ethan.

He seemed absorbed in a book, his expression alternating between deep concentration and bursts of laughter, as if the words were spilling joy directly into his soul. My heart raced, a peculiar mixture of excitement and trepidation washing over me. Could this be fate tapping me on the shoulder, or merely a coincidence, a playful trick of the universe?

Summoning my courage, I made my way toward him. As I approached, he glanced up, a surprised smile blooming across his face. "Well, if it isn't the bookstore keeper who saved me from an umbrella catastrophe!" His voice was warm, resonating like a favorite song. "What brings you to this side of town?"

"Desperate for caffeine," I replied, feeling slightly sheepish. "But maybe the universe had a hand in it too."

"Maybe it did," he said, his eyes sparkling with intrigue. "Care to join me? I promise this book is as good as it looks." He gestured to the tome sprawled on the table, the title obscured by the angle of my view.

I sat down, the warmth of the café wrapping around us like a shared secret. As we talked, the conversation flowed effortlessly, weaving through topics from literature to life dreams, punctuated by laughter and the occasional burst of curiosity. Ethan's passion for stories mirrored my own, and I found myself entranced not just by his words, but by the way he spoke of them—each tale a new adventure, each thought a step into the unknown.

Time slipped by unnoticed, the world outside fading into a soft blur. It was as if we had created our own little universe within those walls, one where nothing existed but the two of us and the stories we shared. The light in the café softened, casting a golden glow around us, and I felt the fluttering sensation return, but this time, it was accompanied by a sense of ease. Perhaps this was what Mrs. Dalrymple had meant—an unexpected story unfolding right before my eyes, each word a thread connecting us in a tapestry yet to be fully woven.

As the night deepened, I realized that sometimes the most unlikely encounters can lead to the most beautiful narratives, waiting to be written.

Days stretched into a haze of sunlight and quiet reflection after that unexpected encounter. The storm had dissipated, but its remnants lingered in my heart like the last drops of rain clinging to a windowpane. Each morning brought with it the familiar routine of dusting off shelves and assisting customers, yet the shadow of

Ethan's laughter danced through my thoughts, adding a new hue to my otherwise monochrome days. I could almost hear his voice echoing through the aisles, a playful reminder that the world outside my bookstore held adventures yet to unfold.

Life in the bookstore had its own rhythm, a soothing hum that I had grown accustomed to. Regulars would come and go, sharing snippets of their lives like the pages of the books I cherished. Mrs. Dalrymple continued to weave her tales of past romances and quirky anecdotes, each story leaving an indelible mark on my heart. But even her tales began to pale against the vibrant memory of that rainy afternoon with Ethan. It was as if I had glimpsed a world beyond the bindings of the novels, a world where my own story could intertwine with another.

One evening, after closing up the shop, I found myself walking the same path I had taken the day I met Ethan. The familiar streets glistened under the golden glow of streetlights, each puddle reflecting fragments of my thoughts. Just as I rounded the corner by the café, I spotted him through the window, hunched over a table, engrossed in a book. My heart leapt, and without thinking, I pushed open the door, the bell chiming like a welcoming tune.

"Back for more?" he quipped, looking up with that same disarming grin, as if he had been expecting me all along.

"I could say the same to you," I replied, feeling a rush of warmth flood my cheeks. "Is that a new book, or are you just trying to make me jealous?"

He chuckled, motioning for me to join him. "A little bit of both, I suppose. This one's a real page-turner, though. You should give it a try."

As we fell into easy conversation, the café transformed around us into our own sanctuary. The aroma of freshly brewed coffee mingled with laughter and the clinking of cups, wrapping us in an intimate cocoon. We delved into discussions about our favorite genres, from the fantastical realms of epic sagas to the quiet revelations found in literary fiction. With every shared opinion, it felt as if we were stitching together a patchwork quilt of our individual stories, creating something uniquely ours.

"What do you love most about books?" he asked, his gaze unwavering, as if he were unearthing buried treasures within me.

I paused, contemplating. "I think it's the ability to escape reality," I began, feeling the words flow like an unrestrained stream. "Books have this magical quality—they can transport you to worlds you never knew existed, allow you to live a thousand lives in one lifetime. But more than that, they connect us. Each story is a thread that binds us to someone else, a shared experience even if the characters are fictional."

He nodded, a thoughtful expression on his face. "You're right. Stories are the essence of who we are, the blueprints of our existence. They shape our dreams and, sometimes, even our realities." His voice held a weight, as though he understood the power behind those words all too well.

As the night deepened, we lingered over our drinks, oblivious to the café closing around us. It felt as though the universe had conspired to create this moment—two souls meeting amid a chaotic world, finding solace in the shared experience of words and dreams. With each laugh and shared glance, I began to see Ethan not just as a charming stranger but as a potential co-author of my unfolding narrative.

Just as I thought the evening would stretch on indefinitely, he glanced at his watch, his brows furrowing slightly. "I have to get going," he said reluctantly. "But can I see you again? Maybe for a bookshop visit, or we could grab coffee and discuss our reading lists?"

A rush of excitement coursed through me, and I nodded eagerly. "I'd like that. Very much."

As we stepped outside, the cool night air felt electric, crackling with possibility. We walked together for a while, our conversation fading into comfortable silence, the city buzzing around us. He paused at the corner, turning to face me, the streetlights casting a warm glow on his features. "Tonight was really great," he said softly, his blue eyes sparkling with sincerity. "I'm glad you came in."

With that, he leaned in, his lips brushing against my cheek in a gentle goodbye. The warmth of his breath sent a shiver down my spine, igniting a spark of hope I hadn't realized I craved. I watched him walk away, my heart thrumming with the realization that perhaps this was the beginning of a story worth telling.

In the days that followed, anticipation fluttered in my chest like the pages of a well-loved book waiting to be opened. We exchanged messages, sharing quotes from our favorite novels and recommendations that sparked endless conversations. Each text felt like another thread weaving our lives together, creating a tapestry of shared interests and undeniable chemistry.

But just as our connection began to deepen, the specter of doubt crept in, its fingers brushing against the edges of my excitement. I had grown comfortable in my solitude, a haven where I could wrap myself in the familiar embrace of literature. What if stepping into this new chapter brought chaos rather than the beauty I imagined? The thought of risking my heart was both exhilarating and terrifying.

Yet, as the sun rose and set in a cycle of hope and hesitation, I found myself drawn back to the stories that had once anchored me. They spoke of love, loss, and the beauty found in the delicate dance of vulnerability. I had always believed that life mirrored art, and perhaps it was time to embrace the unpredictability of my own narrative.

One evening, as I flipped through a particularly poignant novel, my phone buzzed with a new message from Ethan. "Let's meet tomorrow," he wrote. "I found a little bookstore that's supposed to be amazing. I want to explore it with you."

A surge of determination flooded my veins. I could feel the familiar flutter return, but this time it was accompanied by a sense of purpose. I was ready to step outside my comfort zone, ready to see where this story could lead us. As I put down the book and gazed out the window, watching the world bathe in the golden hues of twilight, I realized that every great adventure begins with a single step into the unknown.

With my heart racing, I texted him back, a smile tugging at the corners of my lips. "I'd love to." In that moment, I understood that sometimes, the most beautiful stories are the ones that unfold when we least expect them, inviting us to turn the page and discover the magic hidden within the chapters of our lives.

Chapter 3: Pages and Heartbeats

The afternoon sun streamed through the dusty windows of "Whispers of the Past," casting a warm, golden glow over the shelves crammed with books whose spines had seen better days. The aroma of freshly brewed coffee wafted through the air, mingling with the faint scent of old pages, creating an intoxicating atmosphere that wrapped around me like a beloved old sweater. I nestled into my usual spot in the corner, a battered armchair that seemed to have been stitched together by the hands of countless readers, each one leaving a mark of their own. It was my sanctuary, a place where time slowed down, and the outside world faded into a soft hum.

Ethan slid into the seat across from me, his presence electrifying in the muted chaos of the café. He had an easy charm, his smile crinkling the corners of his blue eyes as if he were perpetually amused by some private joke. His dark hair fell carelessly over his forehead, and when he spoke about the books that filled our conversations, he transformed into a storyteller, weaving narratives that sparked something within me.

On this particular day, the café bustled with life, a medley of laughter and soft chatter surrounding us. I cradled a steaming mug in my hands, feeling the heat seep through the ceramic, grounding me in this moment. Ethan leaned in, his voice barely rising above the noise. "What's your favorite book?"

I hesitated, lost in a labyrinth of titles and characters that had woven themselves into the fabric of my existence. "I think it has to be The Great Gatsby," I finally admitted, the words tasting bittersweet on my tongue. "There's something about the longing for something just out of reach that resonates with me."

Ethan nodded, a thoughtful expression crossing his face. "F. Scott Fitzgerald captured the essence of hope and disillusionment so beautifully. It's like he was speaking directly to the hearts of the lost."

As we continued our literary exchange, I felt the walls I had built around my heart begin to crack. Each shared book became a bridge, connecting us in ways I hadn't anticipated. The vibrant descriptions of characters' lives and the emotional landscapes we navigated felt like threads weaving us closer together, pulling me from the cocoon of solitude I had wrapped around myself for far too long.

Then, as if sensing the delicate moment between us, Ethan leaned closer, his voice a soft murmur that sent a shiver of anticipation down my spine. "Have you ever thought about writing your own story?" The question hung in the air like a sweet, forbidden fruit, daring me to reach out and taste it.

I swallowed hard, my heart racing in tandem with my thoughts. Writing had always been my secret desire, a flickering flame buried under layers of self-doubt and fear of failure. I had filled countless journals with half-finished tales, snippets of poetry, and fragments of memories that felt too fragile to share. But hearing Ethan's gentle inquiry opened a floodgate of emotions I had long kept at bay. "Not really," I replied, trying to mask the tremor in my voice. "I guess I've never thought my stories were worth telling."

His eyes held mine, a silent challenge simmering between us. "That's the beauty of stories, though. They belong to the storyteller. If it matters to you, it matters to someone else. You could inspire someone who's feeling lost, just like we were talking about with Gatsby."

A rush of warmth blossomed in my chest, not only from his encouragement but from the realization that he truly cared about my thoughts and aspirations. My heart pulsed like a drumbeat, louder than the café chatter, and I felt alive, every nerve ending tingling with possibility.

"But what if they're terrible?" I countered, the skepticism creeping back in, the familiar weight of my insecurities pressing down. "What if no one cares?"

Ethan chuckled, a rich, genuine sound that filled the air between us. "What if they're not? You'll never know until you try. Every great writer started with a blank page, wondering if their words would mean anything. It's the act of creating that matters, not the judgment that comes afterward."

His words resonated like a familiar tune, a gentle push against the barricades of my self-doubt. I found myself leaning in, drawn to the light in his eyes as he spoke, a spark igniting in the pit of my stomach. The thought of crafting my own narrative, of shaping characters and breathing life into their stories, sent shivers of excitement through me. Yet, lurking beneath that exhilaration was a twinge of fear. Would I truly have the courage to share my voice with the world?

We spent the rest of that afternoon weaving through our thoughts, our laughter mingling with the gentle clinking of cups and the whispers of fellow patrons. Each moment felt imbued with an intoxicating magic, the kind that lingers long after the sun sets. I could sense the unspoken bond forming, a connection deeper than mere friendship, tethering our hearts together through shared vulnerability.

The world outside blurred into a canvas of vibrant colors, the sky shifting from the warm hues of late afternoon to the cool blues of twilight. As I sipped my coffee, my thoughts danced around the idea of storytelling, and for the first time in years, I felt the stirrings of hope—a yearning to capture the fragments of my life on paper. It was exhilarating and terrifying, yet the idea blossomed within me, blooming like wildflowers in a forgotten field, and I knew that with every word, I would weave my own tapestry of dreams and heartbeats.

As the evening light began to dim, and the chatter in the café swelled into a comforting background hum, I stole a glance at Ethan. He caught my gaze, and in that moment, I saw not just a friend but a kindred spirit—someone who dared to see the flickering flames of potential within me. Perhaps, just perhaps, I could transform those quiet whispers in my heart into a symphony of words that could resonate beyond the confines of my imagination.

As the café dimmed under the weight of twilight, I felt an intoxicating blend of excitement and apprehension swirling within me. The lively chatter around us softened into a muted backdrop, allowing the thoughts that had taken root to flourish unimpeded. I was acutely aware of Ethan's gaze, a gentle weight on my soul that seemed to both challenge and encourage me to dive deeper into this newfound yearning. Each sip of coffee felt like a small step toward an awakening I hadn't anticipated, and I could almost hear the echo of my dreams whispering back to me.

The barista, a sprightly young woman with bright pink hair, came over to refill our cups, her infectious smile momentarily pulling me back from the precipice of my own thoughts. "You two look like you're plotting something delicious," she teased, her eyes sparkling with mischief. I laughed, the sound bubbling up from my core, and Ethan grinned, a knowing look passing between us.

"Just brainstorming ideas for a story," he said, his tone light but his eyes serious. "You know, the kind that would sweep you off your feet."

"Sounds like a bestseller in the making," she replied with a wink, and as she walked away, I couldn't help but feel a spark of validation in her words. Maybe there was something there, some hidden treasure I had yet to unearth.

Ethan leaned back in his chair, his fingers tracing the rim of his cup, a contemplative expression settling over his face. "You should really consider it, you know? The world needs more stories, especially those that come from a genuine place."

"What do you mean by 'genuine'?" I asked, tilting my head slightly as I considered his words.

"Authenticity," he replied, his voice steady. "Everyone has a story to tell. The moments that seem mundane to us can resonate deeply with someone else. It's the way you frame them that gives them life. And I have a feeling your perspective is unique."

A wave of warmth washed over me, and my heart fluttered at the thought that perhaps my experiences weren't as trivial as I had once believed. I thought of my childhood—those long summers spent exploring the woods behind my house, the way the sunlight filtered through the leaves like shimmering gold. I could almost feel the cool breeze against my skin, the exhilaration of discovery tinged with a sense of freedom that felt so far removed from my current reality.

"What would I even write about?" I mused aloud, my voice barely above a whisper. "I'm not sure my life is that interesting."

Ethan tilted his head, a playful smirk dancing on his lips. "That's where you're wrong. Life is full of interesting moments, even the small ones. You just need to learn how to see them."

The corner of my mouth tugged upward, and I shook my head in mock disbelief. "You make it sound so simple."

He shrugged, a teasing glimmer in his eyes. "That's because it is, in a way. The challenge comes from turning the ordinary into something extraordinary. You have to dig deeper, find the beauty in the chaos."

As the words sank in, I found myself lost in thought, imagining characters and plots weaving through the tapestry of my life. The idea of crafting a narrative from my own experiences felt both daunting and exhilarating, like standing at the edge of a cliff, staring into the vast unknown. Could I really harness that energy?

Our conversation drifted seamlessly from storytelling to the layers of our lives, each revelation punctuated by laughter and lingering glances that felt charged with unspoken promises. The world outside the café faded into shadows as the night wrapped around us like a soft blanket, the streetlights flickering to life, casting a warm glow onto the sidewalks.

"Do you ever feel like you're living in a story?" I asked, the question slipping out before I could reel it back in.

Ethan's expression softened, his gaze drifting toward the window where the rain had started to fall, each drop racing down the glass like a fleeting thought. "Every day, actually. Life is the greatest narrative, filled with unexpected plot twists, cliffhangers, and characters who surprise you at every turn. You just have to learn how to read between the lines."

I leaned back, considering his words. Perhaps I had been so focused on the mundane that I had forgotten to look for the extraordinary nestled within it. The world beyond the café was alive with stories waiting to be told, each raindrop a potential spark of inspiration.

The evening slipped by in a haze of conversation and connection, as Ethan continued to coax the dormant words within me into the light. He shared anecdotes from his own life, painting pictures of summer adventures and winter misadventures that had shaped him into the person he was today. I felt a kinship forming, an understanding that transcended the surface of our interactions, pushing us toward a deeper connection.

As the café began to empty, the barista waved goodbye, leaving us with the last dregs of our coffee and the remnants of the warmth that had enveloped us. I glanced at the clock on the wall, disbelief creeping in as I realized how much time had slipped away.

"I should probably head out," I said reluctantly, feeling the pang of disappointment at the thought of leaving this cocoon of creativity and camaraderie.

Ethan, however, wasn't ready to let the evening end. "Wait. Let's do this again. I mean, I'd love to hear more about your ideas. And I think you'd really enjoy the process of writing. Let me help you find your voice."

His words wrapped around me like a cozy scarf, bringing with them the promise of exploration and encouragement. "Okay," I replied, a smile blooming on my lips. "I'd like that."

As I stepped outside into the cool, damp air, the world felt transformed. Each raindrop was a reminder of possibility, each breath a declaration of newfound courage. I glanced back at the café, the lights twinkling like stars against the dark canvas of the night. Perhaps, just perhaps, I could let my voice resonate in the same way, weaving a narrative that would connect the dots of my life into something beautiful.

With every step away from "Whispers of the Past," I felt the lingering warmth of possibility radiate through me, an ember of inspiration that had ignited a fire within. The journey ahead was unknown, but for the first time in a long while, I felt ready to embrace it—ready to write my own story, one heartbeat at a time.

The following days after that conversation felt like a delicate dance, a choreography of thoughts and emotions swirling around my mind. Each time I entered "Whispers of the Past," the familiar aroma of roasted coffee beans and baked pastries washed over me like a warm embrace, yet this time it felt different. I found myself looking for Ethan not just to exchange book recommendations but to share something deeper, an exploration of those timid dreams that had begun to unfurl within me.

He had become my confidant, the unexpected catalyst for a transformation I hadn't known I craved. On our next visit, I settled into the worn armchair, feeling both nervous and exhilarated, a delicate balance of anticipation hanging in the air. When Ethan arrived, the light in his eyes seemed brighter, as if he were a fellow traveler, equally eager to navigate the uncharted territory of creativity.

"Hey there, dreamer," he said, his voice a playful tease as he slid into the seat opposite mine. "Ready to talk about your story?"

I took a deep breath, the weight of the question hanging in the air like a ripe fruit, ready to be plucked. "I think I'm ready to explore the idea," I admitted, my heart fluttering at the prospect of finally bringing those buried thoughts to the surface. "But I'm not sure where to start."

Ethan grinned, his enthusiasm infectious. "Let's break it down. What's the first thing that comes to mind when you think of writing?"

I paused, letting the silence envelop us for a moment, feeling the gears in my mind begin to turn. "Memories, I guess. Moments that shaped me."

"Perfect. Let's dig into that. What's a memory that sticks out?"

I could almost feel the door to my past creaking open, the dust of forgotten stories swirling around me. "There was this summer when I was ten," I began, my voice steadying with each word. "I spent weeks exploring the woods behind my house, the sunlight filtering through the trees like a thousand tiny spotlights illuminating my path. I remember feeling so free, like I could do anything."

Ethan leaned in, his eyes sparkling with interest. "That sounds beautiful. What did you find there?"

My mind danced back to that sun-drenched summer, where every corner of the forest seemed to hold magic. "I found a stream," I said, my heart warming at the memory. "It felt like a secret, a hidden world away from everything else. I would sit there for hours, listening to the water and imagining adventures."

He nodded, his expression encouraging. "That's a story waiting to be told. Think about how that sense of wonder shaped you. How did it make you feel? Did you ever find anything unexpected?"

I closed my eyes, letting the memories wash over me. "I did, actually. One day, I found a tiny, abandoned nest on the ground. It was empty, but the way it cradled itself in the grass struck me. I took it home, thinking of all the stories it must hold—of where it had been, the journeys it had taken."

Ethan's smile widened. "Now that's a metaphor if I've ever heard one. A nest symbolizes home and growth. You could weave that imagery into your narrative. It could be about finding your voice, about reclaiming those stories that felt lost."

His words struck a chord deep within me. The concept of reclaiming what was once lost resonated in ways I couldn't fully articulate. There was a sense of urgency in my chest, a feeling that this was more than just a story; it was a reclamation of my identity.

"Can you help me?" I asked, vulnerability lacing my tone. "Help me figure out how to write it?"

Ethan leaned back, contemplating my request with a thoughtful expression. "Absolutely. But first, we need to set the stage. You need a character, someone who embodies those feelings you're trying to express. Who were you back then? What did you want?"

I felt the wheels of creativity begin to turn again, the characters of my childhood starting to take shape in my mind. "I was brave, I think. I wanted adventure. I wanted to feel like I belonged somewhere."

He nodded, taking it all in. "Good. Now, let's create a landscape for this adventure. What was the world like around that stream? What obstacles did you face?"

I felt the forest come alive in my imagination—the trees stood tall, their branches whispering secrets, while the stream bubbled over rocks, singing a song of freedom. "There were thorns, prickly bushes, and the occasional scare from a startled deer. It felt wild and unpredictable."

"Just like storytelling," Ethan replied, a gleam of inspiration lighting up his face. "You need those obstacles to make the journey worthwhile. It's what keeps readers engaged. They want to root for your character as she navigates her way through challenges."

Our discussion flowed effortlessly, weaving a tapestry of ideas that ignited my passion. Hours slipped away unnoticed, and I could have easily spent the entire night lost in this world we were creating. As I spoke, I felt my confidence building, layer by layer, like a brick wall turning into an intricate mosaic.

Just when I thought the night couldn't become any more surreal, Ethan shifted the conversation toward something more personal. "Tell me about your fears," he said, his tone gentle yet probing. "What's holding you back from writing?"

The question struck a nerve, sending ripples of vulnerability coursing through me. "I guess... I'm afraid it won't be good enough," I confessed, the admission feeling like a weight lifted. "What if I put myself out there and it all falls flat?"

Ethan's expression softened. "Every writer feels that way, I promise you. But remember, it's not about perfection; it's about connection. Your truth will resonate with someone, and that's what matters."

I met his gaze, finding solace in the sincerity of his words. The weight of my fears began to feel a little lighter, as if the act of sharing them had transformed them from daunting shadows into mere whispers.

That evening was a revelation. By the time we said our goodbyes, the stars had begun to peek through the veil of clouds, twinkling like distant possibilities. I left the café, my heart buoyant with newfound determination, the ember of inspiration roaring into a warm flame.

Over the next few weeks, the forest in my mind flourished with stories, each visit to "Whispers of the Past" deepening my understanding of the craft. I wrote late into the night, pouring my heart into the pages, creating characters who echoed the parts of myself I had hidden away. Each word felt like a step forward, each sentence a bridge toward the self I was learning to embrace.

Ethan became not only my confidant but also my cheerleader, his encouragement wrapping around me like a warm blanket. We exchanged snippets of my writing over coffee, his insights sharp and illuminating, guiding me through the maze of emotions and experiences that had once felt insurmountable.

As I embraced this journey, I discovered that storytelling was not merely an act of creation; it was a way to reclaim the narrative of my life. I found myself writing not just about the past but about the hopes I held for the future, each page a testament to the resilience I had nurtured.

With every story I crafted, I began to realize that my voice was worth sharing, that the echoes of my experiences could resonate beyond the confines of my imagination. And in that realization, I found the courage to step into the light, ready to embrace the unfolding story of my life—one heartbeat at a time.

Chapter 4: Reawakening Inspiration

A soft glow illuminated my cluttered desk as dawn crept through the half-drawn curtains, casting playful patterns on the worn wood. The quiet of the early morning enveloped me, a stark contrast to the cacophony of thoughts that had kept me tossing and turning throughout the night. The remnants of sleep clung to my eyelids, yet the weight of inspiration pulled me from the comforts of my bed. With hesitant resolve, I slid out from under the blankets and made my way to the dusty corner of my room, where my old journal lay forgotten beneath a stack of neglected books and half-empty coffee mugs.

Picking it up felt like discovering a long-lost friend, the spine creaking softly as I opened it to pages yellowed with time. The familiar scent of aged paper enveloped me, mingling with the faintest trace of lavender from the candle that flickered in the corner. My heart raced with an excitement I hadn't felt in years. As I settled into the embrace of my well-worn armchair, I realized this was my sanctuary, the very spot where dreams and reality blurred into a dance of possibility.

My fingers trembled slightly as I clutched the pen, a trusty companion in this journey of self-discovery. I pressed it to the page, and like a torrent unleashed, words began to flow. I wrote of sprawling fields kissed by golden sunlight, of a narrow dirt road winding through the mountains that cradled my small town of Cedar Creek. The air here was thick with nostalgia and possibility, infused with the earthy scent of pine and the sweet tang of summer rain. I could almost hear the rustling leaves whispering secrets, urging me to delve deeper into my imagination, to set free the vibrant characters and untold stories waiting patiently in the shadows of my mind.

As I wrote, my surroundings faded away, replaced by vivid scenes unfolding like a movie reel. I pictured a young woman, daring and adventurous, standing at the edge of a cliff, wind whipping through her hair as she gazed out at the endless horizon. Her heart pulsed with the thrill of the unknown, a spark of wildness that mirrored my own dormant desires. What if she, too, was searching for something beyond the mundane? What if she longed for love and adventure, just like me?

But with every stroke of the pen, a nagging doubt slithered into my thoughts. The elation of creativity was shadowed by a familiar fear: what if my words were nothing more than echoes of my fantasies, doomed to remain unshared and unheard? I glanced at the pile of rejection letters that had long since lost their sting, remnants of a battle fought and lost in the pursuit of publishing. Each letter felt like a reminder that perhaps I didn't possess the talent I so desperately wished for.

Yet, as I gazed back at my writing, a small spark of hope ignited within me. The pages held not only my dreams but the very essence of who I was, a reflection of my heart and soul. I allowed myself to imagine a future where my words resonated with others, a possibility where my stories could bridge the gap between my solitary existence and the vibrant lives of those I had yet to meet.

The sun climbed higher, bathing the room in warmth as I continued to write. I crafted vivid descriptions of my fictional landscapes, where wildflowers danced beneath an expansive sky and laughter echoed through sunlit meadows. The characters emerged from the depths of my imagination, each with their own stories to tell, their hopes and dreams intertwining with mine. I envisioned a charming bookstore nestled in the heart of Cedar Creek, a haven where locals gathered to share tales of love and loss, where my protagonist might find solace and perhaps even romance among the dusty shelves.

As my pen glided across the pages, I could almost hear the gentle chime of the doorbell ringing, welcoming visitors into this cozy refuge. I pictured the warm glow of string lights, twinkling like stars against the backdrop of the evening sky, inviting weary souls to seek refuge in the written word. The aroma of freshly brewed coffee wafted through the air, mingling with the scent of old books, a heady blend that sparked an unquenchable thirst for stories yet untold.

But even as I poured my heart into the pages, doubt still lingered like a specter in the corner of my mind. I paused, tapping the pen against my chin, wondering if I could truly breathe life into these characters and settings. What if they failed to resonate with anyone else? What if my passion, my desperate longing to share my voice with the world, was met with indifference? The thought made my chest tighten, a knot of anxiety forming as I struggled to silence the inner critic that threatened to overshadow my creativity.

In that moment of vulnerability, I remembered why I had started this journey in the first place. It wasn't about validation or recognition; it was about connection, the timeless dance of hearts reaching out through words. I had witnessed the transformative power of storytelling, the way a single sentence could spark a flame of understanding between strangers. Perhaps it was enough to write for myself, to embrace the joy of creation without the burden of expectation.

Taking a deep breath, I allowed myself to write freely, unburdened by doubt or fear. The pages became my canvas, each word a brushstroke painting the intricate tapestry of my soul. I let go of perfection and surrendered to the beauty of imperfection, finding solace in the rawness of my thoughts. Each sentence crafted was a step toward reclaiming a piece of myself that had long been hidden, a testament to resilience and the enduring spirit of creativity.

The day wore on, and as the sun dipped low, casting golden rays through the window, I felt lighter, unshackled from the chains of self-doubt. The journal transformed into a sanctuary where I could explore the depths of my imagination, where the possibilities were endless, and my voice could finally be heard. I closed the journal with a satisfied sigh, feeling a renewed sense of purpose surge through me. I was ready to dive back into this vibrant world I was creating, ready to embrace the adventure that awaited just beyond the pages.

As the ink dried on the final strokes of my thoughts, I leaned back in my chair, the sun now casting a golden hue across the room, illuminating the piles of books that had become my silent companions. A rich tapestry of stories surrounded me, each spine whispering its own secrets and dreams. The world beyond my window had transformed; vibrant greens glistened under the bright light, and the gentle rustling of leaves filled the air like a symphony, urging me to embrace my own story as fervently as I had embraced theirs.

A soft knock interrupted my reverie, and my heart leaped. It was Annie, my neighbor and best friend since childhood, who had an uncanny ability to appear precisely when I needed a spark of energy—or a distraction. She popped her head through the door, a whirlwind of bright red curls bouncing with enthusiasm. "You look like you've seen a ghost!" she exclaimed, her voice lilting with mischief. "Or maybe a muse?"

I chuckled, feeling the warmth of her presence wash over me like a cozy blanket. "More like a muse that finally decided to show up after a long vacation," I replied, motioning for her to join me. She plopped down in the chair opposite mine, the fabric squeaking in protest, and settled in as if she owned the space.

"What's brewing in that head of yours?" she asked, glancing at the open journal on my desk. "Are we talking wild romances or daring adventures?"

"Both, perhaps," I said, flipping the pages to reveal scrawled sentences bursting with life. "I've been diving into my dreams and fears, trying to weave them into something tangible. It's like I've finally given myself permission to explore."

Annie's eyes sparkled with curiosity as she leaned forward, her fingers itching to touch the pages. "I've always believed you have a gift for storytelling. You just needed to shake off the cobwebs."

Her words flitted through the air, each syllable igniting a small flame of confidence within me. "I don't know if it's a gift," I replied, half-heartedly. "What if it's just... words? What if they don't mean anything to anyone but me?"

Annie rolled her eyes, a gesture so familiar it felt like a comforting ritual. "You know better than that. You've always had a way of making people feel something. Remember the time you told that story at the campfire? We were all sitting there, wrapped up in your words like they were the softest blankets, hanging onto every single one."

A flush of warmth crept into my cheeks as I recalled that night—the crackling fire, the stars winking overhead like old friends, and the rapt expressions of my friends as I spun a tale that felt alive. "It's different now," I murmured, a hint of self-doubt creeping back in. "I don't know if I can capture that magic again."

She leaned in closer, her voice lowering as if sharing a secret. "You're not trying to recapture anything. You're building something new. Your voice has changed, just like you have. Lean into that. Let it be messy and real. You'll find your rhythm."

I inhaled deeply, letting her words settle in my heart. Maybe she was right. Maybe this was the beginning of something entirely different, a fresh canvas where my dreams could dance freely without the chains of expectation. The thought sent shivers of exhilaration down my spine.

As the afternoon light filtered through the window, a sudden idea flickered in my mind. "What if I write about Cedar Creek? About us? Our adventures, our secrets, the little moments that define us?" The notion felt like a leap into the unknown, an exhilarating plunge that sent my heart racing.

"Now that's a story worth telling!" Annie's enthusiasm was infectious, her laughter ringing out like a bell. "We've had our fair share of escapades—who wouldn't want to read about that?"

In that moment, inspiration surged like a tidal wave, washing over me and infusing my thoughts with vivid imagery. I could see us now, a duo of misfits embarking on small-town adventures that left imprints on our souls. There were summer evenings spent lying on the grass, sharing dreams under a sky painted with stars; lazy afternoons exploring hidden trails that wound through the whispering pines; and spontaneous road trips, where we belted out our favorite songs, our laughter echoing into the night.

"I can already see it!" I exclaimed, the excitement bubbling within me. "The way you always insisted we take the scenic route, even if it meant getting lost for hours. The time we snuck into that abandoned house to uncover its secrets..."

"Or the day we turned an ordinary picnic into a full-blown scavenger hunt!" Annie interjected, her eyes sparkling. "We had everyone running around like crazy, and we were just sitting there, eating cupcakes and pretending we were in a grand adventure."

Our shared laughter enveloped the room, weaving a tapestry of memories that inspired me to keep writing. I felt the chains of self-doubt slowly loosening, replaced by a newfound determination to share our stories—the laughter, the heartaches, the moments that shaped us into who we were.

"I think I'll start with a chapter about our escapades," I declared, a gleam of mischief lighting my eyes. "And maybe sprinkle in a little romance along the way. After all, what's a good story without a touch of love?"

Annie raised an eyebrow, a playful smirk on her lips. "Are you implying you have a secret crush you're planning to write about?"

I feigned shock, pressing my hand to my chest dramatically. "Me? A crush? How scandalous! I'd never..."

"Right," she teased, her laughter cascading through the room like sunlight breaking through clouds. "You know I'm here for all of it—the stories, the romances, and the heartaches. Just promise me one thing: if you ever write about our lives, make us look really cool."

As our laughter faded into the warmth of the room, I felt an undeniable sense of purpose settle within me. This was my time, my journey, and with every stroke of the pen, I would reclaim the power of my voice. I was ready to dive into the vibrant world of Cedar Creek and breathe life into the pages that had once felt so daunting.

With my heart ablaze and my spirit renewed, I leaned over my journal, the blank pages inviting me into the depths of my imagination. I was not just an observer in my life; I was its creator, ready to embrace the beautiful chaos of my story as it unfolded, one word at a time.

With a renewed sense of purpose coursing through me, I flicked open my journal to a fresh page, heart racing with the thrill of embarking on a new adventure. As my pen met the paper, I could practically hear the whispers of Cedar Creek, coaxing me to share its magic and mysteries. The sun dipped low outside, casting long shadows that danced across the room, a perfect backdrop for the world I was about to create.

I envisioned Cedar Creek as more than just a backdrop; it was a character in its own right, pulsating with life and personality. The sleepy town, nestled between undulating hills, was cloaked in a serene beauty that belied the stories hidden within its confines. Each brick in the quaint buildings lining Main Street held a tale of its own, echoes of laughter and tears that hung in the air like the scent of fresh pastries wafting from the local bakery. I could picture Mrs. Reynolds, the elderly owner, dusting flour from her apron as she set out warm blueberry muffins, her laughter as hearty as her recipes.

The corners of my mouth curled into a smile as I wrote about the ramshackle old library that stood on the edge of town, its sagging roof and peeling paint telling stories of a forgotten time. Inside, the scent of aging paper mingled with the faintest trace of mustiness, creating a comforting embrace. I could almost feel the weight of those books, each one a portal to another world, filled with adventure and heartbreak. It was a place where I'd spent countless afternoons lost among the shelves, dreaming of far-off lands and daring heroines, filling my mind with tales that ignited my own ambitions.

Yet, amidst the charm, Cedar Creek had its secrets—those whispered hushed in the shadows of alleyways and echoed among the gossiping townsfolk. As I let my imagination run wild, I crafted characters who would breathe life into these stories, intertwining their lives with the very fabric of the town. I introduced Lily, a spirited artist who had recently returned after a decade spent in the bustling chaos of the city. Her heart was heavy with the weight of past mistakes, yet her spirit burned bright, determined to reclaim her voice through vibrant canvases splashed with color. In my mind's eye, I could see her sitting on the bank of the creek, brush in hand, capturing the sunset's glow in a riot of hues, her laughter echoing through the trees.

Then there was Marcus, the brooding bookshop owner with a mysterious past. He had an air of quiet intensity, the kind that drew people in and left them wanting to know more. I pictured him perched on a stool in his cozy shop, surrounded by the musty smell of old books, his dark hair tousled as he lost himself in thought. Rumor had it that he had traveled the world, gathering stories and experiences, only to find solace in the heart of Cedar Creek. The dynamic between him and Lily was electric, an unspoken tension that thrummed beneath the surface, waiting for just the right moment to ignite.

As the words flowed from my pen, I wove their lives together, crafting a tapestry of connection, hope, and second chances. Each character became a reflection of my own longings and fears, and I realized that perhaps I was writing not just their stories but my own—a narrative threaded with the intricate dance of love and redemption. I wrote of stolen glances and quiet conversations, of late-night strolls under a canopy of stars where secrets slipped into the cool night air, each confession a step closer to unraveling the barriers that held them apart.

With every line, the world around me faded further into the background, leaving only the vibrant landscape of Cedar Creek and its inhabitants. I lost track of time, consumed by the rhythm of the words as they poured from me like water from a spring, each drop shimmering with the essence of my emotions. I could see the vibrant colors of Lily's paintings come to life on the pages, each stroke carrying a story of its own, while Marcus's literary world blended seamlessly with the rich tapestry of the town.

As the sun sank below the horizon, I finally set my pen down, a satisfied sigh escaping my lips. The journal lay open before me, pages filled with dreams and desires, reflections of my journey intertwined with those of my characters. Yet, as the ink dried, a new thought flickered at the edges of my mind—a pulse of possibility that sent shivers down my spine.

What if I took this further? What if I shared these stories beyond the confines of my journal? The mere notion was electrifying, sending a rush of adrenaline through my veins. I envisioned an entire collection, a vibrant mosaic of Cedar Creek's tales, each one revealing the depth and richness of the human experience. I could almost hear the clink of glasses in a packed café as I read snippets to an eager audience, their faces illuminated by the glow of candlelight, hanging on to every word.

My heart raced at the thought of setting my stories free, of connecting with others through the very essence of my existence. I could almost feel the warmth of a welcoming community, where voices intertwined in laughter and tears, celebrating the triumphs and trials of life. But the flicker of excitement was swiftly tempered by the shadow of doubt. What if they didn't resonate? What if the stories remained buried, much like my own fears?

Just then, a soft knock interrupted my spiraling thoughts. It was Annie again, her expression a mix of curiosity and concern. "You've been awfully quiet in here. What's going on?" she asked, her gaze flitting to the open journal filled with my scrawl.

I glanced up, feeling a spark of courage ignite within me. "I think I want to share these stories. All of them. About Cedar Creek, about Lily and Marcus, and about... me."

Annie's eyes widened with delight, and I could see the joy radiating from her. "That's incredible! You've always had a way with words, and this place—this town—is bursting with stories waiting to be told. You need to share it with the world."

Her encouragement wrapped around me like a warm embrace, and the weight of uncertainty began to lift. I could picture myself standing in front of an audience, my heart racing, as I shared the tales that had once lived only in my imagination. There was magic in the idea, an invitation to connect and resonate with others, to break free from the cocoon of doubt that had held me captive for far too long.

As night settled over Cedar Creek, the stars began to twinkle overhead, and I felt a sense of clarity wash over me. The journey ahead would be filled with challenges and unknowns, but I was ready to embrace it all. With each word penned, I would forge connections, breathe life into dreams, and, perhaps most importantly, find my voice in the symphony of life. And in that moment, surrounded by the memories of my past and the hope of the future, I knew I was no longer hidden—my story was ready to unfold, vibrant and alive, just like the town that had nurtured it.

Chapter 5: Storms of the Heart

The bookstore hummed with the palpable energy of creativity, a warm haven in the cool embrace of twilight. The wooden shelves, lined with dog-eared novels and fresh paperbacks, seemed to lean closer, eager to catch snippets of the evening's offerings. Warm, golden light spilled from an antique chandelier, illuminating faces that glowed with the soft flicker of anticipation. A gentle aroma of brewed coffee and well-worn pages wafted through the air, mingling with the scent of fresh pastries. Every corner of the shop held a story, a memory tucked between the pages of a book waiting to be discovered.

As the poetry reading unfolded, I felt the intoxicating rush of vulnerability swell within me, coaxing me closer to the edge of my own insecurities. It was a vibrant gathering, the crowd a kaleidoscope of humanity—students scribbling notes, seasoned poets clutching their dog-eared collections, and curious patrons drawn in by the siren call of words. I spotted Ethan among them, a lighthouse amidst the swirling sea of faces. He leaned slightly forward, his dark curls catching the light like the shiniest of treasures, his green eyes glimmering with an appreciation that made my heart race.

When my name was called, I swallowed hard, my hands clammy against the worn paper of my poem. The microphone felt foreign in my grasp, an alien entity that magnified the echo of my pulse. I glanced at Ethan, who offered a reassuring nod, and in that moment, the world around me faded into a comforting blur. I took a deep breath, each word a fragile thread weaving the tapestry of my emotions. The verses spilled from my lips, each line a revelation of heartache and hope, a dance between joy and sorrow. I could feel the weight of my vulnerability thrumming in the air, a shared heartbeat between me and the audience.

When I finished, the silence hung for a heartbeat longer than expected, thick and charged, before the applause erupted. Ethan was the first to stand, his enthusiasm a beacon that cut through the remaining haze of my self-doubt. His hands clapped together with genuine fervor, and I felt the heat of a thousand glances turn toward me, but it was Ethan's pride that warmed me from within, a glow that wrapped around my insecurities like a tender embrace.

Later, as the crowd thinned, we found ourselves on the bookstore's quaint porch, the wooden planks creaking underfoot. The air was tinged with the sweet promise of a coming storm, a hushed energy that electrified the atmosphere. Ethan leaned against the railing, the fading light casting shadows across his face, accentuating the contours of his features in a way that made him look almost ethereal. I couldn't help but admire the way he seemed to absorb the world around him, his gaze sweeping across the horizon as if searching for answers hidden in the clouds.

It began as lighthearted banter, the kind that danced effortlessly between two souls searching for connection. We traded anecdotes about our lives, laughter ringing out like bells against the backdrop of the impending storm. But as the clouds thickened and the wind began to whisper secrets of change, the conversation shifted. Ethan's demeanor grew serious, a weight settling into the lines of his forehead. He glanced at me, vulnerability creeping into his expression, and I felt a shiver of recognition; we were both navigating storms within our hearts.

"I've been feeling lost, you know?" he confessed, the words tumbling out like leaves caught in a gust of wind. "Being a graphic designer seemed like a dream, but it's not what I thought it would be. I'm stuck in a rut, and it's like I'm just going through the motions." His voice was a low rumble, full of longing and frustration, echoing my own silent fears.

I listened intently, my heart aching with empathy. I understood that feeling, the gnawing sense of dissatisfaction that whispered late at night when the world had quieted down. "I get it," I replied, my voice steadying. "I've been feeling the same way in my writing. It's like I'm pouring my heart into these pages, but sometimes it feels as though no one is reading what I have to say." There was a rawness in my admission, a crack in the façade that I carefully maintained. It was refreshing to share these unvarnished truths, the kind of authenticity that felt rare and precious.

Ethan looked at me, his eyes wide, as if he had just discovered a kindred spirit in the most unexpected of places. The storm clouds above seemed to echo our turmoil, rumbling softly as if urging us to dig deeper. "Maybe we're both searching for something more," he said, the corners of his mouth turning upward in a hopeful smile that warmed the cool evening air. "Something beyond what we've settled for."

I nodded, feeling the stirrings of possibility weave through our conversation. "Perhaps we can help each other," I suggested, the words dancing on the edge of my lips, imbued with a sense of purpose. "You can inspire me to push my boundaries in writing, and I can help you rediscover your passion for design. Maybe together, we can navigate our storms."

Ethan's laughter rang out, light and bright, cutting through the heaviness that had settled over us. "I like the sound of that," he replied, the storm clouds seeming to part slightly, allowing a glimmer of moonlight to break through. The warmth of our connection wrapped around us like a cozy blanket, shielding us from the tempests of our uncertainties. In that moment, with the world on the brink of a storm, we stood together, two souls caught in the swirling winds of change, yet grounded in the knowledge that we were not alone in our journey.

The air shifted around us, thick with unspoken thoughts and the distant rumble of thunder, as if the universe was conspiring to mirror our internal dialogues. I leaned against the weathered railing, the wood warm from the day's sun, grounding me amidst the swirling chaos of emotions. Ethan's laughter lingered like a sweet melody, but beneath its surface was the stark reality of our mutual uncertainties. The flickering porch light cast soft shadows, dancing against our faces as the wind tousled his hair, making him look both boyish and deeply contemplative.

"Do you ever feel like you're just treading water?" he asked, his tone shifting to one of quiet reflection. "Like you're expending so much energy but never really getting anywhere?" His words struck a chord deep within me. It was a sentiment I had clung to in the silence of my writing space, a relentless worry that whispered to me in the darkest hours of the night.

I nodded, finding solace in the shared weight of our vulnerabilities. "Absolutely. It's as if we're all in this race against ourselves, and the finish line keeps moving further away." The storm outside began to break, a soft patter of rain tapping against the porch roof, lending a rhythm to our conversation that felt both soothing and intense. Each drop seemed to echo the unsettled feelings we had shared, punctuating the air with the promise of transformation.

Ethan shifted closer, intrigued by my words. "What if we made it our mission to find that finish line together?" His eyes glimmered with a light that could ignite sparks in the darkest of corners. "I mean, why not shake things up a bit? You write, and I design. We could blend our talents, create something that speaks to both of our storms."

His suggestion hung between us, electric and exhilarating. I envisioned a collaborative project, our minds weaving together narratives and visuals like threads in a rich tapestry. The prospect ignited a flame within me, the kind that ignites when inspiration strikes, and I could feel the corners of my mouth curl into a smile. "That sounds amazing," I replied, my enthusiasm bubbling over. "But what would we create? A book? An art installation? Maybe a graphic novel that combines your designs with my storytelling?"

His eyes sparkled, a glint of mischief surfacing as he pondered. "How about a collection of poems paired with illustrations? Something that captures both the raw emotion of your words and the vibrancy of your imagination." The idea blossomed in the air between us, taking on a life of its own. I could almost see it—pages filled with my verses and his art, each piece telling a story that wove through the tumult of life.

The rain picked up, a steady rhythm now, and I felt the world around us fall away. It was just the two of us, cocooned in the intimacy of our shared dreams, our laughter mingling with the sound of the storm. It was a comforting realization that our struggles didn't have to be solitary endeavors; we could create something beautiful from the chaos.

With each moment, I felt the weight of our confessions lift, replaced by a lightness that had been absent for far too long. "I can't help but think," I mused, leaning a little closer to Ethan, "that this could be the start of something transformative for both of us. It's as if we've been searching for a creative outlet and stumbled upon each other just in time."

He grinned, his smile infectious and bright, like a flash of lightning illuminating the darkened sky. "Then let's not waste any more time." His determination was contagious, and I felt my heart race with the thrill of possibility. "Let's set aside some time this week to brainstorm. Who knows? We might even uncover something that could help us both find our way back to what we love."

As the storm raged on outside, the weight of our shared aspirations swirled in the air, turning our fears into something tangible, something hopeful. I couldn't help but feel that perhaps our storms, while tumultuous, were leading us toward something significant—a rekindling of passions, a reawakening of dreams that had lain dormant for far too long.

With our plans made, the mood shifted back to lightness. The rain was relentless now, but it felt like a cleansing, washing away the remnants of doubt and fear that had clouded our minds. We started exchanging ideas, throwing out concepts and imagery that danced like sparks in the air. I could see the gears turning in Ethan's mind as he began to sketch concepts, his hand moving with a grace that mirrored the ebb and flow of the rain.

Time slipped away unnoticed, the evening darkening around us as our voices filled the space with warmth and laughter. We brainstormed until the last vestiges of sunlight disappeared, leaving us bathed in the glow of the porch light. The world outside was a blur of shadows and shapes, but in our little bubble, everything felt electric and alive.

Eventually, the laughter subsided, and we found ourselves lost in a comfortable silence, a mutual understanding weaving through the quiet. The storm continued its symphony, a fitting backdrop to our newfound ambitions. I felt a profound sense of connection with Ethan, a bond that had blossomed under the weight of our candid conversations and shared dreams.

"Can you believe how fast the evening went?" I asked, my voice barely above a whisper. "It feels like we've been on this porch for hours, yet it's all just flown by."

"Time has a funny way of disappearing when you're doing something you love," Ethan replied, his gaze drifting toward the rain-soaked street. "It's a reminder that we should pursue what ignites our spirits, don't you think?"

His words resonated deep within me, echoing the sentiment I had felt earlier in my writing. Here we were, two storm-tossed souls finding light in each other's company, ready to chase the shadows away. As the rain continued to fall, I couldn't help but feel that this was just the beginning—of something beautiful, something that would allow us to harness our storms and transform them into art.

With that thought nestled in my heart, I smiled at Ethan, my resolve solidified. Together, we would navigate this unpredictable landscape, turning chaos into creativity and vulnerability into strength, all while finding our way back to the paths we were meant to walk.

The rain continued its steady serenade, drumming softly against the roof and merging into the whispers of the night. The world felt suspended, as if time had chosen to wrap itself in the cozy cocoon of our shared dreams and aspirations. I could still feel the warmth of Ethan's presence beside me, an anchor amidst the swirling uncertainty that often engulfed my thoughts. The porch light flickered softly, illuminating his face with a golden hue that danced in harmony with the shadows.

Ethan leaned back, a look of contemplation etched on his brow. "You know," he mused, his fingers idly tracing the grain of the railing, "there's something about this place—this bookstore—that just fuels my creativity. I think it's the stories trapped within these walls. They're all waiting for someone to let them out." His eyes gleamed with the kind of passion that made me believe he could unleash the very soul of the books around us.

I tilted my head, considering his words. "Every corner holds a history, doesn't it? Each book is a doorway to another world, waiting for someone to take the plunge. That's what I love about writing—there's always a story lurking beneath the surface, just begging to be told." I leaned closer, my heart fluttering with excitement at the thought of our potential collaboration. "What if we let those stories guide us? What if we created pieces inspired by the very essence of this place?"

Ethan's eyes sparkled with intrigue, the prospect of breathing life into our visions igniting a fire within him. "We could set up a makeshift studio right here on the porch. Bring our supplies, let the world fade away while we work." The idea flowed between us, as fluid as the rain that fell, each drop fueling our creative fire. "We can play with the boundaries of poetry and visual art, letting each element inform the other."

As we brainstormed, the evening unfolded with a rhythm that echoed the patter of raindrops. The stories began to take shape, characters and scenarios springing to life in the space between us. I envisioned a series of poems inspired by the everyday lives of the bookstore's patrons—an elderly man who found solace in the pages of his favorite mystery novels, a young couple who met at the very first reading, their love story woven through sonnets and stanzas. The possibilities were endless, each narrative blossoming into a vibrant tapestry of emotions and experiences.

Ethan, meanwhile, sketched concepts that melded beautifully with my ideas, his artistic instincts sharpening the focus of our collaboration. He described how he could capture the essence of each poem through color and form, infusing life into the characters that danced through my verses. "Imagine an illustration of the old man surrounded by books, the covers forming a protective wall around him, his eyes alight with the thrill of discovery," he suggested, his voice infused with enthusiasm.

As our conversation deepened, the rain began to let up, the pitter-patter softening into a gentle whisper, allowing a silvery moonbeam to pierce through the cloud cover and cast a magical glow over the porch. I felt a sense of liberation wash over me, an exhilarating awareness that we were no longer alone in our storms. We were companions navigating through the tempest, ready to create our own shelter from the chaos.

In that moment, with our hearts laid bare, I found myself drawn to Ethan in a way I hadn't anticipated. The gentle rain had washed away the layers of uncertainty, leaving us vulnerable yet empowered. "It's rare to meet someone who understands this," I said softly, my voice barely above a whisper. "To find someone who feels as deeply as I do about their craft." I could see him processing my words, a flicker of understanding passing between us.

"Maybe that's why we're here," he replied, his gaze steady and unwavering. "Maybe it's fate or some cosmic alignment that brought us together at this moment, in this space." There was a sincerity in his eyes that left me momentarily breathless, a connection that felt significant and profound.

We sat in silence for a heartbeat, the world around us forgotten as the stars began to peek through the dissipating clouds. The night was alive with possibilities, a canvas waiting for our strokes of creativity. The conversations of the bookstore patrons still echoed in my mind, blending with the rustling leaves and distant laughter, creating a backdrop for the art we were about to create.

"Let's do it," I finally declared, a sense of determination rising within me. "Let's turn this porch into our sanctuary for creativity." The words hung in the air, and I could see the realization dawn on Ethan's face, the thrill of shared purpose igniting the spark of inspiration.

Ethan's laughter rang out, bright and infectious. "I can already envision the chaos of paint splatters and paper strewn about, the caffeine-fueled late-night brainstorming sessions." His excitement was contagious, and I felt a rush of joy surge through me, mingling with the remnants of uncertainty that had plagued us both.

As we made plans to gather our supplies the following day, the air shifted around us once more, the weight of the night slowly dissipating. A sense of renewal enveloped the porch, like the first light of dawn breaking through after a long, dark night. We stood, our hearts racing with the thrill of possibility, ready to embark on this journey together.

With a final glance at the shimmering street and the remnants of the rain pooling at the edges of the porch, I turned to Ethan, my heart swelling with gratitude for this unexpected turn of events. "I have a feeling this is just the beginning," I said, my voice brimming with hope.

"Me too," he replied, his eyes shining with the same fervor that ignited within me. "And who knows where this will take us? Our stories, our art—they could reach places we can't even imagine right now."

As we stepped away from the porch, our laughter echoed into the night, intertwining with the soft murmur of the rain as it finally gave way to stillness. We were embarking on an adventure unlike any other, armed with nothing but our dreams, our talents, and the unshakeable bond we had forged under the stormy skies. With the world before us, we were ready to embrace the unpredictable journey ahead, turning our storm-tossed hearts into something vibrant and alive, something that would resonate long after the last drop had fallen.

Chapter 6: The Boundaries of Friendship

The streets of Maplewood sparkled like a scene from a dream, awash in the golden glow of late summer. As we strolled along the charming brick sidewalks, the heady scent of popcorn from a nearby vendor mingled with the faint sweetness of blooming magnolias, wrapping around us like an invisible blanket. I could hear the distant laughter of children chasing each other, their shouts mingling with the soft strumming of a guitar from a street musician perched against a weathered lamppost. It was one of those perfect evenings that felt plucked from the pages of a fairy tale, and yet, there was a heaviness in my heart that contrasted sharply with the magic around me.

Ethan walked beside me, his laughter echoing off the brick facades of the old storefronts that lined the street. I stole glances at him, his profile outlined against the flickering light of the café signs, and I couldn't help but admire how the amber light caught the tousled strands of his hair, framing his face with an almost ethereal glow. He had this way of bringing the mundane to life, of turning an ordinary walk into an adventure, and for that, I was grateful. But with every moment spent together, every shared laugh that sent ripples of warmth through my chest, my feelings began to weave themselves into something far more complicated than I had anticipated.

As the evening wore on, the atmosphere thickened with unspoken words and lingering glances. I felt a magnetic pull between us, palpable and electrifying, but it was tangled in a web of anxiety and self-doubt. When our fingers accidentally brushed against each other, I felt an undeniable spark—a jolt of energy that raced up my arm and settled somewhere deep within my chest. In that fleeting moment, everything shifted. The laughter faded into the background, the music transformed into a distant hum, and all I could focus on was the warmth of his skin against mine.

But as quickly as the moment had arrived, insecurity washed over me, like the sudden rush of cold water. What if I ruined the best friendship I had ever known? The question hung in the air, heavy and oppressive, twisting my insides into knots. I had watched too many friendships disintegrate under the weight of unreciprocated feelings, the silence that followed a confession, the awkwardness that loomed like a dark cloud. I couldn't let that happen to us.

Ethan's laughter snapped me back to the moment, a reminder of the reality we were both navigating. We turned a corner, and suddenly the world transformed. The quaint shops gave way to a small park, where the grass shimmered like emeralds under the streetlights. An old oak tree stood tall and proud, its branches swaying gently in the breeze, as if beckoning us to sit beneath its comforting shade. I hesitated, my mind swirling with the possibilities. We had spent countless afternoons here, our laughter spilling into the air, but this time felt different. The air was thick with an energy I couldn't quite name.

"Let's sit," Ethan suggested, his voice warm and inviting, breaking through my spiraling thoughts. I nodded, swallowing the knot in my throat as we settled beneath the tree. The grass felt cool beneath me, grounding me even as my heart raced.

"Do you remember that time we built that ridiculous fort in the backyard?" he asked, his eyes dancing with mischief. "You insisted on using those neon pink sheets, and it looked like a circus tent."

I chuckled, the memory flooding back—how we had laughed until we cried, our creation collapsing under the weight of our enthusiasm. "And you kept insisting it was a 'luxurious castle.'"

"Hey, it was a castle worthy of royalty," he defended, feigning seriousness, and I laughed again, the sound bubbling up from a place deep within me. In those moments, the tension eased, and I felt the familiar comfort of our friendship wrap around me.

But as the laughter faded, so did the ease. The silence that followed felt charged, the air thick with everything unsaid. I could feel the weight of his gaze on me, searching, waiting, and it took every ounce of strength not to look back. My heart pounded in my chest like a drum, echoing the rhythm of my conflicting thoughts. What if I turned to face him and found something more? What if that unspoken connection burst forth like a dam breaking, flooding us both with the truth we had been skirting around?

"Lily," he said softly, his voice breaking through my internal battle. I dared to look at him, and the intensity in his eyes stole my breath. "Can I ask you something?"

The world around us faded, the distant laughter and music muted into a soft whisper. It was just the two of us beneath that old oak tree, two souls caught in a moment suspended in time. My stomach knotted with apprehension, a thousand possibilities racing through my mind. "Of course," I replied, my voice barely above a whisper, the vulnerability hanging between us like a fragile thread.

"I've been thinking about us," he said, his words deliberate, as if each one carried the weight of the universe. My heart lurched, a whirlwind of hope and fear crashing together. "I just... I feel like there's something more here. Do you feel it too?"

The air crackled with anticipation, and I felt my heart leap at the prospect of his words. But in that moment, I was paralyzed by the fear of what lay ahead. The thought of crossing that boundary between friendship and something more loomed large, threatening to shatter the delicate balance we had built. So instead of answering, I looked away, my gaze falling to the grass, where the shadows danced like fleeting whispers of what could be. I wanted to tell him yes, to let go of my fears, but the words stuck in my throat, caught in a tangle of uncertainty.

"I—" I started, the weight of my hesitation pressing down on me. The truth of my feelings clawed at the edges of my heart, desperate for release, but fear held me captive. How could I unravel the beautiful friendship we had woven together? How could I risk everything for a chance at something I had longed for but feared would slip through my fingers like sand?

The silence stretched between us, heavy and pregnant with anticipation, and I knew that in that moment, I stood at the precipice of change. A choice loomed ahead of me, and my heart raced with the realization that I could either leap into the unknown or retreat into the safety of the familiar.

Ethan's gaze lingered on me, searching, and the gravity of that moment pressed down like the summer humidity, thick and heavy. The world around us faded into a blur, but the warmth of his presence remained undeniable. It was as if the universe held its breath, waiting for me to respond, and in that suspended silence, I felt the weight of my indecision grow ever heavier. My heart raced with the realization that the choice was mine alone to make—either step forward into the uncharted territory of possibility or cling to the comforting familiarity of our friendship.

"Lily?" His voice, barely above a whisper, cut through the tension, a gentle nudge urging me to break free from my reverie. I hesitated, caught in the web of my thoughts, and for a heartbeat, I felt utterly lost. Yet, there was an undeniable beauty in the way he looked at me, as if he could see beyond the layers of uncertainty that wrapped around my heart. I wanted to reach out, to tell him that yes, I felt it too, that I had dreamed of us more times than I could count, but the words felt like lead, heavy and unyielding.

What if I told him how I felt, only to watch his expression shift from longing to pity? The very thought of it made my stomach churn. I could almost hear the echoes of my past, the specters of friendships that had crumbled under the weight of unspoken truths.

Those voices whispered insidiously, telling me I was foolish to even consider risking what we had. Yet another part of me—the part that ached for something deeper, something more—screamed in defiance, demanding to be heard.

"Ethan, I—" The words danced on my lips, but hesitation held me captive. My heart thrummed in my chest, a steady reminder of my beating hopes and fears. I needed to find a way to express the tangled mess of emotions swirling inside me.

But before I could collect my thoughts, he took a deep breath, his eyes widening slightly, as if he were about to reveal a secret that had been buried too long. "I don't want to make things awkward, but I can't shake this feeling that we might be more than friends." His words spilled forth, raw and unfiltered, and in that moment, I felt both relieved and terrified.

I turned my gaze away, the weight of his confession settling in my chest like a stone. "It's complicated," I finally managed to say, each syllable tinged with the flavor of regret.

"I get that," he replied, leaning closer, his earnestness captivating me. "But isn't it worth exploring? What if we're missing something incredible by not even trying?"

In his eyes, I saw a flicker of hope, a glimmer of something that felt dangerously close to desire. It was as if he held out a hand, inviting me to leap into the unknown, but the abyss of uncertainty loomed large, filled with shadows of past failures and the fear of what lay ahead. "What if it doesn't work?" I whispered, the words escaping before I could rein them in.

Ethan's brow furrowed, and he shook his head. "What if it does? We're two people who care about each other, Lily. I can't help but think that's a strong foundation."

A foundation. His words swirled in my mind, igniting a spark of courage amid my hesitation. Perhaps he was right; perhaps this friendship, which had blossomed in laughter and shared secrets, could withstand the weight of something more. But as my heart leaped at the possibility, my mind waged war against it, battling the fears that threatened to hold me back.

"I don't want to lose you," I finally admitted, the vulnerability spilling from my lips like the last rays of sunlight sinking beneath the horizon.

He moved closer, and the warmth radiating from his body wrapped around me like a comforting embrace. "You won't lose me," he promised, his voice steady and reassuring. "No matter what happens, you'll always have a place in my life."

It was an anchor in the storm of my emotions, a lifeline that offered both comfort and challenge. My heart danced in response, tempted to take a step forward, to let go of the fears that had held me captive for so long. Yet the thought of putting everything on the line made my stomach twist.

"Okay," I breathed, feeling the tension begin to ease slightly as I weighed my words carefully. "Okay, let's explore this."

Ethan's face broke into a smile that lit up his features, and the joy that radiated from him made my heart swell. But as the moment lingered, I could still feel the weight of uncertainty pressing down on us, a reminder that while the door to something new had cracked open, it was far from fully ajar.

"I'm glad," he said, his voice softening, as if acknowledging the fragile nature of this new chapter we were stepping into. "Let's just take it slow, see where it leads us."

I nodded, my pulse quickening as I tried to suppress the thrill of excitement dancing through me. We could take our time, ease into this new dynamic, and perhaps redefine what it meant to be "us."

As we sat beneath the ancient oak, a gentle breeze rustled through the leaves above, whispering secrets of change and possibility. The stars began to twinkle into existence, dotting the sky like scattered diamonds, and I couldn't help but feel a sense of wonder at how life had twisted and turned to bring us to this moment.

The air felt charged, electric, and I could almost taste the anticipation lingering between us. I leaned back, letting the cool grass cradle me as I stole a glance at Ethan, who was now gazing up at the stars, his expression soft and contemplative. There was a sense of peace in the air, a quiet promise that maybe—just maybe—we could navigate the unknown together.

We spent the next few moments in comfortable silence, lost in our own thoughts yet tethered together by a shared understanding that something new was blooming between us. The sounds of the world around us faded, replaced by the rhythm of our hearts beating in sync with the unfolding moment.

"Hey," I said softly, breaking the silence, wanting to bridge the gap between our old selves and the new possibilities. "No matter what happens, I want you to know I value our friendship."

He turned to me, his eyes brightening. "Same here, Lily. We've built something special, and that will always be the foundation."

I smiled at his words, feeling the warmth of hope blossom within me. The boundaries of our friendship were shifting, becoming something richer, more vibrant, and the fear that had once gripped me loosened its hold, allowing me to breathe a little easier.

As we sat beneath the stars, the universe around us felt expansive and inviting, filled with potential and adventure. I didn't know what lay ahead, but for the first time, I felt ready to face it alongside Ethan. Together, we would navigate this uncharted territory, trusting that our bond was strong enough to weather any storm that might come our way.

The following days felt like a delicate ballet of hesitations and half-smiles, where every glance exchanged was laden with unspoken words. Maplewood transformed into a canvas for our evolving relationship, with its winding streets and vibrant parks becoming the backdrop for our journey. The scent of fresh bread wafted from the local bakery, mingling with the robust aroma of coffee from the café where we often sat, our conversations flowing as effortlessly as the streams that danced through the nearby park. I could almost taste the sweetness of what could be, but the bitterness of doubt lingered on the edges of my thoughts, refusing to be drowned out.

One afternoon, we found ourselves perched at our usual table, a cozy nook under the sprawling shade of an oak tree. The warmth of the sun filtered through the leaves, dappling the wooden table in soft, golden light. Ethan sipped his coffee, his eyes animated as he recounted a story about a ridiculous encounter with a raccoon at a campfire. I laughed, my heart fluttering with the ease of our connection, yet beneath the surface, my thoughts churned with uncertainty.

"Lily, you're not even listening," he teased, a playful smirk on his lips.

"I am! I just... I was thinking about how we always seem to find ourselves in these ridiculous situations," I replied, forcing a smile while trying to shake off the weight of my musings.

"You mean I find myself in ridiculous situations," he corrected, leaning forward with mock seriousness. "You just happen to be my lucky charm."

The laughter that erupted between us felt like a balm, soothing the frayed edges of my worries. But as the afternoon wore on, the conversations took on a new hue, a deeper shade that hinted at the complexities we had yet to explore.

"Have you ever thought about what happens next?" Ethan asked, his tone suddenly serious, pulling me back from the reverie I had retreated into.

"What do you mean?" I responded, tilting my head slightly, trying to decipher the shift in his demeanor.

"I mean, with us. I don't want to be just friends, not anymore."

The declaration hung in the air, palpable and intoxicating. My heart raced, caught between exhilaration and fear. "Ethan, I—"

"Just hear me out," he interrupted, his eyes locked onto mine. "I know this is complicated, but what if we took a chance? What if we explored this connection?"

His words ignited a fire within me, a yearning I had been carefully stifling. The notion of risking everything for the possibility of love was terrifying, yet it also filled me with a wild, exhilarating hope. I wanted to lean into that spark, to explore the warmth of his smile and the way his laughter made the world around us fade. Yet the fear of losing the incredible friendship we had built held me back, a looming shadow in my mind.

"Ethan, I can't lose you. You mean too much to me." My voice trembled, the weight of my emotions spilling into the space between us.

"Trust me," he said, his voice dropping to a gentle whisper. "I don't want to lose you either. But I feel this... this thing between us, and I can't just ignore it. We've always been more than friends, haven't we?"

My heart fluttered at his words, the truth of them resonating deep within me. But I also felt the heaviness of doubt settle in my stomach. "What if it doesn't work? What if we can't go back?"

Ethan's gaze softened, and he reached across the table, his fingers brushing against mine, sending a thrill coursing through me. "Then we figure it out together. Isn't that what we do? We navigate this crazy life side by side."

I looked down at our hands, a tantalizing promise of what could be. Perhaps this was the moment I had been waiting for—the chance to leap, to embrace the unknown that shimmered enticingly in front of me. Slowly, I allowed my breath to steady, letting the warmth of his touch calm the tempest inside me.

"Okay," I whispered, meeting his eyes. "Let's see where this goes."

A grin broke across his face, pure and bright, like the sun breaking through the clouds after a storm. "Really? You mean it?"

I nodded, my heart racing with a mix of excitement and fear. There was no turning back now, and the thought sent shivers down my spine.

As we left the café, hand in hand, the vibrant streets of Maplewood seemed to pulse with a newfound energy, each corner imbued with the promise of adventure. The fairy lights twinkled above us, like stars come down to earth, and I could feel the magic of the moment wrapping around us, pulling us closer together.

The next few weeks unfolded like the petals of a flower, revealing layers of color and fragrance that I had never noticed before. Every shared glance became charged with meaning, and every brush of our hands sent ripples of warmth coursing through me. Ethan and I explored the depths of our connection, taking long walks through the park, where we found hidden nooks perfect for whispered conversations and shared dreams.

The world around us transformed, blooming into a vibrant tapestry of possibilities. I found myself laughing more, the kind of laughter that felt like sunlight on my skin, banishing the shadows of doubt that had lingered for too long. Together, we discovered cozy little cafés tucked away in alleyways, each one offering a new adventure, a fresh blend of flavors that mirrored the excitement growing between us.

But with the sweetness came the sharp edges of reality. As the initial thrill began to settle, I felt the pressure of expectations creeping in. What if we couldn't sustain this? What if the real world intruded upon our idyllic bubble? I began to sense the undercurrents of tension, the complexities of emotions that were threatening to disrupt the delicate balance we had forged.

One evening, as we wandered through a local festival, the air alive with laughter and the scent of caramel corn, I felt a twinge of unease. Ethan's hand was warm in mine, and yet, I could feel the weight of our uncharted territory pressing down. The festival buzzed around us—families milling about, couples dancing under the fairy lights—but my mind was racing with doubts.

"Are you okay?" Ethan asked, his brow furrowing as he noticed my silence.

"Yeah, just thinking," I replied, forcing a smile that felt a little too tight.

He squeezed my hand, his touch grounding me. "You know you can talk to me, right?"

I took a deep breath, the laughter of the festival fading into the background as I wrestled with my thoughts. "It's just... things are changing. I don't want to mess this up."

Ethan paused, a flicker of understanding crossing his face. "I get it. Change can be scary, especially when it feels so good. But maybe it's okay to embrace the uncertainty. Isn't that part of what makes this worth it?"

His words resonated, igniting a spark of courage within me. "You're right. We just have to navigate this together, no matter where it leads."

His smile returned, and I felt the tension begin to ease, if only slightly. Perhaps this was a journey, one filled with peaks and valleys, laughter and tears, but it was ours to explore.

As the night deepened, the festival lights flickered around us, illuminating the world in a soft, ethereal glow. I leaned into Ethan, allowing the warmth of his presence to envelop me, a cocoon against the uncertainties that threatened to unravel everything we had built.

The possibilities stretched before us, shimmering like stars in the night sky, and I felt a thrill of anticipation pulse through me. Together, we would embrace whatever came our way, navigating the beautiful chaos of friendship turned love, one step at a time.

Chapter 7: Confronting My Fears

The neon lights of the city flickered like fireflies caught in the throes of night, illuminating the scattered remnants of a summer storm that had drenched the streets hours earlier. I leaned against the cool, damp brick of the café wall, savoring the scent of rain mingling with the rich aroma of fried dumplings and sweet and sour chicken wafting from the takeout boxes in our hands. Each bite was a delightful escape, a burst of flavor that punctuated the air around us. Ethan and I found a small table outside, the remnants of the rain adding a sheen to the pavement that reflected the vibrant hues of the nearby signs.

"Are you really going to eat that whole thing?" he teased, a half-smile playing at the corners of his lips as he gestured toward my nearly empty container. The casual banter hung between us, light and teasing, yet beneath the surface, I felt the heaviness of unsaid words pressing down. We both had our shields up, encasing our vulnerabilities in the clinking of chopsticks and laughter.

"I can't help it if they're delicious," I retorted, grinning as I licked a morsel of sauce from my fingers. The heat of the food complemented the cool evening breeze, but it was the warmth in Ethan's gaze that truly melted the barriers I had erected around my heart. Each glance was an invitation, a silent promise that he was ready to delve deeper.

But then, just as the moon dipped behind the clouds, casting us into shadows, he leaned forward, the smile fading as he narrowed his eyes. "What are you afraid of?" he asked, the question cutting through the jovial atmosphere like a knife through soft butter. My heart raced as if it had suddenly stumbled into an uncharted territory, one where honesty was required but felt terrifyingly out of reach.

A myriad of fears unfurled in my mind, like the tangled threads of a frayed tapestry. What if he saw me as just another fleeting moment, a casual fling amidst the chaos of life? The thought twisted in my stomach, knotting it in uncertainty. "I'm afraid of... rejection," I admitted, my voice barely above a whisper. I focused on the splatters of rainwater on the pavement, avoiding his intense gaze. "And failure. I've always had this feeling that I'm not good enough, you know? Like I'll never measure up."

The silence that followed was heavy, laden with the weight of my admission. I stole a glance at Ethan, who was now staring at his takeout, the chopsticks resting idly in his hand. For a heartbeat, I thought I had crossed a line, laid bare my insecurities without his invitation. But as the seconds slipped away, I saw something shift in him, a flicker of understanding and perhaps even relief.

"I thought I was the only one," he finally said, lifting his eyes to meet mine. "I guess we all wear masks, pretending to be okay when we're really scared shitless."

His confession took me aback, a mix of surprise and kinship washing over me. Ethan, with his confident demeanor and charming smile, hiding his own fears beneath layers of humor and bravado. I had always admired his unwavering spirit, but it was in this moment that I saw him as more than just a facade. We were two kindred souls, adrift in a sea of uncertainties, desperately seeking an anchor.

We spent the night unraveling the threads of our lives, weaving through our histories with each spoken word. The city buzzed around us, unaware of the little universe we were creating at that tiny café table. I spoke of the countless rejections I had faced, the job interviews that turned into polite goodbyes, and the friendships that faded like old photographs. Each story poured from my lips like an overflowing fountain, an outpouring of the raw, unfiltered version of myself. And with every confession, I felt lighter, as if the weight of my fears was dissipating into the cool night air.

Ethan shared his own struggles, a boy who had once been overshadowed by his siblings' achievements, always trying to catch up but never quite managing to outrun the ghosts of expectations. I listened, my heart aching with empathy as he spoke of late nights spent studying, hoping to prove himself in a world that seemed determined to measure him against impossible standards.

Somewhere between the shared laughter and the poignant moments of vulnerability, dawn crept up on us. The sky shifted from deep indigo to soft lavender, and the first rays of sunlight broke over the horizon, painting the world anew. The café around us was beginning to stir; the barista inside flicked on the lights, filling the space with a warm glow. But we remained in our bubble, insulated from the chaos of the waking world.

As the sun climbed higher, I realized that our late-night confessions had acted as a catalyst, pulling back the curtain on the insecurities we had hidden for far too long. In that moment, vulnerability felt less like a weakness and more like the thread that tied us together, weaving a tapestry of trust and connection. I smiled at Ethan, my heart swelling with a newfound courage, a desire to forge ahead without the shackles of my fears.

The city was alive now, bustling with the sounds of traffic and laughter, but in that instant, all I could focus on was the warmth radiating from his gaze. Maybe vulnerability wasn't a precipice from which to fall but rather a bridge that could lead us to something beautiful, something real. And for the first time in a long time, I felt a flicker of hope, igniting within me a belief that love, too, could be waiting just beyond the horizon.

The sun fully broke through the horizon, casting a golden hue over the city, and with it came the bustle of a new day. The café we had inhabited felt different now, filled with the aromas of fresh coffee and baked goods. I watched as a barista expertly crafted lattes, steam curling like tendrils in the air, creating a cozy cocoon around us. Ethan leaned back in his chair, a satisfied smile gracing his lips as he caught me staring.

"Penny for your thoughts?" he asked, tilting his head, the sunlight catching the flecks of green in his hazel eyes. Those eyes—deep and inviting—had become my refuge through the night, grounding me in the tumult of my emotions. I marveled at how such a simple question could dissolve the weight of our midnight revelations. In that moment, the walls I had spent years building crumbled away, revealing a landscape ripe for possibility.

"Just thinking about how different today feels," I replied, searching for the right words that wouldn't betray the depth of my newfound courage. "It's like the world has transformed overnight."

Ethan's laughter chimed, a soft melody that danced through the air. "You mean the magic of confessions and greasy takeout?" He raised an eyebrow, and I couldn't help but join in his mirth, the remnants of our shared vulnerability now a foundation for a deeper connection.

As we chatted, I could feel the thrill of something awakening inside me—a sense of hope that had been buried under layers of doubt and fear. I dared to consider the possibility of what lay ahead. With every exchange, we peeled back the layers of our identities, revealing the raw, unrefined parts that often went unseen. My heart raced with a mixture of excitement and trepidation; for the first time, the thought of love didn't feel like a distant fantasy but a tangible reality waiting to be embraced.

"Let's go for a walk," Ethan suggested, rising from the table and grabbing his half-finished coffee. The invitation sent a spark of exhilaration racing through me. I followed him out into the sunlight, where the city sprawled before us, alive with a symphony of sounds. The laughter of children echoed from a nearby park, and the distant strum of a street musician's guitar filled the air with a sense of freedom.

As we meandered down the bustling streets, I felt a gentle sway of connection between us, as if the very ground we walked on was weaving our stories together. The vibrant colors of the city enveloped us—the deep reds and burnt oranges of brick buildings, the emerald green of trees lining the sidewalks. It was as if every detail danced in rhythm with my heartbeat, amplifying the thrill of this new beginning.

"So," he started, casting a sideways glance my way, "what's your idea of a perfect day?"

The question lingered, inviting me to step deeper into the realm of possibility. I hesitated, a sense of vulnerability creeping back in. My mind raced, pulling memories of sun-soaked afternoons spent wandering through art galleries, laughing with friends over shared secrets, or simply curling up with a good book in a cozy nook. "I think it would start with a morning at a local farmers' market," I said, the vision taking shape. "Fresh produce, flowers everywhere, the smell of baked bread wafting through the air. Then maybe a picnic in the park?"

Ethan listened intently, nodding as I spoke. "That sounds amazing. But where's the adventure? What about a spontaneous road trip?"

His suggestion ignited a spark of excitement within me, and suddenly, the mundane felt alive with possibility. "Okay, yes! A road trip! We could get lost somewhere—preferably near a beach, with the sound of waves crashing against the shore."

As we discussed our dream adventures, the conversations flowed effortlessly, weaving an intricate tapestry of shared dreams and aspirations. I found myself laughing freely, the weight of my fears lifting as the sun climbed higher in the sky. We were two souls, wandering through the labyrinth of our desires, and with each moment, the connection between us deepened, a shimmering thread binding our hearts.

Yet, beneath the surface, a flicker of anxiety stirred within me. Could I truly let go of the fear of rejection? Was I ready to risk my heart for a chance at love? The doubts lingered, but Ethan's presence felt like a balm, soothing the frayed edges of my heart. In the gentle touch of his hand brushing against mine as we walked, I sensed a promise, an assurance that I was not alone in this journey.

We arrived at a park, a lush expanse of green cradled by towering oak trees that offered refuge from the sun. Children laughed and played, their joy infectious as they darted around the playground. Ethan and I found a quiet patch of grass, where we spread out our picnic blanket, a vibrant plaid that seemed to capture the spirit of our day.

As we settled down, I caught sight of a small dog running wildly across the lawn, its fur glistening in the sunlight. "What do you think its name is?" I mused, pointing at the ball of energy.

"Probably something like Charlie. The classic dog name," Ethan replied, smirking. "But it could also be something like Captain Fluffykins, if we're being adventurous."

We erupted into laughter, the sound blending seamlessly with the chorus of life surrounding us. In those moments, I realized how intoxicating it felt to be free—to let go of my fears and embrace the joy of being in the present. The shadows of my insecurities faded with every laugh shared, every moment seized, and I felt the magnetic pull of something deeper taking root in my heart.

As the afternoon sun began its descent, painting the sky with strokes of pink and gold, I found myself lost in thought. I glanced at Ethan, whose gaze was fixed on the horizon, lost in a reverie of his own. I could see the way the sunlight kissed his features, highlighting the gentle curve of his smile and the softness in his eyes. In that moment, I felt the rush of vulnerability again, but it was different this time—less daunting and more exhilarating.

"Hey, Ethan," I said softly, my heart racing. "What if we really went on that road trip? Just you and me, exploring the world beyond this city."

He turned to me, his eyes sparkling with mischief and excitement, the promise of adventure hanging in the air. "I'd say, why not? Let's make it a reality."

And just like that, with the sun setting behind us and the world stretching ahead, I felt as though I had stepped into a story that was uniquely ours. A tale woven from the threads of courage and love, daring me to embrace the unknown and find joy in every fleeting moment. The fears that once held me captive began to dissolve, replaced by the warmth of possibility and the intoxicating scent of adventure.

The sun dipped lower in the sky, casting long shadows across the park, creating a whimsical interplay of light and darkness that felt almost poetic. I sat cross-legged on the blanket, savoring the last bits of our picnic—a smorgasbord of half-eaten sandwiches and crumbs of cookie dough. Ethan leaned back, his hands supporting him as he gazed out over the expanse of green. The world around us was alive; children's laughter rang out like music, blending seamlessly with the chirping of birds flitting from branch to branch.

The atmosphere hummed with possibilities, a vibrant energy that beckoned me to step further into this newfound connection. "What's next for us?" I asked, breaking the comfortable silence. The question hung in the air, its weight both thrilling and intimidating, much like the thrilling chaos of life itself.

Ethan turned to me, his eyes narrowing thoughtfully. "Well, we could start with that road trip. Just the two of us, no plans. Maybe a little spontaneity?" His voice was laced with an infectious excitement that sent a rush of adrenaline through me. The idea felt like a breath of fresh air, invigorating and liberating.

"What if we get lost?" I countered, unable to suppress the nervous laughter bubbling up inside me. "You know I'm not exactly a seasoned adventurer."

"Ah, but therein lies the charm! Getting lost can lead to the most unexpected discoveries," he replied, leaning closer, the sunlight illuminating the contours of his face. "We'll make memories, stories to tell later. What could be more thrilling than that?"

I felt my heart flutter at the prospect of it all—a spontaneous road trip, a chance to escape the mundane and dive headfirst into adventure. The thought sent waves of exhilaration washing over me. "Okay, let's do it! But we have to have at least one playlist dedicated to cheesy love songs."

He laughed, a rich sound that vibrated in the air around us. "Agreed! It wouldn't be a proper road trip without some cringeworthy sing-alongs."

As the sun began to set, painting the sky in hues of orange and pink, the park transformed into a magical wonderland, the shadows stretching and merging, creating a canvas of silhouette against the vibrant backdrop. It was here, amidst the enchanting glow of twilight, that I felt a stirring within—a realization that transcended fear and doubt. The moment felt sacred, as if we were caught in a time warp, suspended between what had been and what could be.

As we packed up our things, the city came alive around us, its rhythm quickening as people strolled, couples lingered, and families gathered for evening picnics. The ambiance buzzed with laughter and chatter, creating a backdrop to our own budding story. The scent of nearby food trucks wafted through the air—savory grilled meats and sweet funnel cakes—tempting our senses and igniting a sense of indulgence.

"Let's grab something sweet before we head home," Ethan suggested, nodding toward a bright red food truck that promised decadent desserts. My mouth watered at the thought of gooey chocolate chip cookies, warm and melting.

"Lead the way!" I replied, my spirit buoyed by the thrill of our day, now spilling into the evening. As we approached the food truck, its bright colors stood out against the darkening sky, a beacon of comfort amidst the whirlwind of urban life. The smell of sugar and cinnamon enveloped us, wrapping around us like a warm hug.

Ethan placed our order, and as we waited, I couldn't help but steal glances at him. The way he animatedly chatted with the vendor, his laughter bright and unrestrained, made my heart race. It was in these small moments that I realized the depth of my feelings for him—beyond the adventure and spontaneity, it was the simplicity of shared experiences that captured my heart.

We found a small bench nearby, our hands filled with warm pastries, the world blurring around us as we took our first bites. The sweetness exploded in my mouth, mingling with the warmth of his smile. "This is amazing," I murmured, wiping crumbs from my chin, feeling utterly carefree.

"I knew you'd love it. Nothing beats dessert after a day of adventure." His eyes sparkled with mischief, and in that moment, I couldn't shake the feeling that this was just the beginning.

We devoured our treats, laughter spilling between us like music, and with every passing moment, the weight of our earlier confessions faded, replaced by the thrill of discovery. As the last rays of sunlight dipped below the skyline, the city transformed, the lights flickering on, casting a glow that felt almost magical.

"Let's walk a bit more before we head back," I suggested, the evening air crisp and refreshing. The prospect of more moments with him filled me with a lightness I hadn't felt in ages.

We strolled hand in hand, weaving through the streets as the nightlife awakened. The vibrant atmosphere buzzed with energy—musicians played soulful tunes on street corners, artists showcased their work, and the laughter of strangers mingled with the scent of street food wafting from nearby stalls. It felt like we were in a world painted in vivid colors, where everything was possible, and the boundaries of our lives melted away.

"Look at that!" Ethan exclaimed, pointing at a street performer juggling flaming torches. The crowd gathered, clapping and cheering as he spun and twirled, mesmerizing us with his skill. My heart raced, not just from the excitement of the performance but from the palpable energy shared between Ethan and me.

We joined the crowd, the heat from the flames flickering against our skin, casting dancing shadows around us. Ethan leaned closer, his breath warm against my ear as he whispered, "I can't believe we're here, experiencing this together."

In that moment, I felt a rush of affection swell within me. This was more than just an evening out; it was a journey into the unknown, a leap into a life that felt more vibrant with every shared moment. I turned to him, our eyes locking, and in that gaze, I saw a reflection of the courage I had mustered throughout the day.

"Thank you for pushing me," I said, the words tumbling out before I could think twice. "For making me confront my fears and reminding me what it feels like to be alive."

He smiled, a soft, genuine smile that lit up his entire face. "You didn't need me to push you. You were ready for this all along."

A warmth spread through me at his words. As the final act of the street performer concluded with an explosion of applause, I felt a sense of resolution settle within me. I was ready to embrace whatever came next—ready to explore the depths of this connection, to dive into the vast ocean of possibilities ahead.

And as we walked away from the crowd, the city buzzing with life around us, I understood that confronting my fears was not just about vulnerability—it was about forging bonds, discovering love, and allowing myself to truly live. The adventure had only just begun, and with Ethan by my side, I felt an exhilarating sense of hope that promised to illuminate every corner of my journey ahead.

Chapter 8: The Dance of Desire

The night of the charity gala unfolded like a scene from a dream, painted in rich hues of silk and satin, where every detail whispered of luxury and purpose. The moment I stepped through the grand entrance of the historic estate, my senses ignited, each element vying for my attention. High above, crystal chandeliers hung like glittering constellations, casting a warm glow over the room, illuminating faces both familiar and foreign. Lush arrangements of roses and peonies adorned every corner, their fragrance mingling with the distinct, tantalizing notes of fine champagne that floated through the air.

Ethan stood beside me, a vision of sophistication and confidence, his tailored navy suit hugging his frame in all the right places. My heart fluttered like a trapped bird as I caught glimpses of his relaxed smile, the playful gleam in his dark eyes that had so often made my pulse quicken. I could hardly believe I was here with him, surrounded by the elite of the city, yet in that moment, it felt as though we were the only two people in the universe.

As we moved into the ballroom, the music enveloped us, a soft, melodic waltz that beckoned me to the dance floor. The other couples glided gracefully, their movements fluid and effortless, as though they were one with the rhythm of the evening. I glanced at Ethan, my stomach swirling with anticipation. He held out his hand, his expression encouraging, and I took it, feeling the warmth of his palm envelop mine. A rush of electricity coursed through me, igniting a fire I hadn't expected.

We stepped into the dance, and the world around us faded into a blur. The soft fabric of my gown swirled around my legs, each step guided by Ethan's gentle lead. He was surprisingly light on his feet, and I soon found myself lost in the moment, entranced by the way he moved, the way his presence filled the space with an unspoken promise. I tilted my head back slightly, catching the sparkle of the chandeliers above, their lights shimmering like stars in the night sky, and for a fleeting moment, I imagined we were the only ones there.

With each twirl, my heart raced, and I could feel the unyielding chemistry between us intensifying, coiling tightly like a spring ready to snap. The warmth of his breath against my ear sent shivers down my spine, and I caught myself leaning in closer, savoring the intoxicating scent of his cologne, a blend of cedarwood and citrus that felt so uniquely him. I knew, at that moment, I was teetering on the edge of something profound—a realization, a confession, perhaps even a leap of faith.

But just as I began to weave my thoughts around the idea of what could blossom between us, a familiar voice broke through the harmony of the moment, sending ripples of confusion through my heart. "Ethan! Is that really you?" The words were sharp, cutting through the air like a knife, and I felt my stomach drop. The voice belonged to a woman, striking and confident, with cascading auburn hair and a dazzling smile that could outshine the chandeliers above us. She was a specter from Ethan's past, and I instantly felt my resolve waver.

Ethan's grip on my waist loosened slightly as he turned to face her, and I could feel the shift in his demeanor—the way his shoulders squared and his expression morphed into one of polite surprise. The laughter around us faded into a muffled buzz, and I became acutely aware of the way the music transformed from a soft embrace into an awkward tension. I stepped back slightly, just enough to give him space, but not enough to let the distance grow too wide.

"Claire," he said, his voice laced with disbelief and a hint of nostalgia. "It's been ages. How are you?"

I stood there, heart hammering in my chest, observing the way the past loomed over them like a thundercloud ready to unleash its storm. Claire stepped closer, her laughter light yet tinged with something sharper, a reminder of all the possibilities I was not. The easy camaraderie between them felt like a dagger, and I fought the urge to recoil, to step out of the narrative they seemed to weave so effortlessly.

As they exchanged pleasantries, I felt like an outsider looking in, a mere spectator in a play where I had hoped to be the leading lady. Ethan's eyes flickered toward me, searching for reassurance, and I offered him a small smile, though I felt as though it cracked under the weight of uncertainty. Was I really prepared to navigate this landscape of emotions, this burgeoning connection, while standing in the shadow of someone who once meant so much to him?

The warmth of the dance floor began to dissipate, replaced by an unsettling chill as Claire's presence loomed larger. The music continued, its melody now an undercurrent to the ebb and flow of their conversation. I could feel the laughter of the other guests rising and falling around us, their moments of joy turning into an echo that felt painfully distant.

In that whirlwind of confusion and longing, I knew I had a choice to make. I could slip back into the background, a wisp of a thought in Ethan's memory, or I could stand tall, embracing the connection we had forged amidst the clamor of life. I took a deep breath, feeling the soft fabric of my gown against my skin, grounding me in the present moment. I would not allow the past to dictate my future, nor would I let Claire's shadow dim the light I had begun to see in Ethan's eyes.

As I turned to face Ethan, my heart steadied, a resolve blossoming within me. It was time to reclaim my place, to dance not just for him, but for myself. With a flicker of courage igniting within, I stepped forward, ready to join the conversation and reclaim the moment, even as the air thickened with tension.

As I stepped back into the moment, that swirling haze of perfume and laughter, I felt the air between Ethan and me shift, an electric current hanging tantalizingly close. Claire stood there, a radiant reminder of possibilities past, her laughter like a chime in a windstorm, stirring up the tendrils of doubt that had begun to creep into my heart. I could see the way Ethan's demeanor softened, his familiar smile reshaping itself into something nostalgic, even affectionate, and I momentarily felt lost in the undertow of that emotion.

I took a breath, grounding myself in the moment, remembering why I was there—my hopes dancing in tandem with the rhythm of the waltz, a fragile tapestry of new beginnings that I didn't want to unravel. The music pulsed on, a steady heartbeat that anchored me. I felt the smooth fabric of my gown hugging my curves, reminding me of the beauty I had sought to embody for this night.

With newfound determination, I stepped forward, summoning every ounce of confidence I possessed. "Ethan," I said, my voice steady, yet softer than the fabric of the gown that glimmered under the soft lights. "It's lovely to see you enjoying yourself. Claire, isn't it? How have you been?"

I felt his eyes shift toward me, surprise mingling with appreciation as I inserted myself into their conversation. Claire turned, her expression a mix of curiosity and scrutiny. The dance floor swirled around us like a kaleidoscope of color and light, the guests' laughter cascading like a gentle wave, oblivious to the shifting dynamics in our little triangle.

"Yes, it's Claire," she replied, her tone playful, with a hint of edge. "Ethan and I go way back. We were quite the pair, weren't we?"

Her eyes sparkled with mischief, and I could sense the narrative she was eager to weave, one that I was determined to alter. "Oh, I'm sure there are many great stories to tell," I said, my smile unwavering. "But it seems he's found a better partner to dance with tonight."

Ethan's gaze flickered between us, the tension crackling like static in the air. I could see the hint of admiration in his eyes as he looked at me, and I reveled in the warmth it ignited within. Claire's smile faltered, just a fraction, but it was enough to embolden me. The unspoken challenge hung between us, and I was ready to rise to it.

"Do you remember that time we got stuck in the elevator after the gala?" Claire asked, her eyes narrowing slightly as if testing the waters. "That was quite the adventure, wasn't it, Ethan?"

A nostalgic smile played on his lips, and I could almost see the memories playing out in his mind, their laughter echoing against the backdrop of the night. I felt a twinge of jealousy but pushed it aside, reminding myself that I was here, present, and forging my own narrative.

"Ah, yes," he replied, laughter lacing his tone. "That was definitely a night to remember. But I think this night is shaping up to be even better."

He turned to me, his eyes searching mine, and the warmth that spread through me was intoxicating. I felt a pulse of confidence surge as I realized that I was not merely a spectator in this tale. The chemistry we had ignited couldn't be snuffed out by a mere memory, no matter how vibrant.

"Ethan," I said, my voice lower, deliberately drawing his attention back to me. "Why don't we show Claire how it's done? Let's give them something to talk about."

A flicker of surprise crossed his face, swiftly replaced by a grin that made my heart flip. I felt as though I had summoned the essence of boldness that lay dormant within me. We moved closer, the music rising to a crescendo, and in that moment, we became a new story. I twirled toward him, my skirt flaring around me, embodying all the confidence I could muster. Ethan stepped in closer, and we began to dance once more, our movements seamlessly blending with the rhythm.

The whispers of the past faded as we lost ourselves in the moment. As I spun, I could see Claire's expression shift, frustration mingled with admiration, her eyes narrowing in determination as I turned the tide. Each step I took felt like a reclamation, an assertion of my place beside him. The soft fabric of my gown brushed against his suit, a tactile reminder of the connection we shared. My laughter echoed in the air, light and free, and I could feel the warmth radiating from Ethan as he guided me through the dance, his confidence bolstering my own.

With each spin, I felt the walls of uncertainty crumble, leaving behind a burgeoning sense of freedom. The world around us blurred, and in those moments, it felt as if we were writing our own love letter, etched into the very fabric of the night.

"Where did this boldness come from?" he teased, his eyes sparkling as we found a rhythm all our own.

I grinned back, reveling in the spontaneity of it all. "Maybe it was always here, just waiting for the right moment."

The music slowed, transitioning into a soft ballad that enveloped us in its embrace. I found myself gazing up at him, the flickering candlelight reflecting in his eyes, casting a soft glow that seemed to highlight the delicate contours of his face. This was no longer just a dance; it was an unspoken promise, a whisper of what could be. The world around us faded to mere background noise, and for that moment, we were two souls entwined in the dance of desire.

Just then, the melody shifted again, and the atmosphere vibrated with the pulse of anticipation, drawing us closer. I felt the heat radiating from Ethan as he leaned in, his voice low and intimate. "You have a way of surprising me. I like this side of you."

"Just wait until you see the rest," I replied, a mischievous smile playing on my lips.

As I spun away from him, inviting him to join me in a playful flourish, I caught sight of Claire from the corner of my eye. Her expression was a mix of disbelief and admiration, the flickering candlelight dancing across her face, illuminating a moment that felt as fragile as glass yet so intensely charged. I felt a surge of triumph;

this night, with its cacophony of emotions and unexpected encounters, was shaping into something extraordinary.

I turned back to Ethan, his gaze steady and unwavering. Together, we twirled under the sparkling chandeliers, the music weaving a tapestry of connection and longing that enveloped us both. With each step, I felt the pull of the moment, the thrill of what lay ahead, and the exhilarating promise of desire, unbound and unyielding.

The dance floor had transformed into a canvas of our shared energy, vibrant and alive, each step imbued with a pulsating thrill that surged between us. The soft notes of the ballad wrapped around us like a warm embrace, cradling our whispered words and stolen glances. I leaned in closer, my heart beating in rhythm with the music, the world beyond our bubble fading into an abstract haze of colors and laughter.

Ethan twirled me once more, his grip firm yet gentle, guiding me through the ebb and flow of the crowd. I caught fleeting glimpses of guests enraptured in their own stories—couples exchanging secret smiles, friends celebrating reunions, and acquaintances deep in conversation, their words a blur of excitement. But all of it paled against the electric connection pulsing between Ethan and me. It was intoxicating, an exhilarating dance not just of bodies but of souls, where unspoken promises lingered just beneath the surface.

As the final notes of the ballad faded into a hushed silence, I felt Ethan's breath hitch slightly, his gaze piercing through me, seeking something deeper. I had lost myself in the moment, but the reality of Claire's presence hovered like a specter, threatening to pull me back into a realm of doubt and uncertainty. I caught her watching us from the edge of the dance floor, her expression a mix of surprise and steely determination. The air thickened with a palpable tension, and I wondered how far I could push this newfound boldness before it all came crashing down.

"Do you want to take a breath?" Ethan asked softly, his eyes never leaving mine, as though he could sense the turmoil brewing just beneath my surface.

"Definitely," I replied, my voice steadier than I felt. I wasn't ready to back down, not yet. This night was too precious, too filled with the possibility of something beautiful. I nodded toward the terrace, a space draped in soft, twinkling lights and adorned with blooming jasmine that cast its fragrant spell over the evening. It beckoned like a secret garden waiting to be explored, a sanctuary away from prying eyes.

Ethan offered me his arm, a gesture that felt both protective and inviting, as we navigated through the lively throng of guests. The air outside was cooler, refreshing against my flushed cheeks as we stepped onto the terrace. The stars twinkled overhead, each one a tiny beacon illuminating the night sky, and I couldn't help but marvel at how magnificent everything felt—the venue, the people, and, most importantly, Ethan.

We found a cozy corner, secluded enough to feel intimate yet close enough to hear the music still pulsing inside. I leaned against the railing, the smooth wood cool beneath my fingertips, as I gazed out at the sprawling city skyline, the lights of the buildings twinkling like a sea of stars mirrored on earth. "Isn't it beautiful?" I asked, my voice softening.

"It really is," he agreed, leaning beside me. His presence was warm, grounding, yet charged with an undeniable energy that sent a thrill coursing through me. "But I think the view is even better up close."

Our eyes locked, and for a moment, the world around us faded entirely. I could see the flicker of excitement in his expression, a reflection of my own hopes and fears swirling together in a delicate dance. "Ethan, I—" I began, the words bubbling up within me, desperate to spill forth, but I hesitated, the enormity of my feelings momentarily paralyzing.

Before I could finish, Claire's voice sliced through the night, her laughter ringing like a bell as she joined us on the terrace, the very picture of elegance and confidence. "Mind if I join the two lovebirds?" she quipped, her gaze flitting between us with an air of playful mischief.

Ethan's smile faltered slightly, but he regained his composure quickly. "Of course not, Claire. We were just enjoying the view."

The three of us stood there, an awkward triangle forged by the interplay of past and present. I could feel the tension thickening again, a silent battle of wills emerging in this unexpected reunion. Claire leaned against the railing, her stance confident as she eyed me. "So, you're the one who's captured Ethan's attention tonight. I must say, I didn't see that coming."

The way she said it held an edge, a challenge that sent a prickling heat up my spine. I refused to let her words unsettle me. "Well, it takes a certain kind of magic to hold someone's interest at a gala like this," I replied, trying to sound more assured than I felt. "But I guess it's all in the performance."

She raised an eyebrow, her smirk transforming into something more contemplative. "Is that so? Perhaps I've been too serious in my pursuits. Maybe I need to loosen up a bit." Her voice dripped with a playful sarcasm, yet there was a hint of sincerity that caught me off guard.

Ethan stepped between us, his presence an anchor in the swirling tide of unspoken competition. "Let's not turn this into a game," he said, his tone light yet firm. "We're all here for a good cause, after all. There's plenty of room for everyone to shine."

I admired him for that, for his ability to navigate the complexity of the situation with grace, but part of me wished he would take a firmer stand. Claire's presence loomed, challenging the newfound connection I'd felt blooming like wildflowers beneath the sun.

As if sensing my thoughts, Ethan turned to me, his eyes earnest. "I'm glad you're here with me tonight. You make this event much more enjoyable."

A spark ignited within me at his words, emboldening me to step further into this tangled web of emotions. "Thank you, Ethan. I'm glad to be here too," I said, the sincerity evident in my voice. "It's been an incredible night."

Claire seemed to sense the shift, and while her expression remained playful, I could see the challenge glimmering in her eyes. "Well, why don't we see just how incredible it can get? I heard there's a contest for the best dance moves inside. What do you say we join in?"

Ethan's eyes lit up with mischief, and I could see the flicker of competition igniting within him. "Are you up for it?" he asked, glancing at me with a playful challenge of his own.

"Absolutely," I replied, the adrenaline pumping through my veins, spurred on by both Claire's invitation and Ethan's excitement. This was my moment to claim my place, to assert my growing feelings, and to show both of them that I was not to be underestimated.

As we turned to head back inside, I felt a rush of exhilaration. I wasn't just competing for Ethan's attention; I was showcasing who I was and what I could bring to the dance. The thrumming music reached us before we entered, a lively tune that demanded energy and confidence.

Stepping onto the dance floor again, I could feel the collective energy of the guests swirling around us, an intoxicating mix of anticipation and celebration. I glanced over at Claire, and to my surprise, there was a flicker of camaraderie in her gaze, an acknowledgment that we were both players in this enchanting game.

THE PATH BETWEEN WORDS

As the first notes rang out, I found my rhythm, letting the music guide me. Ethan fell into step beside me, his movements fluid and instinctive. Together, we became a whirlwind of laughter and spontaneity, the worries of the world outside dissolving into the background.

With each spin and leap, I felt my confidence swell, rising with every laugh that escaped my lips and every twinkling glance Ethan sent my way. The contest became an exhilarating showcase of our playful connection, each moment drawing us closer and sparking a deeper bond.

And there, amidst the whirlwind of the night, I realized that perhaps I wasn't just competing for his heart; I was crafting a narrative of my own—a tale of resilience, bravery, and the intoxicating magic of new beginnings. The dance floor became our world, and I was no longer afraid to claim my place within it.

Chapter 9: Love's Complications

The clinking of glasses and the hushed laughter of the crowd swirled around me like a warm breeze as I made my way through the dimly lit bar. The scent of aged whiskey and fresh lime hung in the air, dancing with the rhythm of the jazz band in the corner. Each note was a playful caress, a reminder of the joyous evening I had imagined—a night filled with laughter, intimate glances, and the electric spark of a budding romance. Instead, I found myself wrestling with an unexpected tempest, a whirlwind of emotions threatening to pull me under.

Ethan had been radiant that evening, a rare smile lighting up his face as he shared stories of his latest adventures. I adored his passion, the way his blue eyes sparkled when he recounted a day spent hiking in the Appalachian mountains, each word spilling forth like a rush of adrenaline. He was magnetic, a vibrant force of nature that drew people to him. I sat, nestled comfortably beside him, my heart fluttering in response to his every word, feeling as if I had stepped into a painting of a perfect moment. Until she arrived.

Chloe slipped into the scene like a wisp of smoke, her presence undeniable, magnetic in its own right. She was stunning—tall, with cascading waves of chestnut hair that glimmered under the bar's low lights. Her laughter echoed through the space, bright and infectious, wrapping around Ethan like an embrace, and I felt the weight of my own existence begin to crumble. How was it possible that she could weave her way into our moment so effortlessly, with an ease that seemed to amplify everything I feared? I clenched my drink tightly, feeling the ice crack beneath my grip, a physical manifestation of the fractures forming within me.

I excused myself, needing a moment to gather my thoughts, to remind myself that I was not a mere shadow in the periphery of their reunion. The restroom offered a brief sanctuary, a place where

I could wash away the rising tide of jealousy and insecurity. Staring into the mirror, I scrutinized my reflection—a cascade of auburn curls framing my face, cheeks dusted with a flush that came not from the cocktails I'd enjoyed but from the knot of anxiety tightening in my stomach. I was adorned in a soft green dress that hugged my curves, something I had chosen for its ability to accentuate my features without overshadowing me.

Yet, even as I examined myself, doubt crept in. Was I truly worthy of his affection? Chloe had a lightness about her, a vivacity that was intoxicating, while I felt like a worn book on a neglected shelf. I sighed, splashing cool water on my face, hoping it would wash away the invasive thoughts that had taken root. As I straightened up, I whispered a mantra to myself—You are worthy of love; you are worthy of this moment. But it felt fragile, like a thin thread poised to snap under the weight of reality.

When I returned, the sight before me was disheartening. Ethan leaned closer to Chloe, their conversation flowing like the whiskey being poured at the bar. Her laughter was a siren's call, and he was captivated, ensnared in a web of nostalgia and allure. I felt as if I was observing from behind a glass wall, separate from the vibrant world they inhabited. It was a cruel twist of fate—one moment of bliss upended by the arrival of someone who was not merely a reminder of Ethan's past but an embodiment of my own insecurities.

As the minutes dragged on, I took a deep breath and pushed my way back into the fray. I plastered a smile on my face, determined to reclaim my footing in this chaotic tableau. "What are you two scheming about?" I asked, injecting a lightness into my voice, though it felt foreign, as if it belonged to someone else entirely.

Chloe turned to me, her smile radiant and disarming, her bright eyes holding a spark of mischief. "Just reminiscing about our wild adventures. Did you know Ethan nearly fell off a cliff during a hike?

I still have the video!" Her words floated through the air, sweet as honey but with a sting that pricked my heart.

Ethan chuckled, his laughter mingling with hers, and I felt my smile wavering, threatening to slip into a frown. "It wasn't that dramatic," he countered, his gaze flickering between us, a spark of recognition in his eyes. But as I looked at him, hoping for a lifeline, I found only a glimmer of the bond he once shared with Chloe, and the fear of being an afterthought clawed at my insides.

I steeled myself, desperately trying to inject my own experiences into the conversation, weaving tales of my recent escapades, hoping to reclaim a piece of his attention. Yet, with every word, I felt Chloe's presence overshadow me like a towering oak. The way she leaned in, the way she touched his arm—it was as if I were watching a play unfold where I had forgotten my lines, standing on the sidelines as the main act took place without me.

The evening wore on, and my attempts to engage felt more like shadows, stretching but never quite reaching him. I was determined to not be the wallflower, to break through the glass barrier that felt so impenetrable, but every effort seemed to vanish into the ether, lost in the magnetic pull of their connection. With every shared glance between them, my heart sank further into a chasm of doubt, threatening to swallow me whole. I couldn't help but wonder—was I simply a fleeting spark in Ethan's life, destined to flicker and fade? Or could I carve my own place in his heart, amidst the complexities of love and the echoes of past relationships?

I stood there, feeling like a ghost at my own gathering, watching Ethan's blue eyes sparkle as he exchanged laughter and stories with Chloe. Each smile that crossed his lips felt like a dagger, carving deeper into my heart. I could sense the easy chemistry between them—a dance of familiarity that I desperately wished I could join. The world around me blurred, the vibrant laughter and chatter dimming into a muffled hum. My fingers clutched the edge of the bar, the polished surface cool against my palm, grounding me as the waves of insecurity threatened to wash me away.

With a deliberate effort, I nudged my chin up, forcing my feet to move towards them. It was absurd how quickly I could feel my courage wane, yet I couldn't let the evening end like this. I was here, I belonged here, and I refused to be overshadowed by a memory. The distance between us felt insurmountable, each step a battle against my own trepidation.

"Ethan, what's this I hear about a cliff?" I interjected, my voice surprisingly steady. The moment I spoke, I felt the atmosphere shift. He turned to me, a look of surprise mingled with delight breaking across his face. I saw the flicker of acknowledgment, a small flame of hope igniting within me.

Chloe's smile faltered just a bit as she tilted her head, and I could almost hear the gears turning in her mind, assessing me as a potential rival. I couldn't let her see how much her mere presence rattled me. "Oh, just a little hike gone wrong," Ethan laughed, his tone light, but I noticed the hint of a blush creeping up his neck, a color I had not seen before, perhaps from embarrassment or the effects of the whiskey. "It was a breathtaking view, but the trail had its... challenges."

I seized the opportunity, launching into a story of my own, one where I triumphantly navigated a tricky hiking trail, a solo adventure that had tested my limits and rewarded me with stunning vistas. I painted the scene with my words, allowing the images of fiery sunsets and sprawling landscapes to come alive in the air between us. "You see," I said, my voice bubbling with enthusiasm, "the key is to embrace the challenge. It's about finding balance and knowing when to trust your instincts."

Ethan's eyes sparkled as they met mine, and I felt a rush of warmth. Chloe, however, leaned back slightly, her expression now a mix of amusement and skepticism. The flicker of competition ignited between us, and I relished the subtle game, keen to prove that I, too, could hold my own in this delicate dance.

"Is that how you tackle life, too? With the same zeal?" Chloe asked, her tone teasing yet pointed.

"Absolutely," I replied, matching her tone with playful confidence. "Every hike, every challenge—it's a little piece of the adventure. Besides, it's far more enjoyable when you have someone to share it with."

I could see Ethan's intrigue, the way his gaze lingered a moment longer than necessary. Perhaps I hadn't been so far off the mark after all. For every time I felt unseen, there seemed to be a small glimmer of hope flickering in his eyes, and I clung to that like a lifeline.

As the evening progressed, the rhythm of conversation flowed like a well-crafted melody, each note building on the last. Chloe, in her attempts to shine, brought up tales of shared friends and adventures from their past. I listened, feeling a mix of admiration and annoyance as her anecdotes unfolded, punctuated with laughter that rang out like chimes in the air. Still, I was determined not to let jealousy consume me. Instead, I focused on the edges of her stories, searching for a way to weave my own experiences into the narrative.

I found my footing in snippets of shared memories and laughter that echoed with familiarity. I brought up an old college friend, and Ethan jumped in, recalling their mutual acquaintance, turning the spotlight back to me. My heart soared for a moment, the way his enthusiasm mirrored my own. Yet, I could still feel Chloe hovering nearby, a vibrant specter from his past, casting shadows on our budding connection.

"Tell me," she said, a playful lilt in her voice, "how do you manage to keep up with all your adventures? You must be busy with work, too, right?"

Her question was layered, a subtle challenge wrapped in curiosity. I smiled, my fingers dancing over the rim of my glass. "I believe life is meant to be lived fully. Sure, I have responsibilities, but finding balance is key. Besides, adventure doesn't always mean grand escapades. Sometimes, it's simply enjoying the moment."

Chloe's expression shifted, perhaps gauging the authenticity of my words. I leaned in, letting the passion of my convictions infuse my tone. "I believe that every day holds potential—whether it's discovering a new café around the corner or finally trying that hiking trail you've been eyeing. Life's richness lies in the simple pleasures."

Ethan nodded, clearly resonating with my perspective, a soft smile spreading across his face. I could see the admiration reflected in his eyes, and for a fleeting moment, I felt empowered, momentarily overshadowing Chloe's radiant presence.

As the evening wore on, the initial tension between us began to dissolve into a camaraderie that I hadn't anticipated. The three of us shared stories and laughter, a tangled web of pasts and presents, woven together by the shared fabric of life experiences. With each shared moment, I felt more anchored, the fear that had once threatened to engulf me now retreating like shadows at dawn.

But just when I thought I had a solid grasp on this delicate balance, Chloe leaned closer to Ethan, her voice dropping to a conspiratorial whisper. "Remember that time we got lost in the mountains? You were so sure you knew the way, and we ended up in that little diner…"

A wave of nostalgia washed over him, and I felt my stomach knot again as he laughed, his eyes sparkling with warmth as he reminisced about their escapade. Chloe continued, each word drawing him deeper into the past, and for a moment, I felt as if I were watching a film unfold, the screen flickering with memories I wasn't a part of.

The warmth of the room faded slightly as the chill of uncertainty crept back in. Just when I thought I could stake my claim, I felt Chloe's magnetic pull sweeping Ethan away into the depths of a shared history I couldn't penetrate. I reminded myself of my worth—of the vibrant life I had built, the adventures I had crafted with care and passion.

With a deep breath, I chose to reclaim my moment. "Lost in the mountains? Now, that sounds like a story worth hearing!" I interjected, injecting a playful tone into the atmosphere. "What kind of diner serves the best post-hike comfort food?"

Chloe turned to me, her surprise quickly morphing into a gracious smile. "Oh, you wouldn't believe it! They had the best milkshakes, and Ethan insisted we try everything on the menu."

Ethan laughed, the sound warm and infectious, and I felt a wave of relief. It seemed the night had room for all of us, weaving our stories together in unexpected ways. The three of us laughed and shared anecdotes, the atmosphere slowly morphing into something lighter, where the past and present could coexist without overshadowing one another.

As the night unfurled, I found a renewed sense of purpose. I realized that perhaps love wasn't about outshining someone else, but about embracing the light that each of us carried. And as I glanced at Ethan, laughter echoing between us, I felt hope blossom—a promise that perhaps this night, this connection, was only the beginning of something beautifully complex.

The night carried on like a high-tension wire, crackling with energy, every laugh and whispered word building to a crescendo that both exhilarated and terrified me. I watched as Chloe animatedly shared another story, her gestures wide and expressive, weaving a tapestry of memories that made me feel increasingly small, as if I were merely a backdrop in a play where she commanded the stage. Ethan leaned in, captivated, and for a moment, I could almost see the threads of their shared history enveloping him, pulling him deeper into a world I had yet to enter.

"Remember that time we got lost at the festival? You were so convinced that taking that shortcut would save us time, and we ended up miles from where we needed to be!" Her laughter danced around us, infectious yet tinged with a sweetness that made my heart ache.

I took a sip of my drink, willing the warmth of the bourbon to chase away the chill settling in my bones. The ice clinked against the glass, a sharp reminder of the reality I was trying to escape. Every detail of Chloe's narrative was vivid, painted with the kind of brush that ignited nostalgia in Ethan's eyes. I felt a pang of longing, the realization that I wanted to create similar memories with him—ones that echoed with laughter and warmth, not overshadowed by the brilliance of another.

"Yeah, we were lost for hours! But we did find that amazing taco truck," Ethan interjected, his voice filled with genuine delight as he recounted their escapade. His enthusiasm was electric, and I could see the way Chloe's presence acted like a magnet, drawing his focus away from me, from the here and now.

"It was the best!" Chloe chimed in, her eyes sparkling like stars in the night sky. "We couldn't stop laughing, and those tacos..." She let out a soft sigh, as if savoring the memory of the food as much as the company.

The bar around us faded into a blur of warm hues and indistinct chatter, my attention honing in on the connection they shared. Yet, amidst my swirling emotions, a small flicker of defiance ignited within me. I would not let this moment slip away without making my mark.

With a soft clearing of my throat, I leaned forward, injecting my own story into the fold. "Tacos always have a way of making a bad situation feel like an adventure," I quipped, the lightness of my tone surprising even me. "I had a similar experience at the street fair last summer. I accidentally joined a conga line, and by the end, I was covered in glitter and half-eaten funnel cake. I couldn't help but laugh at how ridiculous I must have looked."

Laughter erupted, a sound that felt like a bridge forming between us, connecting my experiences with theirs, reminding me that I, too, could share in the vibrant tapestry of the evening. Ethan's laughter rang louder, and I noticed his gaze flicker towards me, that glimmer of appreciation I craved illuminating his features.

"See? You're already making memories," he said, a warmth threading through his voice.

The conversation shifted, the three of us flowing like the melodies from the band, each anecdote rich with flavor and life. We traded stories and laughter, weaving our paths together in that cozy bar, where the air was thick with possibilities. Yet as the minutes slipped by, I couldn't help but notice how often Chloe returned to tales of her past adventures with Ethan, moments that seemed etched in his mind with the care of a cherished photograph. Each recollection felt like another step deeper into a realm where I struggled to find my footing.

At one point, Chloe playfully nudged Ethan, her fingers brushing against his arm, and I felt an unwelcome rush of heat flooding my cheeks. "You were always the most daring, weren't you? Remember that time you tried to impress me by climbing that rock wall and got stuck halfway up?"

Ethan laughed, a rich, rumbling sound that echoed against the bar's wooden beams. "I thought it would be a smooth ascent, but I realized halfway up that I had no idea what I was doing. I'm pretty sure I embarrassed myself in front of everyone."

"I think you managed to pull it off with style," Chloe teased, and for a fleeting moment, I felt my stomach twist. She had a way of weaving words that made everything sound like a romantic adventure, and I couldn't shake the feeling that she was painting a picture of him that I could never hope to replicate.

But then I realized—perhaps I didn't need to replicate anything. I could forge my own path, create memories that were distinctly mine. It was a revelation that sparked a newfound resolve within me.

"Let me tell you about my most embarrassing moment," I said, my voice steady. "During a rock climbing lesson last fall, I thought I'd impress my instructor by trying to scale a particularly challenging route. Let's just say I ended up more tangled in ropes than reaching the top. I like to think of it as my 'artistic interpretation' of climbing," I laughed, allowing the moment to swell with levity.

Ethan's eyes sparkled with laughter, and for the first time, I sensed a shift in the dynamic. "You must have looked like quite the sight," he teased, clearly enjoying the visual.

"Believe me, I had all the grace of a newborn deer," I replied, my cheeks warming with the shared laughter. "But the best part was how supportive everyone was. It turned into a team effort to get me untangled, and by the end, we were all laughing together."

Chloe's expression softened, and I sensed a flicker of appreciation in her gaze. "It sounds like you really embraced the spirit of adventure," she remarked, her tone shifting as if she recognized the bond we were forming in that moment.

As the evening unfolded, I reveled in the rhythm of conversation, each exchange drawing me closer to Ethan while Chloe's stories began to weave a different narrative. She shared more about her travels, her experiences, and the lessons she had learned, but it was becoming clear that the essence of her tales was shifting from nostalgic to appreciative. Perhaps she, too, could recognize the beauty of forging new connections, the exhilarating energy of shared laughter.

I found myself laughing more easily, feeling the walls I had built around my heart beginning to crack. The three of us formed an unlikely trio, a blend of past and present that opened up unexpected pathways. I caught Ethan stealing glances at me, his admiration now clearer than ever, and I felt emboldened to step into the light, no longer hiding in the shadows of Chloe's memories.

As the clock ticked on, the bar began to fill with the lively buzz of the weekend crowd. The air pulsed with energy, laughter spilling over the edges like a frothy drink. The band switched to an upbeat tune, a lively rhythm that made it impossible to remain seated. Without thinking, I rose, the music pulling me toward the dance floor. "Come on! Let's dance!" I called, an impulsive invitation escaping my lips.

Ethan glanced at me, surprise flickering across his features, before a grin broke through. "You're on!" he exclaimed, his voice ringing with enthusiasm as he joined me.

Chloe followed suit, laughter bubbling as we made our way to the center of the bar. As we began to sway to the music, the tension of the evening melted away, replaced by a sense of liberation. The three of us moved together, a spontaneous trio lost in the moment, the rhythm carrying us into an exuberant bubble of joy.

With each step, I let go of the doubts that had plagued me. The air felt electric as we danced, our movements synchronizing effortlessly. Laughter erupted, filling the space as we let the music take over, weaving our own narrative through the lively beats.

As the song reached its peak, I caught Ethan's eye, and in that instant, the world around us fell away. He pulled me closer, our laughter merging into something deeper, a connection that thrummed in the space between us.

It was in that moment, amid the warmth of camaraderie and the thrill of the music, that I finally understood the heart of love. It wasn't merely about the past, the shadows of old memories; it was about the connections we built, the stories we created, and the moments that took our breath away. In the chaos of laughter and the glow of newfound friendship, I felt the promise of something beautiful, something uniquely ours.

Chapter 10: Shadows of the Past

Sorting through the eclectic array of old books at "Whispers of the Past" felt like stepping into a living museum of forgotten tales. The scent of aged paper mixed with a hint of dust danced in the air, wrapping around me like a comforting shawl. Each spine I brushed against told its own story, from the faded gold lettering to the creased edges that hinted at countless hands flipping through the pages. It was during one of those sun-dappled afternoons, where the golden rays filtered through the tall windows, that I unearthed the diary.

Nestled among the heavy volumes of classic literature, its presence was almost ethereal. The cover was a tapestry of browns and faded reds, resembling the last embers of a dying fire. As I opened it, the brittle pages crackled softly, like whispers of the past beckoning me closer. The handwriting was an elegant flourish, each letter imbued with emotion. The ink had faded but was still legible, a testament to the feelings captured within those pages. I felt as if I had cracked open a treasure chest, its contents gleaming with the light of a thousand forgotten moments.

The words danced before my eyes, weaving tales of love and loss, dreams that were nurtured only to be shattered, and the mundane magic of everyday life. With each turn of the page, I felt myself being pulled into the life of the writer—a woman who, despite the decades that separated us, felt achingly familiar. Her thoughts on heartbreak resonated deep within me, as if I were holding a mirror reflecting my own fears and desires.

That evening, I couldn't resist the urge to share this discovery with Ethan. As the sun began to set, painting the sky with shades of orange and purple, I invited him over for coffee. The familiar warmth of our small kitchen enveloped us, contrasting with the chill creeping in from the autumn air outside. I brewed a pot of rich, dark coffee, its aroma filling the space with a cozy embrace. The gentle hum of the kettle was soothing, a sound that seemed to anchor us in the moment.

Ethan arrived just as the last rays of sunlight slipped away, bringing with him a smile that lit up the dim room. He slipped off his jacket, revealing the soft flannel shirt that seemed to carry the warmth of home with it. As we settled at the kitchen table, I placed the diary between us, my fingers trembling slightly with anticipation. "You have to see this," I said, my voice a mix of excitement and reverence.

He leaned closer, curiosity sparkling in his deep-set eyes, and I could see the corners of his mouth curve upwards as I began to read aloud. The passages spoke of quiet evenings spent in small towns, the kind where everyone knows your name, and the stars seem to twinkle just a little brighter in the absence of city lights. It was a world far removed from our bustling lives in the city, but it felt achingly close, as if we could reach out and touch it.

"'I found myself in the comfort of his embrace,'" I read, my voice thickening with emotion. The words seemed to linger in the air, hanging between us like the last leaves clinging to autumn branches. I glanced up to find Ethan's gaze fixed on me, a mixture of understanding and intrigue in his expression.

"Do you think she found what she was looking for?" he asked, his tone soft and thoughtful, breaking the silence that had enveloped us. The question hung between us, heavy with implications. I could feel the pulse of our shared moment, as if the very air around us was charged with unspoken truths.

"I want to believe she did," I replied, feeling the warmth of his presence seep into my bones. There was a vulnerability in our conversation that both terrified and exhilarated me, an invitation to dig deeper into our own stories. As we read further, we began to stitch our lives into the fabric of the writer's words, transforming her struggles and triumphs into our own.

The words flowed freely, an effortless exchange that began to blur the lines between her life and ours. "What's your greatest dream?" I asked suddenly, breaking the rhythm of the reading. The question hung in the air, filled with the weight of anticipation. Ethan paused, his brow furrowing as he considered the query.

"I want to build something that lasts," he finally admitted, his voice steady but laced with vulnerability. "Something that people will remember, that will have an impact." His gaze drifted out the window, lost in thought, and for a moment, I saw the contours of his dreams etched in the twilight.

"And you?" he countered, turning the question back to me, his eyes searching mine for a glimpse of my truth. I hesitated, my heart racing as I considered the depth of my aspirations.

"I want to create spaces where people feel seen," I confessed, the words spilling from me like secrets I had long kept. "To help them find their stories, to weave them into something beautiful. Just like this diary." The admission felt liberating, a release of emotions that had long been bottled up.

With every revelation, our connection deepened, and the energy between us crackled with the potential of what could be. We laughed and shared, weaving a tapestry of dreams and fears, both of us stepping delicately into the shadows of our pasts, hoping to find light along the way.

As we read more, the diary became a conduit for our truths, transforming the kitchen into a sanctuary of shared vulnerability. The coffee grew cold, forgotten in the swell of our stories. And outside, the world continued to turn, the night wrapping its arms around the city, while we remained cocooned in our own intimate universe, lost in the whispers of the past that guided us toward an uncertain but hopeful future.

The conversation flowed like the gentle stream I had often imagined when reading about quaint little towns. Our words wrapped around each other, creating a tapestry of shared hopes and quiet fears. I marveled at how easily we fell into this rhythm, a dance of vulnerability that neither of us had anticipated but both desperately craved. The diary became our muse, a link between the intimate world we were carving out together and the past that still held us captive.

With the autumn night deepening outside, a chilly breeze rustled the leaves in the trees, creating a soft symphony that added to the warmth radiating from the kitchen. I looked up to find Ethan's eyes shining with that familiar spark of mischief, as if he were about to share a secret that had been lodged in his heart for too long. "You know," he began, his tone teasing yet contemplative, "reading these entries feels like eavesdropping on someone else's life. I half-expect her to pop out from behind the cover and shush us for reading her innermost thoughts."

I chuckled, picturing a spectral figure with wild hair and a spirited glint in her eye, scolding us for our audacity. "Maybe she's just grateful we're giving her words a second chance," I replied, allowing the thought to linger in the air.

"Or she's hoping we'll take her advice," he shot back, a smile playing on his lips. It was moments like these that reminded me of the easy rapport we shared, a bond that had been nurtured in the fertile soil of laughter and understanding.

As we continued to explore the diary, we stumbled upon passages that reflected the writer's fierce longing for adventure, the kind that bubbled beneath the surface of her day-to-day existence. She described a yearning that thrummed in her chest, a desire to escape the mundanity of her small town for something larger than life. I couldn't help but feel a kinship with her; my own dreams had often danced tantalizingly just out of reach, like fireflies in the twilight.

"Do you ever think about leaving everything behind?" I asked, the question slipping out before I could filter it. "Like packing a bag and just going?"

Ethan's brow furrowed for a moment, and then he nodded slowly. "Sometimes. But I think it's not so much about the physical place as it is about finding a sense of home. I've chased that feeling all my life."

There was something poetic about his words, a lyrical truth that resonated in my heart. The idea of a physical journey becoming an emotional quest struck me deeply. I wondered if, amidst the comforts and chaos of our lives, we could both be searching for that elusive sense of belonging.

"Where do you think you would go?" he asked, leaning forward with genuine interest.

I paused, pondering the question. "I think I'd love to wander through the streets of New Orleans," I replied, my voice softening as I painted the picture in my mind. "The jazz music, the vibrant colors, the stories hanging in the air—it all seems so alive. Like every corner has a tale waiting to be told."

Ethan's gaze sharpened, as if he were trying to see into my very soul. "And what would you do there?"

"I would find a little café, maybe one with outdoor seating, where the air is heavy with the scent of beignets and coffee," I mused, lost in the vision. "I'd sit and write, letting the stories spill out of me while the world bustled around. It feels like there's magic in the chaos."

His eyes sparkled with enthusiasm. "That sounds incredible," he said, his tone laced with a hint of awe. "Maybe one day we can both go. Find that chaos together."

A warmth spread through my chest at the idea. I could almost envision us there, wandering the vibrant streets, sharing laughter and dreams over sweet pastries and the heady notes of a saxophone drifting through the air. The thought was intoxicating, a promise of adventure woven into the very fabric of our connection.

Our conversation flowed back to the diary, and as we continued reading, it became a shared tapestry of our lives. Each passage ignited our imaginations, leading us to create characters and scenarios that intertwined with our own narratives. We were no longer just two people sitting in a cozy kitchen; we had become collaborators in a world shaped by ink and paper, crafting a reality that was both familiar and wonderfully foreign.

Suddenly, a passage about the writer's first love caught my attention. She wrote of the exhilarating rush of youthful romance, the way it felt like soaring high above the clouds, only to come crashing down to earth with an aching thud. I glanced up at Ethan, a mischievous smile breaking across my face. "Did you ever have a first love?" I asked, eager to draw him into the web of confessions we had been weaving.

He laughed lightly, the sound deep and rich, filling the room with warmth. "Oh, you mean the one that makes you feel like your heart is about to burst out of your chest? Yes, unfortunately."

"What happened?" I leaned in, my curiosity piqued.

He took a deep breath, as if he were about to unravel a piece of his soul. "It was a summer fling, hot and intense, like a wildfire that spread too quickly to control. But when the leaves turned and the summer sun faded, so did she. It was like losing a part of myself that I didn't even know existed."

A soft sigh escaped my lips. "That's both beautiful and heartbreaking."

"Such is the nature of love, I suppose," he replied, his voice thick with nostalgia. "It teaches you, shapes you, sometimes breaks you. But you keep coming back for more, don't you?"

There was a weight to his words, a resonance that struck a chord deep within me. It was true. Love was a wild creature, elusive and intoxicating, one that could lead to the most profound joy or the deepest sorrow. In that moment, I realized that our stories, while uniquely ours, were all part of the grand tapestry of human experience—woven together by threads of joy, loss, laughter, and longing.

As the evening deepened, we lingered over the diary, our coffee now a forgotten memory, the pages illuminated by the soft glow of the kitchen light. With each shared story, each intimate revelation, I felt the walls I had built around my heart begin to crumble, replaced by something softer and infinitely more vulnerable. The world outside may have been shrouded in the cold grip of autumn, but inside, warmth blossomed like the first hints of spring. In that cozy sanctuary, where the past intertwined with our present, we found solace in each other's company, two souls embracing the uncertainty of what lay ahead.

The night deepened around us, a soft blanket of darkness draping over the neighborhood, while inside the cozy confines of my kitchen, the atmosphere crackled with intimacy. The diary lay open before us like a portal to another time, its pages whispering secrets that felt both personal and universal. I could hardly believe how quickly we had descended into this abyss of shared emotions, where laughter and silence danced hand in hand, creating a beautiful tension that made my heart race.

The flickering candle on the table cast playful shadows, their forms twisting and turning as if trying to eavesdrop on our thoughts. I caught Ethan watching me, his expression a blend of amusement and contemplation. "You know," he said, leaning back in his chair, "for someone who owns a bookstore, you're quite the amateur detective. You might have a future in uncovering hidden stories."

I laughed, the sound bubbling up effortlessly. "Who needs sleuthing when you can just read other people's diaries?" I quipped, trying to deflect the compliment. The truth was, I was reveling in the connection we were forging through this shared experience. The warmth of his gaze felt like sunlight breaking through a cloudy day, illuminating the hidden corners of my heart.

As we flipped through more entries, we stumbled upon a passage that detailed the writer's experience of friendship, the kind that felt like coming home after a long journey. The description of late-night conversations, the kind that stretched until dawn, resonated with me, tugging at the strings of nostalgia. It was a reminder of the bonds I had forged over the years, some strong enough to withstand the test of time, while others had crumbled like old buildings under the weight of neglect.

"What do you think makes a friendship last?" I asked, my curiosity piqued.

Ethan considered the question, his brow furrowing slightly. "I think it's a combination of honesty, humor, and the willingness to be vulnerable. If you can share your worst days and still laugh together, that's magic."

"Magic," I repeated, letting the word linger in the air. It held a weight that felt profound. "I've had friends who seemed perfect on the surface but fell apart when life got tough. It's the ones who stay, who lean in when things get messy, that matter."

He nodded, his gaze steady, a hint of something deeper flickering behind his eyes. "It's like the diary itself. It holds the messy, beautiful truths of a person's life. Sometimes, the imperfections are what make a story worth telling."

There was something so comforting about discussing the intricacies of friendship and connection with him. Each revelation felt like peeling back the layers of a hidden treasure, revealing not just who we were, but who we could become.

"Speaking of stories," I said, my voice lowering conspiratorially, "I think we need to write our own."

Ethan raised an eyebrow, the glimmer of mischief returning to his eyes. "And what would our story be? A romantic comedy where we navigate the ups and downs of book hoarding?"

I feigned a gasp. "Hey, that's a serious profession! We could be the poster children for literary enthusiasts!" The playful banter made the air around us hum with excitement.

Our laughter faded into an easy silence, and I found myself drifting back to the diary, my fingers brushing over the yellowed pages. I realized that within this sacred space of sharing, I had let go of my guard just a little more. The fear of revealing my vulnerabilities seemed to shrink beneath the warmth of Ethan's presence.

"Let's write about our own adventures, then," I suggested, my tone earnest. "Not just the grand gestures, but the quiet moments that make life rich. The mornings spent drinking coffee while the world wakes up, the laughter shared over silly inside jokes. I want to remember those, too."

Ethan's face softened, and I could see the wheels turning in his mind. "I like that idea. It's like creating our own little world, where we can store our memories, much like this diary."

As he spoke, I felt an unexpected rush of joy. The thought of creating something together, capturing our lives in a way that was raw and honest, filled me with an exhilaration I hadn't anticipated. The thrill of collaboration ignited a fire within me, and I felt as if we were standing on the precipice of something beautiful and transformative.

"So, how do we begin?" he asked, his voice low and inviting.

"Let's start small," I suggested. "We could write down our favorite moments, the little things that bring us joy. The laughter, the warmth, the unexpected surprises. It'll be like a time capsule we can revisit whenever we need a reminder of what matters."

He nodded, enthusiasm flickering in his eyes. "I love that. It's like we'll be crafting our own mythology."

I could envision it, us tucked away in my little kitchen, crafting narratives that painted our lives in vibrant colors, each story a brushstroke in the masterpiece of our friendship. The world outside might be vast and chaotic, but within those walls, we would create our own sanctuary—a refuge filled with laughter, memories, and connection.

As we spoke, I felt the excitement swell between us, igniting a desire to pour our hearts onto the page. We picked up pens, their tips gliding smoothly over paper as we jotted down our favorite memories: the time we had gotten lost in the city, wandering aimlessly until we stumbled upon that quirky little bakery with the best pastries, or the evening we had spent under the stars, sharing our dreams and fears until the dawn broke.

With every word, the weight of our unspoken thoughts lifted, leaving behind a buoyancy that filled the air. It was exhilarating to watch our stories intertwine, forming a tapestry rich with color and texture, a beautiful homage to our shared experiences.

Hours passed unnoticed as we delved deeper into our creative project, each memory illuminating our connection, pulling us closer together. The more we wrote, the more I felt as if I were unveiling not only the intricacies of our friendship but also the quiet depths of my own heart.

Finally, as the candle flickered one last time, casting gentle shadows around the room, I placed my pen down, the ink drying on the page. "This feels like the beginning of something," I murmured, the words escaping my lips like a spell.

Ethan looked at me, the intensity of his gaze making my heart race. "It is," he said, his voice steady and filled with promise. "It's the beginning of us."

In that moment, surrounded by the remnants of our laughter and shared stories, I understood that we were no longer merely two people navigating life's complexities; we were co-authors of our own narrative, crafting a beautiful story that had just begun to unfold, full of shadows and light, laughter and tears, and everything in between. The weight of the past still lingered, but we were weaving our own threads into a tapestry that promised to be just as rich and complex as the lives we had read about, the lives we would soon cherish and remember.

Chapter 11: Torn Pages

The gallery was a riot of colors, each canvas shouting for attention in a chorus of reds, blues, and yellows that mingled and clashed like a crowd of revelers at a summer carnival. I stood amidst this symphony of artistry, my heart thumping a frantic rhythm, partly from the beauty that enveloped me and partly from the man standing beside me. Ethan. He was a magnetic force, his presence commanding yet gentle, and I felt like a child lost in the towering spires of a whimsical fairy tale, trying to make sense of the world. His eyes darted from one piece to another, each glance a spark of inspiration, while I found myself lingering in the shadows, battling a sense of insignificance that threatened to pull me under.

As we navigated through the sea of eclectic expressions, I caught Chloe's gaze flitting back to Ethan more times than I could count. She was like a storm cloud looming just on the periphery of my sunny day, her striking auburn hair catching the overhead lights and framing her face with an effortless beauty that had men turning their heads. I felt like a wisp of a breeze, unseen and barely felt, while she took center stage. The delicate knot in my stomach tightened, twisting my insides into a tight coil as I forced myself to focus on the artwork. Yet, each brushstroke seemed to echo my insecurities—vivid and chaotic, revealing more than I cared to admit.

Ethan turned toward me, his lips curving into a smile that felt like the sun breaking through a heavy overcast. "What do you think of this one?" he asked, pointing toward a chaotic swirl of colors that reminded me of a tempest. I hesitated, my thoughts scrambling to form a coherent response. The artist had captured a wildness I both admired and envied. "It's... intense," I finally managed, my voice slightly breathless. "It feels alive."

His eyes danced with excitement as he nodded, clearly enamored by the raw energy. "Exactly! The emotion practically leaps off the canvas." I couldn't help but marvel at how effortlessly he connected with art, his passion igniting a fire in his eyes that made my heart flutter. But as I stood there, cloaked in my own doubts, I couldn't shake the feeling that while he was passionate about art, he might not be as passionate about me.

We drifted further into the gallery, the cacophony of voices and laughter wrapping around us like a vibrant shawl. Each piece was a new world waiting to be explored, but my mind remained fixated on Chloe. She lingered a few paces behind us, her laughter ringing out like a siren's call, coaxing Ethan's attention back toward her. The way he occasionally turned to answer her questions, his gaze lighting up in a way that made my heart ache, sent my mind spiraling. Was I simply the backdrop in this unfolding story?

An installation caught my eye—a series of torn pages from books, meticulously arranged to create a semblance of a life once lived, now scattered like leaves in autumn. The pages whispered stories of love, loss, and longing, an echo of what lay within me. I stepped closer, feeling an undeniable connection to the fragmented narratives. My fingers brushed the edges, each torn corner a reminder of how I felt; pieces of myself scattered, trying to fit into a world that seemed so whole without me.

"Hey," Ethan's voice broke through my reverie, warm and inviting. I turned to face him, forcing a smile that I hoped concealed the tempest inside. "You okay?" he asked, genuine concern etched across his features. There was a tenderness in his gaze that made me want to spill my fears, but I bit my tongue, unwilling to show my vulnerabilities. Instead, I nodded, a simple gesture that felt too heavy for the weight of my unspoken emotions.

"Just admiring the art," I replied, gesturing toward the installation. "It's beautiful, isn't it?" He moved closer, and I caught the faint scent of his cologne—something crisp and woodsy, reminiscent of pine forests and open skies. He stepped beside me, our shoulders brushing once again, an electric connection that sent sparks flying through the air.

"Yes," he said softly, his eyes scanning the pages. "It's like each piece tells a story." I wanted to lean into him, to share the fragments of my own story—how I had wandered through life, always searching for my place, for belonging. But I hesitated, the weight of Chloe's presence a heavy anchor dragging me down.

As the evening wore on, the gallery pulsated with life. Laughter bubbled up around us, punctuated by the clinking of glasses and the rustle of cocktail napkins. I tried to lose myself in the artwork, but my heart remained tethered to the budding jealousy that crept in like a shadow. Each glance I caught between Ethan and Chloe made me feel more like an outsider, watching a world of color while I remained in grayscale.

When the exhibit reached its crescendo, a performance unfolded—a local poet weaving words like a delicate thread, stitching together the hearts of everyone present. I stood captivated, letting his verses wash over me, even as my mind tangled with the insecurities that fluttered like moths around a flame. The poet spoke of love and loss, of dreams deferred and hopes ignited, and I felt each word resonate within me, stirring emotions I had buried too deep.

But then I caught a glimpse of Ethan, his eyes glued to Chloe as she laughed, her head thrown back in carefree joy. The weight of those moments pressed down hard, a realization crystallizing in my chest. My heart raced as I understood that every torn page of my life was intertwined with the unwritten chapters that lay ahead. With every passing minute, I sensed my own story still unfolding, vibrant yet fragile, waiting for me to gather the courage to turn the page.

The energy in the gallery buzzed like the neon signs of a bustling city, every laugh and murmur adding to the vibrant tapestry of the evening. I was floating on a sea of emotions, the waves crashing against the shore of my thoughts. As the poet's words reverberated through the crowd, I felt a yearning swell within me—a desire to connect, to be seen, to be part of the beautiful chaos surrounding me. But as Chloe continued to shine, her laughter contagious and her spirit magnetic, I felt increasingly like a phantom drifting through a world I couldn't quite touch.

The crowd surged toward the exit, and I found myself trailing behind, caught in my web of insecurities. Ethan moved effortlessly, weaving through the throngs with the grace of a dancer. When he turned, his gaze searching for mine, the warmth in his eyes felt like sunlight breaking through dark clouds. I forced a smile, willing myself to step closer, to absorb his energy like a sponge soaking up water. But as I drew near, my heart sank when I caught Chloe's lingering gaze on him, her admiration too palpable to ignore.

We exited into the cool night air, the sky a velvet expanse dotted with stars, twinkling as if sharing secrets of their own. I took a deep breath, inhaling the scent of freshly cut grass mingling with the distant aroma of street food, a heady mix of familiarity and adventure. I longed to revel in this moment, to lose myself in the serenity of the night, but the tension coiling in my chest wouldn't release its grip.

"Did you enjoy it?" Ethan asked, his voice rich and melodic, pulling me from my thoughts. He stepped closer, creating a bubble of intimacy that seemed to shield us from the lingering doubts.

"It was inspiring," I replied, my voice steadier than I felt. "Especially that installation with the torn pages. It really struck a chord." I gestured toward the gallery, where a handful of people still lingered, sharing their thoughts in hushed tones, their voices blending into the night.

Ethan's eyes sparkled with understanding. "Yeah, it's amazing how a few torn pages can tell a story. It's like each fragment is a piece of someone's soul, discarded yet still holding meaning." His words wrapped around me, comforting in their depth.

Just then, Chloe emerged from the crowd, her cheeks flushed from excitement. "Hey, you two! What did you think of the poet?" She was radiant, and her presence felt like a sudden gust of wind that stirred the air around us, displacing the warmth between Ethan and me.

"He was great!" Ethan responded, enthusiasm spilling from him like a glass tipped too far. "He had this way of weaving words that made you feel everything."

I stood by, a shadow in the spotlight, as Chloe's laughter rang out again. "I could listen to him for hours! There's something magical about the way he captures raw emotion."

I offered a polite smile, but inside, a tempest brewed. Chloe seemed to embody everything I admired—confidence, charm, and an effortless connection to the world around her. And here I was, just a quiet observer, fumbling through my feelings like a child in a game of hide and seek, never quite sure if I'd be found.

Ethan turned his full attention to Chloe, their conversation flowing like a river, swift and unyielding. I felt like a stone in the water, slipping away from the current, longing to be part of their dialogue yet too timid to leap in. The distance between us widened, and I was left on the banks, watching the tide carry him further from me.

Feeling an ache deepen in my chest, I glanced away, focusing instead on the stars dotting the dark canvas above us. Each pinprick of light held the potential for a wish, a dream yet to be realized. I closed my eyes and inhaled deeply, allowing the chill of the night air to settle over me like a cool blanket, but the comfort it offered was fleeting.

"Do you want to grab a bite to eat?" Ethan's voice broke through my reverie, pulling my attention back to him. His brow furrowed with concern, and I could see the flicker of worry in his eyes, as if he could sense the dissonance in my spirit.

"Sure, that sounds nice," I managed, my voice catching slightly as I fought to maintain a facade of confidence. But my heart raced—would it be a night of laughter and camaraderie, or would it further deepen the chasm I felt widening between us?

As we ambled toward a nearby diner, the neon lights flickered like fireflies against the midnight sky, casting a glow that felt both inviting and intimidating. The bell above the door jingled as we entered, and the comforting aroma of burgers and fries enveloped us. I found solace in the familiarity of the space, with its vinyl booths and checkered floors, but even here, the shadows of my insecurities danced at the edges of my mind.

Seated in a cozy booth, I tried to immerse myself in the banter, but the conversation felt like a balancing act. Ethan and Chloe seemed to click effortlessly, sharing jokes and stories that made me want to lean in and contribute, yet I often found myself hanging back, waiting for the right moment to weave my voice into the tapestry they were creating.

"Remember that time we got lost during the road trip?" Chloe laughed, her eyes sparkling with mischief. "We ended up at that random gas station with the questionable hotdogs!"

Ethan chuckled, the sound rich and infectious. "I still can't believe we actually ate those. I thought we'd end up with food poisoning for sure!"

Their laughter filled the space, warm and buoyant, and I felt like an outsider peering through a window, longing to be part of the warmth inside. I picked at the edges of my fries, forcing a smile as they exchanged stories, but the more they laughed, the more I felt like a character in a story who had lost her narrative thread.

"Don't you think we should do another trip soon?" Chloe suggested, her voice light and airy. "We could hit the coast! I've always wanted to see the sunset over the ocean."

Ethan's eyes lit up, a spark igniting between them that felt too bright for my presence. "That would be amazing! Just imagine it—sand between our toes and the sound of waves crashing." He turned to me, a question in his gaze. "What do you think? Are you in?"

I hesitated, my heart clenching at the thought of joining them in a setting that felt foreign, a world where I was the third wheel, the odd piece in a perfectly fitting puzzle. "I don't know... I'm not great with spontaneous trips," I replied, my voice barely above a whisper, laced with uncertainty.

"Come on," Chloe chimed in, her smile wide and inviting. "It'll be fun! A little adventure never hurt anyone."

Ethan nodded, his gaze encouraging, but the thought of being swept away in their whirlwind left me feeling unsteady. Adventure had always felt like a distant land, a place I could only watch from afar, and now, the prospect of joining felt like stepping off a cliff into the unknown. I wanted to say yes, to grab hold of that thread of possibility, but the fear of falling held me back.

As they continued to weave their plans, I realized that this was the crux of it all. Beneath the layers of laughter and camaraderie lay my own fears—of inadequacy, of being unworthy, of losing myself in someone else's story. I was torn between the desire to connect and the instinct to retreat, caught in a struggle that felt painfully familiar, like a song I had heard too many times yet couldn't help but sing along to.

With each passing moment, the space between us felt both close and impossibly vast, a dance of emotions swirling in the dim light of the diner. I wanted to break through the noise, to articulate my heart, to lay bare my hopes and fears, but the words remained stuck, waiting for courage to emerge.

The chatter of diners filled the air, blending with the sizzle of fries in the fryer and the clink of silverware against plates, creating a comforting yet frenetic backdrop. I sat across from Ethan and Chloe, the booth's faux leather seat molded to my form like an embrace that felt just slightly too tight. They were lost in a whirlwind of memories, a tapestry woven from laughter and shared experiences, while I sat as a solitary thread, uncertain of my place in this colorful fabric of their friendship.

"Remember that crazy karaoke night?" Ethan laughed, his eyes sparkling with nostalgia as he leaned back, relishing the moment. "Chloe totally stole the show with that power ballad!"

"Only because you dared me!" Chloe countered playfully, her grin infectious. "You were supposed to be my backup, but you bailed before the first note!"

I took a sip of my soda, the fizz tickling my nose, while their laughter washed over me like a gentle wave. The taste was familiar—comforting, yet I felt out of sync, a note played slightly off-key in a melody I yearned to join. My heart raced with the weight of unspoken words, the urge to contribute clawing at my throat, but I hesitated, unsure how to navigate the space between them.

"Don't you have a karaoke night planned soon?" I interjected, eager to carve out a space for myself in their laughter. "That could be fun."

Ethan's gaze turned toward me, and I felt a flicker of hope, a brief moment where it seemed like he noticed my presence beyond the periphery. "Yeah! We should definitely all go. It's always a riot. I promise I'll sing this time!" He nudged Chloe playfully. "And you can't bail on me!"

Chloe rolled her eyes, the gesture light-hearted and teasing. "I'll hold you to that. I've got to see you tackle some of those cheesy 80s songs!"

The playful banter between them was a melody that wrapped around me, and for a moment, I felt a bit lighter, a fleeting sense of belonging seeping into my bones. Yet, beneath the surface of my smile, the same insecurities bubbled up again, sharp and insistent. What if they didn't want me there? What if I was simply an afterthought, a shadow in the glow of their friendship?

As we finished our meals, I found my gaze wandering to the diner's vintage decor, the faded photographs of the town's past lining the walls like silent witnesses to countless stories. Each frame told a tale—a young couple laughing at a picnic, children playing in a field, friends gathered around a table much like ours, their expressions frozen in time. I longed to be part of a narrative that felt as vibrant and alive as those snapshots. But was I creating my own story, or was I merely a spectator in theirs?

Once we left the diner, the crisp night air greeted us like an old friend, a refreshing contrast to the warmth inside. The streets shimmered under the glow of streetlamps, casting long shadows that danced playfully with each step we took. As we strolled, I couldn't help but notice how effortlessly Ethan and Chloe moved together, their laughter echoing like music, while I trailed behind, caught in a tangle of emotions.

"Have you two ever been to the old bookshop down the street?" I asked, hoping to draw them into a conversation where I could find my footing. "It has the most amazing collection of rare books. We should go sometime!"

Ethan's face lit up at the mention of books. "I love that place! They have a fantastic poetry section. Remember, Chloe? We spent hours browsing last time!"

"Yes! And you found that obscure book of poems," Chloe added, her eyes gleaming with excitement. "You've got a knack for finding hidden gems."

Their camaraderie made my heart swell, yet I couldn't help but feel like a puzzle piece that didn't quite fit, my edges jagged while theirs interlocked seamlessly. I longed to share in their laughter, to become part of the tapestry of stories they spun together, yet the nagging sensation that I didn't belong lingered like an unwelcome guest.

As we approached the bookshop, the soft glow from the windows beckoned us inside, illuminating the dusty tomes and cozy nooks that seemed to invite whispered secrets. The scent of aged paper and leather enveloped me as I stepped over the threshold, the familiar aroma grounding me amid the swirling doubts.

"Let's split up and explore!" Ethan suggested, excitement bubbling in his voice. "I'll check out the poetry, and you two can browse the fiction."

Chloe and I exchanged glances, and I could see her enthusiasm mirrored in my eyes. "Sounds perfect!" she replied, her voice a buoyant melody.

We wandered into separate aisles, and as I slid my fingers along the spines of books, I felt a sense of calm wash over me. Each title was a door to another world, a chance to escape into the pages where anything was possible. I pulled out a novel, its cover faded yet somehow beautiful, the tale of a lost love and the bittersweet ache of longing waiting to be uncovered.

In that moment of solitude, I allowed myself to breathe, the cacophony of my insecurities quieting, if only for a moment. I felt a tug at my heart, a whisper that perhaps I could carve out my own space in this story—my own narrative intertwined with theirs, yet distinctly mine.

When I emerged from my reverie, I noticed Ethan and Chloe sharing animated laughter in the poetry section, their heads bent together, a world built on shared words and dreams. The sight filled me with a mixture of warmth and sadness, like watching a sunset bathe the horizon in colors that were stunning yet fleeting.

"Hey, check this out!" Chloe exclaimed, holding up a book of poems that seemed to shimmer in the soft light. "It's by that new author I mentioned! The one who writes about love and loss with such raw emotion."

Ethan leaned closer, his eyes shining with intrigue. "I've heard about this one! I've been wanting to read it."

As they continued to explore, I felt a desire to step closer, to join them in their excitement. But as I approached, the words in my throat felt heavy, the weight of my fears settling back in like an unwelcome fog.

"What do you think, Lily?" Ethan suddenly called out, catching my gaze. "Do you have a favorite poet?"

The question hung in the air, charged with possibility, yet it felt like a spotlight aimed squarely at me. I hesitated, scrambling to pull my thoughts together, my mind racing through the many poets I adored. But as I opened my mouth to respond, the weight of expectation loomed larger than ever.

"I, um, I really like Rumi," I stammered, trying to summon confidence. "His words are so beautiful and full of longing. They resonate with me."

"Great choice!" Ethan replied, his smile genuine. "He has a way of capturing the essence of love and connection that's just breathtaking."

Chloe nodded enthusiastically. "You should share some of your favorite poems with us sometime. I'd love to hear how they speak to you."

I felt a flicker of hope, a glimmer of acceptance, as they turned back to the books. Maybe this was my moment to embrace vulnerability, to intertwine my story with theirs, even if it felt daunting.

"Actually," I began, my voice steadying as I approached them. "I've been working on some poems of my own. It's just something I do for myself, but I'd love to share them with you both."

Ethan's eyes widened with genuine interest, and I felt a rush of warmth at his response. "You write poetry? That's incredible! I'd love to read them."

Chloe's expression mirrored his enthusiasm. "Yes! Sharing poetry is such a beautiful way to connect. I can't wait to hear yours."

With those simple words, the weight I had carried for so long began to lift. It felt like the first rays of dawn breaking through the darkness, illuminating the path ahead. I realized that my story, with all its torn pages and insecurities, was worthy of being shared. I was no longer a mere observer in their world—I was becoming an integral part of it, a voice in the vibrant symphony we were creating together.

As we continued to explore the bookshop, I found myself caught in a tapestry of possibility, woven together with the threads of friendship, poetry, and the promise of new beginnings. The insecurities that had once anchored me felt lighter, replaced by the exhilarating notion that, perhaps, my narrative could intertwine with theirs, crafting a story that was uniquely our own. And in that moment, surrounded by the warmth of their laughter and the scent of old books, I felt the first stirrings of hope. The pages of my life were still being written, and I was ready to turn them, one word at a time.

Chapter 12: A Window to the Soul

The evening air wrapped around me like a comforting shawl as I settled into the sanctuary of my bookstore, nestled on a quaint corner of a bustling street in the heart of Portland. The soft, warm glow from the vintage Edison bulbs cast playful shadows across the shelves, illuminating the spines of books that whispered tales of adventure and heartbreak, each one inviting me into its world. The scent of aged paper mingled with the faint aroma of freshly brewed coffee from the small café nook in the back, creating an intoxicating atmosphere that always made me feel at home.

I pulled my journal from the wooden counter, its well-worn cover a testament to my many late-night musings and confessions. The pages, filled with my jagged handwriting, had become a refuge for my thoughts, a place where I could untangle the complexities of my heart. Tonight, however, the familiar act of writing felt more like a necessity, a desperate attempt to clear the fog that had settled over my mind. As I settled into the plush, overstuffed armchair by the window, I could see the world outside fading into dusk, the streetlights flickering to life like tiny stars trying to pierce the growing shadows.

With each stroke of my pen, the frustrations that weighed heavy on my heart began to ebb away. I wrote about my fears—how I constantly felt like a puzzle with too many pieces, some missing and others fitting together just wrong. The narrative flowed, a stream of consciousness that revealed not only my insecurities but also my burgeoning desire to confront them, to strip away the layers of self-doubt and show Ethan the real me. The idea filled me with a mix of exhilaration and terror. Would he still want to be around me once he knew the true depths of my struggles?

Just as I put my pen down, a sudden jingle of the doorbell snapped me from my reverie. I looked up to find Ethan stepping into the store, his presence like a breath of fresh air on a summer's day. The surprise etched on his face quickly transformed into a warm smile that sent a flurry of butterflies swirling in my stomach. He was a whirlwind of energy, effortlessly charming, with his tousled dark hair and the casual way he wore a denim jacket over a simple white T-shirt. It was as if he had walked straight out of one of the romantic novels lining my shelves, a character meant to unravel the tightly wound plot of my life.

"Didn't expect to find you here," he said, his voice smooth and inviting. He strolled over to where I sat, glancing at my journal with a curious tilt of his head. "What's the secret?"

I hesitated for a moment, grappling with the instinct to shield my vulnerabilities behind a veil of nonchalance. Yet, as I looked into his eyes, I sensed a flicker of understanding that encouraged me to lower my guard. There was a depth there, a sincerity that beckoned me to share my truth. "Just some thoughts on life and...well, feelings," I replied, the admission hanging in the air like the scent of rain on pavement.

"Feelings, huh?" He chuckled softly, the sound resonating within the cozy confines of the bookstore. "That sounds deep. Care to elaborate?"

I chuckled, the nervous energy dissipating, replaced by a budding confidence. We settled into an easy conversation, the awkwardness of my earlier thoughts fading with each word exchanged. We talked about the art exhibit we'd both seen the week before—the vibrant colors, the passion that spilled from each canvas. I recounted how the piece that had struck me most was a chaotic blend of reds and blues, the artist's turmoil and longing apparent in every brushstroke.

Ethan listened intently, leaning forward as if my words were the very air he breathed. "Art has a way of peeling back the layers, doesn't it?" he mused, his gaze steady and earnest. "It shows us what we hide from ourselves."

His insight sent a shiver down my spine, awakening something deep within me. There it was again—the notion that perhaps I didn't need to hide behind my insecurities, that showing my true self wouldn't lead to rejection but to connection. I couldn't help but admire how effortlessly he navigated the conversation, his genuine curiosity making me feel seen and heard in a way I hadn't experienced before.

"Exactly!" I said, my excitement bubbling over. "It's like you can glimpse into the soul of the artist, feel their heartbeat in the strokes of their brush. I want to do that—to be that open."

Ethan nodded, a smile breaking across his face, illuminating the corners of his eyes. "Then why not start with the people around you?" His words wrapped around me, each syllable a gentle nudge toward the edge of vulnerability I had long feared to approach.

As the conversation continued, I shared fragments of my story—the fear that clung to me like a shadow, the struggle of wanting to be more than what I believed I could be. Each revelation felt like a weight lifting, the heaviness in my chest easing with the understanding that I wasn't alone in my journey. Ethan didn't flinch; instead, he leaned in closer, his presence a comforting anchor amidst the tempest of my emotions.

With each exchange, I felt the invisible walls I had built around my heart beginning to crumble, revealing the tender, pulsating core that had been hidden for far too long. I was stronger than I thought, and perhaps, just perhaps, that strength was enough to let Ethan see the real me—the woman grappling with her fears while striving for the light.

The warmth of the conversation wrapped around me like a cozy blanket, making the outside world feel distant and unimportant. Each exchange with Ethan felt like a gentle unraveling of the threads that had tightly woven my heart into a protective cocoon. I dared to dive deeper, encouraged by the light in his eyes and the genuine interest he showed in my words. It was exhilarating, like swimming in a clear blue lake, the water cool against my skin, refreshing and invigorating.

As our laughter echoed softly within the walls of the bookstore, I noticed how the streetlights outside began to flicker on, casting a golden hue across the polished wooden floor. The world outside faded further into darkness, leaving our intimate little bubble untouched by time. I savored this moment, a sanctuary amid the chaos of life, where the weight of my insecurities felt lighter with every story shared.

"Have you ever felt like you were living in someone else's story?" I asked, my fingers absentmindedly tracing the rim of my coffee cup. The steam curled upward, mixing with the warm atmosphere that enveloped us. "Like you were just a character in a plot you didn't choose?"

Ethan's brow furrowed slightly, a thoughtful look crossing his face. "All the time. Sometimes, it feels like we're following a script written by someone else's expectations." He paused, and I could see him grappling with his own experiences. "But I think there's beauty in the moments we take control, where we can scribble our own lines into the narrative."

The clarity in his words struck a chord within me. I thought of the days I'd spent arranging my life to fit neatly into what I thought others wanted—a well-structured plot devoid of unexpected twists. Yet here we were, exploring the rawness of our experiences, allowing the real characters to emerge. I wanted to be brave enough to step into my own spotlight, to take the pen and write my own story, messy as it might be.

Ethan leaned back in his chair, the flickering overhead lights casting playful shadows across his features. "What about you?" he asked, his tone earnest and inviting. "What would your story look like if you had complete control?"

I took a moment to ponder the question, letting it settle like a leaf on the surface of a pond. "It would be filled with color and spontaneity," I began, my voice gaining momentum as my imagination ignited. "There would be adventures that take me off the beaten path, encounters that shake my worldview, and moments of vulnerability that build the strongest connections."

As I spoke, I imagined myself wandering through the vibrant streets of New Orleans, the air rich with jazz and the scent of beignets. I could almost hear the laughter of strangers mingling with the sound of street musicians, each note a reminder of the freedom to explore life's unpredictable rhythms. My mind danced through snapshots of sun-soaked days at the beach, where I could build sandcastles without worrying about tides or time. Each vision was a slice of life, filled with vibrant hues, laughter, and joy.

Ethan watched me with rapt attention, and I couldn't help but feel buoyed by the warmth of his gaze. "What about romance?" he asked, a playful smirk dancing on his lips. "Is there a love story in your script?"

My cheeks flushed, a mixture of embarrassment and excitement bubbling within me. "Oh, absolutely," I admitted, a playful glint in my eye. "It would be a rollercoaster of emotions—passionate and tumultuous, where every stolen glance holds a thousand unsaid words. I'd want a love that feels like coming home, yet always keeps me on my toes."

Ethan's laughter rang out, brightening the cozy atmosphere even further. "I think we'd all like that kind of story," he said, his voice teasing but sincere. "One filled with spark and unpredictability, where love is as thrilling as it is comforting."

With a grin, I nodded, feeling emboldened by the connection we were forging. "Yes, a love that challenges you to grow and embraces your flaws. The kind that feels like a favorite song—one you can listen to on repeat, never getting tired of the familiar chorus, yet always discovering something new in each note."

Our conversation continued, weaving through the nuances of life and dreams, passions, and fears. We shared tales of our childhoods, moments that shaped us, and those we wished to forget. The more we opened up, the deeper the bond felt, like an invisible thread tying our hearts together in a tapestry of shared experiences. I felt an unfamiliar warmth blossoming in my chest, something akin to hope. Maybe this was what it felt like to truly connect with someone, to peel back the layers until you reached the core—raw, unfiltered, and real.

As the night wore on, I glanced out the window, noticing the moon hanging low in the sky, casting a silvery light on the pavement outside. The world seemed to pause, holding its breath as if to witness the moment unfolding between us. I wondered if this was the turning point in my narrative, the moment I would look back on and realize that I had chosen to rewrite my own story.

Just then, Ethan's gaze caught mine, and for a heartbeat, the air crackled with an unspoken understanding. "I want to see you step into that narrative, you know?" he said, his voice low and earnest, as if he were revealing a precious secret. "You have so much to offer, and I think the world deserves to see the real you."

My heart fluttered, a delicate butterfly taking flight. I felt a rush of gratitude, intertwined with a flicker of apprehension. What did it mean to show my true self, to allow someone like Ethan to witness my journey? Yet, standing in this sacred space filled with dreams and aspirations, I realized that perhaps the fear of vulnerability was far less daunting than the regret of never trying.

With renewed determination, I looked into his eyes, feeling the warmth of connection radiating between us. "Then let's embark on this journey together," I said, a smile breaking across my face, my heart open to the possibilities that lay ahead. "Let's write our own stories, filled with laughter, adventure, and maybe a little bit of chaos."

Ethan returned my smile, and in that moment, a silent promise hung in the air. We would forge our paths, one step at a time, embracing the beautiful messiness of life together. I felt a sense of liberation wash over me, as if I were finally shedding the heavy layers of doubt that had long shackled my spirit. This was only the beginning—a canvas waiting to be painted with the vibrant hues of our stories, rich with the potential of the unknown.

The conversation blossomed between us like wildflowers in a sun-drenched meadow, vibrant and alive. Each shared thought and flicker of laughter wove us closer together, the fabric of our connection growing richer and more intricate. I felt an exhilarating freedom in revealing my thoughts, peeling back the layers I had kept so carefully guarded. Ethan was the sun to my shy blooms, coaxing me into the light with each question, each thoughtful nod, his genuine curiosity inviting me to flourish.

I caught a glimpse of myself reflected in his eyes—an image I hardly recognized. There was a glint of resilience there, the kind I had thought existed only in the pages of my favorite novels. I had always prided myself on being the dependable friend, the shoulder to cry on, but never the one who opened up completely. Yet, with Ethan, I felt a stirring within me, a longing to share the stories that shaped me, the dreams that danced just out of reach.

"I've always believed that the heart is like a garden," I said, my voice taking on a lyrical quality as the metaphor took shape. "It requires nurturing, patience, and sometimes, a little bit of wildness. If you tend to it, it can blossom beautifully, but it can also get choked by weeds if you're not careful."

Ethan leaned in, his expression encouraging. "So, what's been choking your garden?" he asked gently, his words a gentle nudge, urging me to dig deeper.

I hesitated, the weight of vulnerability settling like a heavy cloak on my shoulders. "I think it's the fear of disappointment," I confessed, my fingers curling around the warm ceramic of my mug. "I've spent so much time trying to live up to expectations—family, friends, society. It's exhausting. I feel like I've been playing a part, but now I want to break free and plant my own seeds."

Ethan nodded, understanding glimmering in his gaze. "What if you allowed yourself to fail? To not live up to those expectations for once?"

His question reverberated through me, igniting a flicker of hope mixed with apprehension. The notion of embracing failure was terrifying yet liberating. What if I could untangle myself from the web of expectations and cultivate a life that felt authentic? The possibility sent ripples of excitement through my veins, and I allowed myself to imagine what that might look like.

"I guess I've been so focused on the 'shoulds' that I've forgotten about the 'wants,'" I said, my voice growing firmer. "I want to travel, explore new places, learn to dance like nobody's watching, and dive headfirst into experiences that scare me."

Ethan's smile broadened, and I could see a flicker of admiration in his eyes. "Then why not start with a little adventure?" His enthusiasm was contagious, as if he was offering me a key to unlock the door to my hidden desires.

"Adventure?" I echoed, half-laughing, half-intrigued. "What kind of adventure do you have in mind?"

"Let's go to that new art gallery opening downtown this weekend," he suggested, the light in his eyes dancing with mischief. "I hear they're showcasing some up-and-coming local artists. It could be a perfect way to immerse ourselves in creativity and maybe even meet some fascinating people."

My heart raced at the prospect, a delightful flutter of excitement coursing through me. "You really think so? I mean, what if it turns out to be a disaster?"

"Then it will be a story worth telling," he replied with a grin, as if he were inviting me into a world where nothing was predetermined, where every twist and turn could lead to something extraordinary.

The thought of stepping into the unknown ignited a spark within me. I realized that this was more than just a spontaneous trip to an art gallery; it was a chance to step beyond the confines of my self-imposed limitations. "Okay, let's do it," I declared, my voice trembling with exhilaration.

As we continued to plan our impromptu adventure, the conversation shifted seamlessly into light-hearted banter, each laugh punctuating the air like a burst of confetti. I relished the feeling of camaraderie, the effortless flow of dialogue that felt both intimate and invigorating.

Before I knew it, the night had deepened, and the cozy bookstore had transformed into a cocoon of laughter and shared dreams. I glanced at the clock, realizing how quickly the hours had slipped away. "I should probably close up," I said reluctantly, a sense of sadness washing over me at the thought of ending our conversation.

"Let me help," Ethan offered, rising from his seat with a casual grace. Together, we began tidying the space, rearranging books and wiping down surfaces, all the while sharing stories of childhood adventures and the quirks that made us who we were. I found comfort in the mundane act of cleaning, the simplicity of working side by side with someone who genuinely wanted to be there.

With each book I returned to its rightful place, I felt an increasing sense of belonging—not just in the bookstore, but in this newfound connection with Ethan. The world outside faded, the streetlights casting soft glows that danced against the windows, reminding me of the vibrant colors we'd soon encounter at the gallery.

As we finished up, Ethan leaned against the counter, his gaze locked onto mine. "You know," he said, his tone shifting to something more earnest, "I'm really glad we met. I can't remember the last time I felt this kind of connection with someone. It's refreshing."

A blush crept across my cheeks, and I felt a warmth radiate from within. "I feel the same way," I admitted, my voice softer now. "It's like I've been waiting for someone to see the real me, and you...you've managed to look past the surface."

In that moment, the air crackled with unspoken possibilities. I caught the glimmer of something profound in his gaze, a promise that this was just the beginning of a journey yet to unfold. My heart swelled with hope, as if we were on the precipice of a new chapter—one filled with adventure, laughter, and the exquisite messiness of life.

Ethan's smile widened, and I felt a surge of courage within me. Maybe, just maybe, I was ready to embrace the wildness of my own story, to step boldly into the unknown and trust that the universe would catch me. With Ethan by my side, I sensed that I could navigate this uncharted territory, where every moment was a chance to plant new seeds, nurture them, and watch them bloom into something beautiful.

As we stepped outside, the crisp night air enveloped us, filled with the scents of possibility. The moon hung low, a watchful guardian over our unfolding tale. Hand in hand, we took our first steps into the unknown, ready to paint our own vivid masterpiece amidst the swirling colors of life.

Chapter 13: Through the Looking Glass

The air crackled with the crisp energy of autumn as I weaved through the bustling streets of Maplewood, my senses alive with the scents of cinnamon and caramel wafting from nearby stalls. Pumpkins adorned every corner, their bright orange skins glowing like little suns against the backdrop of fiery red and golden leaves. Children darted past me, their laughter ringing like wind chimes in the gentle breeze, their cheeks flushed from the chill. It was a quintessential fall day, the kind that held the promise of warm cider and stories shared under a blanket of stars.

My heart fluttered with the anticipation of the annual fall festival, a vibrant celebration that seemed to breathe life into our small town. I had set up a booth for my bookstore, surrounded by the warm glow of fairy lights strung overhead, casting a whimsical light across the rows of books. The wooden table, polished and smooth, was an inviting surface for the carefully curated selection of novels and cozy mysteries. I had picked each book with love, hoping to connect readers with worlds that mirrored their dreams or whisked them away from the mundane.

As I organized the titles, arranging them like a careful puzzle, my mind wandered to Ethan. He had promised to be here, to help me share my passion, but as the minutes stretched into hours, his absence hung over me like a storm cloud. I brushed off the growing worry, engaging with customers who were drawn to the colorful display. Each conversation was a spark of joy, a reminder of why I loved this town and the people in it. I shared stories of characters who had become my friends, and soon, my booth was alive with laughter and the sound of pages turning.

Yet, as the sun dipped lower in the sky, painting the horizon with strokes of orange and violet, an unsettling sense of urgency gripped me. I scanned the festival grounds, filled with vibrant booths and swirling decorations, searching for a familiar face. My heart sank as I caught a glimpse of him across the field, laughing and chatting animatedly with Chloe. They were bathed in the golden light of the setting sun, and in that moment, everything felt surreal, like a scene from one of the novels I adored.

A lump formed in my throat as I watched the two of them, the way their laughter danced through the air, intoxicating and unguarded. Chloe, with her bright smile and effortless charm, was everything I felt I could never be. She was the kind of person who turned heads and captivated attention without even trying. I could feel the weight of my insecurities dragging me down as I stood frozen, unsure of whether to approach or retreat into the safety of my booth.

A surge of determination flooded through me. I had to confront this rising tide of feelings or risk drowning in a sea of uncertainty. I couldn't let fear dictate my actions any longer. Drawing in a deep breath that tasted of apples and promise, I took a step forward, leaving the comfort of my booth behind. Each stride felt like a declaration of my intent, a quiet rebellion against the anxiety that had gripped me since I'd first glimpsed Ethan with her.

The laughter of the festival faded into a dull hum as I approached them, and my heart raced with the thunderous rhythm of anticipation. The vibrant lights seemed to twinkle more brightly, illuminating the path ahead, urging me on. As I drew closer, I could see Ethan's face, a blend of joy and warmth that always made my heart flutter. My resolve deepened with every step; this was a moment I needed to seize, to carve out my own place in this unfolding narrative.

"Ethan!" I called, my voice steady despite the wild fluttering in my stomach. He turned, his laughter catching in his throat as our eyes met. In that instant, the world around us faded away, leaving only the two of us suspended in a fragile bubble of possibility. Chloe glanced between us, her expression unreadable, but I pushed past the instinct to retreat. I was here, and I had every right to be.

"Ethan," I repeated, stepping closer, the distance between us closing like the final pages of a well-loved book. "Can we talk?"

His brow furrowed, concern flickering in his eyes as he excused himself from Chloe. The chatter of the festival, once a comforting hum, now felt intrusive as we stood together, the air thick with unspoken words. I could see the questions swirling behind his gaze, mirroring the chaos in my own heart.

"What's up?" he asked, his voice soft yet curious, like a warm embrace that pushed back the cold.

I hesitated, the weight of everything I wanted to say pressing against my chest. How could I articulate the whirlwind of emotions that had taken root within me? Instead, I took a step back, reclaiming my space, the flickering lights overhead reflecting the turmoil inside. "I just... I wanted to see you. I was worried when you didn't show up, and I thought maybe we could—"

"Sorry, I got caught up talking to Chloe," he interjected, but the sincerity in his tone cut through the rising tide of disappointment.

"That's fine," I said, forcing a smile that felt shaky at best. "I just miss spending time with you. This festival feels different, you know? I want us to enjoy it together." My heart raced as I spoke, the truth spilling out like leaves tumbling in the wind, each word more liberating than the last.

Ethan's expression shifted, the laughter in his eyes fading into something more serious. He stepped closer, the distance between us now charged with unspoken possibility. "I miss that too," he confessed, his voice a soft balm against my anxiety. "I just didn't know if you wanted me here."

"Of course I do," I replied, feeling the weight of my insecurities begin to lift, if only for a moment. "I want us to share this, to figure it out together."

His gaze held mine, a flicker of something deeper passing between us, a shared understanding that whispered promises of more to come. As the festival buzzed around us, our connection blossomed like the autumn leaves, vibrant and full of potential, waiting for the right moment to unfurl.

The air was thick with the sweet aroma of candied apples and the earthy smell of freshly turned leaves, blending seamlessly into the tapestry of sounds that filled the festival. The laughter of children, the cheerful bickering of vendors, and the distant strum of a guitar created a symphony that pulsed in time with the heartbeat of Maplewood. As the last slivers of sunlight faded, I could feel the excitement in the air building to a crescendo, and with it, my determination hardened.

Ethan's gaze still lingered in my mind, his laughter an echo that refused to dissipate. I studied him as he talked with Chloe, her animated gestures drawing him into her orbit. Every laugh that escaped his lips was like a dagger, stirring feelings I had kept hidden beneath layers of hope and fear. In that moment, the world around us faded, the colors brightening into surreal hues that seemed to mirror my emotional upheaval. This was my chance—a moment suspended in time where I could either sink into the shadows of doubt or step boldly into the light of possibility.

Taking a deep breath, I stepped closer, weaving through the crowd, my heart pounding with each stride. The familiar faces of friends and neighbors flashed by, their joyful smiles a stark contrast to the storm swirling inside me. With every step, I could feel the warmth of the festival enveloping me, urging me forward like a cosmic force. I reached them just as Ethan turned away from Chloe, his expression shifting from carefree laughter to something more contemplative, something that made me think he felt the tension too.

"Hey," I said, my voice steady but light, as if I were testing the waters. His eyes lit up, and a smile broke across his face, banishing the shadows that had momentarily clouded it.

"Hey!" he replied, his enthusiasm returning like the sun breaking through clouds after a rainstorm. "I was just telling Chloe about the new mystery novel I found in your shop. I think you're going to love it."

Chloe's eyes sparkled with curiosity, and for a brief moment, I felt an unexpected swell of pride. "What mystery?" I asked, leaning in as if the mere act of sharing this moment could solidify my place in it.

"Something about a haunted library and a missing author," he said, his enthusiasm infectious. "You know, it has that perfect blend of eerie and charming that I know you appreciate."

I grinned, feeling the tightness in my chest loosen just a fraction. "You have no idea how much I love a good library ghost story. It's practically a genre of its own," I said, my voice dipping into conspiratorial delight.

Chloe laughed, her laughter ringing clear and bright in the warm evening air. "Sounds perfect for a chilly October night. You two should host a ghost story reading at the bookstore. I'd come!"

"Absolutely," I replied, caught up in the energy of the moment, the flutter of hope beginning to chase away the remnants of doubt. "It could be our first event of the season."

Ethan's eyes met mine, and there was a flicker of something unspoken between us—a spark of connection that pulsed in the spaces where words failed. The chatter of the festival around us began to fade, the world narrowing down to just the three of us, a bubble of warmth amidst the bustling chaos.

"What about you, Chloe? Do you have a favorite ghost story?" Ethan asked, turning the conversation back to her, yet the gaze he held me with lingered like an unspilled secret.

"I do! There's this old tale about a librarian who never left her library. She helps lost books find their way home, even after she's gone," she replied, her eyes lighting up as she recounted the story.

"Now that's a story worth telling," I said, savoring the moment, the intertwining of our lives like threads in a rich tapestry. I could almost feel the weight of my own thoughts lift, swirling away like autumn leaves caught in a playful gust of wind.

But the moment was fleeting. As the laughter echoed around us, a shadow fell across my heart—a reminder of the uncertainty that still loomed. Just as I was savoring the simplicity of this gathering, the reality of what I needed to say surged forward, a tide I could no longer ignore.

"Ethan," I began, my voice rising above the laughter and music, tinged with an earnestness that surprised even me. "I really value our friendship, and I've been thinking... about us."

His smile faltered, and for a moment, time stood still, the world around us fading back into the background. Chloe, sensing the shift, glanced between us before excusing herself to grab some hot cider, leaving us enveloped in a space that felt suddenly expansive and intimate.

"Yeah?" he replied, his tone cautious but attentive, as if he were bracing himself for a storm.

"I don't want to complicate things, but I've realized that what I feel for you goes beyond friendship. I like you, Ethan. More than I probably should," I confessed, my heart racing. I could almost hear the whispered encouragement of the festival around us, the rustle of leaves and distant melodies urging me on.

He shifted slightly, his gaze dropping to the ground as he processed my words. A silence stretched between us, thick and charged, like the stillness before a summer storm. My heart thudded in my chest, each beat a reminder of the vulnerability I had just laid bare. I wanted to reach out, to touch him, to close the space that felt like a chasm opening up beneath us, but I stayed still, afraid of the answer that might ripple back.

"I had no idea you felt that way," he finally said, his voice low and contemplative, as if weighing every word carefully.

"I didn't either, not until today. But seeing you with Chloe, it made me realize how much I don't want to miss my chance," I admitted, my cheeks flushing as the words poured out, raw and real. "I didn't want to be the friend who waited too long."

He met my gaze again, and in his eyes, I could see the flicker of uncertainty mirrored back at me. "I like you too, but I didn't know if you saw me that way. I thought maybe I was just someone you enjoyed hanging out with," he confessed, his voice carrying a hint of relief mingled with hesitation.

"I want to be more than that," I said, emboldened by his honesty. "I want us to explore what this could be. Together."

He stepped closer, a tentative movement, yet charged with potential. "I'd like that. I really would."

A smile broke through the tension, blooming like the vibrant colors around us, and in that moment, the world felt lighter. The festival buzzed back to life as if it had been holding its breath, ready to celebrate this new chapter, this leap into the unknown. The connection between us shimmered with the promise of something beautiful, vibrant, and real, as we stood there beneath the glittering lights, open to whatever paths lay ahead.

With the exchange of unspoken words lingering in the air like the remnants of a beautiful song, Ethan and I stood at the edge of a new beginning, each moment stretching deliciously before us. The festival swirled around us, a kaleidoscope of energy and color that perfectly matched the flutter of excitement in my chest. Laughter bubbled up from nearby booths, children darted past with sticky fingers clutching caramel apples, and the sounds of an acoustic guitar drifted through the crisp evening air. I could feel the pulse of life in Maplewood—alive and electric.

As the initial rush of adrenaline settled into a warm, steady hum, I found my courage blossoming like the marigolds lining the pathway. "So, what do we do now?" I asked, my voice laced with playful curiosity, hoping to keep the momentum of our newfound connection alive.

Ethan chuckled, the sound rich and inviting, sending a rush of warmth through me. "How about we check out the pie-eating contest? I heard Mrs. Hargrove made her famous apple pie this year. It's supposed to be legendary," he suggested, his eyes sparkling with mischief.

"Legendary, huh? I don't think I can resist a challenge," I replied, the playful banter flowing effortlessly between us. It felt liberating to share this lightness, a contrast to the heaviness that had shadowed my heart earlier.

Together, we navigated the festival, threading our way through crowds of smiling faces and colorful booths, where vendors peddled everything from homemade candles to intricate crafts. The night enveloped us in a cozy embrace, and the fairy lights above twinkled like stars caught in a gentle breeze. Each step felt like a dance, an unspoken rhythm we were beginning to share.

We found our way to the contest area, where Mrs. Hargrove stood behind a table overflowing with golden-brown pies, each one beckoning with the promise of sweetness and spice. She beamed at us, her round face framed by curly gray hair, a halo of warmth and nostalgia. "Ah, if it isn't my favorite bookshop owner and her charming friend! Are you here to indulge in some pie or to witness the chaos?"

I grinned at her, feeling a rush of affection for this woman who had become a cornerstone of the community. "A little bit of both, I think! I might just have to sample the competition, too."

As we settled in on the sidelines, I caught sight of the contestants: a motley crew of local daredevils, ranging from spirited teenagers to seasoned adults, each brimming with the determination to devour as much pie as possible within a set time. I exchanged a look with Ethan, laughter dancing in our eyes as we shared a moment of collective disbelief at the absurdity of it all.

The whistle blew, and the chaos erupted. Faces smeared with apple filling, grins wide enough to rival the Cheshire Cat, and shrieks of laughter filled the air. I felt the weight of the day slip away, my worries fading into the background, overtaken by the sheer joy of the moment.

"This is a perfect representation of fall in Maplewood," I mused, leaning in closer to Ethan, the scent of cinnamon and apples enveloping us. "People letting go of their inhibitions, just enjoying life. It's what I love about this town."

Ethan turned to me, the warmth of his gaze igniting something deep within. "It's also the perfect setting for us to be ridiculous together," he said, a teasing smile on his lips. "Should we join in on the madness next year?"

I laughed, the sound bubbling up uncontrollably. "Oh, absolutely! You're on!" The thought of us, side by side, faces covered in pie as we competed for glory, filled me with a sense of joy I hadn't expected.

As the contest wrapped up, we ambled over to Mrs. Hargrove's booth to grab slices of her famed pie. "Two slices, please!" I said, handing her a few bills, my excitement palpable.

She handed us generous portions, the flaky crust glistening with a hint of sugary glaze. I took a bite, the flavor exploding on my tongue—a perfect balance of tart and sweet, with hints of nutmeg and cinnamon. "Oh my god, this is incredible!" I exclaimed, savoring every morsel.

Ethan mirrored my enthusiasm, his laughter infectious as he wiped a crumb from the corner of his mouth. "I think I might have found my new favorite food group."

"Pie?" I teased, nudging him playfully.

"Absolutely. No contest," he shot back, and in that moment, everything felt right. The air buzzed with an energy that pulsed between us, threading our lives together in a tapestry woven from laughter and sweet memories.

With the night deepening, the festival glowed under a blanket of stars, the sounds of music and laughter rising around us like a soft wave. "Let's take a walk," Ethan suggested, motioning toward the edge of the festival grounds where the trees stood tall and proud, their leaves rustling in the night breeze.

As we strolled, the path lined with flickering lanterns casting gentle shadows, our shoulders brushed, sending delightful shivers down my spine. The cool air filled with the earthy scent of fallen leaves and the distant warmth of bonfires. Each step felt like a journey deeper into connection, a step further into understanding one another.

"Do you remember the first fall festival you attended?" he asked, breaking the comfortable silence that enveloped us.

"I do! I was so nervous. I had just moved here and didn't know anyone. I remember standing by the dunk tank, watching my neighbor get soaked, and thinking how strange and wonderful this town was," I replied, nostalgia coloring my tone.

He chuckled, "And look at you now. The town's unofficial book ambassador, charming the pants off everyone."

I laughed, warmth blooming in my chest. "I wouldn't say unofficial. I'll take that title proudly."

As we wandered deeper into the festival, we stumbled upon a small stage where local musicians played folk tunes, their melodies twirling into the night. Ethan and I paused, letting the music wash over us, the sweet notes mingling with the laughter and chatter around us. It felt like a scene from a romantic movie, the kind where everything suddenly makes sense, where the world narrows down to just two people in a universe of possibilities.

"Dance with me?" Ethan asked, his voice a gentle invitation.

I hesitated, glancing at the small crowd around us, but he took my hand, the warmth of his touch igniting sparks of courage. "Come on, it'll be fun," he encouraged, his eyes glimmering with mischief.

With a smile that felt like the sun breaking through clouds, I nodded, allowing him to pull me into the small clearing. As the music enveloped us, I melted into the moment, surrendering to the rhythm. We swayed together, lost in a bubble of laughter and warmth, my heart racing in time with the music.

Ethan's hands found their way to my waist, grounding me as I moved closer. The world around us faded into a blur, and suddenly, it was just us—two souls dancing in the glow of fairy lights, the laughter of the festival fading into the background.

"I'm glad you're here," I said, the sincerity flowing freely as I gazed up at him, his face illuminated by the warm light, and in that moment, everything felt right.

"Me too," he replied, his voice a soft promise hanging in the air between us. The distance we had once feared was now a bridge built on connection, laughter, and a shared love for this little town that had brought us together.

As the song reached its crescendo, I knew this was a night I would cherish forever. The festival, the laughter, the pie—everything came together in a beautiful mosaic that mirrored the hope I felt blooming within me. In this vibrant world, amid the colors and lights, I found not just Ethan but a part of myself I had been searching for, and it felt like magic, rich and alive, whispering the promise of new beginnings.

Chapter 14: The Truth Unfolds

The festival pulsed around us, a cacophony of color and sound blending into a backdrop of flickering lanterns and a warm, golden glow that set the night ablaze. I stood before Ethan, an island of anxiety amidst the swirling crowd. The air hung thick with the scent of roasted corn and candied apples, a sweet aroma that usually coaxed laughter from my lips, but tonight, it lodged in my throat like a stone. His blue eyes, usually a source of comfort, now swirled with uncertainty. I could almost feel the weight of unspoken words hanging between us, thick and suffocating, as if the very fabric of the universe had shifted beneath our feet.

"Can we talk?" I murmured, my voice trembling like a leaf caught in the wind. Ethan's brow furrowed, and I could see the flicker of concern dance across his face. In an instant, the infectious laughter and the vibrant music faded into a muted hum, our world narrowing down to this singular moment of vulnerability.

We slipped away from the festive throng, wandering toward a secluded nook just outside the reach of the lights. The hum of the festival turned into a distant melody, the joyous shouts of friends and families dimming into a whisper. The cool night air brushed against my skin, sending a shiver down my spine that had nothing to do with the temperature. I tucked a loose strand of hair behind my ear, a nervous habit that had betrayed me countless times before.

"Ethan," I began, my heart pounding against my ribcage like a wild animal desperate to escape. "I need to be honest with you." My eyes searched his, hoping to find reassurance, but instead, I was met with a cautious curiosity. "I've been thinking about you and Chloe... and I can't shake the fear that I'll lose you to her." Each word felt like a stone thrown into a still pond, sending ripples of unease across the space between us.

His gaze softened, and for a heartbeat, the world around us seemed to freeze. "You're the one I want to be with," he replied, his voice steady yet filled with an undercurrent of hesitation. I felt a spark of hope ignite within me, flaring brightly before it was shrouded in shadow. The words hung in the air, heavy and profound, but they were soon followed by a caveat that twisted my stomach into knots. "But I don't want to hurt her either."

Reality crashed down like a tidal wave, and my heart plummeted into the depths of despair. I could see it now, the intricate web of emotions we were all tangled in, each thread representing a choice, a possibility. I had hoped for a straightforward resolution, a moment of clarity that would dissolve our complications like sugar in hot tea. Instead, I stood on the precipice of heartache, my hopes precariously balanced on the edge of a delicate precipice.

"Ethan, it's not just about her," I insisted, desperation creeping into my voice. "I've spent too many sleepless nights wondering if I'm not enough for you. If you're drawn to her, then maybe I should just... step aside." The idea of relinquishing him felt like a dagger twisting in my chest. How could I so easily dismiss the connection we had built, the moments we shared, the laughter that echoed in the corners of my heart?

His expression shifted, a mixture of frustration and sadness flickering across his features. "No, you don't understand. You're everything I want," he said, stepping closer, his warm breath mingling with the cool night air. "But Chloe's been my friend for so long. I don't want to hurt her feelings. It's complicated." The sincerity in his voice only deepened the ache inside me.

"Complicated doesn't mean impossible," I replied, my voice stronger now, fueled by the heat of my emotions. "We have something special, Ethan. It's not fair to either of us to pretend otherwise." The truth of my words settled over me like a comforting blanket, yet the weight of reality pressed down on my shoulders, reminding me of the tangled web we found ourselves in.

He glanced away, his jaw tightening as he considered my words. The chaos of the festival faded into a mere echo as the world around us continued to twinkle with laughter and joy. My heart thudded, each beat echoing the urgency of the moment. I yearned to reach out, to close the distance between us and grasp the undeniable chemistry that thrummed just beneath the surface.

"Do you remember the first time we met?" Ethan asked suddenly, a ghost of a smile flickering on his lips. The tension between us lightened for a moment, and I couldn't help but smile back, recalling the clumsy introductions at the community center. "You spilled your drink all over my shoes," he chuckled softly, a warmth spreading across his face. "You were so mortified."

"I was just trying to impress you," I teased, my heart momentarily buoyed by the shared memory. "Clearly, I failed spectacularly." We laughed together, a brief interlude that offered a reprieve from the weighty conversation, but I could see the clouds of uncertainty still swirling in his eyes.

"I just wish it could be easier," he said, his voice softening. "But I don't want to hurt anyone." The earnestness in his expression tugged at my heartstrings, the conflict evident in every line of his face.

"I get that," I replied, my tone gentle yet firm. "But what about us? Don't we deserve to be happy too?" The question lingered in the air, charged with unspoken possibilities, the path ahead veiled in uncertainty.

He paused, studying my face as if searching for an answer within the depths of my eyes. I held my breath, every second stretching into infinity, hoping he could see the sincerity of my feelings, the truth that thrummed beneath the surface of our friendship. The festival lights flickered above us, illuminating our fragile moment of honesty, weaving a tapestry of hope and desire that was as bright as the stars twinkling in the night sky.

The air between us crackled with an electric tension, the kind that happens when two people are standing at a crossroads but aren't quite ready to choose a direction. I could see Ethan grappling with the weight of the moment, the dilemma etched into his brow, and I felt a pang of sympathy for the predicament we found ourselves in. A festival that should have been a backdrop of carefree joy now felt like a pressure cooker, each heartbeat echoing the urgency of our conversation.

"I never wanted this to become a mess," he finally admitted, running a hand through his tousled hair, the moonlight highlighting the gentle waves. "I thought I could just keep things simple." The honesty in his tone washed over me like a refreshing wave, yet it only intensified the disquiet in my heart. Simplicity seemed a distant fantasy now, buried beneath the complexities of our lives, like the way the sun sets behind a mountain range, beautiful yet unreachable.

"Maybe simple isn't what we need," I countered, my voice steadier than I felt. The laughter of festival-goers danced on the edges of our conversation, a reminder of the world we were stepping away from. "Maybe we need to be brave enough to admit what we really want." My words hung in the air, heavy with unspoken feelings that swirled like the colors of the festival's decorations—vibrant, chaotic, and full of potential.

Ethan's eyes narrowed thoughtfully, his gaze drifting to the flickering lanterns above us, their glow casting soft shadows that played across his handsome features. The light illuminated the sharp angles of his jaw, and for a moment, I could see how the weight of his decision rested on him like a heavy cloak. "You really think we could just... ignore everything else and focus on us?" His question was laden with a hint of disbelief, yet the flicker of hope in his expression was unmistakable.

"Yes," I said, the conviction rising from my core. "I think we can. But it has to start with us being honest—not just with each other but with ourselves." I could feel the urgency of the night pressing down upon us, urging him to see beyond the fear of hurting others. It was a delicate dance of feelings and choices, one that required not only trust but a leap of faith.

"I'm scared, you know?" he admitted, his voice dropping to a hush, almost as if the world beyond our little sanctuary might overhear. "What if I make the wrong choice? What if we hurt her more than we intend to?" His concern was valid, a voice of reason in the storm of emotions swirling between us, yet it tugged at my heartstrings. I longed to reassure him that love didn't have to be a battleground of guilt, but rather a journey of shared truths and open hearts.

"We're all just trying to figure it out, Ethan," I said, leaning in closer, my eyes locking onto his. "No one's going to emerge from this completely unscathed. But isn't it worth it to find out what we have?" The festival pulsed behind us like a heartbeat, reminding me that life was filled with fleeting moments, and I didn't want to let this one slip through my fingers.

He took a deep breath, as if collecting all the pieces of his uncertainty, and I felt a pang of empathy wash over me. "I just don't want to lose what I already have, you know? Chloe's been my friend forever." The raw honesty in his voice sent a shiver through me, and I couldn't help but wonder if friendship, while essential, was enough to anchor him when the tides of passion and connection surged so strong.

"Friendship can be a beautiful foundation, but it can also grow into something deeper," I offered, trying to weave our possibilities into a tapestry of hope. "What we have... it's different. It's real." As I spoke, I felt a flutter of vulnerability, my heart laid bare before him.

He regarded me with an intensity that sent warmth blooming in my chest. "I want to believe that," he murmured, his eyes reflecting the flickering lights above. "I want to be brave enough to follow this feeling, but—"

"No more 'buts,'" I interjected, my voice firm yet laced with a hint of playfulness. "Just let yourself feel this moment. Let yourself feel us." The sincerity of my words hung in the air, intertwining with the soft melodies that drifted from the festival, the lively sounds now a gentle reminder of the life we had outside our intimate bubble.

For a heartbeat, it felt like we were the only two people in the universe. The distant laughter echoed like a fading symphony, leaving only the quiet thrum of our hearts. And then, slowly, Ethan's features softened, a flicker of resolution sparking in his eyes.

"You're right," he said, his voice steady. "I want to explore this. I want to see where it leads." Relief flooded through me, warm and consuming, yet it was tinged with a new kind of apprehension. The road ahead was unclear, a winding path shrouded in uncertainty, but at least now we were walking it together.

As if on cue, a firework exploded overhead, scattering brilliant colors against the inky sky, each burst a testament to the magic of the night. I glanced up, the brilliance captivating my senses. It was a moment where joy collided with fear, where hope mingled with trepidation, and I couldn't help but smile at the audacity of it all.

"See that?" I pointed skyward, where the last sparkles of light faded into the darkness. "That's life. It's unpredictable and beautiful all at once."

He turned to me, and the corners of his mouth lifted into a genuine smile, the kind that crinkled the edges of his eyes. "Maybe you're right. Maybe we just have to embrace the chaos."

The warmth radiating between us felt electric, igniting a flame of possibility that danced in the air. I took a step closer, feeling the heat of his body radiate against the cool night air. For the first time in what felt like an eternity, I sensed that we had stepped beyond the boundary of friendship, the moment teetering on the edge of something profound.

As the sounds of the festival swirled around us, laughter bubbling up and mixing with the distant melodies, I knew that whatever lay ahead—challenges, joys, or heartaches—we would face it together. I wanted to embrace this new beginning, to savor each second as we crafted our own story amidst the vibrant chaos of life, the colors of our journey exploding like fireworks in the night sky.

The festival's heart continued to beat wildly around us, a vibrant backdrop to our fragile moment, where laughter danced in the air and the intoxicating scent of fried dough mingled with the sweet aroma of caramel apples. I could still hear the distant strains of live music floating through the night, notes curling around us like a warm embrace, but the world beyond our little haven felt both exhilarating and intimidating, teetering on the precipice of potential change.

Ethan's face, lit by the soft glow of fairy lights strung above us, was a canvas of conflict. "It's complicated," he repeated, as if those two words could encapsulate all the swirling emotions and uncertain futures hanging in the balance. I wanted to reach out, to bridge the distance between what he feared and what we could become.

"Complicated might just mean that it matters," I replied, my heart quickening at the thought of our connection. "It's not easy, but nothing worth having ever is." My voice trembled slightly, but the warmth in my chest urged me to speak my truth, to dismantle the barriers that threatened to keep us apart. I took a tentative step closer, feeling the gravity of the moment pulling us together, as if the universe conspired to weave our fates.

Ethan's brow furrowed in thought, a momentary crease deepening between his eyes, but the tension in his shoulders eased slightly as he absorbed my words. "What do you want?" he finally asked, his voice low, almost reverent. The question hung in the air, heavy with unspoken hopes and fears.

"I want to explore this," I confessed, feeling the pulse of the festival thrumming in my veins. "I want to see what we could be." The honesty of the moment washed over us, each word a tiny wave eroding the rocky foundation of uncertainty between us. "Life is too short to play it safe, to let fear dictate our choices."

His gaze shifted, searching mine, and for the first time, I saw a flicker of determination ignite behind the veil of doubt. "You make a compelling argument," he said, the hint of a smile tugging at the corners of his mouth. "I just... need to figure out how to navigate everything without causing pain."

"Pain is inevitable," I replied, a note of intensity lacing my voice. "But I'd rather embrace the risk than remain in the shadows of what could have been." I reached for his hand, my fingers grazing his palm, the warmth of our connection igniting a fire deep within me.

He hesitated, the heat of my touch sending shivers up my arm, before finally intertwining his fingers with mine. "Okay," he breathed, the weight of his acceptance felt monumental, as if we had crossed an invisible threshold into a realm of possibilities.

Just then, a chorus of cheers erupted nearby as a firework exploded in the sky, sending a shower of brilliant colors cascading against the dark canvas above us. We looked up, momentarily entranced by the beauty of the moment, and as the vibrant lights flickered in our eyes, I couldn't help but feel that we were witnessing our own potential unfold in a dazzling display.

"Let's take this one step at a time," Ethan suggested, turning back to me, the smile now genuine and warm. "We'll figure it out together." His words were a balm to my racing heart, soothing the frayed edges of anxiety.

"Together," I echoed, the word resonating like a promise. The thrill of the unknown buzzed in the air, but so did a sense of relief.

As we stood there, hand in hand, I felt the invisible threads of connection strengthen, weaving our lives together with a delicate but unbreakable bond.

The festival began to wind down, families and couples drifting toward food stalls and carnival rides, laughter ringing through the air like chimes. But we remained in our little bubble, the world around us fading into a backdrop, a stage where only our emotions played out in vivid colors.

"Do you want to grab some food?" I suggested, the thought of sharing cotton candy or funnel cake suddenly appealing. "I hear the caramel apples are to die for."

Ethan's eyes lit up, a spark of mischief igniting within them. "Only if you share it with me," he replied, the warmth in his gaze making my heart flutter.

As we made our way through the remnants of the festival, the crowd parted like the sea, laughter swirling around us, our hands still intertwined. The atmosphere felt charged, vibrant, alive with possibility, as if we were the stars of our own movie. I felt like I was floating, buoyed by a concoction of excitement and trepidation, as if the universe itself was holding its breath in anticipation of our next move.

"Look!" I exclaimed, pointing to a booth with brightly colored lights twinkling like fireflies. "The ring toss! We should try it." Ethan laughed, his joy infectious, and we approached the booth, where the cheerful vendor grinned at us.

"Win a prize for your girl!" he said, winking at Ethan, who rolled his eyes but couldn't suppress a smile.

"Alright, let's see what you've got, champ," I teased, nudging him playfully. The stakes felt lighthearted, yet every throw echoed with an undercurrent of significance. With each ring tossed, a shared laugh or an exaggerated groan only deepened our bond, the air around us brimming with warmth and ease.

After a few attempts, Ethan finally managed to ring a bottle neck, and the vendor clapped his hands in delight. "Congratulations! Pick your prize!"

Ethan grinned and turned to me. "What should I choose?"

"Something silly!" I urged, unable to suppress my laughter at the plush unicorns and oversized sunglasses displayed behind the vendor. He glanced at the options, and without hesitation, he chose a comically large stuffed monkey, its goofy grin making it impossible to resist.

"I think this will match your personality," he joked, his laughter ringing out, infectious and light, filling the air with joy.

"Very funny," I shot back, clutching the ridiculous monkey as if it were a treasured possession. "I'll name him Gerald."

We continued wandering, the world around us fading into a vibrant blur of colors and sounds. The thrill of new beginnings enveloped us, the future stretching out like a vast canvas waiting to be painted. Every laugh, every shared glance, and every moment of intimacy only intensified the feeling that we were teetering on the edge of something extraordinary.

As we reached the edge of the festival, we found a quieter spot overlooking the sparkling lake, the water reflecting the stars above. The moon bathed the scene in silver light, casting a serene glow over everything. We settled down on a bench, the stuffed monkey resting awkwardly between us, an unlikely but fitting symbol of our whimsical journey.

"This feels... perfect," I breathed, gazing out at the shimmering water. The night air was cool against my skin, but the warmth of Ethan's presence enveloped me like a cozy blanket.

"Yeah," he replied, his voice low and sincere. "It really does." He leaned slightly closer, the subtle shift sending a thrill racing through me.

"Do you think we'll figure it out?" I asked, the vulnerability creeping back in, tinged with a hint of anxiety.

"I believe we will," he answered, his gaze steady and reassuring. "It won't always be easy, but we'll take it one step at a time. Together."

A comfortable silence enveloped us, each moment stretching into eternity as we soaked in the beauty of our surroundings and the reality of our newfound connection. The festival was just a backdrop, a mere whisper of the journey we were embarking upon, and I felt exhilarated at the thought of every twist and turn that lay ahead.

As the night deepened, the stars began to twinkle in the vast expanse above us, a tapestry of light and darkness woven together like the threads of our lives. I knew that whatever challenges awaited us, whatever heartaches or joys lay ahead, we were ready to embrace them, hand in hand, forging a path together.

Chapter 15: Crossroads

A gust of wind flared through the narrow streets of my small town, causing the leaves to dance in a chaotic rhythm reminiscent of my own tangled thoughts. The crisp air had begun to carry the subtle chill of autumn, promising the arrival of cozy sweaters and pumpkin spice lattes. I reveled in this change, holding onto the fleeting moments of warmth as I stood behind the counter of the bookstore. The musty scent of well-loved pages mingled with the fresh aroma of coffee from the little café at the back, creating a cocoon that made the world outside seem distant and unimportant.

Every day felt like a new chapter, yet the narrative remained the same: my heart caught between the tender affection I felt for Ethan and the looming shadow of his friendship with Chloe. Their shared laughter echoed in my mind, a melody that contrasted sharply with the dissonance in my chest. I'd been attempting to convince myself that their friendship was innocent, just a couple of souls caught up in the warmth of familiarity, but every time I saw them together, it was like watching a slow-motion train wreck. My heart would clench, a visceral response I could never prepare for.

Ethan arrived one evening, his silhouette framed by the door as he stepped into the warm glow of the store. The familiar tinkle of the bell announced his presence, and I straightened up instinctively, as if adjusting my own scattered emotions. He looked weary, the kind of exhaustion that seeps into the bones and hangs in the air like a fog. My heart surged, a familiar tug of affection, but it was accompanied by an undercurrent of dread. There was something on his mind, and the way his eyes darted around the room told me he was searching for the right words—words I feared would change everything.

"Can I come over? I need to talk," he said, his voice tinged with uncertainty. I nodded, even though my stomach twisted at the thought of what he might reveal.

THE PATH BETWEEN WORDS

The walk to my apartment felt longer than usual, each step echoing with unspoken words. I unlocked the door, and we entered the small space that was a chaotic collage of mismatched furniture and shelves brimming with books. My sanctuary, where stories breathed life into the silence, now felt stifling. I gestured toward the couch, my heart racing as I settled in across from him, the distance between us feeling like an insurmountable chasm.

"I—" he began, but the words fell short, hanging in the air like an unsung song. He ran a hand through his tousled hair, the gesture so familiar and yet charged with an unfamiliar intensity. "Chloe confronted me."

My heart skipped, a sudden rush of adrenaline coursing through my veins. It was as if the world had paused, leaving just the two of us suspended in this delicate moment. "About us?" I asked, my voice barely above a whisper, as if raising it could shatter the fragile bubble of our conversation.

He nodded, his eyes searching mine for a spark of understanding. "Yeah. She's been noticing how much time we've been spending together. She asked if there was something going on between us." His voice wavered slightly, revealing the inner turmoil that had been haunting him. "I didn't know what to say. I mean, I care about her, but..." He trailed off, the weight of his unspoken words heavy in the air.

The silence stretched between us, taut like a string ready to snap. I wanted to reach out, to bridge that distance, but fear held me back. "What did you say?" My voice cracked slightly, and I hated how vulnerable I felt.

"I told her we're just friends, but..." He hesitated, and the pause felt like an eternity. "But I don't think that's true anymore."

Those words fell between us like a stone, heavy and undeniable. My heart raced, a wild flutter that filled the space with both hope and fear. I could feel the warmth of his gaze, the way it lingered on me, and I wanted nothing more than to dive into that warmth, to forget the complications that loomed overhead.

"Ethan, I—" I started, but he cut me off, a spark igniting in his eyes.

"I've been thinking a lot about us," he said, his voice firm yet laced with uncertainty. "This connection we have, it feels different. It's real. And I can't ignore it anymore."

The admission hung in the air, crackling with an electric tension that was both exhilarating and terrifying. My mind raced, grappling with the implications of his words. The thrill of potential loomed before me, but so did the fear of losing him entirely. Love, I had learned, was rarely uncomplicated.

"Ethan, you know how much Chloe means to you. You've been friends for so long. What if this...whatever this is, ruins that?" My voice trembled, a wave of anxiety crashing over me. I was terrified of being the one to unravel the delicate threads of their friendship.

He sighed, the weight of the world etched across his features. "I know. But I also know I can't keep pretending that what we have isn't special." He leaned forward, the air thickening with unspoken possibilities. "I don't want to choose, but I also can't keep living in this limbo. It's exhausting."

I nodded, my heart a cacophony of conflicting emotions. Here we were, standing on the precipice of something beautiful, yet fraught with potential heartache. The bookstore, with its comforting familiarity, faded into the background as I focused solely on him—his earnest expression, the way his hands fidgeted as he spoke, betraying his own uncertainty.

"What do we do?" I whispered, barely able to contain the hope blooming within me, alongside the fear that it could all slip through our fingers. In that moment, I realized we were standing at a crossroads, the paths ahead shrouded in mist, each direction fraught with its own dangers and delights. Would we embrace the risk, or would we retreat back into the shadows, forever wondering what could have been?

The days that followed felt like an intricate dance, each step laden with uncertainty and electric anticipation. Mornings greeted me with the gentle sunlight filtering through the bookstore's windows, casting playful shadows on the wooden floors, and each afternoon was filled with the rich aroma of coffee blending with the crisp scent of new paperbacks. I found solace in the familiar routine, but the underlying tension tethered to my relationship with Ethan clung to me like a second skin.

Every encounter with him became a delicate negotiation, a balancing act between the sweet thrill of burgeoning feelings and the bitter sting of jealousy. I watched him with Chloe as they navigated their shared history, their laughter intertwining in a way that felt both joyful and painful. Each smile exchanged between them felt like a dagger aimed at my heart, and I fought the impulse to withdraw into the comforting embrace of solitude. My heart, however, rebelled against such seclusion, yearning for connection and warmth.

One rainy afternoon, while I restocked the romance section, my thoughts spiraled in circles around Ethan and Chloe, like a whirling dervish. I could hear the soft patter of rain against the window, creating a soothing backdrop that almost drowned out my anxiety. Just as I was lost in my reverie, the bell above the door chimed, and in walked Ethan, his hair slightly damp and a hint of urgency in his stride.

"Hey," he greeted, his voice low, almost a whisper. He stepped closer, his eyes intense and searching. "Can we talk?"

The world outside faded into a blur as I nodded, leading him to the small nook nestled between shelves filled with novels. A cozy armchair sat beneath a dim lamp, casting a warm glow that felt like an invitation to confide in each other. As we settled into the intimate space, the air thickened with unspoken words and lingering tension.

"I've been thinking about what we talked about," he began, his voice steady but laced with emotion. "Chloe confronted me again. She can't shake the feeling that something is different between us." His admission sent a shiver down my spine, an electric current coursing through the air, igniting every nerve in my body.

I could feel my heartbeat quicken, a frantic rhythm that resonated in my ears. "What did you say?" I managed to ask, my throat dry, as if the very act of speaking could unravel the fabric of our fragile situation.

"I told her I was confused. I said I needed time to figure things out," he confessed, running a hand through his hair, a gesture I found both endearing and heart-wrenching. "But I can't keep lying to myself or to her. I don't want to hurt her, but I can't ignore what I feel for you."

A wave of relief washed over me, mingling with the anxiety that had become my constant companion. His honesty was a breath of fresh air, but the implications settled heavily in the pit of my stomach. "Ethan, it's not fair to Chloe. She's your friend, and she deserves to know the truth."

"I know," he replied, his voice earnest. "But what if the truth ends up hurting everyone? What if we end up losing each other in the process?"

The dilemma hung between us, a palpable force that demanded resolution. I wanted to reach out, to comfort him, but the fear of stepping too close to the flames held me back. Instead, I searched his eyes for answers, seeking clarity in the depths of his uncertainty. "What do you want?" I asked, my voice barely above a whisper, each word trembling with the weight of its significance.

His gaze held mine, fierce and unwavering. "I want to be with you," he said, each syllable resonating deep within my chest. "But I don't want to be the reason Chloe is hurt. She's been there for me through so much, and I can't just turn my back on that."

A storm of emotions brewed inside me—desire, compassion, guilt. I understood the complexity of his predicament, yet my heart ached for the possibility that lay before us. "It doesn't have to be a choice between us and her," I said softly, willing the words to hold weight. "We can find a way to navigate this. It's going to be messy, but maybe it's worth it?"

He studied me, the tension in his brow easing slightly as he considered my words. "You're right. Maybe we can figure out a way to handle it without causing too much pain. But I don't want to put you in the middle of this. You shouldn't have to bear that burden."

I felt my heart swell at his thoughtfulness, even as the reality of our situation hung heavy. "We're already in the middle, Ethan. We just have to be honest with each other and with her."

The sincerity in my voice seemed to reach him, and the corners of his mouth lifted in a tentative smile. "You're incredibly brave," he said, his tone softer now. "I don't know if I can handle this without you."

With those words, I could feel the barriers around my heart slowly beginning to dissolve. He reached out, his fingers brushing against mine, igniting a spark that coursed through my veins. In that moment, the bookstore, with its haphazard arrangement of stories and dreams, faded away, leaving just the two of us suspended in the delicate balance of hope and uncertainty.

As we navigated the conversation, the intimacy of the moment deepened, pulling us closer together even as the world outside raged on with its complexities. We spent hours exploring our fears and dreams, our laughter weaving through the silence like a balm against the tension. Each word we shared seemed to build a bridge over the chasm of confusion, solidifying the bond we were beginning to forge.

But even as I reveled in the connection, a flicker of doubt loomed at the edges of my mind. The consequences of our choices were yet to reveal themselves, and I knew that the path ahead would be fraught with challenges. I couldn't ignore the reality of Chloe's presence in our lives, nor the weight of the decision we were about to make.

Yet, as I looked into Ethan's eyes, filled with a mixture of hope and apprehension, I found comfort in the knowledge that we were both committed to navigating this labyrinth together. Love, I realized, was never a simple equation; it was a series of intricate intersections where paths crossed, diverged, and sometimes tangled together. We would have to face the music, but for now, in this quiet corner of the world, we embraced the promise of something extraordinary waiting just beyond the horizon.

The following days unfurled like the delicate petals of a blooming flower, each one carrying the intoxicating scent of possibility mingled with a hint of danger. Autumn settled into the town, painting the landscape in hues of gold and crimson, as if nature itself conspired to mirror the tempest of emotions swirling within me. Each morning, the bookstore buzzed with customers seeking solace in stories, their laughter and chatter acting as a backdrop to my inner turmoil. I lost myself in the familiar rhythm of arranging books and serving coffee, yet my mind lingered on Ethan and Chloe, an incessant hum of worry and yearning.

Ethan's confession had cast a shadow over my thoughts, yet it also illuminated a path forward, fraught with uncertainty but pulsating with potential. Each time I caught sight of him, whether in the aisles of the store or during our tentative meetings, an electric current surged between us, binding us in an unspoken agreement that we were on the brink of something profound. Our conversations deepened, filled with shared secrets and fleeting touches that ignited sparks of hope and fear in equal measure.

Yet, every interaction with him was tainted by the specter of Chloe. I found myself often glancing toward the door, half-expecting her to waltz in, with her carefree laugh ringing like a bell, blissfully unaware of the emotional tug-of-war unfolding around her. It wasn't that I disliked her; on the contrary, she had a vibrant spirit that drew people in, making her effortlessly likable. But therein lay the conflict—how could I encroach upon a friendship that had been steadfast long before my feelings had entered the equation?

On one particularly brisk evening, as golden leaves rustled outside and a soft rain began to tap gently against the window panes, I settled into my favorite corner of the bookstore. The scent of coffee wafted through the air, mingling with the mustiness of old books. The atmosphere felt both sacred and suffocating, a safe harbor from the storms raging within my heart. I flipped through the pages of a novel, but my mind was a swirling vortex, circling back to Ethan and the inevitable confrontation with Chloe that loomed like a thundercloud on the horizon.

A few days later, as I was meticulously rearranging the mystery section—aligning the spines just so—Ethan stepped through the door. The familiar thrill of seeing him coursed through me, but a new layer of anxiety settled in. This time, his expression was unreadable, a tight mask of determination and something deeper that sparked my curiosity.

"Can we talk?" he asked, his voice low and firm, slicing through the soft murmur of customers browsing nearby. I nodded, my heart pounding in a rhythm that mirrored the rain outside as he led me to the café's back corner, a secluded nook where we could escape the prying eyes of the world.

"I talked to Chloe," he began, and I felt my heart seize at the revelation. "I couldn't put it off any longer. She deserves to know the truth."

My breath hitched. "What did you say?" The weight of the question lingered between us, heavy with consequence.

"I told her about us," he confessed, his gaze locking onto mine, searching for a reaction. "I explained how I felt and that I couldn't keep pretending everything was fine." The words hung there, raw and potent, swirling around us like smoke from a dying ember.

The silence stretched, thick with tension. I felt a cocktail of relief and apprehension swirling in my chest. "How did she react?" I finally managed to ask, my voice trembling at the edges.

Ethan ran a hand through his hair, a familiar gesture that tugged at my heartstrings. "She was hurt, understandably. But she also...she wants me to be happy. I think she knew something was off for a while." His voice faltered slightly, revealing the gravity of his confession.

"Does she hate me?" The question slipped out before I could catch it, laced with vulnerability. The thought of Chloe harboring resentment toward me clawed at my insides.

"No," he said quickly, shaking his head. "She was upset, yes, but she knows it's not your fault. It's complicated, but she cares about you. I think she's trying to process everything."

A wave of empathy washed over me. Chloe didn't deserve to be caught in the crossfire of our emotions, and I felt an overwhelming urge to reach out, to ease her hurt in some way. "What do we do now?" I asked, the uncertainty of the future stretching before us like a vast, uncharted ocean.

"I don't know," Ethan replied, his voice softer now, almost tender. "But I want to figure it out with you."

His gaze bore into mine, igniting the sparks of hope I had tried to contain. "Together," I whispered, the word hanging in the air between us, a promise that felt both exhilarating and terrifying.

Days turned into a haze of anticipation and tension as we navigated the aftermath of Ethan's confession. I found myself looking for Chloe in every corner of the bookstore, imagining her laughter mingling with the sound of the rain as it fell against the roof. Each time the bell above the door chimed, my heart would race, wondering if she would walk in, ready to confront me or offer forgiveness.

Then, one day, she did. Chloe stepped into the store, her presence as vibrant as ever, yet there was a shift in the air, a weightiness that hadn't been there before. My breath caught in my throat as she approached, a nervous smile playing on her lips.

"Hey," she said, her voice light yet tinged with something deeper. "Can we talk?"

I nodded, suddenly feeling small under the intensity of her gaze. We moved to the same nook where Ethan and I had shared our pivotal conversation. The atmosphere was charged, and I could feel the walls closing in around us as we settled into the worn armchairs.

"I wanted to say I'm sorry," Chloe began, her voice steady despite the emotional gravity of the moment. "I didn't mean to confront Ethan like that, but I could see something was changing. I was just...worried."

"Worried?" I echoed, unsure how to respond. I could see the hurt flickering in her eyes, and it tugged at my heart.

"Yeah," she admitted, taking a deep breath. "I felt like I was losing him, you know? He's been my best friend for years. I just didn't want to lose that connection."

"I never meant to come between you two," I said, my voice barely above a whisper. "I care about him, but I care about you too. I don't want to hurt either of you."

Chloe regarded me for a moment, the tension in her shoulders easing as understanding flickered in her gaze. "I know. And I appreciate you saying that. I think... I think we can figure this out. I want Ethan to be happy, and if that's with you, then I want to support that."

Relief flooded through me, and I could feel a weight lift off my chest. "Thank you for saying that. I didn't want to hurt you. You're an amazing person, and it means a lot that you understand."

Chloe smiled, a genuine warmth spreading across her features. "We're both navigating uncharted waters, but maybe we can do it together. I want to remain friends, even if things feel different now."

Our conversation unfolded like a delicate tapestry, each thread woven with honesty and vulnerability. As we spoke, I could feel the tension dissipate, replaced by a burgeoning camaraderie that felt both fragile and profound. By the time we parted ways, I realized that we were all intertwined in a web of feelings, each strand pulling us closer together, even amid the chaos.

As I left the bookstore that evening, the sky had turned a soft lavender, the first stars flickering to life against the deepening dusk. My heart felt lighter, buoyed by the possibility of healing and the promise of new beginnings. I looked forward to the future with renewed hope, believing that love, in all its complexities, was worth every heart-wrenching moment.

Chapter 16: The Weight of Choices

The air was thick with the scent of coffee and old paper, a comforting embrace that wrapped around me as I settled into my favorite corner of the bookstore. The heavy, wooden shelves loomed like sentinels, their tomes filled with whispers of worlds I had yet to explore. I loved this little sanctuary in the heart of Boston, where the muted buzz of conversations intermingled with the soft rustle of pages turning. Rain drummed against the glass windows, a soothing symphony that provided the perfect backdrop for the cacophony of thoughts swirling in my mind.

With each stroke of my pen, I poured out my soul, the ink flowing like a river, carving paths through the intricate landscapes of my imagination. Words became my refuge, a place where I could lose myself and, paradoxically, find myself in the chaos of emotions and experiences that had become my existence. It was here, surrounded by characters who defied reality and tales that transcended time, that I began to untangle the threads of my life.

I had taken a step back from the whirlwind of relationships and expectations, yearning for a moment of clarity amidst the clamor of my heart. I knew I needed to rediscover the rhythm of my own heartbeat, to learn the dance of self-love before inviting another into my life. The realization felt like a gentle nudge, an echo of wisdom reminding me that the foundation of any true connection must begin within.

Yet, the ghosts of my past clung to me, shadows dancing on the edges of my consciousness. Ethan. His name was a bittersweet melody, haunting yet comforting, like a familiar song played on an old vinyl record. Our connection had ignited something in me, a spark that felt both exhilarating and terrifying. Even as I sought solitude, a part of me couldn't help but wonder about him, about us.

I found myself tracing the delicate outlines of our shared moments, each memory a brushstroke on the canvas of my heart.

The rain intensified outside, and the world beyond the window transformed into a blurred watercolor painting. I welcomed the gloom; it matched my introspection perfectly. My fingers paused mid-sentence, hovering above the page as my thoughts drifted like the droplets cascading down the glass. I imagined Ethan, his disarming smile and playful banter, a stark contrast to the tempest brewing inside me. The more I tried to distance myself from him, the more he seemed to linger, an intoxicating presence woven into the fabric of my being.

Just as I began to surrender to the solitude, the bell above the door jingled, and I looked up, startled from my reverie. There he stood, drenched from the downpour, his hair a dark tousle, sticking to his forehead, droplets clinging to the edges of his jacket like tiny jewels. He was a vision of warmth amid the chill, his smile radiating like the sun breaking through the clouds. My heart stuttered, caught between disbelief and joy, a jolt of electricity zipping through the space between us.

"Fancy seeing you here," he said, his voice a low rumble that sent shivers down my spine. He took a step closer, shaking off the rain like a dog emerging from a bath, and I couldn't help but laugh, the sound bubbling up uncontrollably.

"What are you doing here?" I managed to ask, my heart pounding in my chest as I battled the conflicting emotions surging through me.

"Looking for you," he replied simply, and in that moment, the weight of the universe shifted, tilting in favor of the connection we shared. "I was hoping to escape the storm and maybe find some inspiration," he added, glancing around the cozy bookstore with a spark of mischief in his eyes.

I motioned for him to join me at my table, the sight of him warming me against the chill of the damp air. As he settled into the chair opposite me, I couldn't help but notice how the dim light of the bookstore danced across his features, accentuating the determined line of his jaw and the depth of his hazel eyes, which held a glimmer of something unspoken.

"Are you working on something?" he asked, leaning forward, genuine curiosity etched on his face. There was a magnetic pull between us, an invisible thread weaving our stories together.

I hesitated for a moment, uncertainty gnawing at me. I had poured my heart into this piece, an exploration of love and self-discovery, and sharing it felt like exposing my vulnerabilities. But as I looked into his eyes, I realized that this was part of the journey—embracing the risks that came with connection, even when it terrified me.

"Just trying to figure things out," I admitted, my voice barely above a whisper. "You know, about love, and... myself."

Ethan nodded, his expression softening, understanding etched in the lines of his brow. "That's the hardest part, isn't it? Figuring out how to love yourself before you can truly let someone in."

His words resonated within me, echoing the thoughts I had been wrestling with in the solitude of my writing. As the rain continued to fall, a steady rhythm that seemed to match the pulse of our conversation, I felt the walls I had built around my heart begin to crack, revealing the vibrant colors beneath.

The air was thick with the scent of rain-soaked earth and the warm aroma of coffee wafting from the corner café. I looked up from my pages, the ink still wet, and found Ethan standing there, a vision of chaos and charm. His hair, darkened by the rain, clung to his forehead in rebellious strands, while droplets cascaded off his jacket, pooling at his feet. He was a sight to behold, as if the storm had conspired to sculpt him from the very essence of weather itself—wild, unpredictable, yet utterly captivating. In that moment, time felt suspended, the world around us fading into a soft blur, leaving only the electricity of our connection crackling in the air.

Ethan flashed a smile, the kind that had the power to light up even the grayest of days. My heart thudded with a familiar rhythm, each beat a reminder of the countless conversations we'd shared, each one weaving a tapestry of laughter, vulnerability, and an undeniable bond. I had vowed to focus on myself, to nourish my own spirit before intertwining it with another's, yet here he was, a beacon of everything I had longed for during those solitary hours spent in my thoughts.

"Mind if I join you?" he asked, his voice rich with warmth, pulling me from my reverie. Without waiting for an answer, he made his way to my table, shaking off the remnants of the storm like a playful dog. I gestured to the seat across from me, and our eyes locked, the universe once again aligning in a way that felt almost scripted.

As he settled into the chair, I took a moment to observe him. The way his smile danced with mischief, the way his eyes twinkled like stars behind the veil of clouds. It was moments like these that reminded me how easily we could lose ourselves in someone else's orbit. I had been so consumed by my own journey, my own desires, that I hadn't fully realized how deeply intertwined our lives had become.

"What are you working on?" he asked, peering curiously at my notebook, where ink trails crisscrossed like a secret map of my thoughts.

"Just trying to figure things out," I replied, a hint of hesitation creeping into my tone. I hadn't wanted to dive into the intricacies of my emotional labyrinth just yet. Instead, I offered a vague smile, hoping it would suffice for now.

"I get it," he nodded, his gaze steady, as if he could see through my guarded exterior. "Sometimes the best way to untangle our thoughts is to spill them out onto the page."

His words resonated, and I couldn't help but chuckle softly. It was a truth I had embraced, yet hearing it from him felt like a gentle nudge, a reminder that vulnerability wasn't something to be feared. In the midst of our conversation, I felt a weight lift, like the clouds parting to reveal a bright patch of sky.

We fell into an easy rhythm, words flowing like water between us. We shared snippets of our lives, laughter echoing through the bookstore as we recounted our quirkiest moments. With every shared story, the invisible thread connecting us tightened, weaving a fabric rich with possibility and unspoken understanding.

Yet beneath the laughter, a lingering thought danced in the back of my mind. As Ethan spoke animatedly about his latest adventure, I couldn't shake the feeling that I was standing at a crossroads, two paths stretching out before me. One path called for self-exploration, a deep dive into my own soul, while the other beckoned me towards him, an alluring promise of companionship and shared dreams.

A soft rain pattered against the window, and I turned to gaze outside, the world a blur of colors and movement. The storm mirrored the tempest within me—both chaotic and beautiful. Just as the rain nourished the earth, I knew that I needed to nourish my own heart before opening it fully to anyone else, including Ethan. But how could I explain that to him without tearing at the delicate fabric of our connection?

As if sensing my internal struggle, Ethan leaned closer, his voice dropping to a softer, more intimate tone. "You know, I've always believed that the most important journey we can take is the one within ourselves. It's where we find our strength, our truths, and ultimately, the love we can share with others."

His words struck a chord, echoing my own reflections. Perhaps this moment was not a divergence but rather a stepping stone, a chance to weave our individual journeys into something greater. I smiled, the tension within me easing ever so slightly. Maybe it was possible to embrace this connection while still honoring my own path.

"Sometimes," I began, hesitant yet determined, "I think we rush into relationships, seeking answers outside of ourselves when we really need to look within."

Ethan nodded, his expression thoughtful. "It's easy to get caught up in the idea of love, but true connection comes from knowing who we are first."

His words hung in the air, the weight of their truth settling around us like a warm embrace. It was as if we were dancing on the edge of a revelation, both of us inching closer to understanding the depth of our bond while still respecting the individual journeys we had embarked upon.

The conversation flowed seamlessly, morphing into discussions about dreams, fears, and the wild unpredictability of life. We spoke of the moments that had shaped us, the choices that had led us here, and the unknown paths that lay ahead. With each shared story, I felt the universe nudging us closer, urging us to explore this newfound connection without losing ourselves in the process.

As the sun dipped lower in the sky, casting a golden hue over the bookstore, I realized that this moment was a gift—an opportunity to embrace the uncertainty while holding tight to my own aspirations. I could cherish the warmth of Ethan's presence while continuing my journey of self-discovery. Our laughter mingled with the sound of the rain, creating a symphony of life that echoed the complexity of human connection. In that moment, I felt alive, teetering on the precipice of something beautiful, fragile, and infinitely promising.

The chatter of other patrons faded into a comforting hum, and for a moment, it felt like Ethan and I were the only two people in the world. The flickering overhead lights cast gentle shadows across the pages of my notebook, where thoughts and dreams collided in a chaotic dance of ink. I leaned back in my chair, allowing the atmosphere of the bookstore to envelop me, the scent of old books mingling with fresh coffee providing a sensory embrace that felt both invigorating and nostalgic.

Ethan, ever the effortless conversationalist, began to share stories of his latest escapades—hiking through mist-covered trails and stumbling upon hidden waterfalls, his enthusiasm spilling over with every word. He spoke with a reverence for nature, his eyes sparkling like sunlit waters as he described the way the sunlight filtered through the trees, casting dapples of light on the forest floor. It was a reminder of how life could be both tumultuous and serene, a duality I had been grappling with in my own heart. I couldn't help but admire the way he embraced life's unpredictability, diving headfirst into every adventure with childlike wonder.

"I've been thinking," he said, tilting his head slightly, the playful curls of his hair framing his face like a work of art. "We should explore together sometime. You've been so caught up in your writing; you deserve a little adventure."

His suggestion stirred something within me—an invitation to break free from the confines of my solitude. But as the thought flitted through my mind, another wave of uncertainty washed over me. Could I truly balance the thrill of exploration with the introspection I had promised myself? Yet the idea of sharing those moments with Ethan, of experiencing the world together, tugged at the corners of my heart, beckoning me toward a more vibrant existence.

"Adventure sounds wonderful," I replied, a tentative smile dancing on my lips. "But I need to figure some things out first."

He nodded, a flicker of understanding crossing his face. "I get it. I just thought it could be fun to share a few experiences together."

The honesty in his voice resonated deeply, reminding me of the importance of human connection. As much as I craved solitude, I also yearned for companionship—the kind that nurtured growth rather than stifling it. Perhaps this was the balance I sought: a relationship that allowed for individual exploration while building something extraordinary together.

Our conversation meandered from dreams of travel to the intricacies of our favorite books, each new topic adding another layer to the tapestry of our connection. I discovered that Ethan had an affinity for stories that blurred the lines between reality and fantasy, tales that transported him to distant lands filled with mythical creatures and daring heroes. His passion for storytelling ignited a flame within me, a reminder of the magic that words could weave, and I found myself opening up about my own aspirations as a writer.

"I've always wanted to create a world where readers can lose themselves," I confessed, my heart racing with the vulnerability of sharing my dreams. "A place that feels real but allows them to escape the ordinary."

His eyes sparkled with genuine interest, and in that moment, I felt seen. "I think you have the talent to do just that," he replied, a hint of admiration in his voice. "You've already created so much beauty on these pages. Just imagine what you could accomplish if you let your imagination run wild."

The sincerity of his words washed over me, a wave of encouragement that bolstered my resolve. I realized then that my writing wasn't just a solitary pursuit; it was a bridge to connect with others, to invite them into the depths of my imagination. And as I sat across from Ethan, the lines between our worlds began to blur, the possibilities unfurling like petals in the sunlight.

But just as the warmth of our exchange enveloped me, a flicker of doubt nagged at the edges of my mind. How could I reconcile this burgeoning connection with my need for self-discovery? In the midst of the chaos, I found myself grappling with the realization that I couldn't simply write my own narrative without acknowledging the plot twists life threw my way.

With a hesitant smile, I turned the conversation towards the uncertainties that loomed ahead. "What if we're both on different paths?" I asked, the weight of my words hanging in the air. "What if this connection leads us astray from where we need to go?"

Ethan regarded me thoughtfully, the corners of his mouth quirking upward in a knowing smile. "Every journey has its challenges," he replied. "But sometimes the paths that seem the most divergent can lead to the most unexpected destinations."

His perspective struck a chord, and as I contemplated his words, I couldn't help but feel a flicker of hope. Perhaps embracing this connection with Ethan didn't mean sacrificing my individuality. Instead, it could enhance my journey, providing companionship as we navigated the labyrinth of life together.

As the day wore on, the rain outside began to ease, the clouds parting to reveal patches of blue sky. With each passing moment, the uncertainty that had once felt insurmountable began to dissolve, replaced by the promise of new beginnings. I realized that my path didn't have to be solitary; it could be enriched by the laughter and support of someone who understood my struggles and dreams.

With a newfound resolve, I leaned forward, meeting Ethan's gaze with determination. "Maybe we should plan that adventure," I suggested, the thrill of possibility coursing through me. "Let's discover new worlds together—both in our lives and in our stories."

Ethan's smile widened, illuminating the space between us. "I'd love nothing more," he replied, his voice warm and inviting. "Just think of the stories we'll create."

In that moment, the weight of uncertainty lifted, replaced by the exhilaration of possibility. We were two souls, intertwined in a journey that held the promise of growth, discovery, and a connection that defied the ordinary. As I returned to my writing, my heart swelled with hope, ready to embrace whatever came next—both in my story and in the unwritten chapters of our lives. The pages of my life were ready to turn, and I was eager to see where they would lead.

Chapter 17: Between the Lines

A warm haze of golden light spilled into the cozy nook of my apartment, casting a soft glow on the walls adorned with eclectic art—an assortment of thrift store finds and hand-painted canvases that spoke of dreams and late-night musings. The smell of freshly brewed coffee lingered, mingling with the remnants of a garlic-infused dinner that had long since gone cold. Outside, the rhythm of the city pulsed, a chaotic symphony of laughter, car horns, and the distant strains of a street musician playing a haunting tune that danced on the edge of my consciousness.

Ethan entered, shaking off the remnants of the storm that had just rolled through. Raindrops clung to his tousled hair like tiny jewels, sparkling momentarily in the ambient light before falling away to pool at his feet. He looked like a tempestuous artist, full of life and unpredictability, the kind of person who could turn an ordinary day into a whirlwind of color and chaos. I felt a flutter in my stomach as he settled onto the worn-out couch opposite me, his presence igniting the air like a spark in the dark.

We spoke, the conversation flowing effortlessly, as if we had been crafting this moment for lifetimes. Our voices mingled with the light patter of rain against the window, creating a comforting backdrop. I found myself sharing pieces of my soul, unraveling the tapestry of my dreams and fears, each thread a revelation that brought us closer. I talked about my ambitions, the art I longed to create, and the fear of never quite living up to the expectations I had set for myself. With each word, I saw the flicker of understanding in Ethan's deep-set eyes, a reflection of the uncharted territories of his heart.

He, too, bared his vulnerabilities—his dreams of being a musician, the struggles with self-doubt that gnawed at him in the quiet hours of the night. I could see the conflict etched on his face as he spoke of his ambitions. Music flowed through him, a living, breathing entity that resonated with every note he played. In those moments, I believed we were suspended in our little universe, a world devoid of the noise and chaos that often drowned out our dreams.

Yet, as the clock ticked on, shadows danced across his features, dimming the warmth that had enveloped us. It was a fleeting glimpse, a whisper of the turmoil lurking just beneath the surface. His eyes flickered away from mine, a crack in the intimacy we had forged, and I felt my heart plummet. In that moment, the weight of unspoken words hung heavy in the air.

He sighed, the sound carrying the weight of the world, and confessed that Chloe had asked him to a party that weekend. My heart constricted painfully, an unexpected twist in the narrative we were weaving. The ground beneath me felt unstable, the comforting world we had built starting to tilt dangerously. Ethan's admission was a quiet storm, a crack in our carefully crafted reality, and I found myself grappling with the shifting tides of our relationship.

The mention of Chloe twisted something deep within me. She was the light-hearted whirlwind that swept through our lives, her laughter infectious, her energy captivating. I could never quite decide if I envied her or admired her, but the thought of Ethan spending time with her—being pulled into her orbit—made me feel like a ship lost at sea, tossed about by waves of uncertainty. I had tried to brush it off, to convince myself that it didn't matter, but the truth was as tangible as the raindrops cascading down the window, relentless and inescapable.

"Are you going?" I managed to ask, my voice barely above a whisper, a tremor betraying the composure I desperately tried to maintain.

He ran a hand through his hair, a nervous gesture that made my heart ache. "I... I don't know yet. I mean, she asked, but..." His words trailed off, leaving a gaping silence between us, thick with unspoken tension.

I searched his face for any sign, any indication of where we stood. Did he see her as just a friend, or was there something more lingering beneath the surface? The thought alone sent a fresh wave of panic washing over me. The vulnerability of our connection felt fragile, like a delicate glass sculpture that could shatter at any moment.

"What if you do?" The question slipped from my lips, raw and unguarded, a piece of me laid bare.

He met my gaze, his expression shifting from uncertainty to something resembling resolve. "I want to be here, with you. But..." His voice faded again, leaving behind the lingering scent of possibilities unfulfilled.

The air between us crackled with tension, every moment stretching painfully. I wanted to grab him, to pull him closer, to remind him of the laughter we had shared, the stories that had woven us together, but the words eluded me. Instead, I sat there, a storm of emotions swirling within me—fear, jealousy, longing—all of them coalescing into a single, desperate thought: how could I fight for something that felt so precarious?

As Ethan stared into the distance, I caught the glint of rain on the window, reflecting the chaos of my heart. In that moment, I realized that I could either embrace the uncertainty or retreat into the shadows, away from the warmth of the connection we had built. The world outside raged on, but inside, I was caught in a web of my own making, struggling to find a way through the tangled threads of my emotions.

The rain drummed a persistent rhythm against the window, a backdrop to the tension that thickened the air between us. I felt the urge to fill the silence, to bridge the widening gulf that had opened since his revelation. But how does one find the right words when every syllable threatens to tip the precarious balance of everything you hold dear?

Ethan's gaze was distant, lost somewhere in the shifting shadows of my living room. I watched him, this beautiful enigma who had entered my life like a sudden storm, leaving traces of warmth and confusion in his wake. His features, usually so animated, were now clouded by uncertainty. I couldn't help but wonder if he was contemplating his next steps, weighing his options like a tightrope walker poised above the ground. My heart ached for him, yet I felt the familiar tendrils of jealousy creeping in, their icy fingers curling around my resolve.

"I just don't want things to change," I finally managed to say, my voice cracking slightly, betraying my vulnerability. "Everything feels so good right now, and I don't want to risk losing that." The confession hung in the air, a fragile thread of honesty that felt both liberating and terrifying.

He turned to me, surprise flickering across his face, and for a moment, the storm outside faded, replaced by the tempest brewing within our own hearts. "Neither do I," he replied, his voice steady, but the weight of his words pressed down on us like the low-hanging clouds outside. "But I can't ignore what's happening with Chloe. She's…she's been in my life for a long time, and it's hard to just dismiss it."

My stomach twisted, a bitter knot tightening at the thought of Chloe—her laughter, her easy confidence, the way she seemed to dance through life while I often stumbled. I wanted to be the person Ethan looked at with that kind of admiration, the one whose presence lit up a room. Yet here I was, desperately trying to hold on to something that felt as though it was slipping through my fingers like grains of sand.

"It's not like I'm asking you to dismiss her," I replied, frustration creeping into my tone. "But you have to understand that I feel…I don't know, threatened? It's hard not to when you talk about her like she's some kind of muse."

A flash of understanding crossed his face, and I could see the gears turning in his mind. "I get it. I really do," he said softly. "But it's not what you think. Chloe and I—" he paused, searching for the right words. "We have a history, but that doesn't mean there's anything between us now. I just... I don't want to hurt anyone, you know?"

I nodded, feeling a mix of empathy and frustration swirling within me. His desire to protect everyone, including me, felt noble but also complicated. "What do you want?" I pressed, desperate to peel back the layers that concealed his true feelings. "What do you really want?"

He hesitated, and in that moment of stillness, I sensed a shift in the air, a crack forming in the fortress of indecision that had surrounded him. "I want you, but... I'm not sure if I'm ready to let go of the past. It's like this tug-of-war inside me. Chloe is part of my life, and I've always been drawn to her light."

His words pierced through me, each syllable a reminder of the invisible tether that connected him to her, and my heart sank further. Light. Chloe was light, and I felt like the shadow that hovered at the edges, forever longing to step into the glow. I tried to swallow the bitterness, the sense of defeat that threatened to drown me. "So what does that mean for us?" I asked, my voice barely a whisper.

Ethan took a deep breath, and for a moment, I thought he might reach across the distance between us, grasp my hand, and pull me back into the warmth. But he stayed put, the space between us both comforting and suffocating. "I don't know," he admitted, his eyes searching mine as if looking for answers I didn't have. "I don't want to string you along, but I also don't want to lose you."

The honesty in his words cut through the haze of confusion, leaving me feeling exposed and vulnerable. I wanted to scream, to demand that he choose me, but that wouldn't be fair. Love wasn't a game of elimination; it was a complex tapestry woven from trust and understanding. "What if we don't have to lose each other?" I ventured cautiously, my heart racing. "What if we can figure this out together?"

His expression softened, and I could see the flicker of hope ignite in his eyes. "What does that look like?"

I shrugged, my mind racing to piece together a plan, a vision of a future where we could coexist without the weight of unspoken fears. "Maybe we could take things slow? I mean, if you want to explore what's happening with Chloe, that's okay. But I need to know that you're here with me, too, and that you're willing to fight for what we have."

Ethan regarded me, the storm that had clouded his face beginning to clear. "I want that. I want to fight for us." His voice was steady now, infused with determination that sent warmth flooding through me.

In that moment, the chaotic symphony of the city outside faded into the background. The rain became a gentle lullaby, a reminder of the storm we had weathered together, and I felt a flicker of hope spark to life within me. Perhaps we could navigate this tangled web of emotions, find our way through the uncertainties that loomed like dark clouds.

As I sat there, the weight of our conversation still palpable in the air, I realized that we were on the precipice of something new. Whatever lay ahead, I knew we would face it together. And with that knowledge, the shadows that had once threatened to engulf us began to dissipate, leaving space for the possibility of a brighter tomorrow.

The air between us thickened, a charged current pulsing with unspoken words and half-formed thoughts. The warmth of our earlier conversation felt distant now, replaced by a chilly uncertainty that sent shivers down my spine. I watched Ethan, his brow furrowed, eyes darting away as if seeking answers in the cluttered corners of my living room. Each moment stretched like taffy, sweet yet agonizing, and I could feel the knot in my stomach tighten as the reality of his connection with Chloe sank in.

I took a deep breath, filling my lungs with the rich scent of coffee and something sweet—perhaps the remnants of a dessert I had devoured earlier in a moment of distraction. "What if I told you I was scared?" I asked, my voice barely above a whisper. The admission hung between us, vulnerable and raw, yet it felt liberating to say it out loud.

His eyes met mine, and for a fleeting moment, the storm clouds of uncertainty were pierced by a ray of understanding. "I think we're both scared," he replied, the corners of his mouth twitching in an attempt to smile, a gesture that did little to ease the weight pressing down on us. "But fear doesn't have to dictate our choices."

"I want to be brave," I said, my heart racing with the desire to believe in our connection. "But I can't shake the feeling that I'm standing on the edge of a cliff, and one misstep could send me tumbling down."

Ethan shifted closer, the warmth radiating from him like sunlight breaking through a storm. "Then let's take a step back, together. We don't have to rush into anything." His words wrapped around me like a comforting blanket, and for the first time that evening, I felt a flicker of hope ignite in my chest.

"Together," I echoed, the word a balm against the jagged edges of my anxiety. "I like the sound of that."

He smiled then, a genuine warmth spreading across his face, and in that moment, I could see glimpses of the future woven into the fabric of our connection. Perhaps it wasn't a matter of choosing one path over another but of finding a way to merge our journeys into something new, something beautiful.

As we leaned into the conversation, the rain outside began to soften, its intensity fading to a gentle patter, like a lullaby that promised calm after the storm. We began to talk about the things we loved—music, art, the vibrant pulse of the city that felt like a living entity, always changing and evolving. It felt so easy, so fluid, as if we were two rivers converging into a single flow, each contributing our unique colors to create something breathtaking.

Ethan spoke about his passion for songwriting, the way the notes danced in his head, begging to be released onto paper. I could hear the excitement in his voice, the love for crafting melodies that could resonate with others. "I want to tell stories through my music," he said, his eyes lighting up. "Just like you do with your art. We both want to capture life, to immortalize these fleeting moments."

It was an understanding that deepened our bond, a realization that we both yearned for connection in different forms. I shared my love for painting, how each stroke of the brush felt like an extension of my soul. The vivid colors were a reflection of my emotions, swirling together to create something both chaotic and beautiful. "I believe art has the power to change perspectives," I mused, my heart swelling with the truth of it. "To evoke feelings and memories that linger long after the last note has faded or the paint has dried."

Ethan nodded, his gaze unwavering. "And that's exactly what I want to do with my music. I want to create songs that people can hold onto, songs that speak to their hearts."

Our voices entwined like a melody, creating a harmony that echoed through the room. The previous tension began to dissipate, replaced by a shared understanding that felt both new and familiar. We were two souls on a similar path, navigating the complexities of love, ambition, and the intertwining of our lives.

Yet, the memory of Chloe lingered in the back of my mind like a distant storm cloud, threatening to overshadow our moment. I took a chance, deciding to voice the nagging concern. "What about Chloe? If she's part of your life, how do we fit into all of this?"

Ethan hesitated, his expression shifting as he processed my question. "She's a friend, and I care about her, but I also feel something different with you. Something deeper."

The admission sent a wave of warmth rushing through me, mingled with the cool remnants of uncertainty. "But if you spend time with her at this party, won't it complicate things?" I asked, my voice tinged with the fear of losing the fragile connection we had forged.

"Maybe," he conceded, running a hand through his hair in a familiar gesture of frustration. "But I want to be honest with you about everything. I don't want to hide anything."

As I listened to him, I felt a flicker of understanding bloom within me. It wasn't just about navigating a relationship with him but about confronting the insecurities that bubbled beneath the surface. "Honesty is key," I said thoughtfully. "But I also think we need to define what we want. Can we keep exploring this—whatever this is—without the shadow of Chloe hanging over us?"

He smiled, the corners of his mouth lifting as he reached out to take my hand, the warmth of his touch sending a rush of reassurance coursing through me. "Yes, I want to keep exploring. You matter to me, and I want to see where this goes."

Our eyes locked, a silent agreement passing between us, a promise to be brave together, to embrace the unknown and allow our connection to grow in its own time. Outside, the rain had turned to a gentle drizzle, and I imagined the clouds parting just enough for the sun to peek through, a glimmer of hope illuminating the path ahead.

As the evening wore on, we continued to share pieces of ourselves, revealing our dreams and aspirations like delicate petals unfolding under the morning sun. The world outside faded into a muted backdrop, our laughter echoing in the quiet corners of my apartment. With every passing moment, the fear of losing him ebbed away, replaced by a growing sense of possibility.

And in that cozy nook, where vulnerability and understanding intertwined, I felt a sense of peace settle over us—a fragile but tenacious connection, like a vine beginning to sprout through the cracks of concrete. With each shared laugh and earnest word, we built a foundation strong enough to withstand the storms that life might throw our way. Whatever challenges lay ahead, I knew we would face them together, hand in hand, ready to navigate the complexities of love and life, embracing the chaos and beauty that came with it.

Chapter 18: Fractured Bonds

The day of the party arrived, the air thick with anticipation and a hint of autumn chill. I pulled my sweater tighter around me as I navigated the streets of our small town, where every house felt like a canvas painted with the vibrant hues of change. Leaves danced down from branches like confetti, their fiery reds and burnt oranges mirroring the tumult of emotions swirling within me. With each step, I felt the familiar weight of uncertainty settle onto my shoulders, a constant reminder of the fractured bonds I was here to face.

As I approached the old community center, I could hear the distant thrum of music leaking through the walls, mingling with the delighted laughter of our neighbors. It was the kind of laughter that wrapped around you like a warm embrace, promising good times and shared stories. But I knew beneath that surface lay the cracks in my world, the unspoken words and unshed tears that haunted the corners of my heart. Today, those bonds would be tested, perhaps shattered.

Inside, the scene was almost surreal. Strings of twinkling lights hung from the ceiling like stars plucked from the night sky, casting a soft glow on the faces of my friends and acquaintances. The aroma of spiced cider wafted through the air, mingling with the sweetness of baked goods, creating a sensory tapestry that was both comforting and disorienting. I moved through the crowd, my gaze darting around, absorbing the cheerful chaos that enveloped me. I spotted familiar faces: Lydia from the book club, her curls bouncing as she animatedly recounted her latest literary obsession, and Mark, ever the jokester, attempting to juggle plastic cups with exaggerated flair.

But it was Ethan who caught my eye, standing in a corner with Chloe, his laughter rich and inviting, cutting through the music like a beacon. A pang shot through my chest as I watched him lean closer to her, their heads bent together, sharing a moment that felt unbearably intimate. My breath hitched in my throat, and I forced my feet to move forward, each step a battle against the tide of doubt pulling me back. I was determined to face him, to confront whatever it was that had morphed our friendship into a tangled mess of silence and resentment.

As I approached, their laughter became more pronounced, punctuated by the occasional warmth of shared stories. I could almost envision the glowing sparks that flickered between them, an electric energy that made my heart pound with a mix of anger and longing. They were entwined in a world that felt impossibly far from mine. I steeled myself, breathing in the scent of cinnamon and apples, hoping to gather enough courage to say something—anything.

"Ethan," I called out, my voice barely rising above the cheerful din. He turned, those familiar eyes meeting mine, and for a moment, the world around us faded into the background. But just as quickly, the moment shattered. I overheard Chloe's laughter ringing out like a bell, bright and carefree, and I could feel the weight of her presence like an anchor dragging me down. She was everything I wasn't: effortlessly charming, with a smile that seemed to light up the room.

"Hey, I was just telling Chloe about that hike we took last summer," Ethan said, his smile genuine but tinged with something unreadable, a flicker of discomfort as if he sensed the tension coiling between us.

"Right, the one where we got lost for hours?" I managed, forcing a laugh that felt hollow, a ruse to mask the tightness in my chest.

"Yeah! You were so determined to find the trailhead," he said, chuckling, but the warmth in his voice didn't reach my heart. It only made the distance between us more palpable, a chasm filled with unresolved feelings and painful memories.

Chloe interjected, her voice sweet but clipped. "Oh, I've heard that story! Ethan always has the best adventures." She turned her gaze toward me, her eyes sparkling with a mix of mischief and curiosity. "You should join us next time, it sounds like a blast."

The suggestion hung in the air like a threat, a reminder of the space that had grown between us all. "Maybe," I replied, forcing a smile that didn't quite touch my eyes. My heart raced, and I could feel the heat creeping up my cheeks as the realization hit me hard: I was competing for a place in Ethan's life, and it terrified me.

The laughter around us swelled again, but it felt distant, muted, as if I were trapped behind a glass wall. Every joke, every shared glance between them felt like a strike against the fragile remnants of our friendship. In that moment, I could feel the walls closing in, suffocating in their closeness, yet I remained trapped in this uncomfortable space, teetering on the edge of confrontation.

Just as I prepared to speak again, to voice the whirlwind of feelings crashing within me, the world shattered once more. The words I had been holding onto evaporated when I overheard a conversation just behind me, a hushed exchange that sent shockwaves through my heart. "Did you hear about Sarah?" a voice whispered, tinged with concern. "They say she's moving away. No one saw it coming."

The weight of those words slammed into me, pulling me under like a sudden undertow. Sarah, my childhood friend, the one who had shared all my secrets and dreams. The thought of her leaving felt like the final straw in a life already teetering on the brink of chaos. I turned back to Ethan and Chloe, but they were lost in their own world, oblivious to the storm brewing inside me.

All I wanted was a moment of clarity, a chance to reach through the noise and grab onto something solid, something real. Instead, I felt myself slipping, spiraling into uncertainty, desperate for an anchor as the vibrant world around me blurred into a kaleidoscope of emotions—fear, anger, and a deep, aching sorrow that threatened to drown me.

I blinked, trying to ground myself amidst the chaos of swirling emotions. Sarah's name echoed in my mind like an uninvited guest at a party, her impending departure weaving itself into the very fabric of my anxiety. It felt surreal, like a cruel joke. How could she leave without saying goodbye? The thought of her packing up her life, leaving the very streets we had once roamed together, was like an avalanche, burying me under a pile of memories—late-night talks under star-speckled skies, whispered dreams, and promises that felt etched in stone.

I turned away from Ethan and Chloe, their laughter now muted, the colors of the party bleeding together as my thoughts spiraled. My pulse quickened as I pushed through the crowd, seeking solace in the quiet corners of the community center. Each face blurred into the next, the vibrant atmosphere morphing into a chaotic whirlpool of sound and color. I stumbled into a small alcove, where the twinkling lights overhead flickered like distant stars, casting a gentle glow over a table laden with pastries and punch.

My fingers traced the edges of a cupcake, the frosting adorned with little sprinkles that glimmered like confetti. I picked one up, the sugary sweetness of it reminding me of simpler times, of birthday parties and carefree summers. I took a bite, the frosting melting on my tongue, but even that familiar taste felt bittersweet. I wished it could drown out the gnawing worry in my chest, but no amount of sugar could mask the growing pit of despair.

A sudden burst of laughter pulled my attention, and I glanced up to see Lydia approaching, her eyes sparkling with a mischief that usually signaled trouble. "You look like you've just bitten into a lemon. What's going on?" she asked, her voice warm and inviting.

I attempted a smile, but it fell short, revealing the cracks that had formed beneath my cheerful facade. "Just... processing a lot, I guess. Did you hear about Sarah?"

Lydia's expression shifted, her laughter fading as she nodded solemnly. "Yeah, I heard. I can't believe she's leaving, either. She was supposed to be the one who stayed."

A lump formed in my throat. "It feels like everyone is moving on while I'm stuck here," I admitted, the words tumbling out before I could catch them. "Ethan is here with Chloe, and it feels like a reminder that I'm the one left behind."

Lydia leaned against the table, crossing her arms as she regarded me with a knowing look. "You're not left behind. You just need to figure out where you fit in now. People grow and change, but that doesn't mean you're stuck. You have your own path to carve."

Her words sank in, and I felt a flicker of warmth amidst the cold dread pooling in my chest. "But what if I lose the people I care about? What if I can't find a way to connect with them anymore?"

"Then you'll find new connections," she replied, her tone steadfast. "You're not just a background character in someone else's story, you know. You're the protagonist of your own life. So go out there and write your own narrative."

With that, a sense of determination welled up within me. I could stay trapped in my fears, or I could take a step forward. With a deep breath, I pushed myself away from the table, the taste of frosting lingering sweetly on my lips as I navigated back into the crowd, the pulsing music beckoning me like a siren.

Ethan and Chloe were still deep in conversation, and I could hear snippets of their playful banter as I approached. The air buzzed with the rhythm of laughter and music, and for a brief moment, I stood there, uncertainty dancing on my skin like static. But I was here, ready to reclaim my space among them.

"Ethan," I called out again, my voice stronger this time, and he turned, his expression shifting as he registered my presence. Chloe smiled at me, but there was a fleeting shadow of confusion in her eyes, as if she couldn't quite place the nature of our connection.

"Hey!" Ethan said, his smile lighting up his face like the fairy lights surrounding us. "We were just talking about that time we got lost in the woods and thought we were going to have to survive off acorns."

"Ah yes, the great acorn famine," I quipped, unable to resist. Laughter erupted, a ripple of sound that wove us closer together.

"Exactly!" Ethan chuckled, and for a moment, the atmosphere shifted, the tension dissipating like morning fog. "You were so resourceful. I thought we were going to be eating leaves and twigs."

I felt a warmth blooming in my chest, the kind of connection that used to come so easily. "I'm just glad I had snacks hidden in my bag. A true survivalist always comes prepared."

Chloe laughed, and the sound, once jarring, now felt welcoming. "So you were the true hero of that adventure. I need you to teach me your snack-hiding skills."

"Consider it a masterclass in outdoor survival," I replied, feeling the heaviness in my heart lift just a little. I was finding my footing again, inch by inch.

Ethan looked at me, his gaze searching, as if he were trying to decipher some unsaid words hanging in the air between us. "You okay?" he asked softly, concern creeping into his voice.

I nodded, pulling together the fragments of my bravado. "Yeah, just dealing with a lot of changes, you know? Like with Sarah. I didn't expect it to hit me this hard."

"Change can be tough," he said, his eyes earnest. "But it doesn't mean everything's falling apart. You've got us, right?"

His words wrapped around me like a lifeline, and in that moment, I realized that my fears of being left behind didn't have to become a reality. Change was inevitable, yes, but so was the possibility of new beginnings.

As the evening unfolded, I found myself surrounded by laughter and warmth, the party transforming into a tapestry of moments—shared stories, smiles, and an undeniable sense of connection. I looked around at the faces of my friends, their joys and struggles weaving together into something beautiful and raw. It was a reminder that while some bonds may fracture, others could mend, and new ones could emerge from the ashes of what was lost.

With a renewed sense of purpose, I plunged into the swirling sea of voices and laughter, ready to navigate this new chapter of my life, even if it meant embracing the unknown. The evening was just beginning, and perhaps, just perhaps, it would lead to a horizon bursting with possibilities I had yet to imagine.

The warmth of the party enveloped me as I navigated the sea of familiar faces, but underneath that cozy blanket was an unsettling tension, a tugging at the corners of my heart. I hadn't fully processed the weight of Sarah's potential departure, and now the weight of everything felt as heavy as a leaden sky threatening to rain. I was desperate to put on a brave face, but the ache in my chest and the swell of emotions fought against me, threatening to spill over.

Yet, as the minutes turned into hours, I felt a subtle shift in the atmosphere around me. With every shared laugh, every exchanged glance, I began to stitch together the remnants of my scattered thoughts and fears. The music pulsed like a heartbeat, vibrant and alive, urging me to lose myself in its rhythm. I watched Lydia command a small crowd, animatedly recounting the time we all hiked up to the old lighthouse, her gestures grand and theatrical. It was moments like this that made me realize how intertwined our lives were, how the bonds of friendship were not merely about proximity but about shared experiences, laughter, and even the occasional heartache.

As I shifted my focus, I noticed Ethan standing on the periphery of the gathering, his gaze flickering between Chloe and the jubilant crowd. I felt an undeniable pull toward him, a need to reconnect amidst the swirling chaos. I could sense he was searching for me, too, as if he were a lighthouse keeper in the fog, hoping to spot a familiar light in the distance. I took a step forward, my heart racing with every heartbeat, and caught his eye.

"Hey," I said, breaking through the din as I approached him. The warmth of his smile was an instant balm, soothing the jagged edges of my worry. "How's it going?"

"It's great! Just listening to Lydia's latest tall tale," he chuckled, the sound wrapping around me like a warm blanket. "You know how she can get."

"True! She has a flair for the dramatic." I felt a surge of warmth as I matched his smile, the tension between us slowly dissolving.

Chloe, sensing the shift, chimed in, "I'm glad you two are back together! It was getting boring just watching Ethan flounder without his partner-in-crime."

The playful jab felt like a lifeline, anchoring me back into the moment. "Well, someone has to keep him in check," I shot back, raising an eyebrow at Ethan. He pretended to look offended, placing a hand dramatically over his heart, causing Chloe to burst into laughter.

In that moment, the knot in my chest loosened. Perhaps I wasn't as isolated as I felt. Maybe the bonds we had built could weather the storm of change, adapt and grow in unexpected ways. I glanced at Chloe, who looked back at me with a mix of amusement and understanding, as if she were an ally rather than an adversary.

As the night wore on, I allowed myself to be swept up in the energy of the party, the music wrapping around us like a warm embrace. I found myself engaging in conversations with familiar faces, each exchange adding another thread to the tapestry of my life.

I caught up with old friends, reminiscing about shared experiences, from awkward school dances to spontaneous road trips.

But through it all, I couldn't shake the underlying current of uncertainty regarding Sarah. The idea of her leaving loomed over me like a shadow. In between bursts of laughter and lively discussions, I felt that familiar sense of loss creeping in, tugging at my heartstrings.

"Can I ask you something?" Ethan leaned closer, his voice just above a whisper, cutting through the laughter and music. I turned to him, intrigued. "What's really bothering you? I can tell something's off."

His gaze was steady, genuine, and I could feel the sincerity in his words. My defenses crumbled, and for a moment, I considered voicing my fears, spilling my heart out. But then the heaviness returned, swirling around us like a dark cloud. I hesitated, unsure of how to articulate the whirlwind of emotions without sounding melodramatic or needy.

"I just... I've been feeling a little overwhelmed with everything," I finally said, my voice barely rising above the din. "With Sarah possibly moving away, and then seeing you and Chloe..."

Ethan nodded, his expression softening with understanding. "Change is hard. I get that. I've felt it too—like I'm being pulled in different directions."

"What do you mean?" I asked, my curiosity piqued.

He took a moment, his brow furrowed in thought. "Well, with Chloe moving in closer and all, I feel like I'm trying to balance my past and my present. It's like I'm on this tightrope, and one wrong step could send me tumbling."

The honesty in his voice resonated with me. We were both standing at a crossroads, feeling the weight of choices that could shape our futures. "That makes sense," I replied, feeling the tension ease between us. "It's tough to find that balance."

Before he could respond, a loud cheer erupted from across the room. Lydia had rallied the crowd for a game of charades, the excitement palpable as everyone scrambled to join in. "Let's go!" I said, unable to resist the allure of spontaneous fun.

Ethan's eyes lit up, and together we surged toward the gathering. The air crackled with energy as the game unfolded, laughter spilling over like the punch that had been spilled on the floor. I watched as friends mimicked absurd gestures, their exaggerated movements eliciting waves of laughter. The night took on a whimsical quality, transforming into a joyous carnival of silliness.

"Okay, my turn!" Lydia exclaimed, stepping up to the center of the circle, and soon enough, her wild motions had everyone guessing wildly.

As I stood there, surrounded by laughter and camaraderie, I felt the fragile threads of connection tightening around me. Maybe change didn't have to mean loss. Maybe it could be an opportunity to create new memories and strengthen old bonds.

The game continued, and soon it was my turn. Heart racing, I hopped to the front and struck a pose, arms flailing dramatically as I pretended to climb a mountain. Laughter erupted around me, and for a moment, I was wholly present, lost in the joy of the moment. I caught Ethan's eye across the room, and he grinned, his encouragement lifting me higher.

As the game rolled on, I reveled in the sheer absurdity of it all, my worries gradually fading into the background. Surrounded by my friends, I felt a renewed sense of purpose. Life was messy and unpredictable, but amidst the chaos, there was beauty—friendship, laughter, and the promise of new beginnings.

With every laugh and shared moment, I began to accept that fractures could lead to healing, that bonds could be reformed and fortified. The night deepened, and with it, my understanding of what it meant to truly connect with those around me. No longer just a spectator in my own life, I was stepping boldly into my story, ready to embrace whatever came next.

Chapter 19: A Bitter Truth

The setting sun painted the sky with a riot of colors, transforming the horizon into a canvas of fiery oranges and deep purples. I stood at the edge of the park, hidden behind a cluster of tall pines, their needles whispering secrets as the breeze rustled through them. It was the kind of early evening that promised nostalgia, wrapped in the scent of freshly mown grass and blooming lilacs. Children's laughter echoed nearby, the sound punctuated by the rhythmic thumping of basketballs on asphalt. A distant ice cream truck chimed its familiar tune, a siren song to summer's sweet memories.

But here I was, an unwilling observer, wrapped in a cocoon of my own insecurities as I watched Chloe and Ethan. They sat on a weathered bench beneath the sprawling branches of an old oak, its gnarled limbs reaching out like protective arms. Chloe leaned in closer, her laughter tinkling like chimes, filling the space between them with a warmth I craved but could never seem to grasp. I could barely hear the words they exchanged, but the way her head tossed back in glee sent my heart spiraling into a tempest of envy.

I had always thought of myself as the grounded one—the reliable friend who offered support when it was needed. Yet, in moments like this, I felt more like a ghost haunting my own life, invisible and longing to be seen. I wrapped my arms around myself, not for warmth but as a makeshift shield against the pangs of jealousy that gnawed at my insides. What was it about Chloe that made her so effortlessly magnetic? The way her dark curls bounced with each laugh, the spark in her hazel eyes that seemed to outshine even the brightest summer days—it all made me feel painfully ordinary in comparison.

Ethan, with his easy smile and thoughtful gaze, had become the sun in our little solar system. I knew I was drawn to him; the way he listened with genuine interest, his brow furrowing slightly when he was deep in thought, was the kind of attention I had yearned for, yet never managed to articulate. But there, watching him lean closer to Chloe, his body language as open as the blue sky above, I felt like a bird caged in a world where freedom was tantalizingly close yet forever out of reach.

The moment his gaze flicked toward me was electric, a jolt that surged through my veins and forced my heart to stop for a breath. His surprise morphed into concern, and as he walked toward me, the playful atmosphere faded into the background like the last notes of a song. "Are you okay?" he asked, and despite the tenderness in his voice, a chasm opened between us.

I swallowed hard, my throat constricting as I tried to formulate a response, but the words were like scattered leaves in the wind—here one moment, gone the next. The truth of my feelings loomed over me like a storm cloud, dark and threatening, ready to unleash a downpour of emotions I had kept bottled up for far too long. I wanted to scream, to cry, to throw myself into his arms and lay bare the confusion that twisted inside me. Yet, the moment felt too fragile, too precarious, and I feared breaking it with my raw honesty.

"Yeah, I'm fine," I finally managed, my voice trembling like a leaf in the breeze. The lie tasted bitter on my tongue, and I could see the flicker of disappointment in his eyes. "Just... lost in thought."

He nodded, though his expression suggested he saw right through me. "You sure?" His concern felt both comforting and suffocating. "You looked like you were about to start a fire with your stare."

The heat in my cheeks flared at his teasing, and for a split second, the familiar warmth of his laughter almost melted away my anxiety. But the moment was fleeting, overshadowed by the realization that I was standing in the middle of a battlefield, my heart armed with feelings I had no idea how to express.

"Just trying to figure things out," I mumbled, my gaze falling to the ground, unable to meet his penetrating stare. The grass beneath my feet was lush and inviting, a stark contrast to the turmoil inside me. Every blade seemed to whisper the truth I had buried deep—my heart was a tangled mess, caught between friendship and something much deeper, something I feared would shatter the fragile equilibrium we had established.

"Sometimes it helps to talk about it," he suggested gently, stepping closer, bridging the gap between us. I could smell the faint hint of his cologne, a mixture of cedarwood and something fresh, like rain on pavement. It filled my lungs, grounding me in a reality that felt both comforting and terrifying.

But how could I talk about it? How could I lay bare my soul when the risk of losing him felt like a precipice I wasn't ready to leap from? My heart hammered against my ribcage, a wild bird flapping its wings against the confines of its cage. I took a deep breath, feeling the weight of my unsaid words pressing down on me, heavy and suffocating.

As I glanced back at Chloe, still laughing with Ethan, a familiar resolve began to bubble within me. The moment was slipping away, but maybe this was my chance—my moment to reclaim my voice and my feelings, to step into the light instead of lingering in the shadows of envy.

The world around me faded into a muted blur, the laughter of children and the distant sound of the ice cream truck receding into an echoing void. All that remained was Ethan, the intensity of his gaze pulling me into an orbit where every heartbeat felt amplified. As he stepped closer, the familiar warmth of his presence collided with my swirling emotions, igniting a spark that made me acutely aware of how deeply I cared for him.

"Maybe we should talk," he suggested, the soft insistence in his voice cutting through the fog that clouded my thoughts. I hesitated, searching for the right words, but my mind was a jumbled mess of memories and emotions, like a puzzle with missing pieces. Should I admit that my feelings had morphed from platonic to something far more complicated, something that terrified me? Or should I maintain the facade of the dependable friend, the one who offered laughter and lightness while hiding the tumult beneath?

"Yeah, okay," I finally replied, trying to sound nonchalant. The casualness of my tone felt like a lie as I led him away from the bench, toward a small grove of trees that offered a measure of privacy. The branches formed a natural canopy, dappling the fading sunlight on the ground beneath our feet. Each step felt like a leap into the unknown, the gravity of our friendship pulling me in one direction while my heart yearned for another.

Once we were ensconced in the cool shade, I turned to face him, the uncertainty bubbling up like a fizzy drink I had shaken too hard. I wanted to tell him everything—the pangs of jealousy, the confusing cocktail of emotions that mixed friendship with longing. Instead, I found myself staring at the ground, tracing patterns in the dirt with the toe of my shoe, the silence stretching between us like an unspoken promise.

"I didn't mean to pry," he said softly, breaking the quiet with the gentleness of a whisper. "I just... you seemed off."

His sincerity disarmed me, and for a brief moment, I thought of how easy it would be to spill everything. To lay bare my heart, to confess that every time he smiled, a part of me fluttered, and every laugh we shared felt like a secret language that only we understood. But would he understand? Or would it change everything?

"I just... I feel like I'm in the middle of something I can't quite figure out," I said, the words slipping from my lips before I could think better of it. "It's just hard to articulate."

He tilted his head slightly, his dark hair catching the light in a way that made him look impossibly handsome, a fact that only added to my flustered state. "Sometimes it helps to put it out there, you know?" His voice was steady, encouraging, and my heart raced as I sensed the vulnerability behind his calm exterior.

"Okay," I began, the weight of the moment settling on my shoulders. "I think... I think I might have feelings for you." The admission hung in the air like a suspended breath, my heart pounding so loudly that I feared he could hear it. "More than just friends."

There it was, the truth spilled out like ink on a blank page. I couldn't look at him; my gaze remained fixed on the ground, where ants marched with unwavering purpose, oblivious to my inner turmoil. I waited for the silence to shatter, for the ground to open up and swallow me whole, but all that met my confession was the steady rustle of leaves in the gentle breeze.

Ethan's reaction was delayed, as if he were processing each word like a complex math problem. Finally, he took a step closer, a hint of disbelief mingling with something softer in his eyes. "You're not joking, are you?" he asked, his voice barely above a whisper.

I shook my head, the heat of embarrassment creeping up my neck. "I wish I were," I murmured, the gravity of my feelings suddenly feeling like a weight I couldn't bear. "But I can't help how I feel. And I've been trying to push it away, but... it just keeps coming back."

His expression shifted, the initial surprise melting away to reveal a vulnerability I hadn't seen before. "I had no idea you felt that way," he said, his brow furrowing as he processed my words. "I mean, I've always thought we had a connection, but I didn't want to overstep."

Relief washed over me, a tidal wave of emotion crashing through my chest. "You felt it too?"

"Yeah, I just didn't know how to bring it up," he admitted, rubbing the back of his neck sheepishly. "I didn't want to ruin our friendship."

My heart soared, and for a fleeting moment, the weight of my confession felt lighter, buoyed by the knowledge that he shared my feelings. But then the gravity of what lay ahead sank in, a realization that both thrilled and terrified me. "So... what do we do now?" I asked, my voice barely above a whisper.

Ethan's gaze softened, and he stepped even closer, the distance between us shrinking until the air crackled with tension. "We take it one step at a time," he replied, his voice steady yet laced with the excitement of uncharted territory. "Let's explore this together. I don't want to lose what we have, but I also don't want to ignore what could be."

With those words, a flicker of hope ignited within me, illuminating the path ahead. Perhaps this was the moment we had both been waiting for, the chance to redefine our connection, to venture beyond the comfortable borders of friendship into something more profound. I could feel the weight of my insecurities begin to lift, replaced by a burgeoning sense of possibility.

As we stood there, the sun dipped lower in the sky, casting golden rays that danced around us like fireflies. The park, once filled with laughter and joy, now faded into the background, becoming a distant memory as we stood on the precipice of something new. In that suspended moment, everything felt alive—the world bursting with potential, as if nature itself conspired to bless this fragile yet thrilling leap into the unknown.

Our hands brushed, a fleeting touch that sent sparks cascading through the air, and I could almost taste the sweetness of what lay ahead. Perhaps this was the start of a new chapter, one filled with laughter, uncertainty, and a bond that could grow stronger with each passing day. My heart soared at the thought, a promise lingering on the horizon, waiting for us to seize it.

As Ethan's eyes searched mine, the world around us seemed to blur into a haze of color and sound, a distant backdrop to the moment that now unfolded between us. The air hung thick with unspoken words, each of us standing at the precipice of vulnerability. I could feel the weight of my confession linger in the space between us, an electric charge that sent shivers down my spine. It felt as if the trees themselves were holding their breath, their leaves trembling in anticipation of the truth.

"Are you sure?" he asked, breaking the silence, his voice steady yet laced with uncertainty. "I mean, you really feel that way?"

The sincerity in his tone sent my heart racing. I nodded, my resolve crystallizing as I allowed myself to fully embrace the warmth of my feelings. "I do," I said, my voice gaining strength. "I've tried to ignore it, but it just keeps growing. I can't pretend anymore."

A flicker of something—hope, perhaps—sparked in his gaze, his lips curling into a tentative smile that sent warmth flooding through me. "I'm glad you said something. I've felt it too, but I didn't know how to approach it. I thought I might ruin everything."

The weight of his admission washed over me, a tide of relief mingling with the thrill of shared emotions. "You could never ruin anything," I whispered, stepping closer, drawn in by an invisible thread. The tension between us shifted, charged with a newfound energy that made my heart race.

For a moment, we stood in a cocoon of silence, the park around us fading into a mere background noise. The children's laughter felt distant, and the vibrant hues of sunset cast a golden glow around us, transforming the mundane into something magical. The realization that we were on the cusp of something beautiful filled me with an intoxicating mix of excitement and fear.

"What if we take it slow?" Ethan suggested, his brow furrowing in thought. "I don't want to rush into anything and risk what we have."

"Slow sounds perfect," I replied, my heart swelling at the idea of exploring this new dynamic together. "I want to enjoy this without losing the foundation we've built."

His smile widened, and it felt like the sun had broken through the clouds, illuminating everything in its path. "Great. Let's start by just being honest with each other. No more hiding."

As we began to step away from the gravity of the past and into the uncharted territory of our shared feelings, a sense of liberation enveloped me. I had spent too long harboring emotions that felt like secrets, yet now they floated freely in the air between us. The world felt lighter, the colors more vivid, and I found myself drawn to him like a moth to a flame.

Days turned into weeks, and our relationship blossomed in the soft glow of shared moments. We meandered through sun-drenched afternoons, exploring quaint cafés where the air was thick with the scent of fresh pastries and rich coffee. We shared laughter and late-night conversations that twisted into the early hours, our words weaving an intricate tapestry of understanding and connection.

I cherished the way he would lean in to hear me, his attention unwavering as I spoke about everything and nothing all at once. There were quiet moments in the park where we would sit side by side, our fingers brushing against each other, a gentle reminder of the bond we were nurturing. Ethan had a way of making the simplest things feel monumental—the way he would run his fingers through his hair when he was deep in thought, or the way his eyes sparkled when he laughed. It made every shared moment feel electric, pulsating with a rhythm that echoed in my heart.

Chloe, ever the vibrant spirit, was delighted to see the change in us. "You two are so cute together!" she would tease, her laughter bubbling up like a playful melody. While her words filled me with a sense of belonging, I couldn't shake the remnants of my earlier insecurities. There were moments when I caught myself wondering if

I was enough for Ethan, if he truly saw me as someone worthy of his affections.

One evening, as we settled into a cozy booth at our favorite diner, the jukebox humming softly in the background, I decided to voice my concerns. "Ethan," I began, hesitating as I met his gaze. "Do you ever worry that this—us—might not last?"

His expression turned serious, the light in his eyes dimming momentarily as he considered my words. "Honestly? Sometimes, yeah," he admitted, his voice low. "But I think every relationship has its uncertainties. What matters is how we navigate those together."

His honesty resonated deeply, yet the fear still gnawed at me. "But what if I'm not enough?" The question slipped out before I could catch it, vulnerability painting my cheeks a soft shade of crimson.

Ethan reached across the table, his fingers wrapping around mine. "You are more than enough," he reassured me, his thumb brushing over my knuckles in a soothing gesture. "You've brought so much light into my life, and I don't want to lose that."

In that moment, a warmth spread through me, washing away the shadows of doubt. I believed him—truly, I did—but the lingering fear of inadequacy remained, a silent specter haunting the edges of my thoughts.

As summer deepened, our bond strengthened, yet the whispers of uncertainty never fully disappeared. I often found myself reflecting on the nature of love, the way it could bloom in unexpected places and yet carry the weight of vulnerability. Each shared moment felt like a step forward, yet the remnants of fear hung like cobwebs in the corners of my mind, ever-present, a reminder of the fragility of our connection.

One warm evening, as the sun dipped below the horizon, casting a golden light across the park, I felt a shift in the air. Chloe had invited us to a gathering, a casual affair filled with laughter and music. I sensed an underlying tension, a bittersweet note that hung heavy as we arrived, the shadows of our past insecurities mingling with the vibrant energy of the evening.

As the night unfolded, laughter echoed around us, and I caught glimpses of the happiness radiating from Chloe. Yet, the warmth of the evening was marred by a gnawing anxiety that coiled tightly in my stomach. I watched as Ethan and Chloe exchanged banter, their chemistry undeniable, and despite my efforts to rein in my insecurities, I felt a familiar twinge of jealousy rise within me.

I stood at the edge of the gathering, an unwilling observer, a sense of isolation creeping in despite the vibrant atmosphere. The laughter and music blended into a distant hum, a world I felt increasingly disconnected from. As I glanced at Ethan, the laughter in his eyes tugged at my heart, but the specter of doubt loomed larger.

"Hey," Chloe's voice broke through my thoughts, and I turned to face her, forcing a smile. "You okay? You seem a little off."

"Just tired," I replied, the words tasting bitter on my tongue.

"Come on, join us! We're about to play some games." She gestured toward a group gathered in the middle of the lawn, the glow of string lights illuminating the space.

With a deep breath, I stepped back into the fold, the warmth of camaraderie enveloping me. The laughter was infectious, and as we played, I felt the tension in my chest slowly ease. The games were lighthearted, full of silly antics and friendly competition. I even found myself laughing, the sound bubbling up from deep within me. But as the night wore on, I couldn't shake the feeling that a storm was brewing just beneath the surface.

As the gathering wound down, Ethan and I found ourselves stepping away from the crowd, the night air cool against our skin. "You okay?" he asked, his voice low, concern etched on his face.

"Yeah," I said, though my heart didn't fully agree. "Just a bit overwhelmed."

He nodded, the understanding in his eyes both comforting and unsettling. "If there's something bothering you, you can talk to me. I promise I'm here."

His words hung in the air, heavy with meaning. I wanted to pour my heart out, to unearth the fears that had taken root in my mind. But as I gazed into his eyes, the warmth and sincerity there made me hesitate. Instead, I simply smiled, the vulnerability lingering just beneath the surface, waiting for the right moment to break free.

Chapter 20: Fraying Threads

The hum of the street outside my bookstore buzzed like a lively orchestra, each honk and shout composing a chaotic symphony that matched my fraying nerves. The quaint little shop, nestled between a retro diner with a flickering neon sign and an antique store bursting with mismatched treasures, had always been my refuge. I wrapped my fingers around the warm, chipped wooden counter, grounding myself in the comforting scent of aged paper and freshly brewed coffee. As I peered out the window, the late afternoon sun cast a golden hue over the cobblestone street, where the occasional passerby ambled along, lost in their own thoughts, oblivious to the storm brewing within me.

Ethan's eyes had a way of lingering in my mind, like a melody stuck on repeat, haunting yet beautifully poignant. I could still recall how they sparkled that night, mirroring the twinkling fairy lights strung around the garden. We were surrounded by laughter, the air thick with the scent of grilled burgers and sweet, sticky barbecue sauce. But beneath the surface of revelry, I sensed an unspoken tension, a fragile flicker of something deeper that I dared not acknowledge. Our brief moments together—those shared glances, the accidental brush of hands—felt monumental yet fleeting, like dandelion seeds dancing in the wind, beautiful in their impermanence.

As I absently stacked the latest arrivals on the shelf, I couldn't shake the feeling that our connection was as delicate as the books I handled. What if I was just a bookmark in his story, a temporary pause before he turned the page to something new? The thought twisted like a vine around my heart, squeezing tighter with every passing day. I had been here before, lost in a labyrinth of doubt, and the path always seemed to lead to heartache.

I paused, allowing myself to be enveloped by the soft rustle of pages, the whispers of past authors speaking to me like old friends. Their words swirled around me, filling the empty spaces where my confidence used to reside. Each novel I'd read was a refuge, a window into worlds where love triumphed over adversity, where characters braved the odds for their happily ever afters. I envied them—their ability to find resolution, to weave their narratives into something coherent and whole. Meanwhile, I felt like a loose thread, my story unraveling with every heartbeat, hanging precariously between hope and despair.

Outside, a couple strolled past, hands entwined, laughter bubbling between them like a shared secret. The sight tugged at the corners of my heart, igniting a yearning that threatened to swallow me whole. I couldn't help but wonder if Ethan felt the same spark when he looked at me or if my presence was merely an afterthought, a passing moment in his busy life. I set my jaw, trying to quell the rising tide of insecurities that threatened to drown me.

With a resigned sigh, I grabbed a steaming cup of coffee, the warmth seeping into my palms, and retreated to my favorite nook—a cozy corner where sunlight poured in like liquid gold through the large bay window. The mismatched cushions invited me to sink in, and I curled up with my mug, hoping to find solace in the pages of a beloved classic. Yet, the words danced around my mind like fireflies, refusing to settle. The once-joyful stories morphed into distractions, their plots overshadowed by the growing uncertainty I felt about my connection with Ethan.

I thought back to our last conversation, how he'd leaned in close, the scent of his cologne mingling with the evening air, creating a heady mix that left me breathless. I could almost feel the warmth of his breath against my cheek as he spoke, a soft cadence that wrapped around my thoughts, pulling me in. But the memory was tainted by the question that gnawed at me relentlessly: did he really mean what he said, or were those words just the perfumed compliments we exchanged at parties, crafted to flatter and deflect?

The door chimed, interrupting my thoughts. I looked up to see a familiar face, a regular customer who always seemed to drift into my world at the right moment. Sarah, with her wild curls and an infectious smile that brightened the dullest days, strolled in, her arms overflowing with books. Her eyes sparkled with excitement, and for a fleeting moment, I forgot my troubles as she excitedly recounted her latest literary discoveries.

"Have you read this one?" she gushed, brandishing a thick volume like a trophy. "It's all about finding your voice in a noisy world. You'd love it!"

Her enthusiasm was contagious, and I couldn't help but smile, the warmth spreading through me like sunlight breaking through clouds. I admired her resilience, the way she faced her own battles with unwavering spirit. "You always find the best books, Sarah," I replied, genuinely impressed.

As she browsed the shelves, I couldn't shake the feeling that she was somehow a mirror reflecting my own fears and aspirations. Here I was, cocooned in a world of stories, yet trapped in my own doubts. Watching her lose herself in the narratives I cherished reminded me of why I loved this place—the stories that connected us, that breathed life into our dreams, even in the face of uncertainty.

I slipped into the role of the storyteller, guiding Sarah through the aisles, recommending titles, each choice filled with purpose. It felt good to share my passion, to witness the spark ignite in her eyes with every new suggestion. But just as quickly, the nagging ache of unfulfilled longing crept back in. I yearned for that same fire, that undeniable connection that felt so effortlessly woven between us, yet seemed so elusive with Ethan.

As I stood there, surrounded by the stories that had been my lifeline, I realized that maybe, just maybe, I had to take the leap.

Perhaps the only way to discern the truth about Ethan was to embrace the uncertainty, to let my heart guide me through the tangled web of emotions that seemed to bind us.

The thought was both exhilarating and terrifying, a double-edged sword poised to cut through the silence that had grown so thick between us. As the sun began to dip lower, painting the sky with strokes of pink and orange, I felt the first flicker of resolve stirring within me. If I wanted clarity, I needed to confront my fears, to unravel the threads of doubt that had woven themselves into my heart, and allow myself to discover whether Ethan was indeed a fleeting moment or something much more profound.

The bell above the door tinkled again, and I turned to see Sarah still buzzing with enthusiasm, her laughter a light breeze that swept away the lingering shadows in my heart. She clutched a book against her chest like a child guarding a secret treasure. "You know, I think your bookstore has magical powers," she declared, her eyes sparkling. "Every time I walk in, I feel like I'm stepping into a different world."

Her comment stirred something in me, a flutter of hope that maybe this little haven, with its creaking floors and walls lined with stories, could indeed provide the answers I sought. "If only I could find the right spell to enchant Ethan," I replied, a wry smile creeping onto my face, "maybe then I wouldn't feel like I'm floating in this sea of uncertainty."

Sarah chuckled, oblivious to the deeper currents swirling in my mind. "Oh, come on! You just need to show him how extraordinary you are. You're like one of those heroines in a novel, waiting for the right moment to sweep him off his feet!" Her playful insistence was a buoy in my tumultuous sea of doubt, and I couldn't help but feel a spark of warmth at her encouragement.

"But what if he's just not that into me? What if I'm like one of those quirky side characters who adds a bit of color but doesn't really belong in the main story?" I tried to keep my voice light, but the words tumbled out heavier than I intended.

Sarah paused, her expression shifting to one of sincerity. "You're not a side character, not even close. You're the kind of person who lights up a room. Just think about how many people walk through those doors and leave with a smile because of you."

Her words wrapped around me, cocooning me in a warmth I desperately needed. In that moment, I realized that my own perception of myself had become entangled in the web of uncertainty surrounding Ethan. I had allowed my doubts to cloud my self-worth, forgetting the light I brought to the world.

"Okay, maybe I'm not the quirky sidekick," I said, allowing a teasing smile to emerge. "But what's the next step? How do I go from being a friendly face in his life to something... more?"

Sarah's eyes twinkled as if she were crafting a master plan. "Why not invite him here? You can host a little book club! Share your favorite reads, maybe even do a themed evening. Something like a 'mystery night' could be fun! He'll have to show up—how could he resist a chance to unravel a mystery with you?"

The idea ignited a flicker of excitement within me. A book club! The thought sent my mind spinning with possibilities, like pages fluttering in a fresh breeze. It would be the perfect setting, a comfortable space where we could explore our connection amid the familiar surroundings of stories and laughter.

"Okay, maybe I could try that," I mused, feeling a sense of agency return to my heart. "I'll create an event that he can't ignore."

As I began to sketch out ideas, Sarah returned to her book browsing, and I could hear her humming to herself, lost in the world of paperbacks. I watched her with a smile, admiring her innocence and zeal for life. In many ways, she reminded me of my younger self, before the world's expectations had chipped away at my confidence.

Lost in thought, I momentarily forgot about Ethan. My fingers grazed the spines of the books, each title a potential gateway to different lives and worlds. Yet, a nagging part of me wondered if my plans would amount to anything. I could set the stage perfectly, but what if he didn't feel the same? What if he preferred the thrill of the unknown, the chase of a new adventure?

In the following days, I poured my energy into planning the book club event. The bookstore transformed into a cozy haven, filled with flickering candles and the inviting aroma of freshly baked cookies that I had whipped up, hoping to set the right tone. I printed flyers and pinned them to the community board, crafted enticing social media posts, and watched as the anticipation grew. It was exhilarating and terrifying all at once, but I felt a sense of purpose reigniting within me, pushing me forward.

As the evening approached, I decorated the shop with twinkling fairy lights, creating a warm, inviting atmosphere. The chatter of attendees filled the air, a symphony of excited voices mingling with the soft strumming of a guitar in the background. I could hardly believe my idea had blossomed into something tangible.

When Ethan finally stepped through the door, the room dimmed, and my heart raced as I caught his eye. He moved through the crowd with an ease that made my breath hitch, his presence a magnet pulling me closer. The laughter around me faded, replaced by the pounding of my heart echoing in my ears. I felt vulnerable, exposed, like a character stripped of their armor, standing there waiting for him to see me.

He made his way toward me, a lopsided grin spreading across his face that felt like a beacon in the haze of uncertainty. "This place looks amazing! You really outdid yourself," he said, his voice smooth like honey, instantly wrapping around me.

"Thanks! I wanted to create an environment where everyone could feel at home," I replied, my smile widening despite the nervous fluttering in my stomach.

As the night unfolded, we delved into discussions that twisted and turned like the plot of a gripping novel. Laughter erupted over shared stories, and I found myself leaning into the conversations, weaving between moments of silence that felt electric. Each glance exchanged with Ethan felt charged, filled with unsaid words, as if we were dancing around a deeper truth, one that lay just beneath the surface, waiting to be uncovered.

The evening spiraled into a delightful blur of warmth and camaraderie, the atmosphere thick with the fragrance of books and baked goods. Yet, even amidst the laughter, the ever-present doubt nagged at me, whispering questions I was desperate to silence.

As we wrapped up the night, I felt the urgency of a million unspoken thoughts swirling between us. "I'm really glad you came tonight," I said, my voice softer than intended, revealing a sliver of vulnerability I had kept carefully guarded.

"Me too," he replied, his eyes searching mine, and in that instant, it felt as though the world outside faded away, leaving just the two of us suspended in a moment that could tip either way—toward the familiar comfort we had shared or the unknown that lay ahead.

But it was in the uncertainty that I found my resolve. Maybe it was time to unearth the truths lurking beneath the surface, to embrace the messiness of connection. I was ready to weave the threads of our stories together, to risk it all for the chance of something extraordinary. And as the night drifted into a tender silence, I knew I was willing to face whatever came next, hand in hand with the mystery that was Ethan.

The lingering aroma of vanilla and freshly brewed coffee wove itself into the fabric of the evening as laughter and lively chatter filled my bookstore. With each passing moment, I felt the anxiety that had been a constant companion begin to ebb, replaced by a sense of belonging I had longed for. The twinkling fairy lights hung above like stars in a night sky, illuminating the faces of my friends and the familiar warmth of my haven. And yet, even as I reveled in the atmosphere, Ethan's presence remained a magnetic force, drawing me in with the promise of something more.

As the discussions meandered from plot twists to character arcs, I found myself stealing glances at him across the room, his laughter echoing in my ears like a melodic refrain. He was animated, gesturing wildly as he recounted a hilarious mishap from his week, his dark hair tousled just so, as if he'd walked straight out of a novel, a hero trapped in the ordinary world. My heart danced to the rhythm of his words, intoxicated by the sheer joy of watching him thrive among friends.

I couldn't help but marvel at how effortlessly he fit into this environment. Each time his gaze swept over to meet mine, a jolt of electricity surged through the air, lingering like the last notes of a favorite song. We were connected by a silent thread, an unspoken promise that we were both searching for the same thing—validation, connection, perhaps even love. Yet the weight of doubt still hung over me, a cloud threatening to obscure the bright moment we were creating.

"Let's do a round of 'Two Truths and a Lie,'" Sarah suggested, her voice bright and enthusiastic. The idea caught on like wildfire, everyone eager to share their secrets and laugh together. As the game unfolded, I found my own anxiety ebbing away, replaced by the thrill of vulnerability. The room erupted in playful banter, each revelation bringing us closer, unveiling layers of ourselves that often remained hidden beneath the surface.

When it was Ethan's turn, he leaned forward, a mischievous glint in his eye. "Alright, here goes. One: I once hiked to the top of a mountain and didn't realize I'd been wearing two different shoes.

THE PATH BETWEEN WORDS 213

Two: I can juggle three flaming torches. And three: I've never been on a roller coaster."

The room exploded with laughter. "You're lying about the roller coaster," I blurted, an instinctive response that surprised even me. My heart raced at the audacity of my claim, but the truth felt right. How could someone as adventurous as Ethan not have experienced that rush?

He chuckled, leaning back in his chair, his gaze locking onto mine. "You're right! I've been on plenty. The juggling? A party trick I've yet to master," he admitted, his eyes shining with mischief. The playful exchange felt like a daring dance, each step bringing us closer to an understanding that transcended words.

As the game continued, I felt a palpable shift in the atmosphere, a deepening connection that seemed to spiral into the corners of the room. I caught Ethan glancing at me, and the weight of his gaze felt like a promise suspended in the air. I could sense the invitation hanging between us, urging me to unravel the mystery of what lay beneath the surface.

With the game winding down, I seized the moment. "So, what's your next adventure?" I asked, my voice steady despite the fluttering in my stomach. "What's the next thing on your bucket list?"

Ethan leaned forward, the playful glint in his eyes shifting to something more profound. "I've always wanted to travel to a small town in Italy," he began, his voice low and rich, painting vivid pictures in my mind. "I want to wander through the cobbled streets, savor authentic gelato, and lose myself in the stories etched into the walls of ancient buildings. But honestly?" He paused, allowing the anticipation to build. "I'd rather share that adventure with someone special."

The way he spoke resonated deeply within me, each word threading through my heart, weaving together a tapestry of longing and hope. I could feel the weight of my own yearning reflected in his gaze, the unacknowledged truth that perhaps we were both searching for something that had always been just out of reach.

"Someone special, huh?" I replied, a teasing lilt in my voice, trying to mask the sudden vulnerability that gripped me. "Are you looking for that person, or is it more about the journey?"

He smiled, that captivating smile that made the world around us blur into the background. "A bit of both, I suppose. I think the journey becomes richer when shared. It's all about the stories we create together, the memories we build."

At that moment, a soft hush fell over the group, as if the universe had paused to hold its breath, the air thick with unspoken words. My heart raced, knowing I had a chance to weave my own story into his, to forge a connection that transcended the uncertainties that had haunted me. But the question loomed—was I brave enough to step into that unknown?

As the evening wound to a close, I felt the warmth of our conversation linger, wrapping around me like a favorite sweater. When the last guest had left, I found myself alone with Ethan, the dim light casting soft shadows across the room. The silence stretched between us, an invitation to explore what lay beyond the banter and laughter.

"Thank you for tonight," I said, my voice a gentle whisper, filled with sincerity. "It was more than I hoped for."

He stepped closer, a comforting presence. "You've created something beautiful here. This place, your passion—it draws people in, including me."

A thrill of warmth coursed through me at his words, igniting the hope that perhaps we were both ready to uncover the layers of our connection. "Maybe we could do this again? Just the two of us?"

Ethan's smile broadened, lighting up his face in a way that made my heart race. "I'd like that. I really would."

As he reached for the door, pausing just for a moment, our eyes locked in an unspoken promise. It felt as though the world around us faded, leaving just the two of us suspended in a moment that teetered on the brink of something extraordinary. With every heartbeat, I sensed the fabric of our stories beginning to intertwine, threads of uncertainty giving way to possibilities I had once deemed impossible.

And in that moment of shared silence, I knew I was ready to unravel the doubts that had clouded my heart, to embrace the journey ahead. The stories we were crafting together, infused with laughter, vulnerability, and hope, would be the adventure I had yearned for all along. With each step into the unknown, I felt myself awakening to the beauty of uncertainty, ready to weave my narrative with his, one precious thread at a time.

Chapter 21: The Shift

A gentle hum of anticipation buzzed through the air, mingling with the comforting aroma of freshly brewed coffee and the faintest hint of worn paper. My bookstore, a charming little nook nestled between a vintage record shop and a quirky café, was transformed into a haven for bibliophiles. Colorful banners draped from the ceiling, and tables lined with an eclectic array of books sparkled under the warm glow of string lights. Each corner was alive with the whispers of stories waiting to be discovered. I was lost in the thrill of it all, excitement coursing through my veins as I arranged the last few chairs for the event, my heart dancing in sync with the fluttering pages of the latest novels on display.

But then, like an unexpected plot twist, there he was: Ethan. Standing at the back, his easy smile and disheveled hair stirred something deep within me—a blend of hope and nostalgia that felt almost electric. I could still remember the way his laughter filled the spaces between our conversations, how his teasing could lighten the heaviest of moods. It was a long time since I had seen him, but that familiar warmth swelled in my chest, threatening to spill over.

Yet, as if the universe conspired to douse my flames, Chloe appeared beside him. Her laughter, bright and carefree, echoed through the store like a siren's call, enticing and disorienting. I felt an immediate chill as I recalled all those times she had seemed to effortlessly claim every room she entered. She had an uncanny ability to draw attention, her vivacious personality lighting up the corners of any gathering. The sight of her, so easy and free in her interactions with Ethan, knotted my stomach. I could almost hear the echo of my insecurities whispering in my ear, urging me to retreat into the shadows of my own self-doubt.

In that moment, I struggled to maintain my focus. The energy I had intended to channel into creating a magical experience for our authors and readers flickered like a candle caught in a draft. The voices of the attendees around me faded, and the bright decorations began to blur. I shook my head, attempting to cast away the overwhelming sensations. It was time to reclaim my narrative, to remind myself that I was more than a backdrop in someone else's story.

"Just breathe," I murmured to myself, taking in the vibrant surroundings. My eyes landed on a young girl, her face lit with wonder as she clutched a stack of books, her mother hovering nearby with an equally enchanted expression. This was why I had poured my heart into the bookstore—to create a sanctuary for those who sought solace in the pages of novels, to spark connections between authors and readers. The vision of my dream flickered brightly in my mind, warming me against the cold pangs of jealousy.

As I stepped onto the makeshift stage, I took a moment to gaze across the room. Familiar faces peered back at me, some bright with excitement, others just as uncertain as I felt. I could see Mrs. Thompson, the local librarian, seated in the front row, her notebook poised and ready, eager to absorb every word I spoke. Next to her, a trio of aspiring writers exchanged glances, their eyes gleaming with ambition. They were the heartbeat of my bookstore, and for them, I would summon every ounce of energy I had.

"Welcome, everyone!" My voice rang out, surprisingly steady, and a wave of warmth washed over me. "Thank you all for coming to this special author event. Today, we celebrate not just the words in these books, but the connections we form through them." The applause that followed wrapped around me like a warm embrace, pulling me deeper into my role as their guide through this literary adventure.

With each author introduced, my heart swelled with pride. These were individuals who had bared their souls to the world, their stories rooted in truth and imagination. I shared their journeys, the struggles and triumphs that brought them to this very moment. The stories flowed seamlessly, the air thick with inspiration. I felt alive, each word igniting a flicker of joy within me. And as I glanced at Ethan and Chloe, I noticed something unexpected; they were listening, nodding along, their faces lit with genuine interest.

For a fleeting moment, the shadows of my insecurities melted away. My passion for storytelling enveloped me, allowing me to lose myself in the world I had crafted. As the last author finished speaking, the room erupted in applause, and I felt the exhilaration surge through me, anchoring me firmly in my own reality.

But just as the excitement reached a crescendo, a sudden shift rippled through the crowd. Chloe stood, her voice slicing through the applause with an enthusiastic suggestion for a Q&A session. The mood shifted, and I sensed a flicker of competition rise within me.

As hands shot up around the room, I pushed down my insecurities, channeling my energy into this moment. I asked questions, engaged with the audience, and shared laughter as we explored the depths of creativity. It felt as though we were all woven together, a tapestry of shared experiences, emotions, and dreams.

And just like that, I began to understand something profound. I didn't need to compete with Chloe or anyone else for Ethan's attention. The stories I had created and the community I had nurtured were my own victories, standing strong against the current of comparison. I found solace in the shared passion of our literary gathering, and perhaps, in that realization, a flicker of hope kindled anew.

The event wound down, leaving a warm glow in the air, like the afterglow of a beautiful sunset. I was exhilarated yet exhausted, buoyed by the connections made and the stories shared. As I packed up the last of the chairs, I glanced back at Ethan and Chloe. Their conversation seemed effortless, laughter spilling freely between them. Yet, rather than feeling diminished, I felt something shift within me—a growing sense of self, an understanding that my worth was not defined by their dynamics.

My bookstore was more than a backdrop to their story; it was the heart of mine. I had woven something magical here, something worth celebrating. And with that realization came an unexpected clarity. No matter what unfolded in the pages of my life, I would continue to write my own story, one filled with vibrant characters, undeniable courage, and a resilience that would carry me through the chapters yet to come.

The moment the applause faded into echoes, I found myself swept into a delightful chaos that filled the bookstore. Authors mingled with readers, sharing stories over cups of steaming coffee, laughter dancing through the aisles like fireflies at dusk. I took a deep breath, savoring the ambiance that buzzed with the promise of connection. Each interaction was a new chapter, and my heart thumped with the rhythm of their excitement. I moved among them, checking in on the authors, ensuring their tables were stocked with books, and basking in the light of their shared joy.

But amidst the flurry, my gaze kept drifting back to Ethan and Chloe. I couldn't help but notice how easily they navigated their conversation, the way Chloe's laughter rolled off her tongue like a melody, enchanting everyone nearby. It was a melody I had once known well, but now it felt like a haunting refrain echoing through my memories. I attempted to drown out the familiar pang of longing, reminding myself of the rich tapestry I had woven in my own world.

With purpose, I approached a small group of readers discussing their favorite recent releases. Their enthusiasm pulled me in like a magnet. "Have you read the latest by that debut author?" one of them exclaimed, her eyes alight with passion. I leaned closer, eager to hear every detail, and before I knew it, I was swept away in their enthusiasm, sharing my own thoughts and recommendations.

Suddenly, the vibrancy around me felt like a warm embrace, enveloping me in its comforts. I reveled in the stories that filled the air, each one another thread in the fabric of our shared experience. I made a mental note to incorporate their suggestions into the store's inventory, my mind racing with ideas to cultivate this growing community of book lovers.

As the conversations swirled, I caught snippets of Ethan's laughter filtering through the crowd. It drew me like a moth to a flame, and I chided myself for even considering the path of least resistance—slipping away unnoticed. No, I was no longer that girl who retreated into the shadows, her worth measured against the affections of others. I would not dim my own light to accommodate their glow.

With renewed determination, I maneuvered through the crowd, taking stock of the different conversations. At the heart of it all was my love for books, the stories that connected us all, and I embraced that passion. I found myself chatting with a mother and her son, each sharing tales of their favorite reads, laughter mingling with genuine connections. I offered recommendations, my heart swelling as the boy's eyes widened with wonder at the thought of new adventures waiting on the pages.

The bookstore was alive with possibility, and for every moment that I engaged with a reader or an author, I felt a piece of my former self reemerging. Each smile exchanged was a reminder that I could create my own narrative, independent of anyone else's subplot. I glanced over at Ethan again. This time, he was leaning forward, engaged, genuinely invested in whatever Chloe was saying. But instead of feeling that familiar twist of envy, I found a strange kind of clarity washing over me.

The event unfolded like a beautifully crafted novel, the chapters filled with laughter, shared stories, and moments of camaraderie. I moved through the crowd, drawing inspiration from the voices surrounding me. Each smile and every spark of excitement was like a gentle nudge, reminding me that the stories I nurtured in my bookstore mattered, not just to me but to all those gathered here.

As the afternoon sun dipped lower, casting a golden hue over the room, I found myself gravitating toward a quieter corner where an elderly gentleman sat, a tattered copy of Pride and Prejudice cradled in his hands. His gentle smile and twinkling eyes invited me to sit down beside him. I couldn't help but lean in, drawn to the richness of his experiences. "You know," he began, his voice a soft rasp, "this book has been a companion to me through countless seasons. Each time I read it, I find something new."

Listening to him was like uncovering a hidden chapter in a familiar tale. I shared my own thoughts, and we delved into a spirited discussion about love, resilience, and the power of storytelling. Time slipped away as we lost ourselves in conversation, the bustling noise of the event fading into a soothing backdrop. With each word exchanged, I felt more anchored in the moment, my heart swelling with gratitude for this unexpected connection.

Eventually, as the event drew to a close, I stood in the center of the room, eyes sweeping over the lively crowd, my heart bursting with a sense of belonging. The authors exchanged books, the readers shared their newfound treasures, and the air hummed with the promise of more stories yet to be told. I allowed myself a moment to soak it all in, to revel in the warmth that radiated from this community I had cultivated.

The last few attendees trickled out, and I was left with an overwhelming sense of fulfillment. I turned to see Ethan standing nearby, a soft smile gracing his lips. It was a simple gesture, yet it sent a jolt of warmth through me, as if he had acknowledged my journey without uttering a word. I felt a gentle nudge within me, urging me to approach him. This was my moment—an opportunity to connect without the weight of expectation.

"Thanks for coming today," I said, my voice steady as I crossed the distance between us. "It meant a lot to have you here."

His smile widened, revealing a glimmer of genuine warmth that pulled at my heartstrings. "I wouldn't have missed it for the world. You created something special today," he replied, his gaze sincere.

The sincerity in his words sent a ripple of energy through me, intertwining with the euphoria that still lingered in the air. In that moment, standing amidst the remnants of the day, I understood that this was my space, my community, and my story. I didn't need to shrink back in the presence of others. Instead, I could embrace my journey with pride, knowing that each twist and turn had led me to this vibrant gathering of voices, connections, and possibilities.

As we exchanged stories of our favorite books and authors, the world outside faded away, replaced by the exhilarating discovery of shared passions and dreams. It was a gentle reminder that even in the most complex narratives, the beauty often lay in the connections we forge, the laughter we share, and the love we cultivate. And perhaps, just perhaps, my own story was only beginning to unfold, filled with adventures waiting just around the corner.

The vibrant discussions swirled around me, weaving a rich tapestry of voices as I moved through the crowd, each interaction nourishing my soul. Authors spoke passionately, their words punctuated by gestures that animated their tales, while readers leaned in, eager to absorb every detail. The atmosphere was electric, each laughter and exclamation adding to the melody of the day. I felt like a conductor, orchestrating this symphony of creativity, guiding it with care and enthusiasm.

Just then, I noticed a group huddled around a table displaying a local author's book, their faces alight with curiosity. I stepped closer, drawn to their excitement. "This is an incredible debut," I chimed in, my voice infused with genuine admiration. "The way she captures the essence of small-town life and intertwines it with the supernatural is nothing short of magic."

They turned to me, eyes wide with interest, and I basked in their attention. It felt refreshing to share my passion, the energy of their enthusiasm washing over me like a comforting tide. It was moments like this that reminded me why I had dedicated myself to this space—a sanctuary for those seeking the refuge of a good story.

As I continued to mingle, the world outside the bookstore faded into insignificance. Yet, despite the joy swelling within me, my gaze was still drawn to Ethan. The magnetic pull was undeniable, as if his presence anchored me amidst the chaos. But rather than letting insecurity creep back in, I allowed myself to embrace the uncertainty of the moment. I focused on the richness around me, determined to revel in the connections I was fostering.

With each passing moment, I watched as readers shared their discoveries with each other, their faces lit with the thrill of finding kindred spirits among the shelves. The beauty of literature had woven invisible threads between them, binding their hearts in a delicate dance of understanding. I saw myself reflected in their joy, remembering the first time I stumbled upon a book that spoke to my very soul. It was a cherished moment, one that I wanted to recreate for everyone who walked through my doors.

As the event continued, I caught snippets of conversations echoing around me. People were sharing personal stories, their lives intertwining with the narratives crafted by the authors present. It was as if the very walls of the bookstore were absorbing the emotions, turning the air thick with vulnerability and authenticity. I stood back for a moment, allowing the symphony of human connection to wash over me.

But just as I was reveling in the beauty of it all, I felt a familiar weight settle in my stomach as I noticed Ethan and Chloe leaning closer, laughter bubbling between them like champagne. The sight was bittersweet, a cocktail of hope and heartache that danced in my chest. I took a steadying breath, willing myself to focus on the vibrant exchanges happening all around me. They were the heartbeats of my bookstore, the pulse that breathed life into the stories that lined the shelves.

In an effort to drown out the twinge of jealousy, I turned my attention to a group of teenagers discussing their favorite fantasy series. Their enthusiasm was contagious, and I felt myself drawn into their conversation. They animatedly debated the merits of different magical systems, their faces alive with fervor. I shared my thoughts, teasing them about my own fandom experiences, which only ignited their laughter further.

Hours passed in a blur, a kaleidoscope of faces and voices, each interaction stitching another thread into the rich tapestry of the day. It was an exhilarating whirlwind, a celebration of storytelling in all its forms. And amidst this beautiful chaos, I finally found myself standing beside Ethan, the energy between us crackling like static electricity.

"Looks like you've really outdone yourself today," he remarked, genuine admiration sparkling in his eyes.

"Thanks," I replied, a warmth blooming in my chest. "It's so rewarding to see everyone connecting over something we all love."

He nodded, glancing around at the bustling room. "You've built something incredible here. It's not just about the books; it's about the community you've created."

For a moment, our gazes held, and in that fleeting second, I felt a shift. The weight of my insecurities seemed to lift, replaced by a newfound sense of purpose. This bookstore was not just my passion; it was a beacon of connection, a place where stories intertwined with lives, crafting narratives that resonated far beyond the pages.

As the event wound down, the energy shifted. People began to gather their belongings, exchanging hugs and promises to return. I stood by the door, my heart full as I waved goodbye to each person who walked out, hoping they left with the promise of new adventures waiting to unfold in their lives.

Ethan lingered near the exit, his presence an anchor amidst the ebb and flow of the crowd. As the last attendees filtered out, I caught his eye again, and this time, the tension that had hung between us felt different—lighter, infused with possibility.

"I'm glad I came," he said, taking a step closer, his voice low and sincere.

"Me too," I replied, the words tumbling out before I could second-guess myself. "This day has been everything I hoped for and more."

There was a pause, a charged silence that filled the space between us. I could feel the pulse of unspoken words hovering in the air, electric and vibrant.

"I know we've had our ups and downs," he said slowly, "but seeing you in your element today made me realize how special what you've built is. It's inspiring."

His gaze held mine, and in that moment, I felt a surge of vulnerability, as if the walls I had carefully constructed began to crack. "It's a labor of love," I admitted, my voice barely above a whisper. "I wanted to create a space where people could feel connected, where stories could flourish."

"And you've done that beautifully," he said, his tone warm and inviting. "You're doing something incredible here."

Before I could respond, Chloe emerged from behind him, her laughter piercing the moment like a bright ray of sunlight. "Ethan, we should grab a bite to eat! I'm starving," she announced, her exuberance filling the room.

A flicker of disappointment coursed through me, but I held my ground, forcing a smile. "Of course! Enjoy," I said, my heart momentarily deflating.

Chloe glanced at me, her expression shifting slightly, as if she could sense the unspoken tension lingering in the air. "You should join us! It'll be fun," she suggested, her voice light but carrying an undercurrent of challenge.

I hesitated, uncertainty creeping back in. But then, as I looked at Ethan, I saw a flicker of curiosity in his eyes, an invitation to step into the unknown. "I think I will," I found myself saying, surprising even myself with the boldness of my decision.

As we stepped outside into the warm embrace of the evening, the sun dipped below the horizon, casting the world in hues of pink and gold. The sidewalks glimmered with life, laughter echoing down the street, and for the first time in a long while, I felt a surge of hope blooming within me.

Maybe the path ahead wasn't so daunting after all. With Ethan and Chloe by my side, perhaps I could navigate this new chapter with a sense of courage and determination. I had built something beautiful in my bookstore, and it was time to embrace whatever came next, to let my own story unfold amidst the connections I cherished.

As we walked together, the vibrant pulse of the city surrounding us, I felt the promise of new beginnings dancing just out of reach, waiting for me to seize them. This was my moment, a chance to explore the unknown, to let my heart guide me through the intricacies of love and friendship, and to forge connections that would shape my narrative for years to come.

Chapter 22: Words Unspoken

The room buzzed with the quiet hum of anticipation, an electric pulse that made my heart race and my palms sweat. I could almost taste the words swirling in the air, thick with longing and unexpressed thoughts. Around me, a tapestry of faces flickered under the soft glow of pendant lights, each person lost in their own reflections, their gazes fixated on the small stage. Authors of all walks of life were preparing to share their stories, their voices promising to weave together threads of raw emotion and vivid experiences that danced just beyond the fringes of my imagination.

I shifted in my seat, trying to absorb the energy around me, which felt palpable, like a live wire humming with unspent potential. The scent of fresh coffee mingled with the crisp aroma of paper and ink, a fragrant reminder of the stories that had come before and those yet to be told. A vibrant tapestry of words hung in the air, suspended between expectation and reality. As the first author stepped up to the microphone, a hush fell over the crowd, and the world outside faded into a distant memory.

Her voice was rich and inviting, a warm embrace that wrapped around me as she spoke of heartache and resilience. I leaned in closer, captivated by the rhythm of her storytelling, the way she painted scenes with such meticulous detail that I felt as if I could reach out and touch the fragile petals of her memories. The audience laughed, gasped, and even wiped away tears in perfect synchrony, as if we were all bound by the invisible thread of shared humanity. It was intoxicating, a reminder of the power that words could wield, and I found myself craving that same power—the urge to unlock my own story and lay it bare for all to see.

Yet, as the authors continued to share their truths, I felt a strange dissonance within me, a friction between my desire to connect and my instinct to retreat. I glanced around the room, noting the way people nodded in understanding, the way they clasped their hands together as if bracing themselves for the emotional surge that each narrative would inevitably bring. It was beautiful, really, watching strangers bond over shared experiences, and I wanted to be part of it. But in that moment, as the crowd erupted into applause for yet another compelling tale, I felt a tightness in my chest, a sense of being an outsider looking in.

It was then that I saw Ethan standing at the back of the room, his tall frame illuminated by the golden light. He was a portrait of stillness amid the vibrant chaos, and my heart skipped at the sight of him. The way his dark hair fell into his eyes and the casual grace with which he leaned against the wall made my breath hitch. We had shared so much in the short time we had known each other—laughter, dreams, moments that felt etched into the fabric of my being—but there was a heaviness in the air when it came to us, a weighty silence that clung like fog.

He caught my gaze, and for a moment, the world around us fell away, dissolving into a haze of whispered secrets and unexpressed feelings. His lips curled into a smile, the kind that held the promise of something deeper, and I felt an overwhelming urge to cross the space between us, to break through the barriers we had both constructed. But then, the authors' voices rose around me, and I was torn between the pull of the event and the gravity of what lay unspoken between us.

As the evening wore on, I listened intently, hanging onto every word, but my mind drifted back to Ethan. I couldn't shake the feeling that there was a conversation we needed to have, a reckoning of sorts. The intensity of my feelings for him—fierce and unrelenting—complicated the air around us, transforming the very essence of our interactions into something both thrilling and terrifying. He was an anchor in a storm, yet also the tempest itself, stirring emotions I had never anticipated.

Finally, as the event reached a lull, I felt the undeniable urge to seek him out. I moved through the crowd, the rhythmic beat of my heart drumming in my ears. The hum of voices faded as I approached him, and everything around us blurred into a soft focus. The clinking of glasses, the laughter of friends, the lingering scent of coffee—it all evaporated, leaving just the two of us suspended in a moment thick with anticipation.

"Hey," I said, my voice barely above a whisper, as if speaking too loudly would shatter the fragile bubble we existed within.

He turned to me, his expression a mix of warmth and curiosity, and the air shifted again, charged with the weight of unspoken possibilities. The moments stretched between us, so tangible I could almost see them. I wanted to spill everything—the hopes, the fears, the longing that twisted my insides. I wanted to articulate the feelings that felt like fireworks and chaos, beautiful yet terrifying. But instead, all I managed was a polite smile, and I could see the flicker of disappointment in his eyes.

"Great event, right?" he said, his voice steady, but there was an undercurrent of something unspoken that lingered in the space between us.

"Yes," I replied, my words feeling inadequate against the swell of emotions I battled within. I searched his eyes for understanding, for a spark that would ignite the conversation I desperately wanted to have, but instead, doubt pooled like quicksand, threatening to swallow me whole.

We stood there, an invisible wall rising around us, my heart racing in frustration. I wanted to break free, to dismantle the silence that hung like a fog, to let the words flow unrestrained. But as the laughter and chatter swirled around us, I felt tethered, unable to voice what had become an urgent whisper in my heart. All those thoughts and feelings I had wished to articulate morphed into a dense fog, clouding the clarity I sought.

And there we were, caught in the delicate web of what-ifs and maybes, with the potential for connection glimmering just out of reach.

I searched his eyes, looking for a glimmer of the understanding I so desperately craved. Instead, I saw uncertainty mirrored in his gaze. The silence between us felt like a living entity, pulsing and throbbing with each passing moment. I could feel it constricting my chest, the weight of it making it hard to breathe. The laughter and chatter of the surrounding crowd faded into a soft murmur, a backdrop to the unfolding tension between us. Every fiber of my being screamed to bridge the chasm that had formed, to reach out and grasp the strands of conversation that felt as tenuous as spider silk.

"Did you enjoy the last speaker?" he finally asked, his voice steady but laced with an undercurrent of caution, as if he was testing the waters before diving in.

"Yeah, she was incredible," I replied, my words flowing out in a rush, desperate to fill the void. "The way she described her journey... it was so relatable. It's like she was speaking directly to us, right?"

He nodded, a smile flickering across his face, and for a moment, it felt like a bridge had been built, fragile but real. "I know what you mean. I felt every word. It's inspiring, isn't it? To see someone else share their vulnerabilities so openly?"

"Yes! It makes you think about your own story, the things we keep hidden." The moment I said it, I felt the truth of my own words settle in the space between us, heavier than the air around us. I dared to hope that this was my moment, the precipice from which I could leap into the truth of what I felt.

Ethan leaned slightly closer, the faint scent of his cologne enveloping me in a warmth that felt both inviting and intoxicating. "What's your story?" His question hung in the air, an invitation and a challenge all at once. The gentle encouragement in his voice sparked something deep inside me, igniting a flicker of courage I didn't know I possessed.

"I... I haven't really shared it," I confessed, a rush of vulnerability coursing through me. "Not in the way I want to. I'm still figuring it out, to be honest."

His expression shifted, and I could see the wheels turning in his mind, contemplating the depths behind my admission. "I get that. Sometimes it takes time to unravel everything, to understand what you truly want to say. But I think that's part of the journey, isn't it? The discovering?"

I felt a wave of relief wash over me as he spoke. He understood. The words I had longed to say started to form like mist in my mind, coalescing into coherent thoughts. "It is," I replied, my voice firmer now, emboldened by his kindness. "I've always had this narrative in my head about who I should be, how I should present myself. But it's exhausting, trying to fit into a mold."

He nodded, his brow furrowing slightly as if he were peering into a deeper layer of my truth. "We put so much pressure on ourselves. It's easy to lose sight of what matters. But I think sharing those struggles is what connects us."

Our eyes locked, and in that fleeting moment, the unspoken words tangled in my throat began to unravel. I was terrified yet exhilarated, hovering on the edge of revealing the feelings that had been festering, waiting for the right moment to burst forth like a dam breaking.

"Sometimes," I ventured, my voice a whisper that felt heavy with significance, "I wonder if I'm ever going to find the courage to be truly honest about what I feel. About us."

His expression shifted, surprise flickering across his features before he regained his composure. "Us?" he echoed, the syllables hanging like a delicate thread between us.

"Yes, us," I admitted, emboldened by the soft glow of vulnerability that seemed to envelop us. "There's something here, Ethan. Something I can't quite put into words but feel deeply in my bones."

The warmth in his gaze deepened, and I could see the flicker of recognition spark behind his eyes. "I've felt it too," he confessed, his voice barely above a murmur, yet powerful enough to send a thrill racing through me. "But I wasn't sure if you..." His voice trailed off, leaving the weight of his uncertainty hanging like a heavy fog.

"Didn't you think I could feel it? That we both could?" I pressed, searching for confirmation, my heart thundering in my chest as I took a step closer, closing the distance between us.

He inhaled sharply, his eyes widening slightly. "It's terrifying, isn't it? To think about what could be, to put everything on the line when we've both danced around this for so long. I didn't want to ruin what we have."

A rush of warmth flooded through me. "I think what we have is worth taking that risk. I've kept my feelings hidden out of fear, but I don't want to do that anymore."

The corner of his mouth twitched into a smile, and the tension that had woven through our conversation began to unravel. "Then let's not dance around it anymore. I want to know your story. I want to be part of it."

Those words were like an elixir, washing over me with clarity and purpose. The air felt different, charged with the possibility of something beautiful and terrifying all at once. My heart surged with a mixture of hope and trepidation, urging me to push through the lingering doubts that had held me captive for too long.

"Okay," I whispered, my heart pounding with exhilaration. "Then let's share it. Let's lay it all out on the table."

As we stood there, the world around us resumed its rhythm, laughter and voices blending into a comforting hum. But for the first time in what felt like an eternity, I felt anchored, tethered to something real, something worth the leap of faith. The unspoken words that had once hovered like a storm cloud above us began to dissipate, giving way to a bright sky of possibilities.

Ethan's hand brushed against mine, a simple gesture that sent sparks racing up my arm. I caught my breath, the warmth of his touch igniting a fire within me that I never knew existed. We were teetering on the brink of something extraordinary, a precipice filled with potential, the air alive with the weight of shared stories waiting to be told. And as I looked into his eyes, I knew this was just the beginning.

His gaze held mine, a mix of hesitation and determination that sent a flutter of excitement racing through my veins. The world around us faded once more, our bubble of shared vulnerability becoming a sanctuary amidst the clamor of voices and laughter. In that moment, the possibility of what lay ahead felt like an unwrapped gift, shimmering with potential but still sealed tight, begging to be opened.

"Tell me then," Ethan said, his voice steady yet laced with a gentleness that disarmed me completely. "What does your story look like?"

The question hung in the air, pregnant with promise, inviting me to spill the secrets I had long buried beneath layers of self-doubt. I took a deep breath, feeling the words simmering at the surface, clamoring for release. "It's messy," I began, my voice trembling with the weight of honesty. "It's about dreams and failures, the choices that led me here. It's about the fear of not being enough, of not knowing if I'll ever truly find my place."

He nodded, his expression encouraging as if every syllable I spoke carved a path through the fog of uncertainty. "And what do you want?"

The question, so simple yet profound, sent ripples of thought cascading through me. I hesitated, grappling with the myriad of desires swirling within. "I want to be seen. To be understood beyond the surface," I admitted, the truth spilling forth. "I want to create something that resonates with people, to connect with others who've felt lost or afraid."

As I spoke, I found my courage building, fueled by his unwavering gaze. "There's this fire inside me," I continued, "but sometimes it flickers and dims, and I struggle to keep it alive. I've spent so much time worrying about what others think, molding myself into what I believe they want to see. But I realize now that I've neglected my own voice."

Ethan leaned closer, the warmth radiating from him grounding me as I laid bare my soul. "You have a beautiful voice," he said softly, his words a balm against the insecurities that had clung to me for so long. "And it deserves to be heard. We all have our battles, and sharing them only makes us stronger."

His encouragement washed over me like a soothing wave, erasing the scars of doubt that had built up over the years. I felt the tension easing, replaced by an exhilarating sense of clarity. "And what about you?" I asked, the curiosity bubbling up inside me. "What's your story?"

His smile flickered, a hint of something shadowed passing across his features. "My story?" he mused, almost to himself. "It's not much different from yours, I suppose. Just a guy trying to navigate the chaos of life, hoping to find meaning along the way."

I could sense there was more, a deeper layer beneath his words waiting to be explored. "But what do you really want, Ethan? What drives you?"

He paused, the vulnerability evident in his eyes as he pondered the question. "I want to create," he confessed, his voice low and sincere. "I've always had a passion for storytelling, but I've been afraid to share it. The fear of judgment has held me back. But when I see people connect through words, it lights a fire in me. I want to be part of that."

The raw honesty in his admission resonated within me, intertwining our stories in an unexpected yet beautiful way. "Then let's create together," I said, feeling a surge of exhilaration course through my veins. "Let's explore our passions, our fears, and turn them into something meaningful."

His expression shifted, surprise mingling with hope. "You really mean that?"

"Absolutely," I affirmed, the words flowing freely now, emboldened by the connection we were forging. "Let's collaborate, support each other in our journeys. No more hiding behind the shadows."

A slow smile spread across his face, illuminating the room around us as if we had sparked our own light. "I'd love that. There's something about you, a spark that draws me in. I think together we can create something incredible."

The air around us felt charged with possibility, and in that moment, I realized that our stories, intertwined as they were, could form a tapestry richer than anything either of us could create alone. We were two souls navigating the same storm, reaching out to one another in hopes of finding our way to calmer waters.

As the evening wore on, we lost ourselves in conversation, sharing our hopes, dreams, and the little quirks that made us who we were. I told him about my childhood fascination with writing, how I would scribble stories in the margins of my notebooks, crafting elaborate worlds that transported me far beyond my small town. He listened intently, his eyes sparkling with understanding.

"I remember doing something similar," he shared, a wistful smile on his lips. "I used to write short stories about adventures and heroes, but somewhere along the way, I lost my courage. I let the world's expectations drown out my voice."

We spoke late into the night, the glow of the overhead lights casting a warm halo around us. I felt as though we were peeling away layers of armor, revealing the raw, unvarnished parts of ourselves that we had kept hidden for too long. Each word shared was a step closer to forging something new, something real.

The crowd around us gradually thinned, but we remained anchored in our conversation, oblivious to the passage of time. The world outside carried on, bustling and chaotic, yet we were cocooned in our own little universe, where laughter echoed and the air hummed with possibility.

As we reached the end of our dialogue, I found myself laughing at some silly anecdote he shared, the sound bubbling up freely and effortlessly. In that moment, I was struck by how easy it was to connect with him, how the weight of my fears seemed lighter in his presence.

"Promise me something," I said, a sudden seriousness slipping into my tone. "Promise me we won't let fear dictate our paths anymore. That we'll take those risks, even if it scares us."

He met my gaze with unwavering determination. "I promise. No more holding back."

And as he spoke those words, I felt a shift deep within me. It was as if the dam had burst, and the words I had kept bottled up for so long began to flow freely, setting my spirit ablaze. I could finally envision a future where our voices mingled, creating a symphony of stories that celebrated our journeys—the good, the bad, and everything in between.

In that moment, I knew we were on the brink of something extraordinary. The potential for connection, for shared dreams and unfiltered truths, lay before us like an uncharted territory, waiting to be explored. Together, we would navigate the paths of our stories, unearthing the beauty in the chaos and the power in vulnerability, transforming our unspoken words into a vibrant narrative that echoed long after the night had ended.

Chapter 23: The Breaking Point

The air inside the bookstore was thick with the scent of aged paper and polished wood, a comforting aroma that once felt like home but now clung to my skin like an unwelcome reminder of the choices that loomed ahead. The low, amber light flickered overhead, casting shadows that danced across the spines of novels I had cherished, their stories resonating in the silence. I walked the aisles, trailing my fingers along the dust-coated covers, memories swirling in my mind like pages in a windstorm. Every footstep echoed, reminding me that I was alone in this labyrinth, the comforting whispers of familiar tales drowned out by my racing thoughts.

Ethan's name flashed across my screen like a signal flare, and I felt a shiver of anticipation snake its way down my spine. I hesitated, my finger hovering over the screen, thoughts colliding as I considered how to respond. His messages were rarely casual; they were weighted with purpose, and tonight was no exception. With a deep breath, I replied, my heart pounding like a drum as I braced for the impending conversation that felt more like an ultimatum than a simple chat.

When he arrived, the bell above the door tinkled softly, a jarring reminder of the world outside this sanctuary. I turned to face him, taking in the way his brow furrowed with concern, his usually bright eyes dulled with gravity. "We need to talk about Chloe," he said, his voice steady yet punctuated with a tension that made my stomach drop. In that moment, the air around us thickened, and the chaos inside my mind quieted, leaving only the sound of my heartbeat in my ears.

I nodded, a lump forming in my throat, my pulse racing as I attempted to gather my thoughts. Chloe, my enigmatic friend with a smile that could light up the darkest corners of a room, had become a variable in our carefully constructed equation. Ethan had always viewed her through a lens tinted with admiration, and I could sense that his feelings had deepened into something more complex, something that threatened to unravel the delicate threads of our relationship.

"I don't know how to say this," he continued, his voice a low murmur that echoed against the empty shelves. "I care about her, and I don't want to hurt you. But I can't ignore what's happening between us."

The admission hung in the air, heavy and charged, as I processed his words. My heart felt like a caged bird, fluttering wildly against the bars of my ribcage, desperate to escape. In that moment, a strange cocktail of anger and fear bubbled up inside me, and I had to fight against the urge to lash out. "You care about her?" I managed to whisper, the words tasting bitter on my tongue. "What about us, Ethan? What do we even have left if you're feeling this way?"

He stepped closer, his eyes searching mine for answers I wasn't sure I could provide. "That's what I'm trying to figure out. I love you, but..." His voice trailed off, leaving a chasm between us that felt insurmountable. The flickering lights above cast an ethereal glow around him, making him look almost otherworldly, as if he were part of some dream I had yet to wake from.

"Then why are we having this conversation?" I implored, feeling a mixture of desperation and confusion wash over me. "Why are you even considering her?" Each word fell from my lips like stones dropped into a still pond, creating ripples that distorted our reality.

"I don't know," he admitted, running a hand through his tousled hair, frustration evident in the gesture. "It's complicated. She's... she's different. There's something about her that draws me in."

The words cut through me like a knife, leaving a raw ache in their wake. The familiarity of our routine, the shared laughter, the quiet moments in the early hours of the morning—everything felt threatened by his burgeoning connection with Chloe. My mind raced as I tried to reconcile my feelings, to piece together a narrative that could explain this emotional whirlwind.

"Different?" I echoed, my voice barely above a whisper. "Is that what this is about? She's exciting, and I'm... what? Boring?" The accusation tasted sour on my lips, bitterness creeping into the edges of my voice. I wasn't boring; I was a mosaic of dreams, hopes, and aspirations that colored my world. But in that moment, I felt as though I was standing on the edge of a cliff, teetering dangerously close to a fall that could shatter everything I held dear.

"No, it's not like that." His brow furrowed deeper, his gaze piercing through the tension that hung in the air. "I don't want to hurt you. You mean everything to me. But I can't pretend that I don't feel something for her. It's like I'm being pulled in two directions, and it's tearing me apart."

Tears threatened to spill as I fought against the tide of my emotions. The thought of losing him was like watching the world fade to black, colors draining away until I was left in an empty, monochrome existence. I had never envisioned our story unraveling in such a way, yet here we stood, on the precipice of a decision that could alter the course of our lives forever.

I glanced around the bookstore, seeking solace in the familiar surroundings, yet the comforting embrace of the aisles felt suffocating now. The walls seemed to close in, and I realized I had a choice to make. As I looked back at Ethan, his expression a mixture of anguish and longing, I understood that this moment could either bind us closer together or rip us apart.

"What do you want, Ethan?" I finally asked, my voice trembling as I confronted the raw truth of our predicament. "Do you want to be with her? Or do you want to fight for what we have?"

His gaze held mine, and in that fleeting moment, time seemed to dissolve around us. The clamor of the outside world faded, leaving only the heavy silence of our reality, punctuated by the distant thrum of traffic and the occasional rustle of pages. I could almost hear the whispered secrets of the books surrounding us, stories of love lost and found, tales of betrayal and forgiveness that seemed to taunt me with their relevance. "What do you want, Ethan?" I pressed, my heart thudding in my chest as I searched his eyes for answers.

"I don't know," he admitted, frustration etching lines across his forehead. "I feel like I'm being pulled apart. You're everything I've wanted, but she..." He hesitated, the weight of his unspoken feelings hanging in the air, a ghost of what could have been.

"Is she really that special?" I asked, my voice barely above a whisper, laced with a vulnerability I rarely showed. "What is it about her that has you questioning us?"

"It's not just that," he said, stepping closer, desperation softening the edges of his features. "With Chloe, it's like everything is new and exciting. She challenges me in ways I didn't know I needed. But that doesn't mean I don't love you."

A bitter laugh escaped my lips, unbidden and sharp. "Love is supposed to be enough, isn't it? It's supposed to make you want to fight for what you have." My words hung in the air, fragile and trembling, and I felt the tears prick at my eyes again, threatening to spill over like an uncontained flood.

"I want to fight," he insisted, his voice rising in urgency. "I just— I don't want to lose you, but I don't want to pretend either. I can't do that."

His admission struck a chord within me, a haunting melody that reverberated through my chest. The space between us crackled with tension, a mix of fear and longing, and I felt the ground shift beneath my feet. I had always known our love was not without its complications, but this felt like a cataclysm, an earthquake that would leave nothing untouched in its wake.

"Then why don't we take a step back? Just for a moment?" I suggested, my voice trembling as I tried to find the strength to suggest something that felt both radical and necessary. "Maybe some distance will help us figure this out. I can't be your second choice, Ethan."

He looked taken aback, as if the suggestion had blindsided him. "Distance? Is that what you really want?"

"It's not what I want, but it might be what we need," I said, my throat tightening with the effort of suppressing the sob that threatened to escape. "I don't want to compete for your affection, and I certainly don't want to feel like I'm holding you back from something you think you might want."

He stared at me, his expression shifting from confusion to contemplation, as if he were weighing the gravity of my words. "I don't want to lose you," he murmured, his voice barely a whisper. "You're everything I've ever known. Everything feels so tangled right now."

The truth of it struck me like a lightning bolt. The threads of our relationship had become knotted and frayed, and the comfort of familiarity now felt like a gilded cage. I longed to untangle the confusion, to find clarity amidst the chaos. Yet, how could I do that if I was constantly in his orbit, caught in the gravitational pull of our shared history?

As silence enveloped us, the soft rustle of pages turning in the nearby reading nook filled the void, a gentle reminder of the world outside our tumultuous hearts. I had always believed that love could conquer anything, that the strength of our bond would see us through. But now, standing here with Ethan, I realized that love alone might not be enough to navigate the complexities of our emotions.

"I think we should try," I finally said, the words emerging from my lips like a fragile promise. "A little space might give us both clarity. I need to know that I'm not just someone you turn to when things get tough."

His face softened, and for a moment, I could see the struggle etched in his features. "I don't want to hurt you," he said again, his voice hoarse with emotion.

"I know," I replied, wishing to reach out and touch his hand, to feel the warmth of the connection that had once flowed so effortlessly between us. "But sometimes love isn't enough. Sometimes it takes distance to see what really matters."

He nodded slowly, resignation washing over his features. "You're right. Maybe we both need to figure out what we truly want."

As he stepped back, the space between us felt almost sacred, a boundary marked by our unspoken understanding. I glanced around the bookstore, the familiarity of the surroundings offering me some comfort as I prepared to face this new reality. The walls, once a fortress, now felt like a canvas upon which we would paint a different future, one that might be defined by absence rather than presence.

As Ethan turned to leave, the door chimed softly behind him, a bittersweet sound that reverberated through the stillness. I watched him go, my heart heavy with a mixture of hope and fear. The labyrinth of my thoughts swirled around me, filled with questions that would remain unanswered for now.

Would the space between us allow us to grow, or would it fracture what we had built? As I stood there, surrounded by stories of love and loss, I understood that this was a journey—one I had to undertake not only for myself but for us. The path ahead would be uncertain, but perhaps it was time to step into the unknown, to embrace the complexity of our emotions rather than shying away from them.

I breathed in deeply, letting the scent of the bookstore envelop me, grounding me in the present moment. I would cherish what we had, but I also knew that change was the only constant in life. And with that realization, I felt a flicker of hope ignite within me, a promise that I would emerge stronger, no matter the outcome.

The sound of the door closing behind Ethan echoed in my mind, a finality that settled like an unwelcome guest in my chest. The warmth of his presence lingered in the air, mingling with the familiar scents of musty pages and freshly brewed coffee. I sank onto the worn leather couch nestled in the corner of the bookstore, my heart a heavy anchor pulling me deeper into the tumult of my thoughts. I let the silence wrap around me like a blanket, hoping it might soothe the chaos within.

The dim light cast a warm glow over the mismatched furniture, a reflection of the comforting disorder of my life. I had always loved this place—the creaky floorboards, the towering shelves that seemed to whisper stories long forgotten, the little nooks where readers could escape into worlds of adventure and romance. Yet tonight, it felt like a prison, each volume a reminder of the choices that had led me here, to this fragile precipice of uncertainty.

I took a deep breath, focusing on the aroma of coffee still wafting from the little café at the front of the store. It was a scent that usually made my heart swell with contentment, a sensory embrace that promised comfort and community. But tonight, it tasted bitter on my tongue. My thoughts spiraled around Ethan's words, echoing like a haunting refrain: "I can't pretend anymore."

Chloe. The name struck a chord in my heart, a note that resonated with jealousy and confusion. She was the bright star that had captivated Ethan's attention, drawing him in with her effortless charm and vivacity. I recalled the way she had laughed at the event earlier that evening, a sound like music that seemed to hold everyone's attention, including his. I had tried to shake off the creeping discomfort, chalking it up to my own insecurities, but now, the truth hung heavily between us like a specter.

The chatter of customers and the soft clinking of mugs outside my sanctuary faded into the background, replaced by the steady rhythm of my heart. I closed my eyes, conjuring the image of Chloe, with her flowing hair and bright smile, a siren of sorts who could lure anyone into her orbit. I had always admired her, envied her carefree spirit, and now, it felt as though that very spirit was poised to claim something that had once been mine.

The couch beneath me creaked as I shifted, my thoughts like a jumbled puzzle I couldn't quite piece together. I needed clarity. The words of my favorite authors danced in my mind, their stories filled with turmoil, passion, and the messy reality of love. What would they do? What advice would they offer if they were here, seated next to me, cradling their own secrets?

I thought about the stories I cherished, those tales that had once provided me solace and escape, the characters whose struggles mirrored my own. They navigated love, loss, and heartbreak with a grace I could only dream of possessing. Yet here I was, fumbling in the dark, grasping at the edges of my own narrative, desperately trying to find a resolution to this spiraling plot.

As the minutes ticked by, I made my way to the café, seeking the solace of a steaming cup of coffee. The barista, a young woman with wild curls and an infectious smile, greeted me with her usual enthusiasm. "Hey there! The usual?" she asked, her eyes sparkling with a warmth that momentarily distracted me from my turmoil.

"Yeah, thanks," I replied, trying to muster a smile. As she prepared my drink, I glanced around, observing the patrons nestled in their cozy corners, absorbed in their novels or chatting animatedly. They seemed so at ease, as if the world outside held no bearing on their contentment. I envied their serenity, their ability to be lost in the moment, while I felt like I was being swept away by a tide of uncertainty.

When my coffee was ready, I cradled the warm cup in my hands, the heat seeping into my skin, a temporary distraction from the chill in my heart. I took a sip, allowing the rich, bitter flavor to settle on my tongue. The taste was familiar, yet it couldn't mask the growing knot of anxiety tightening in my chest. I made my way back to the reading nook, where the soft light illuminated my favorite armchair.

Settling into the plush fabric, I closed my eyes again, letting the aroma of coffee and old books envelop me. I pictured Ethan's face, the way his eyes sparkled with mischief and warmth, and the familiar way he would lean in when he was about to share something deeply personal. I couldn't deny the love I felt for him, the way he had woven himself into the very fabric of my life. Yet, with Chloe in the picture, everything felt fragile, like a delicate glass ornament teetering on the edge of a shelf.

Suddenly, a quiet laugh pulled me from my thoughts, and I opened my eyes to find a familiar figure seated across from me. It was Mia, my closest friend, her presence a balm against my inner turmoil. She had a knack for showing up at just the right moment, her intuition sharp as a blade. "You look like you've been through a storm," she said, her voice laced with concern.

"Just the usual chaos," I replied, forcing a lightness I didn't feel.

Mia's gaze pierced through my facade. "You can't fool me, you know. What's really going on?"

I hesitated, the truth bubbling just beneath the surface. I hadn't wanted to burden her with my emotional whirlwind, but the weight of my secret was becoming unbearable. "Ethan and I had a talk," I finally admitted, the words tumbling out like marbles rolling across a polished floor. "About Chloe."

Her expression shifted, a mixture of empathy and understanding washing over her features. "I had a feeling that was coming. He's been... different lately, hasn't he?"

"Yeah," I sighed, running a hand through my hair. "He's confused. He has feelings for her, and I can't shake the feeling that I'm losing him."

Mia leaned forward, her eyes softening. "You won't lose him if you fight for what you have. But maybe you also need to think about what you truly want. Is he the one you can't imagine your life without?"

The question hung in the air, a mirror reflecting my tangled emotions. I wanted to scream, to cry, to dig my nails into the fabric of reality and anchor myself against the storm. "I love him, but I don't want to be a consolation prize. I can't be the fallback when things get complicated."

"Then don't be," she urged gently. "You deserve someone who chooses you every single day, not someone who feels torn. Maybe a little space is just what you need to figure it all out."

As we spoke, the weight of my fears lightened, if only just a little. The world outside carried on, oblivious to the tempest within me. I sipped my coffee, letting the warmth seep into my bones, grounding me in this moment of friendship and understanding. Perhaps there was strength in vulnerability, in sharing my fears with someone who genuinely cared.

We spent the next hour nestled in conversation, sharing laughter and stories, the bookstore around us fading into a comforting blur. Each word I exchanged with Mia felt like a step toward reclaiming my narrative, allowing me to breathe a little easier. It became clear that this moment was a pivotal point—not just in my relationship with Ethan, but in understanding myself and my needs.

As the night wore on, I felt a flicker of determination igniting within me. No matter what lay ahead, I would embrace the uncertainty. I would allow myself the grace to navigate this labyrinth, trusting that I would find my way through the twists and turns. Whatever the outcome with Ethan and Chloe, I would emerge from this, not as a victim of circumstance, but as a woman defined by her choices and her courage to face the unknown.

With renewed resolve, I glanced around the bookstore, the light illuminating the shelves like stars in a vast universe. Each book was a story waiting to be told, just like mine. And as I took a deep breath,

I realized that this was just the beginning of my own tale, one I would write with clarity and strength, determined to forge my path forward.

Chapter 24: Confessions

The late afternoon sun slanted through the dusty windows of the old diner, casting a warm golden glow that felt both comforting and suffocating. I sat across from Ethan, my heart pounding in rhythm with the clinking of cutlery and the low hum of conversation swirling around us. The aroma of freshly brewed coffee mingled with the unmistakable scent of sizzling bacon, wrapping me in a haze of nostalgia. This place, with its red vinyl booths and checkered floors, had been our sanctuary, a refuge from the chaos that often loomed just beyond its doors. It had seen our laughter, our secrets, and the many nights we lost track of time over milkshakes and fries.

Ethan leaned back in his seat, the sunlight catching the golden flecks in his hazel eyes. He ran a hand through his tousled hair, a gesture I had come to recognize as a sign of his unease. My heart sank as he began to speak, his voice steady yet laced with uncertainty. "You know, I value our friendship," he said, each word weighted with unspoken fears. "But things have become complicated."

I felt the air thicken, the playful banter we often shared evaporating into an awkward silence. My stomach twisted as he continued, revealing the turmoil that had been brewing beneath his charming facade. He spoke of Chloe, a name that danced in the air like a phantom, beautiful and elusive. My mind raced as I recalled the times Ethan had confided in me about her, his eyes lighting up with excitement and admiration. It was a light that always felt too bright, leaving me in the shadows, my feelings pushed aside like forgotten items on a cluttered shelf.

"I care about you, too," I managed to whisper, my voice barely audible over the clatter of plates. "But I can't be just a consolation prize." The words escaped my lips with an unexpected ferocity, raw and unfiltered. I could feel the sting of tears prick at the corners of my eyes, threatening to spill over and betray the calm demeanor

I desperately tried to maintain. Vulnerability clung to me like the humidity of a summer day, heavy and oppressive.

Ethan's hand reached across the table, warm and reassuring, enveloping mine in a grip that sent shivers down my spine. In that moment, the world around us faded—the clinking glasses, the chatter of patrons, even the distant sounds of the highway outside—until it was just the two of us, suspended in a fragile bubble. His touch ignited a spark of hope, a flicker of something that felt like possibility, yet it was tinged with uncertainty, hanging in the air like the sweet scent of pie cooling on the window sill.

"I don't want to hurt you," he said, his eyes searching mine as if seeking answers I didn't possess. The depth of his sincerity struck me, resonating with the conflict I felt churning within. It was as if we were two ships navigating a stormy sea, desperately trying to find a safe harbor but unsure of where to anchor. The thought of losing him, of being reduced to a mere footnote in his story, tightened around my chest like a vice.

"I just want you to be happy," I said, though my heart twisted at the thought. The words felt heavy on my tongue, laden with sacrifice. What did happiness even look like for him? For me? The uncertainty loomed larger, threatening to engulf us both. I could see the gears turning in his mind, the flicker of confusion clouding his features. He opened his mouth, a hesitant breath escaping him before he fell silent, grappling with his emotions.

The diner, once a place of solace, now felt like a stage for our unraveling. The other patrons, blissfully unaware of the emotional tempest brewing at our table, continued their lives, lost in laughter and conversations that felt worlds apart from our own. I couldn't help but envy them, those who floated through life unburdened by complicated feelings and unrequited love. Outside, a car horn blared, jolting me from my thoughts.

"Maybe we should take a break from this," I suggested, my voice trembling slightly as I withdrew my hand from his grasp, the warmth fading into a chill that settled in the pit of my stomach. I couldn't bear the weight of his indecision, the tug-of-war between friendship and something deeper. I needed clarity, a beacon of light in this murky fog of confusion that clouded our connection.

"Break?" His brows knitted together, concern etching lines on his forehead. "What do you mean?"

"I mean... maybe it's time to step back and figure out what we really want," I replied, the words tasting bitter on my tongue. It felt like a betrayal, like I was walking away from the best part of myself. But I had to protect my heart, even if it meant losing him.

Silence enveloped us once more, thick and heavy. I could feel the eyes of the other patrons drifting our way, curious, concerned, but ultimately indifferent to the storm raging between us. My stomach churned as I glanced out the window, where the sun was beginning its descent, painting the sky in hues of orange and purple, a stark contrast to the turmoil that roiled within me.

"Can we at least promise to talk about this?" he finally said, his voice a whisper, vulnerable yet earnest. I nodded, a small gesture that felt monumental, like planting a flag in uncertain territory. It was a promise wrapped in uncertainty, a flicker of hope clinging to the edges of our tangled emotions.

As we sat there, the laughter of other diners faded into a distant echo, leaving only the sound of our shared breaths, heavy with unspoken words and unresolved feelings. I realized then that this moment, however painful, was also a testament to the depth of our bond. Whatever lay ahead, we were inextricably linked by the stories we had shared, the laughter and the tears, the unyielding hope that perhaps we could navigate this together, even as the winds shifted around us.

The diner felt smaller somehow, the walls closing in as I fought to quell the tumult within me. My gaze drifted to the window, where the last remnants of daylight struggled to break through the darkening clouds. I could almost hear the whispers of the wind outside, coaxing me to step away from this moment and breathe again. But I was trapped in the gravitational pull of Ethan's presence, his brow furrowed in thought, those hazel eyes reflecting a storm of emotions that mirrored my own.

"Maybe you and Chloe are meant to be," I said, the words tumbling from my mouth before I could catch them. It felt like swallowing glass, sharp and painful. My heart hammered against my ribs, each beat a reminder of the reality I was trying to escape. The idea of him finding happiness with someone else—a vision so vivid it felt tangible—stung like salt in a fresh wound.

"I don't know," Ethan murmured, his voice barely above a whisper. The sincerity in his tone felt like a lifeline thrown into turbulent waters. "I care about you both, but it's complicated." Complicated. How many times had I heard that word bandied about like a shield, deflecting the truths that lay underneath? I wanted to shout that feelings shouldn't be categorized or put on a spreadsheet like some data set waiting to be analyzed. They should spill over, raw and unfiltered, like the coffee we both knew was just about to get cold.

The waitress, a petite woman with a name tag that read "Maggie," shuffled by, her hands laden with plates. She glanced at us, and for a fleeting moment, her gaze flickered with concern. But the world outside our little bubble was indifferent; it spun on its axis, blissfully unaware of the heartbreak unfolding within these familiar booths. As she set down two steaming cups of coffee before us, the aroma enveloped me, grounding me in the moment, but it didn't stop the tide of despair that swelled within.

"Do you want cream?" she asked, her voice chirpy as if she were offering an extra spritz of sunshine. I shook my head, managing a weak smile, but the humor of the moment was lost on me. My heart felt heavy, as if I were bearing the weight of a hundred decisions, all spiraling towards an uncertain conclusion.

Ethan picked up his cup, his fingers brushing against mine briefly, a spark igniting between us that contrasted sharply with the melancholy draping over our conversation. "Look," he said, his voice steadier now. "I don't want to lose what we have. You mean a lot to me." The admission hung between us like a fragile thread, swaying precariously in the storm of our emotions. I could see the determination in his eyes, but also the fear of what lay ahead.

I took a sip of my coffee, letting the rich, bitter taste wash over me, hoping it would fortify my resolve. "What do you want, Ethan?" I asked, the question burning on my tongue, demanding an answer I feared he might not have. "You need to figure that out before we can move forward." My heart raced as I spoke, each word carrying the weight of possibility—what if he chose me? The thought felt both exhilarating and terrifying, like standing at the edge of a cliff, staring into the abyss below.

Ethan leaned back in his chair, his expression shifting from uncertainty to contemplation. "I wish I knew," he replied, his tone thoughtful, almost regretful. "Sometimes it feels easier to just go along with what's expected rather than face the messy reality of feelings." The honesty in his words resonated deep within me, illuminating the tension coiling in the air.

Our eyes locked, and in that fleeting moment, I felt a connection that transcended our unspoken fears. "But it's not easy for me, either," I confessed, my voice breaking slightly. "Every time I see you with Chloe, it feels like a knife twisting in my gut." I hesitated, the fear of exposing my vulnerability creeping in. "I want to be happy for you, but I can't help wishing I were the one standing beside you."

The confession felt liberating, like a weight had been lifted off my shoulders.

"I never wanted to hurt you," Ethan said, his voice softening. "I just didn't realize how deep this went for both of us." The sincerity in his gaze was palpable, a beacon of hope amidst the turmoil. I knew there was a part of him that genuinely cared, a thread that wove us together, fragile yet resilient.

We fell into silence once more, the sounds of the diner swirling around us, a symphony of life that felt both comforting and jarring. I could hear laughter erupting from a table across the room, a couple sharing a joke that seemed so far removed from the turmoil sitting just feet away. The juxtaposition struck me—how life continued to unfold around us, even as our world felt like it was crumbling.

Finally, Ethan broke the silence, his voice a mixture of hesitance and determination. "Can we agree to take a step back, just for a little while? I need to sort through my feelings without the pressure of this looming over us." His request hung in the air, heavy and charged. I wanted to argue, to cling to the hope that we could find a solution, but a part of me recognized the wisdom in his words.

"Okay," I whispered, my heart aching with the decision. The thought of a break felt like a double-edged sword, slicing through the comfort we had built, yet it also offered the chance for clarity. "But I need you to promise me one thing."

"Anything," he replied, his gaze earnest, a flicker of resolve igniting within.

"Promise me you won't lose sight of what we have, even if you're figuring things out with Chloe." The request felt both selfish and necessary, an anchor in the swirling sea of uncertainty.

"I promise," he said, his voice unwavering. "You're not just a consolation prize to me. You're so much more than that."

His words wrapped around me like a warm embrace, infusing a flicker of hope into the suffocating uncertainty. As we sat in the fading light of the diner, I realized that this moment, however fraught with tension, was also a testament to our bond. There was a flicker of potential, a promise that perhaps we could navigate these troubled waters together, even if the path ahead remained shrouded in shadows.

With our hearts laid bare and the weight of our emotions suspended in the air, we both knew that whatever the future held, we would face it as allies, bound by the raw truth of our feelings and the steadfast connection we had forged. The rest of the world faded away as we continued to talk, the chaos of the diner becoming a distant hum, leaving us in our own universe of hope, heartache, and the promise of what might be.

The clatter of silverware resumed around us, an indifferent backdrop to the charged atmosphere at our table. The waitress, seemingly oblivious to the gravity of our conversation, bustled past again with a tray piled high with plates, her bright apron a cheerful contrast to the cloud hanging over us. I could see the gleam of the diner's neon sign flickering through the window, casting colorful reflections on the walls, but all I felt was the icy grip of uncertainty around my heart. It was as if the universe had conspired to trap us in this moment, forcing us to confront the tangled threads of our emotions.

Ethan leaned closer, his voice low, barely above a whisper. "What if I told you I don't want to lose either of you?" The admission hung between us, thick and laden with complexity. I could see the conflict brewing in his eyes—a battle between friendship and something deeper. There was a part of me that longed for clarity, for him to declare his heart without hesitation, but I knew that love didn't always fit neatly into a box. It was chaotic, unpredictable, and often painfully messy.

"I don't want to play second fiddle," I replied, my voice trembling with the weight of my vulnerability. The room felt stifling as I wrestled with my emotions, and I fought the urge to retreat into the safety of sarcasm, my usual armor against discomfort. "If you're still caught up in your feelings for Chloe, I can't just sit here waiting for you to decide." My words were edged with both fear and resolve. The thought of being an afterthought clawed at me, gnawing at the edges of my self-worth.

"I'm trying to be honest," he said, his expression softening, that familiar warmth in his eyes making my heart flutter, even amidst the turmoil. "But it's hard to unravel this mess. I care about you, but I also don't want to hurt Chloe." The sincerity in his tone washed over me, a gentle wave amid the tumult of my emotions. Still, the ache of jealousy throbbed in my chest like a persistent drumbeat, reminding me that I was not the one he had fallen for first.

I took a deep breath, steadying myself against the tide of feelings crashing over me. "You need to figure this out. You can't keep me dangling in limbo, Ethan." I locked my gaze with his, willing him to understand the gravity of my words. "We deserve more than that—both of us."

As if on cue, the door swung open, and a gust of chilly air swept through the diner, rustling the paper napkins on the tables and sending a shiver down my spine. I glanced outside, where the evening sky had transformed into a canvas of deep indigo, speckled with the first stars of the night. There was a beauty in that darkness, an allure that felt strangely comforting. Yet, within it, I found myself reflecting on the stark contrast to the warmth that had blossomed between us just moments ago.

"Maybe we need some time apart," Ethan suggested, his voice barely breaking through the cacophony of my thoughts. "Just to think, to breathe." The suggestion hung between us like an unsaid farewell, yet also a glimmer of hope. It wasn't what I wanted to hear, but it felt necessary—a painful acknowledgment of our reality.

"Time apart sounds... terrifying," I admitted, my voice barely above a whisper, the fear of losing him threading through every syllable. "But it might be what we need." The admission tasted bittersweet, a recognition that perhaps distance could illuminate the path ahead.

Ethan nodded, understanding flickering in his eyes. "Let's promise to be honest with ourselves, no matter how hard it gets. No matter what we decide." His words felt like a lifeline, tethering us to a shared understanding as we stood at the precipice of change.

The waitress returned with our check, her presence a reminder that life outside this booth was marching on, indifferent to our struggles. I paid, my fingers brushing against his once more—a fleeting connection that sent another spark through my veins. The goodbye lingered, a subtle ache that settled deep within me as we stood to leave, the promise of a new chapter hanging in the air.

Stepping outside, the cool night air wrapped around us like a shawl, filled with the scent of rain-soaked asphalt and blooming jasmine. The world felt alive, pulsing with energy, even as my heart felt heavy. I glanced at Ethan, the streetlamp casting a soft glow on his features, illuminating the uncertainty in his eyes. "I guess we just... go from here?" I said, my voice wavering, the words hanging like fragile crystal in the air.

"Yeah," he replied, his voice thick with unspoken emotions. "We go from here."

We lingered for a moment, caught in the web of possibilities. I could sense the weight of everything left unsaid hanging between us, as palpable as the mist rising from the sidewalk. Then, in one swift motion, he pulled me into a hug, and I felt the warmth of his body against mine, the familiar scent of his cologne mixing with the night air—a heady combination of comfort and longing.

"I'll figure this out, I promise," he whispered into my hair, his breath warm against my skin. I melted against him, feeling the tension of the day fade away, if only for a moment. I wanted to believe him, to cling to the hope that this wasn't the end, but rather a new beginning, however tentative.

As I pulled away, the space between us felt charged, like the calm before a storm. I managed a small smile, a flicker of determination igniting within me. "And I'll be here, figuring things out myself." There was strength in that resolve, a promise that I would not fade into the background, no matter how complicated our situation became.

With one last lingering glance, we turned and walked in opposite directions, the night enveloping us like a cloak. I felt a mix of emotions swirling within me—fear, hope, and a determination that felt as potent as the night sky above. Each step I took echoed with possibility, a reminder that while the path ahead was uncertain, it was also mine to navigate.

As I walked, the vibrant pulse of the city surrounded me—cars zooming by, laughter drifting from nearby bars, and the distant sound of music spilling into the streets. The energy buzzed in my veins, and as the cool breeze brushed against my cheeks, I embraced it, knowing that my journey was far from over. I was a tapestry of experiences, woven with threads of love and heartbreak, strength and vulnerability, ready to face whatever awaited me on the horizon.

With every heartbeat, I felt the weight of the decision, the leap into the unknown, but there was also a sense of liberation. I was not merely waiting for Ethan to decide. I was stepping into my own light, ready to embrace whatever life had in store. And perhaps, just perhaps, that was the most beautiful beginning of all.

Chapter 25: Clarity in Chaos

The streets of Maplewood glimmered under the fading light of dusk, each storefront casting a warm glow that beckoned passersby to pause, to linger a moment longer. The aroma of freshly brewed coffee wafted through the air from the corner café, mingling with the scent of fallen leaves—crisp and sweet, a fragrant memory of autumn's embrace. I inhaled deeply, letting the cool air fill my lungs, the chill invigorating, yet familiar, much like the bittersweet ache in my heart. It was in this small town, nestled between rolling hills and painted skies, that I began to reclaim my narrative, a tapestry woven from both joy and sorrow.

My footsteps echoed against the cobblestone path, the rhythm steady and reassuring. Each step drew me closer to the bookstore, my sanctuary, where books lined the walls like old friends, each spine whispering secrets and stories of far-off lands. The soft sound of the bell chiming above the door welcomed me back as I entered, and I closed my eyes for a moment, savoring the scent of paper, ink, and imagination. It was a realm where chaos could not touch me, where every character I created held the power to shape their destinies, unlike the unpredictable tide of my own life.

As the sun sank lower in the sky, painting the horizon in hues of orange and violet, I moved to my favorite corner, a cozy nook adorned with an oversized armchair and a small, wooden table. I sank into the chair, letting its embrace wrap around me like a comforting hug. The light from the antique lamp flickered softly, casting playful shadows across the walls, creating an intimate cocoon where my thoughts could flourish. I pulled out my journal, its pages waiting, eager to be filled with the weight of my revelations.

With each stroke of my pen, I felt a shift within me, a liberation from the chains of doubt and fear. The stories I poured onto the page became more than mere words; they transformed into an extension of my soul. I wrote of characters who embraced their flaws, who danced in the rain and laughed in the face of adversity. I wove tales of love that triumphed over distance, of friendships that stood the test of time, and of individuals who found their purpose amidst the clamor of life. It was a cathartic release, a reminder that even in chaos, clarity could blossom like wildflowers in the cracks of concrete.

As I scribbled furiously, the world outside faded into the background. The soft murmur of the townspeople, their laughter and chatter, became a distant melody, a soothing soundtrack to my creative frenzy. The bookstore, usually a hive of activity, transformed into a quiet sanctuary where my thoughts could roam free. Time slipped away like sand through an hourglass, and I lost myself in the rhythm of my writing, each word building upon the last, creating a universe uniquely mine.

When I finally paused to glance out the window, the night had settled like a soft blanket over Maplewood. Streetlamps flickered to life, casting a warm glow over the sidewalks, illuminating the path of those who wandered beneath the stars. I could see couples strolling hand in hand, their laughter mingling with the night air, while children dashed around in a blur of joy, their innocence untainted by the complexities of adulthood. It struck me then—happiness existed in the simple moments, the shared smiles and gentle touches, and perhaps I could find my own version of it, regardless of the chaos that seemed to swirl around Ethan.

My mind drifted back to him, the memories both sweet and bitter. Ethan was a tempest, unpredictable yet magnetic, drawing me in like a moth to a flame. I could still recall the way his laughter reverberated through the air, his eyes sparkling with mischief, and the way he made me feel like the only person in the room, even in the midst of a crowd. But I also remembered the weight of his silence, the uncertainty that lingered between us like a heavy fog. It was time

THE PATH BETWEEN WORDS

to let go of the illusions that clung to me, the hope that I could change him or the circumstances that surrounded us.

As the clock ticked softly in the background, I penned the final words of my entry, a gentle exhale of all I had bottled inside. I felt lighter, almost as if I had shed a layer of skin, revealing a more resilient self beneath. I closed the journal, a sense of satisfaction washing over me, and leaned back in my chair, allowing the stillness of the night to envelop me.

In that moment, I understood that clarity does not emerge from the absence of chaos, but rather from finding peace within it. Life was unpredictable, much like the changing seasons that enveloped Maplewood, and while I could not control the winds that blew, I could learn to sail with them. I could embrace my dreams, my stories, and above all, my worth. My journey was mine to navigate, and I chose to step forward with courage and grace, ready to carve my own path.

With a newfound resolve igniting my spirit, I stood up from the chair, the weight of the world feeling a little less heavy on my shoulders. Tomorrow was a new day, ripe with possibilities, and I was ready to face it, to create my own joy in a world where chaos reigned. The bookstore glimmered softly around me, a beacon of light in the night, and I stepped out into the world, ready to embrace whatever came next.

The following day dawned with a brightness that felt almost tangible, like the world had been washed clean overnight. The sunlight poured through my bookstore windows, illuminating the dust motes that danced in the air, creating a shimmering tapestry that seemed to reflect my own internal shift. I brewed a pot of coffee, the rich aroma curling around me as I set about preparing for the day. Each sip was a small ritual, grounding me in the present moment, and reminding me that I was here, alive, and ready to seize the day.

As I unlocked the door and stepped into the welcoming embrace of the store, a sense of purpose enveloped me. The familiar creak of the wooden floor beneath my feet resonated like a heartbeat, steady and reassuring. I loved this place—the way it held memories of laughter, of late-night edits and spontaneous conversations with customers who shared my passion for words. This was where I could breathe life into my dreams, and today, those dreams felt bolder, richer, and more achievable than ever.

The bell above the door jingled, a cheerful herald of the day's first visitor. It was Mrs. Henderson, her silver hair a striking contrast to the vibrant red scarf wrapped snugly around her neck. She was a regular, always eager to discuss the latest bestseller or recommend her own favorite hidden gems. Today, however, there was a different spark in her eyes, a twinkle of mischief that made me raise an eyebrow.

"Good morning, dear! I hope you're ready for some excitement," she announced, her voice a blend of warmth and mischief.

"Excitement? In this little corner of Maplewood?" I replied with a smile, leaning against the counter. "I thought that was reserved for the weekend farmers' market."

"Oh, no! This is far more thrilling." She leaned closer, her voice dropping to a conspiratorial whisper. "There's a new book club forming, and I signed you up!"

I chuckled, shaking my head in mock exasperation. "You didn't even ask me!"

"Sometimes you need a nudge, my dear. You're far too talented to hide behind those shelves all day. Besides, you might just enjoy it!"

Her enthusiasm was infectious, and as I considered her words, I felt a spark of intrigue flicker within me. The idea of discussing literature with a group of like-minded souls, exchanging ideas and interpretations, ignited a flicker of curiosity. It was a chance to step outside the comfortable confines of my solitude and embrace

THE PATH BETWEEN WORDS

community. Perhaps it was time to expand my horizons, to let the world in, rather than remaining a mere spectator.

"Fine, count me in," I relented, my tone playful. "But if it turns into a chaotic discussion about existentialism, I might just bolt for the nearest exit."

"Trust me, dear, you'll love it," she said with a wink before bustling off, leaving me with a renewed sense of anticipation.

As the day unfolded, customers trickled in and out, each interaction weaving a thread into the fabric of my day. There was something refreshing about embracing the ebb and flow of life, like a river winding through familiar landscapes. I found myself smiling more, laughing easily, and engaging with my patrons, their stories intertwining with my own in ways that felt unexpectedly significant.

In the afternoon, I decided to take a break from the day's bustle. I slipped into the back room, where a plush armchair awaited, inviting me to sink into its embrace. I pulled out my journal, the pages now a canvas for my thoughts, reflecting the vibrancy of my experiences. I wrote about the people who had graced my shop that day—the young couple choosing their first shared novel, the elderly gentleman reliving memories through the poetry of his youth. I captured the essence of their laughter, their excitement, and their love for stories, realizing how deeply connected we all were in this shared human experience.

The sound of laughter drifted in from the front of the store, and I peeked through the doorway to find a small group gathered, animatedly discussing their latest reads. I couldn't help but feel a swell of joy at the sight—this was exactly what I wanted: a community brought together by the love of literature, sharing ideas and perspectives, a symphony of voices blending harmoniously.

Later that evening, I returned home, my heart buoyed by the connections I had nurtured throughout the day. The sun dipped below the horizon, casting a warm golden glow that enveloped the world in a gentle embrace. I pulled out my journal again, eager to pour my heart into its pages, to reflect on the day and the sense of belonging that was beginning to take root in my life.

As I wrote, I thought about the book club Mrs. Henderson had signed me up for. What would it be like to share my thoughts and interpretations, to delve into discussions that might challenge my perspectives? I felt a twinge of apprehension, but also a surge of excitement. This was growth; this was embracing the chaos and discovering clarity within it.

The next day arrived with a blend of nerves and exhilaration. I donned my favorite sweater—a soft, oversized knit that felt like a warm hug—and prepared for my first book club meeting. My heart fluttered with anticipation as I made my way to the community center, a charming brick building adorned with ivy and surrounded by blooming gardens that seemed to thrive in the golden light of early autumn.

Stepping inside, I was greeted by the soft murmur of voices, a mixture of laughter and the rustle of pages. The room was alive, filled with the scent of freshly brewed tea and baked goods, creating an atmosphere that felt both inviting and comforting. I took a deep breath, stepping into this new space, ready to embrace the uncertainty that lay ahead.

As I settled into my chair, surrounded by fellow book lovers, I realized that this was where I belonged—amid the stories and the connections, weaving my narrative into the rich tapestry of the community. This was my next chapter, one filled with promise, friendship, and the courage to face whatever chaos life threw my way.

The following week unfolded with a delightful rhythm, each day flowing seamlessly into the next, like a well-composed symphony. My evenings spent at the book club became a cherished ritual. We gathered under the soft glow of fairy lights strung across the community center, each meeting transforming into a tapestry of shared stories and vibrant discussions. Women and men of all ages brought their perspectives, their unique experiences enriching our conversations. It felt like unearthing hidden treasures, where every opinion offered a fresh lens through which to view the world.

On one particularly memorable night, we delved into a novel that revolved around the intricacies of love and loss, the author deftly weaving a narrative that resonated deeply with everyone in the room. The discussion sparked a passionate exchange, and I found myself sharing more than I had anticipated. My voice trembled slightly as I recounted my own experiences of heartache and clarity, weaving the threads of my life into the fabric of our dialogue.

As I spoke, I glanced around the circle, observing nods of understanding and expressions of empathy that made me feel less alone. The words I had once kept bottled up began to flow, spilling out like ink on paper, raw and unfiltered. Each member of the group added their own stories, creating a rich tapestry of laughter and tears that blurred the lines between our individual lives, drawing us closer together.

Afterward, as we sipped on warm chai and nibbled on homemade cookies, a gentle camaraderie enveloped us. Mrs. Henderson's wise smile radiated warmth, while a younger woman named Sarah, with wild curls and an infectious laugh, proposed we start a reading challenge—each month focusing on a different theme, from classic romances to contemporary thrillers. The idea ignited a wave of enthusiasm, and before I knew it, I was caught up in a flurry of excitement, eager to dive deeper into literature and all the stories it contained.

Yet amidst this blossoming connection, Ethan lingered in the back of my mind, a shadow that sometimes clouded my newfound clarity. I'd see him from time to time, often at the café or strolling through the park, his presence igniting a flicker of nostalgia that danced like candlelight in the corners of my heart. Each encounter was a bittersweet reminder of our past, of moments shared, but also of the distance that had grown between us. I began to realize that while I couldn't change the course of his choices, I could choose how I responded to them.

One crisp Saturday morning, a gentle breeze rustling the leaves outside, I decided to take a different route home from the bookstore. As I ambled down the street, the familiar surroundings transformed into a vibrant canvas, each storefront and garden alive with color. The old-fashioned lampposts dotted the path like sentinels of the past, their charm adding a touch of magic to the mundane. My heart felt light, buoyed by the laughter echoing from a nearby playground where children chased each other, their innocence spilling over into the air.

That's when I spotted Ethan, seated on a bench, sketching in a small notebook. The sight of him drew me closer, like a moth to a flame, despite the internal debate raging within. Should I approach him? Or was it best to maintain the distance I had worked so hard to create?

He looked up, and our eyes met, a moment suspended in time. There was a softness in his gaze that hadn't been there before, an openness that hinted at vulnerability. It pulled at something deep within me, a flicker of hope intertwined with hesitation.

"Hey," I ventured, my voice steadier than I felt.

"Hey," he replied, a smile breaking through the tension. "I was just capturing the world around me. Would you like to see?"

Curiosity piqued, I stepped closer, my heart racing as he turned the notebook toward me. The sketches were delicate yet expressive, capturing the essence of Maplewood with an artist's eye. There was something ethereal about his work, a way of seeing beauty in the everyday that resonated with me. "You have a real gift," I said, my admiration genuine.

"Thanks. It's just a hobby, but it helps me process things," he replied, his voice softening, as if he were sharing a secret. "How's the bookstore?"

"Busy, but in a good way. We started a book club," I said, a spark of enthusiasm lighting my words. "It's been amazing to connect with others and share stories. It feels like a community."

"That sounds wonderful. I'm glad you're finding your place," he said, and for a moment, the walls we'd built between us seemed to waver.

Silence enveloped us, comfortable yet charged with unspoken words. I could sense the unsaid questions lingering in the air, the history that hovered like a ghost between us. "What about you?" I asked, breaking the stillness. "How have you been?"

He looked away for a moment, as if gathering his thoughts. "I've been... figuring things out, I guess. It's been chaotic, but I'm trying to find clarity too."

The acknowledgment struck a chord within me, mirroring my own journey. Perhaps we weren't so different after all, both navigating our own storms, trying to emerge unscathed. It was a shared struggle, an understanding that sparked a flicker of connection, even amidst the complexity of our past.

"I think clarity can come from chaos," I offered, a hint of wry humor lacing my words. "Sometimes you just have to wade through the mess to find the beauty hidden beneath."

He smiled, the warmth in his eyes igniting something in my chest. "You've always had a way with words."

With that simple compliment, I felt the boundaries between us begin to blur, and the barriers I had painstakingly erected started to crumble. We talked for a while longer, lost in conversation, laughter spilling over like the golden light that surrounded us. The chaotic emotions I had carried around felt lighter, dissipating into the air, replaced by the warmth of connection.

As the sun began to set, casting a warm glow across Maplewood, I knew this encounter was significant. I was ready to embrace whatever might come next, whether that meant rebuilding my relationship with Ethan or allowing myself to let go completely. Either way, I was no longer afraid of the chaos. I had found clarity in my choices, the courage to navigate the unpredictable waters ahead, and an openness to whatever possibilities lay beyond the horizon.

With a renewed sense of purpose, I walked away from that park bench, heart lighter and head held high. The world felt vibrant and full of promise, a beautiful chaos just waiting to be explored. And as I stepped into the unfolding chapter of my life, I realized that clarity doesn't mean the absence of turmoil; rather, it's about finding peace and joy within it. In that realization, I felt ready to write my story, one filled with love, laughter, and a touch of magic.

Chapter 26: A New Direction

The warm light filtering through the large bay windows of the bookstore cast a golden hue over the worn wooden floors, illuminating the eclectic mix of mismatched chairs arranged in a circle. The scent of freshly brewed coffee wafted in from the corner café, intertwining with the faint smell of aged paper and ink that clung to the spines of countless volumes lining the shelves. This was my sanctuary, a place where words breathed life into silence, and today it would serve as a crucible for creativity.

As the clock struck six, I felt a flutter of anticipation in my chest, a nervous energy that danced between excitement and doubt. I had spent the past week tirelessly crafting a curriculum for the workshop, merging writing prompts with discussions on the nuances of storytelling. It wasn't just about putting pen to paper; it was about unearthing the soul of every participant, about coaxing their hidden stories into the light. I took a deep breath, inhaling the comforting scent of well-loved books and roasted coffee, and stepped into the room, ready to welcome the aspiring authors.

The first participant arrived, a wide-eyed woman with curly auburn hair that seemed to bounce with every step. She wore a bright floral dress that mirrored the vibrant energy I hoped to cultivate. "Hi! I'm Lily," she chirped, her enthusiasm infectious. Behind her, others trickled in—an eclectic mix of ages and backgrounds. A middle-aged man in a tweed jacket with ink stains on his fingertips, a college student sporting a graphic tee, and an elderly woman with silver hair that sparkled like moonlight. Each person carried the weight of unspoken dreams and stories aching to escape.

As they settled in, I introduced myself, my voice trembling slightly as I spoke about my own journey as a writer—a mix of triumphs and failures, of inspiration gleaned from the heart of the city. "This workshop is a space for all of you to find your voice," I declared, my heart racing with conviction. "We're here to nurture each other's creativity and cultivate a community of storytellers." The words hung in the air, warm and inviting.

The initial awkwardness of strangers quickly faded, replaced by laughter and shared stories. Each participant spoke about their aspirations, the themes they longed to explore, and the characters they hoped to create. As they shared, I felt a swell of pride and joy. Here, in this cozy nook of the city, I was witnessing the birth of a community.

Amidst the voices, I caught sight of Ethan at the back of the room. He leaned casually against a shelf, his eyes twinkling with encouragement. The warmth of his smile ignited a spark within me. I could see the genuine interest in his gaze, as if he believed in every word being spoken. It felt like a secret support, an invisible thread connecting us, grounding me in the present moment.

As the workshop progressed, I introduced a writing prompt: "Write about a moment that changed your life." The room buzzed with the scratching of pens against paper, the soft rustle of pages turning. I wandered around, peering over shoulders, catching snippets of raw, unfiltered emotion that flowed from their pens. There was something intoxicating about witnessing these fragments of vulnerability. Each story, whether a whimsical daydream or a heart-wrenching confession, drew us closer together, like threads weaving a tapestry of shared experience.

Lily's laughter rang out like a bell, punctuating the air as she recounted a disastrous date that ended with her locked out of her apartment in her pajamas. The group erupted in laughter, the kind that bubbles up from the gut and feels like a release. In that moment, the walls that separated us began to crumble, and we were no longer strangers, but a band of dreamers united by our shared ambition.

As I glanced toward Ethan again, I noticed he was jotting down notes, a look of concentration etched on his face. Something about the way he leaned into the moment stirred something deep within me. Was it admiration? Or perhaps a spark of something more? The thought flitted through my mind like a butterfly, delicate yet exhilarating.

After a while, I encouraged everyone to share their writing aloud, an act that felt both daring and sacred. As the stories unfolded, the vulnerability thickened in the air, wrapping around us like a warm embrace. One by one, they bared their souls, allowing the world to catch a glimpse of their innermost thoughts. I watched their faces shift from apprehension to liberation, each word spoken drawing us closer.

When it was my turn to share, I chose a piece that had been brewing in my mind for weeks, a reflection on the bittersweet nature of change. As I spoke, I felt the familiar tug of emotion, the vulnerability rising like a tide. I saw Ethan lean forward, his eyes locked onto mine, and it ignited a fire within me. I poured my heart into those words, capturing the beauty of uncertainty and the courage it takes to embrace the unknown.

The applause that followed felt like a warm blanket wrapping around me, and for the first time in what felt like an eternity, I found solace in my purpose. This wasn't just a workshop; it was a celebration of creativity, a reminder that stories connect us in ways we often overlook. Each participant left a piece of their heart on the page, and together we forged a bond that transcended the ordinary.

As the evening wound down and people began to gather their belongings, the air buzzed with excitement and new friendships. Conversations sparked like fireflies in the night, and laughter echoed against the walls of my cherished bookstore. I couldn't help but smile, my heart swelling with gratitude. This was just the beginning—a new chapter not just for the participants, but for me as well. In that moment, I felt a sense of belonging, a collective heartbeat of creativity that pulsed through us all.

The following week brought with it a tangible buzz of anticipation, a current of energy that flowed through the bookstore like a gentle stream. Each day, the sun crept higher, painting the sky in hues of amber and rose as if the world were an artist's canvas. I found myself swept away by the enchantment of the season, as autumn unfolded its tapestry of crisp air and vibrant foliage. Outside, the leaves began their slow descent, swirling in a dance that mirrored my heart, now alight with the prospect of new beginnings.

With the writing workshop gaining momentum, I prepared for our second session with a blend of excitement and trepidation. I wanted to keep the spirit alive, to foster an atmosphere where ideas blossomed and flourished. I spent hours at the café down the street, sipping pumpkin spice lattes while scribbling notes and prompts on napkins, the ink smudging my fingers like a writer's badge of honor. I reveled in the knowledge that I was crafting a sanctuary for storytellers, a haven for those who sought to give life to their imaginations.

As the evening approached, the sky turned a deep shade of indigo, the first stars twinkling like diamonds scattered across a velvet backdrop. I stood in front of the bookstore, taking a moment to soak it all in—the familiar creak of the door, the sound of laughter wafting from the café, and the rich aroma of books and coffee swirling around me like a warm embrace. I pulled the heavy door open, its brass handle cool against my palm, and stepped into the warmth of my sanctuary.

The room was a blend of familiar faces and newcomers, an eclectic assembly of aspiring authors who had been drawn to this unique gathering. Each person brought a piece of themselves into the space, their nervous energy crackling in the air like electricity. I scanned the room, my heart swelling with pride as I caught sight of Lily, her bright floral dress a beacon of joy, animatedly chatting with the man in the tweed jacket, who now wore a smirk that suggested a playful banter.

My gaze drifted to the corner, where Ethan sat with a notepad, his brow furrowed in concentration, yet there was a lightness in his demeanor that made my pulse quicken. He looked up, our eyes locking for a brief moment, and the world around me faded into a blur. I wondered if he felt it too, this inexplicable connection that hummed between us, a thread woven into the fabric of our shared passion for storytelling.

With a deep breath, I took center stage, embracing the role I had carved out for myself. "Welcome back, everyone!" I called out, my voice steady and warm, a reflection of the community we were building together. "Tonight, we're going to dive deeper into character development. After all, every story hinges on the characters that breathe life into the pages."

As I spoke, I noticed the eager glances exchanged among the participants, their eyes shining with a spark of curiosity and enthusiasm. I introduced an exercise where each writer would create a character profile, delving into their character's hopes, fears, and secrets. The workshop hummed with the sound of pens scratching against paper, punctuated by the occasional giggle as someone recalled a particularly outrageous quirk.

The warmth of creativity enveloped us, and the atmosphere transformed into a cozy cocoon where laughter intermingled with introspection. I moved among the participants, peering over their shoulders, sharing in their triumphs and nudging them toward deeper explorations. Each character that sprang to life was a reflection of someone's dreams, fears, and desires, a testament to the power of storytelling to mirror the human experience.

In the midst of the workshop, I felt a gentle touch on my shoulder. Turning around, I found Ethan standing there, his smile illuminating the room. "Can I share something?" he asked, his voice smooth and inviting. My heart raced at the thought of him stepping into the spotlight.

"Absolutely," I replied, stepping aside to give him the floor.

He cleared his throat, his gaze drifting toward the group. "I've been working on a story about a man who travels across America to find the woman he loves," he began, his voice steady, yet laced with emotion. "He visits iconic places—the Grand Canyon, the streets of New Orleans, the snowy peaks of Colorado. Each location holds a piece of his journey, reflecting his growth and the love that motivates him."

The room fell silent, captivated by his words. He painted a vivid picture of love intertwined with adventure, and as he spoke, I could see the landscapes unfold in the minds of my participants. The way he described the wind rustling through the trees or the taste of gumbo on the streets of New Orleans was mesmerizing. I was lost in his world, a willing passenger on his character's journey.

When he finished, the room erupted into applause, the sound echoing off the walls like a symphony of support and encouragement. I felt a rush of pride, not just for Ethan's story, but for the community we had built together. There was something truly magical about sharing our dreams and aspirations, about weaving our tales into a rich tapestry of collective experience.

As the workshop drew to a close, I gathered everyone for a final circle, a moment to reflect and share our thoughts. I looked around at the faces illuminated by the soft glow of string lights hanging overhead, and my heart swelled with gratitude. "Thank you all for being here and for opening your hearts," I said, my voice thick with emotion. "Tonight, we not only shared our stories, but we also forged connections that will carry us forward."

The participants shared their insights, each one more profound than the last. Lily spoke of her newfound courage to embrace her quirky ideas, while the tweed-clad man discussed how he planned to integrate elements of his own life into his narrative. Ethan, leaning forward, emphasized the importance of authenticity in writing, echoing sentiments that resonated with everyone in the room.

As they departed, I lingered, watching the last few figures fade into the night, their laughter trailing behind them like a melody. I turned to see Ethan still there, lingering in the doorway, his silhouette framed by the dim light of the bookstore.

"Thank you for tonight," he said softly, his gaze steady and sincere. "You've created something truly special here."

I felt my cheeks warm, a mixture of pride and something deeper, more unsettling. "I couldn't have done it without everyone's energy and passion," I replied, brushing a loose strand of hair behind my ear. "This workshop is as much theirs as it is mine."

Ethan stepped closer, the space between us humming with unspoken words. "You're a remarkable leader, you know," he said, his voice barely above a whisper. I looked into his eyes, feeling the gravity of the moment pulling us closer.

For the first time in a long while, I allowed myself to hope—hope for new stories, new connections, and perhaps a new direction that could unfold beyond the pages of my life.

The nights grew longer as the crisp air of autumn settled in, and the city transformed into a tapestry of burnt oranges and deep reds. The bookstore had become a beacon of warmth in the cooling weather, the smell of freshly brewed coffee mingling with the earthy aroma of aging paper. Each evening, as I unlocked the door to my sanctuary, I felt the weight of the world slip away, replaced by the eager energy of aspiring writers ready to share their stories.

With each passing workshop, I became increasingly aware of the tapestry we were weaving together. The group, a delightful motley crew of different ages and backgrounds, began to resemble a quirky family. I adored the way Lily's laugh lit up the room, a buoyant sound that seemed to dance along with her expressive gestures. Then there was Marco, the middle-aged man in the tweed jacket, whose dry humor added a delightful flavor to our discussions, often making us laugh even as he probed deep into philosophical territory.

Ethan had become a regular fixture, often leaning against the wall with that same knowing smile, his presence somehow comforting, like a warm cup of cocoa on a winter's day. With each workshop, he shared snippets of his own writing journey, revealing layers of vulnerability and aspiration. As he spoke of his characters, I felt an inexplicable connection growing between us, like an intricate web of shared passions binding us closer.

One evening, I introduced a new exercise: "Write a letter from your character to someone they love." The prompt invited the participants to explore emotions that often lay dormant beneath the surface. As they settled into their chairs, the air thick with the rustling of paper and the soft scratch of pens, I moved among them, listening to snippets of their thoughts and quietly encouraging them to dig deeper.

The silence enveloped us like a warm blanket, punctuated only by the occasional sigh or the sound of someone flipping a page. I caught Ethan's gaze as he wrote, his brow furrowed in concentration. The way his pen moved across the page was almost hypnotic, as if he were channeling something profound from the depths of his imagination. I found myself entranced, captivated not just by the words he was crafting, but by the man behind them.

After a while, I invited everyone to share their letters. Lily's voice trembled slightly as she read her heartfelt note to her estranged father, a plea for understanding and forgiveness that resonated with everyone in the room. Marco followed, his letter to a long-lost friend filled with nostalgia and regret, each word a testament to the weight of time and choices made. As they shared, I could feel the bonds between us tightening, the vulnerability creating a space where we all felt seen and valued.

THE PATH BETWEEN WORDS 277

Then it was Ethan's turn. He stood, his expression serious yet warm, and read aloud a letter from his character to a lost love. The words flowed effortlessly, infused with a raw sincerity that had everyone hanging on every syllable. As he spoke of longing and missed opportunities, I noticed a flicker of emotion in his eyes, an intensity that seemed to penetrate the very fabric of the room.

When he finished, silence hung heavy for a moment, each of us grappling with the weight of his words. I could see glistening eyes around the room, a testament to the impact of sharing such intimate emotions. The applause that erupted felt like a wave of affirmation, lifting us all, and I could see the pride radiating from Ethan, the sense of accomplishment blooming in his chest.

As the workshop came to an end, I felt an unshakeable sense of belonging, a recognition that we were all navigating the complex terrain of our stories together. With each session, the lines between our lives and our characters began to blur, and I realized that we were not just writers but explorers, diving into the depths of our own hearts and souls.

In the following weeks, the workshop continued to grow. Word spread through the community like wildfire, fueled by social media posts and the enthusiastic recommendations of those who attended. We transformed a small gathering into a vibrant hub of creativity, each participant becoming both a student and a teacher, learning from one another's experiences.

Amid this blossoming community, my relationship with Ethan deepened. We shared conversations that lingered long after the workshop ended, exchanging thoughts on our favorite authors and exploring our aspirations. I found myself wanting to know everything about him—the dreams he harbored, the fears that kept him awake at night, and the stories that had shaped him into the man standing before me.

One evening, as the workshop drew to a close, I asked everyone to share a personal story that had influenced their writing. The room buzzed with excitement, and I could feel the familiar anticipation coursing through me. It was as if we were gathering around a fire, sharing tales that ignited the imagination and forged connections.

Lily spoke of her childhood in a small town, where the library felt like a sanctuary, and every book was a portal to adventure. Marco recounted a transformative trip he had taken to Italy, where he learned the art of savoring life through the simple pleasure of food and laughter. Then it was Ethan's turn. He took a moment, his eyes distant as if recalling something both beautiful and painful.

"I once lost someone very dear to me," he began, his voice steady yet laced with emotion. "It taught me that life is fragile and fleeting, and it fueled my desire to tell stories that honor the beauty of our connections." He paused, the weight of his words hanging in the air like an unspoken truth. "Writing is how I keep them alive. It's how I remember."

The vulnerability in his voice resonated deeply within me, a reminder of the importance of capturing our experiences on paper. I felt an urge to reach out, to comfort him, but instead, I simply nodded, feeling the unbreakable bond that had formed between us. In that moment, we weren't just fellow writers; we were two souls sharing the intricate dance of love and loss, finding solace in the knowledge that our stories mattered.

As the weeks turned into months, the seasons shifted, and the warmth of community enveloped us like a snug blanket. I reveled in the knowledge that I had created something meaningful, a space where dreams took flight and stories found their voice. Every workshop drew in new participants, expanding our circle and enriching the tapestry we were weaving together.

Ethan became my anchor amidst the storm of creativity. His laughter brightened my days, and his insights challenged me to push my own boundaries. Our discussions spilled into coffee dates and late-night phone calls, the conversations stretching until dawn. I began to feel a spark of something beyond friendship, a longing that ignited deep within me.

One night, as the last of the participants filtered out, I found myself alone with Ethan, the air thick with unspoken words. The soft glow of the string lights cast a warm ambiance, illuminating the space we had created together. I turned to him, my heart racing as I contemplated the moment, the possibilities stretching out before us like the pages of an unwritten book.

"I'm really glad you came into my life," I said, my voice barely above a whisper. It was a simple sentiment, but it carried the weight of everything I felt, an invitation to explore the depths of our connection.

Ethan stepped closer, his gaze steady and filled with warmth. "Me too," he replied, the corners of his mouth lifting into that familiar, disarming smile. "You've changed everything for me. You've given me a reason to write again, to dream again."

In that moment, surrounded by the echoes of laughter and the ghosts of stories told, I felt the world shift beneath my feet, as if the universe had conspired to align our paths. The possibilities before us shimmered like starlight, illuminating the way to a future filled with shared dreams and the promise of love. It was a new chapter waiting to be written, and I felt ready to embrace every word, every heartbeat, and every whispered secret that lay ahead.

Chapter 27: Unexpected Revelations

The workshop room was a sanctuary, drenched in the warm glow of late afternoon light filtering through large, dusty windows. The wooden floors creaked beneath the weight of shared dreams and lingering insecurities, each sound a reminder that we were all in this together. The walls, adorned with pages of half-formed ideas and fraying manuscripts, vibrated with the energy of countless aspirations. I loved this place, with its chalkboard that bore the remnants of past lessons and the scattered chairs that had borne witness to laughter, tears, and everything in between. Each session was a tapestry of stories woven together, and I felt lucky to be one of the many threads.

Mia sat across from me, her auburn hair cascading over her shoulders like a curtain hiding her vulnerability. She wore oversized glasses that made her hazel eyes sparkle with intensity. As she spoke, her voice trembled but gradually found strength, capturing the room's attention as effortlessly as the wind rustling through the leaves outside. "I wrote about heartbreak," she began, her hands animatedly gesturing as if to grasp her thoughts and pull them into the open air. "Not the kind you read about in novels where everything is wrapped up neatly by the end, but the real kind. The kind that leaves you feeling like you've been buried alive."

I could see it in her eyes, the way memories flickered behind them like ghostly apparitions. The honesty in her words wrapped around me, drawing me closer, and I felt an inexplicable urge to share my own secrets. The pain I had carried for so long began to bubble up, but before I knew it, I was unearthing the remnants of my relationship with Ethan and Chloe, as if my mouth had been pried open by the sheer force of her honesty.

"When I was with Ethan, it was like swimming in the ocean on a perfect summer day. We floated on waves of laughter and passion, but one day, the tide turned." I took a breath, glancing at the supportive faces surrounding me. Their expressions were warm and inviting, encouraging me to continue. "We drifted apart slowly, almost imperceptibly, like the tide stealing away the shoreline."

A silence enveloped the room, thick and palpable. I could almost hear the collective heartbeat of my fellow writers as they listened intently. I glanced at Mia, who nodded with understanding, her own wounds bleeding onto the table between us. "And then there was Chloe," I continued, my voice gaining momentum. "She was everything I wanted to be. Fearless, unapologetically herself. But being around her made me question who I was, and in the end, I lost myself entirely."

Mia leaned forward, her elbows resting on the table, her gaze piercing through my confessions. "But you found yourself again, didn't you?" she asked, her voice low and sincere. There was a challenge in her question, but also an invitation. An invitation to embrace my journey, however flawed.

"Maybe," I whispered, the weight of my own uncertainty creeping back in. "Or maybe I'm just learning to live with the pieces."

And just like that, I was no longer a solitary island of despair. The room became a vessel of empathy, and as each writer opened up, sharing their stories, we built a bridge of connection. Laughter erupted in unexpected moments, punctuated by moments of solemnity that echoed with authenticity. I could feel the tendrils of healing wrap around me, transforming the atmosphere into something almost electric. It was a strange paradox; the more I spoke, the lighter I felt, as if I were shedding layers of pain with every shared word.

In the following weeks, the workshop became a sanctuary for my soul. Each session unfolded like a beautifully crafted narrative, filled with diverse characters—an ex-lawyer seeking solace in poetry, a retiree rediscovering his passion for storytelling, and a young mother penning letters to her future self. The melting pot of life experiences made every meeting feel like a celebration of resilience, and I found myself lost in the magic of our shared creativity.

One afternoon, as the sun dipped lower in the sky, casting golden rays across our faces, I shared a particularly raw piece of writing. My words, raw and unfiltered, spoke of vulnerability and strength intertwined. They flowed from my pen like water from a hidden spring, each sentence a reflection of the catharsis I experienced in the presence of my fellow writers.

As I read aloud, I noticed the gentle nods of encouragement from my peers, their smiles illuminating the room. When I finished, a soft silence hung in the air, and for a moment, I feared that I had laid bare too much of my heart. But then, Mia's voice broke the stillness. "That was beautiful," she said, her eyes shimmering with unshed tears. "You have a way of making pain feel like poetry."

Her words washed over me like a balm, igniting a flicker of hope deep within my chest. I realized that I wasn't just sharing my journey; I was inviting others to witness it, to participate in the act of healing. With each story shared and each wound laid bare, I felt the tendrils of connection grow stronger, binding us together in an intricate web of shared humanity.

The workshop became a tapestry of my emotions, each thread a story filled with laughter, sorrow, and hope. And amidst that vibrant cacophony of voices, I began to find my own. I learned to embrace my journey, imperfections and all, and with every word I penned, I crafted not just narratives but a new identity, one that was firmly rooted in the knowledge that I was not alone. In that space, I discovered the transformative power of storytelling, a light in the darkness that illuminated the path ahead, a promise of resilience wrapped in the warm embrace of shared experiences.

As I prepared to leave the workshop that evening, the golden glow of the setting sun spilled across the streets, painting the iconic skyline of the city in hues of orange and pink. I inhaled deeply, filling my lungs with the intoxicating scent of possibility. The familiar sounds of the bustling streets wrapped around me, but this time, they felt different. Each honking car, each distant laugh, seemed to carry a note of hope, a reminder that every story mattered. I walked away with my heart lighter, each step echoing the rhythm of newfound strength, knowing that I was part of something beautiful.

I walked home beneath a canopy of stars, each pinprick of light igniting memories I had once buried beneath layers of doubt and fear. The crisp autumn air wrapped around me like a comforting shawl, and I could taste the sweetness of possibility on my lips. My thoughts danced as I replayed the evening's revelations, the energy of my fellow writers a palpable warmth that lingered in my chest. In that moment, I understood the true power of vulnerability—it could transform mere words into lifelines.

With every step, I relished the way the leaves crunched beneath my feet, each sound a reminder of the earth's rhythm, as if it were echoing the pulse of my own newfound clarity. The city pulsed with life around me, the lights twinkling like stars fallen to earth, illuminating the streets where dreams were forged. I passed by a small café, the rich aroma of freshly brewed coffee spilling into the night, beckoning me to step inside. The place had an intimate vibe, with mismatched furniture and walls plastered with local art, each piece telling its own story.

I ordered a cup of steaming hot chocolate, the barista's smile brightening my day further as he slid the warm cup across the counter. With each sip, I felt the warmth spread through my body, fortifying me for the thoughts that began swirling like autumn leaves caught in a gentle breeze. How had I allowed myself to hide for so long? The question lingered, taunting me like a specter in the back of my mind. The workshop had ignited a flame within me that I hadn't realized had been flickering, just waiting for the right moment to blaze back to life.

Seated in a corner nook, I pulled out my journal, the leather cover worn and familiar beneath my fingertips. My heart raced as I flipped through the pages filled with half-formed ideas and frantic sketches, remnants of a time when my thoughts felt too heavy to voice. But tonight, as I began to write, the ink flowed freely, liberated by the connection I felt with Mia and the others.

I penned down my reflections—the fear of losing myself in relationships, the ache of longing for acceptance, the struggle of finding my own voice in a cacophony of expectations. Each word became a cathartic release, like peeling back layers of an onion until only the essence remained. I wrote about Ethan, the way his laughter had danced through the air like music, and how I had once believed our love was an unbreakable bond. Then came Chloe, a burst of color in my grayscale world, always reminding me of what I wanted to be but never quite felt I could achieve.

As I scribbled furiously, I felt an unfamiliar sensation wash over me—gratitude. For the first time, I acknowledged that my experiences had shaped me, carving out the person I was becoming rather than merely defining the struggles I had faced. I closed my eyes for a moment, savoring the realization like a fine wine. This journey was not just mine; it was a collective tapestry of stories, each thread intertwined with others, creating a beautiful, chaotic masterpiece.

Days turned into weeks, and each workshop transformed into a celebration of our creative spirits. We began to hold writing challenges, the kind that pushed us to explore uncharted territories within our minds. I discovered I had a knack for weaving humor into my narratives, crafting characters with quirks that made them relatable and human. One evening, I shared a short story about a woman who accidentally mistook a pie for a hat during a particularly chaotic dinner party. The laughter that erupted in the room was infectious, lifting the spirits of everyone present.

Mia, whose own tales were often steeped in raw emotion, began incorporating humor into her writing as well, bridging the gap between our worlds. We found ourselves exchanging playful banter, our laughter intertwining like old friends rekindling their bond. One night, as we gathered around the table, I caught Mia's eye, and we shared a knowing glance, an unspoken understanding of the healing power of laughter amidst our struggles.

But as I blossomed in this nurturing environment, shadows from my past still flickered at the corners of my mind. I often found myself at a crossroads, torn between the desire to forge ahead and the fear of losing what I had gained. Ethan had reached out sporadically, each message a bittersweet reminder of the love we had shared. While part of me yearned to reconnect, another part hesitated, wary of treading familiar ground that had once left me breathless with heartache.

Then there were the fleeting encounters with Chloe, our paths crossing unexpectedly at art exhibits or cozy bookshops. She carried an air of confidence that was intoxicating, and our conversations danced between the playful and profound. Yet, even in those moments of connection, I couldn't shake the feeling that I was still trying to prove something—both to myself and to her. Would she ever see me as an equal, or would I always remain a shadow in her vibrant world?

One afternoon, the workshop gathered in a park for a special outdoor session, the trees standing tall like guardians over our shared creativity. The crisp air was alive with the scent of pine and the distant laughter of children playing, a reminder that joy often lay in the simplest moments. We sprawled across blankets, notebooks in hand, the sun warming our backs like a gentle embrace.

Mia suggested we write a collaborative piece, an exercise in trust where we would each contribute a line and see where the story took us. As the sun dipped low in the sky, casting golden rays across our faces, the energy in the air was electric. My heart swelled as I watched each of my fellow writers weave their words into a tapestry that reflected our diverse experiences.

When it was my turn, I hesitated, but then I let the words flow. "In the heart of the city, where dreams intertwined with reality, a forgotten park waited for the stories of those willing to listen." With each line that followed, I felt as if I were pouring a piece of my soul onto the page, relinquishing control and embracing the unknown.

As we shared our collaborative creation, laughter bubbled over once more, but there was also a sense of reverence as we acknowledged the depths of our vulnerabilities. It was in this shared space that I felt the chains of my past begin to rust and weaken, replaced by a new resolve. No longer would I shy away from the complexities of love and loss; instead, I would embrace them, recognizing that they were as integral to my journey as the moments of joy that punctuated it.

And as the sun set, painting the sky in hues of lavender and gold, I realized that this was my new beginning—a place where I could be authentically myself, surrounded by a community that uplifted and inspired me. The stars began to twinkle above, and with each one that appeared, I felt a renewed sense of purpose. This was just the start of something extraordinary, a journey where words became wings, and together we would soar into the horizon of our shared stories.

In the weeks that followed, the workshop transformed into more than just a gathering; it became a vibrant community, each member contributing their unique colors to the canvas of our shared experiences. The park where we often convened took on an almost magical quality, its sun-dappled paths winding through the trees like stories waiting to be told. I would often arrive early, eager to carve out my favorite spot beneath a gnarled oak whose branches reached for the heavens, as if trying to catch every whisper of creativity that floated through the air.

One afternoon, while the scent of blooming jasmine wrapped around us, Mia proposed an idea that sent a thrill through the group. "Let's create a narrative that reflects the essence of our workshop—stories of heartache, hope, and healing, but told through the lens of our surroundings. Let's draw inspiration from this park, from the lives intertwined within its shadows and sunlight." Her eyes sparkled with excitement, and I could feel the enthusiasm radiating from her as if it were a palpable force.

We split into small groups, each tasked with observing our surroundings and weaving those observations into our narratives. I found myself with Mia and a retired schoolteacher named Harold, whose quiet wisdom often resonated deeply within the group. We wandered through the park, allowing our senses to absorb every detail: the laughter of children playing tag, the rhythmic rustling of leaves swaying in the wind, and the distant strumming of a guitar serenading the sun as it dipped toward the horizon.

As we paused near a cluster of wildflowers, Mia knelt down, her fingers gently brushing the petals. "These flowers remind me of resilience," she mused, her voice soft. "They bloom in the most unexpected places, don't they? Just like us." I nodded, my heart swelling with understanding. The flowers mirrored our journey—fragile yet unyielding, bursting forth in defiance of adversity.

We returned to our blankets with a flurry of ideas, the energy in the air crackling like the electric anticipation before a storm. I could hardly contain my excitement as I settled down to write, letting the words flow like a stream unfurling after a long drought. My narrative unfolded around a character named Lila, a woman grappling with her past, much like I had been. Through her eyes, I explored the themes of loss and rediscovery, the way heartache could shape but never fully define a person.

Mia contributed a beautiful passage about a young boy who found solace in the shadows of the trees, crafting worlds out of fallen leaves and twigs, while Harold penned a heartwarming tale of an elderly couple who found love again on the very park bench where they had first met. Each story was a thread, weaving together an intricate tapestry of our lives, rich with emotion and human experience.

As the sun began to set, casting a golden hue across the park, we gathered to share our narratives. Laughter mingled with a sense of reverence as we listened to each other's stories, the characters coming to life in the vibrant hues of our words. In that moment, I felt a profound sense of belonging, a realization that our struggles were not meant to be faced alone. With every tale shared, we were not just writers; we were healers, stitching the fabric of our lives with threads of empathy and understanding.

Yet, even in this cocoon of warmth and acceptance, I felt a subtle stirring of conflict. Ethan's text messages had become more frequent, each ping a reminder of the unresolved feelings I harbored. Part of me craved the comfort of familiar arms, while another part feared that surrendering to those emotions would shatter the delicate progress I had made in reclaiming my voice.

One evening, as twilight enveloped the city, I sat at my favorite café, my journal open and the soft glow of fairy lights twinkling around me. I had intended to write, to channel my tangled thoughts onto the page, but instead, my mind was consumed by Ethan's last message. It had been an innocuous invitation for coffee—a simple gesture laden with the weight of our shared history. My heart raced with anxiety, each beat echoing the conflict within me. Would seeing him again drag me back into the familiar whirlwind of emotions I had fought so hard to escape?

The door chimed softly as a couple entered the café, their laughter bright and carefree. I watched them as they leaned into one another, sharing secrets and smiles. A pang of longing washed over me, but then I recalled the warmth of my writing community—the laughter, the tears, and the undeniable sense of connection that had enveloped me in its embrace. I realized that love, in all its forms, was worth pursuing, but it had to be grounded in self-acceptance first.

With newfound resolve, I drafted a reply to Ethan, my fingers dancing across the keys with clarity and intention. "I'd love to catch up," I typed, "but I need to be honest about where I'm at. I've been on a journey of rediscovery, and I want to ensure that we're both on the same page." As I hit send, a weight lifted from my shoulders, a release akin to letting go of a balloon into the wide expanse of the sky.

The next few days passed in a haze of anticipation, my heart racing at the prospect of seeing him again while simultaneously relishing the freedom that had blossomed within me. When the day finally arrived, I found myself standing in front of the café, the scent of roasted coffee beans mingling with the crisp autumn air. I felt a familiar flutter in my stomach, a combination of excitement and trepidation, as I pushed open the door and stepped inside.

Ethan was already there, sitting at a corner table, his fingers absentmindedly tracing the rim of his coffee cup. He looked up as I approached, his smile warm and inviting. But beneath the surface, I could sense the tension—the unspoken words hovering in the air, waiting for the right moment to break free.

We exchanged pleasantries, the conversation flowing easily, as if no time had passed since we last saw each other. Yet, as we delved into deeper topics, I could feel the weight of our history settling between us, a delicate dance of nostalgia and uncertainty. I shared the journey I had embarked upon, the workshops, the connections

I had forged, and the growth I had experienced. Each word felt liberating, a testament to my newfound confidence.

As Ethan listened, his expression shifted from casual interest to genuine admiration. "I always knew you had it in you," he said, his voice tinged with a mix of pride and something deeper. "You've grown into such an incredible person."

But beneath the compliments lay an unvoiced question. Would I allow him back into my life, or would I keep the door firmly closed, safeguarding the progress I had made?

As the evening unfolded, we danced around the edges of our past—sharing memories, laughter, and tentative hopes for the future. Yet, as the sun began to set, casting a golden glow through the café windows, I felt a sense of clarity wash over me. This moment, however beautiful, was just that—a moment. It did not define my journey, nor did it determine my future.

With each sip of coffee, I recognized the strength I had gained from my workshop family, the sense of self that flourished in their presence. I realized that while Ethan held a significant place in my heart, my journey was mine to navigate, and I was not willing to relinquish that power. As I looked into his eyes, I saw the echoes of our past, but I also saw a glimmer of hope for what lay ahead—an acknowledgment of our shared experiences, but a steadfast commitment to my own path.

In the end, our meeting became a symbol, a stepping stone in my journey of self-discovery. I left the café with a heart full of memories and a spirit buoyed by resilience. The city around me buzzed with life, each sound a reminder that I was not alone in my struggles. As I walked home beneath a blanket of stars, I felt the weight of the world begin to lift, replaced by the knowledge that love—both for myself and for others—could exist in tandem, without overshadowing the journey I was destined to embrace.

With every step, I felt more anchored in my own narrative, ready to write the next chapter, whatever it may hold. The world was vast and full of potential, and I was determined to explore every corner, pen in hand, heart open, and spirit ignited.

Chapter 28: The Turning Tide

The evening sun poured through the large windows of the community center, casting warm, golden hues across the polished wooden floor. The scent of fresh paint mixed with the lingering aroma of coffee from the pot in the corner, where we had set up a small refreshment station. As I arranged the rows of folding chairs, I could hear the gentle murmur of my students in the adjacent room, their excitement palpable. This workshop had become my sanctuary, a place where I transformed anxiety into empowerment, and the ripple of change felt almost electric.

Ethan was an unexpected gift to this sanctuary. His arrival had shifted the atmosphere, like a breeze rustling through the leaves of the old oak tree outside. He was a master at logistics, and his sharp wit paired with a heart of gold made him irresistible. The way he threw himself into our mission, ensuring that every detail was attended to, was both admirable and disarming. With every shared glance and half-smile, my pulse quickened. I had never been one to wear my heart on my sleeve, but with Ethan, the walls I had so carefully constructed began to crumble.

"Can you believe we've already filled up this workshop?" I said, breaking the comfortable silence between us as we rearranged the chairs. I tried to sound light-hearted, but my voice caught on the edge of something deeper, something unspoken that seemed to swirl in the air around us.

He paused, his fingers brushing against mine as he set a chair down, the contact sending a jolt of warmth up my arm. "I think it's a testament to how much you've invested in these people. They see that," he replied, his gaze steady and sincere.

There was a moment of silence, a suspension of reality where the world around us blurred. I was acutely aware of the way the light caught the flecks of gold in his eyes, how the playful curve of his lips seemed to beckon me closer. My breath hitched, and for the first time, I realized just how much I wanted him to be more than a friend, more than a co-organizer. But fear is a funny thing—it wraps around you like a suffocating blanket, whispering that you're not enough, that this moment might shatter everything.

As I glanced away, my heart thumped wildly in my chest, the rhythm echoing in my ears. I was unsteady, caught in a whirlwind of emotions that I had thought I could neatly compartmentalize. But there was no ignoring the spark between us, an undeniable chemistry that had been brewing since we first met. Just then, in that crowded room filled with anticipation, I felt the sharp pang of longing, and the fear of loss wrapped around my heart like barbed wire.

The moment stretched and quivered, heavy with unspoken words and what-ifs. I felt a warmth creeping up my neck as he took a small step closer, and our hands brushed again, sending a delightful shock through me. This time, I didn't pull away. Instead, I held my breath, a silent plea for him to understand, to read the script my heart was desperately trying to convey.

Ethan seemed to sense the shift, his eyes searching mine, seeking permission. And when he leaned in, everything else faded into oblivion—the chatter of my students, the world outside, the weight of expectation. It was just us, suspended in this fragile bubble. His lips met mine, soft and hesitant, igniting a fire deep within me that I hadn't realized was still flickering beneath the surface. It was a kiss filled with the sweetness of newfound possibility and the gentle promise of something deeper.

I melted into him, feeling the warmth radiate from his body. The kiss deepened, taking on a life of its own, a beautiful dance that was both exhilarating and terrifying. It felt as if the earth had shifted beneath us, redefining the very ground we stood on. I couldn't help but pull him closer, our bodies fitting together like pieces of a puzzle, each curve and angle seamlessly aligning.

But as quickly as it had begun, reality came crashing back. I pulled away, breathless and wide-eyed, the electric charge between us still humming. "What was that?" I stammered, the words tumbling out as I struggled to piece together the whirlwind of emotions swirling inside me.

He chuckled softly, running a hand through his tousled hair, his eyes bright with mischief. "I think that was me finally acting on what I've been feeling for a while now."

His honesty was refreshing, yet it terrified me. What if I was risking everything I had built? What if this moment fractured our friendship, sending us spiraling into awkwardness? The thought made my heart clench. I had fought so hard to carve out a space for myself in this community, to earn their trust and admiration. But in this instant, it felt like I was also carving out a space for something new, something potentially beautiful.

"Ethan," I began, my voice barely a whisper, "this is all so new. I didn't expect..." I trailed off, searching for the right words, my heart racing. But he held my gaze, and in his eyes, I saw an understanding that soothed my fears.

"Neither did I," he said, stepping closer, closing the gap between us once more. "But maybe it's time for both of us to embrace the unexpected."

And just like that, the air around us felt lighter, charged with hope and endless possibilities. As I looked at him, the tension that had once felt daunting began to transform into something I could grasp, something that beckoned me to dive deeper into this uncharted territory. The workshop, with its buzzing energy and eager participants, suddenly felt like a backdrop to our unfolding story, a canvas waiting for the vibrant strokes of our choices to paint the future.

With every shared moment, every glance, every whispered word, I felt the tide turning—ushering in the promise of love, a bond that could weather the storms and grow stronger through every challenge we faced together.

The energy in the community center transformed as our kiss lingered in the air like a sweet perfume, and I found myself swept away in a whirlwind of emotions. It was as if we had stepped into a different realm, one where possibility reigned supreme and the rest of the world faded into an indistinct blur. Ethan's presence was magnetic, pulling me closer to a side of myself I had only glimpsed in my daydreams—one filled with laughter, warmth, and the flutter of newfound love.

"Let's finish setting up," he said, his voice a low rumble, still rich with the thrill of that shared moment. I nodded, the warmth of his lips still echoing on mine, and turned back to the chairs. The space felt alive, vibrant with anticipation, a silent witness to our uncharted territory. Each chair I positioned seemed to be imbued with a new significance, as if they too understood that the workshop was not just a place for learning, but now a backdrop for something much more profound.

As the evening wore on, laughter and chatter from my students filled the air, creating a comforting hum that seemed to weave itself into the fabric of the room. I glanced over at Ethan, who was chatting animatedly with a couple of participants. His laughter rang out, rich and genuine, and I couldn't help but smile. In that moment, I felt an overwhelming sense of gratitude for the serendipity that had brought him into my life, his passion igniting my own. It was as if the universe had conspired to place us here, in this moment, at the intersection of our dreams.

As the workshop commenced, I dove into my role, guiding my students through the intricacies of Salesforce like a ship's captain steering through uncharted waters. The air buzzed with the excitement of new knowledge, and my heart swelled as I witnessed their transformations. Each question they asked was a bridge leading to deeper understanding, and I reveled in the process, feeling as if I was part of something larger than myself. With each passing moment, I could feel the weight of my past—my doubts, fears, and insecurities—begin to lift.

But amidst the learning and laughter, there was an undercurrent of tension that I could not shake. Every time Ethan glanced my way, a shiver of anticipation raced down my spine. His eyes would catch mine, a spark igniting that sent a ripple of warmth through me, a silent reminder that our relationship had shifted. The sweet thrill of what lay ahead mingled with an apprehension I couldn't quite articulate.

At the end of the session, we gathered to reflect on the day, a small circle of eager faces, and I could see the newfound confidence radiating from my students. Their eyes sparkled with excitement, their questions deeper, their engagement more fervent. In that moment, I felt a sense of belonging, a community forged through shared learning and growth.

As the room slowly emptied, I caught Ethan watching me with a look that held a promise of more than just friendship. It was a gaze that sent butterflies dancing in my stomach, making me acutely aware of the electricity that pulsed between us. "You were amazing today," he said, leaning against the wall, arms crossed, a sly smile on his lips. "The way you inspired them... it's incredible to witness."

"Thanks," I replied, a smile creeping across my face. "But I couldn't have done it without you." My voice was soft, carrying the weight of the unspoken bond we now shared.

Ethan stepped closer, the air thickening around us as the last remnants of the workshop faded away. "I want to be more involved, you know? This means a lot to me." His words hung in the air, laced with sincerity. It was a subtle invitation, one that sent my heart racing. I wanted to say yes, to dive into this unknown with him, but the cautious part of me held back, afraid of the risks.

We locked eyes, and in that instant, everything felt monumental—the moment teetering on the edge of something extraordinary. "What if we take this further?" Ethan suggested, his voice barely above a whisper, the warmth of his breath brushing against my skin. "Not just the workshops, but... us?"

My heart thudded, a mix of elation and fear bubbling within. "Us?" The word rolled off my tongue, tinged with disbelief and hope.

"Yeah," he said, a nervous edge to his tone. "I've never felt this way about anyone before. Not just the work, but..." He paused, searching my eyes for understanding. "I want to explore what this is. I think we can create something really special together."

I took a breath, my mind racing with possibilities, each one more tempting than the last. "You know it won't be easy," I warned, my heart betraying my cautious exterior. "There's so much at stake."

"Nothing worth having ever is easy," he replied, his voice steady, conviction shining through. "But I believe in us, whatever that means."

I wanted to reach for him, to close the distance between us and seal the promise of possibility with a kiss that would redefine everything we had built. But instead, I stepped back slightly, letting the gravity of our situation sink in. The thought of intertwining our lives was both exhilarating and terrifying, a high-wire act that could either lead to a breathtaking new beginning or a catastrophic fall.

"Let's take it slow," I finally suggested, the words tumbling out as my heart steadied. "Let's not rush. We have this amazing thing with the workshop. I want to focus on that for now."

Ethan nodded, his expression a mix of understanding and disappointment, but there was a flicker of hope in his eyes. "Slow sounds good. Just know that I'm here, and I'm all in."

His words filled me with warmth, a promise of companionship in whatever this would become. As we began to clean up the remnants of the workshop—folding chairs, stacking supplies—I felt a sense of peace wash over me. We moved in tandem, our laughter mingling with the fading echoes of the day, the gentle rhythm of our interactions hinting at the potential of something beautifully intricate.

As I stepped back to survey the room, I could feel the walls of my heart slowly peeling away, making room for new experiences. The world outside was vast and full of opportunities, and I was no longer alone in navigating it. I could sense that our journey was just beginning, a delicate dance of vulnerability and connection, and I was ready to embrace the unknown alongside him.

Each day that followed that electric kiss, our interactions danced on the edge of a thrilling precipice. The workshop became our shared canvas, where we painted vibrant strokes of camaraderie and connection, yet the underlying tension pulsed like a hidden current beneath the surface. I reveled in the ebb and flow of our camaraderie, where laughter filled the gaps of our unspoken words. However, every brush of fingers, every lingering glance felt heavy with unexpressed desires and burgeoning possibilities.

With the next workshop approaching, I found myself in the quiet corner of my kitchen, surrounded by a chaotic symphony of papers, whiteboards, and the faint aroma of freshly brewed coffee. My apartment, a charming reflection of my personality, brimmed with knickknacks collected over the years: colorful mugs adorned with whimsical quotes, stacks of books both dog-eared and pristine, and a collection of plants that seemed to flourish under my care. In this cozy chaos, I took a moment to breathe, clutching a steaming mug as I gazed out the window at the bustling streets below. The golden light of the setting sun draped the city in a warm embrace, illuminating the rhythm of life outside—people rushing home, friends gathering for happy hour, lovers strolling hand in hand.

But amidst this beautiful cacophony, my thoughts drifted back to Ethan. His laughter echoed in my mind, that infectious sound that seemed to uplift every dark corner of my life. We had fallen into an easy rhythm, coordinating the logistics for the upcoming session, and yet, the weight of our earlier moment loomed like a cloud. I could still feel the lingering warmth of his lips on mine, the soft brush of his fingers against my skin, as if a spark had ignited something deep within me—a longing I had tucked away for far too long.

As I prepped materials for the workshop, a rush of anticipation coursed through me. Each handout I created felt imbued with my hopes for my students, a chance for them to experience growth and empowerment, to see themselves in ways they had never imagined. I hoped they could find their voice, just as I had begun to with Ethan by my side. The thought of him in the room, his presence a steady anchor amidst the excitement, brought a smile to my face.

The day arrived, and the community center buzzed with energy as participants trickled in, their faces a mix of eagerness and nervousness. I stood at the front, the sunlight pouring in through the tall windows, illuminating the space and highlighting the bright colors of the materials we would be working with. It felt like stepping onto a stage, and as I glanced over at Ethan setting up the projector, I felt a sense of gratitude wash over me. He was an unassuming force, his quiet confidence and infectious enthusiasm grounding me.

"Ready to rock this?" he asked, his eyes sparkling with mischief as he approached me, his presence wrapping around me like a cozy blanket.

I laughed, the nervous tension of the day easing slightly. "As ready as I'll ever be. Let's give them something unforgettable."

With a shared nod, we dove into the session. The first few hours flew by in a whirlwind of knowledge and interaction, our voices blending harmoniously, guiding our students through the intricacies of Salesforce with enthusiasm and humor. I watched as their faces transformed, confidence blooming with each new concept grasped, and the joy that coursed through me felt intoxicating.

But beneath the surface, my heart raced with every exchanged glance with Ethan. Each time our eyes locked, there was a spark—an understanding that we were not just colleagues, but two souls tethered together, caught in a delicate dance of burgeoning affection. The unspoken words hung heavily in the air, a whisper between us that begged to be voiced.

The workshop unfolded like a story, filled with moments of laughter, learning, and a shared sense of accomplishment. I felt buoyed by the collective energy, the students feeding off each other's enthusiasm, and Ethan's presence only intensified the magic of the day. His subtle support was a tether, grounding me even as I soared.

As we wrapped up, the room buzzed with conversations and excitement. People exchanged contact information, eager to stay connected, while I felt a swell of pride. We had created something special together, a community built on collaboration and shared dreams. Yet, my heart raced as the reality of what lay ahead loomed larger—would we take the next step?

After the final participants departed, the remnants of our workshop lingered in the air. Ethan and I began to clean up, the chairs clattering as we stacked them in neat rows. I felt a mixture of relief and disappointment that our shared experience was coming to an end. My heart thudded in my chest, the weight of our earlier kiss still pulsing in the back of my mind.

"Hey," Ethan said, breaking the silence, his voice soft yet filled with determination. "Can we talk? Just for a moment?"

My breath caught as he led me to a quiet corner, away from the fading noise of the community center. The intimacy of the moment enveloped us like a warm embrace, the world outside fading away. I could see the determination etched on his face, the way his brow furrowed slightly as he sought the right words.

"I know things have changed between us," he began, his gaze unwavering. "I can't ignore it, and I don't want to. You mean more to me than just a partner in this workshop."

I held my breath, the air thick with unspoken possibilities. "I feel it too," I confessed, my voice barely a whisper. "But I'm scared. This is so new, and I don't want to jeopardize what we've built."

Ethan stepped closer, the warmth of his presence enveloping me. "I don't think we'll jeopardize anything. I believe we can have both—the workshop and whatever this is between us. It's like you said, let's take it slow. We can figure it out together."

His words resonated deep within me, and as I looked into his eyes, I felt the walls I had carefully constructed start to crumble. There was something about the way he held my gaze that ignited a sense of hope—a glimmer of what could be.

"Okay," I said, my heart racing. "Let's take this step together."

With that simple acknowledgment, I felt a profound shift in the air. The connection that had formed between us solidified, a promise of companionship and trust as we ventured into uncharted territory. I reached for his hand, intertwining my fingers with his, feeling the warmth radiate through our touch.

And in that moment, I understood that this wasn't just about love; it was about growth, both individually and together. As we stepped out of the community center into the golden light of dusk, the world around us felt vibrant and alive, the possibilities stretching infinitely ahead. With every heartbeat, I felt the tide of change surging within me, and I was ready to embrace whatever came next. Together.

Chapter 29: The Aftermath

The sun dipped below the horizon, painting the sky in a mesmerizing gradient of pink and orange, as I found myself staring into the remnants of our kiss, still lingering on my lips like a forgotten secret. The world around us continued its relentless pulse, the rustling leaves whispering promises I was too afraid to acknowledge. We stood there on the edge of Lake Michigan, the cool breeze playing with my hair, the sweet scent of summer's end mingling with the earthy aroma of the shoreline. It felt like I had stepped into a painting, every detail vivid and sharp, yet I was too lost in the chaos of my emotions to appreciate the beauty.

Ethan shifted beside me, his shadow stretching long against the sun-drenched sand. "What does this mean for us?" I had asked, my voice a fragile echo in the warm air, as if the universe itself would answer my plea. He didn't flinch, but there was a flicker of something in his hazel eyes—a mixture of hope and uncertainty. The golden hour was our backdrop, yet my heart felt heavy with questions, tethered to the ground while my mind danced on a tightrope above a chasm of potential pain.

"I don't know," he admitted, his voice barely above a whisper. The honesty in his admission was both a balm and a brand. It soothed my worries but branded me with an awareness that this wasn't just a moment. This was a crossroads, a point of no return, and we were standing at the precipice, teetering on the edge.

I looked out over the lake, the water shimmering like liquid gold under the fading sunlight, and felt a shiver run through me. Each ripple was a reflection of the turmoil within, a chaotic swirl of emotions I couldn't quite grasp. Just days ago, life had been a familiar rhythm, predictable in its cadence. I woke up each morning with a purpose, a structured life that no longer felt like mine. Now, standing

THE PATH BETWEEN WORDS

next to Ethan, I felt like I was learning to dance without music, each step uncertain, yet exhilarating.

As the sun continued its descent, shadows lengthened around us, creeping closer like the doubts inching into my mind. I wanted to reach for his hand, to solidify the fragile connection that had formed between us, but fear clutched at my heart, urging me to retreat. What if this moment was merely a fleeting distraction, a brief escape from our tangled lives? What if we were just two lost souls clinging to each other as we stumbled through the aftermath of our respective storms?

Ethan cleared his throat, drawing me back from my spiraling thoughts. "What do you want this to mean?" His question hung in the air, weighty and profound, like the first drop of rain before a summer storm. The way he looked at me, earnest and sincere, made my heart ache. I wanted to tell him everything—the way his laughter made my stomach flutter, how every shared glance ignited a fire within me that I thought had long been extinguished. But the words tangled in my throat, caught like autumn leaves in a gust of wind.

"I want...," I started, the admission tasting sweet and bitter on my tongue, "I want to know that this isn't just a moment. I want to know that you see me, all of me, and that you want to be part of my story." My voice trembled, and the vulnerability settled in like a heavy cloak. I felt exposed, raw, and desperately alive.

He stepped closer, his gaze intense, as if he were searching for the answers hidden deep within me. "I see you," he said, his voice steady and reassuring. "And I want to be part of your story. But we're both dealing with our own messes, and I don't want to drag you down with me." His honesty struck me like a sudden downpour, unexpected yet refreshing.

I nodded, understanding the weight of his words. We were both piecing together fractured lives, each fragment reflecting a struggle that felt insurmountable at times. But in this moment, standing together with the setting sun framing our uncertainty, I couldn't help but feel a glimmer of hope. Maybe our messes could intertwine, creating a new tapestry rich with our shared experiences.

As darkness began to blanket the landscape, a delicate hush settled over the lake, broken only by the soft lapping of waves against the shore. I could see the stars peeking through the veil of night, twinkling like distant dreams just out of reach. In that quiet moment, it struck me that our journey didn't have to be perfect; it just needed to be real.

"Let's take it slow," I finally said, the words escaping my lips like a sigh of relief. "Let's figure this out together." Ethan's face softened, and I could see a flicker of relief in his eyes, as if he had been holding his breath, waiting for this very moment.

"Together," he echoed, and in that simple agreement, I felt the beginnings of something beautiful take root within me—a fragile yet vibrant possibility, blooming in the fertile soil of our uncertainty.

With the first stars beginning to illuminate the night sky, I took a deep breath, letting the cool air fill my lungs and carry away the weight of doubt. Standing by the water's edge, with Ethan by my side, I felt a renewed sense of clarity and purpose. Whatever lay ahead, we would face it together, navigating the tumultuous waters of our lives hand in hand, embracing the messy, beautiful aftermath of our shared connection.

The first evening stars twinkled overhead, scattered like shards of glass across a deepening blue canvas. As Ethan and I stood there, the warmth of the summer night enveloped us like a familiar blanket, a stark contrast to the electrifying uncertainty that crackled between us. I could feel my pulse in my throat, a rhythmic reminder of how fragile and exhilarating this moment was, caught somewhere between hope and hesitation.

"Let's go for a walk," Ethan suggested, breaking the stillness. The proposal hung in the air, inviting yet fraught with unspoken tension.

I nodded, my heart racing at the thought of moving away from the safety of the shoreline, toward the unknown, where the darkness might reveal hidden truths. The path wound along the lake's edge, flanked by towering oak trees, their leaves whispering secrets I was yet to understand.

With each step, my mind raced, grappling with thoughts that tangled together like the roots of the trees. What did I want? A relationship felt like an enticing risk, a dance on the edge of a precipice, where one misstep could plunge us into a void of uncertainty. Yet the thrill of his presence ignited something within me, a spark that could either fizzle out into disappointment or ignite into a wildfire of passion.

Ethan walked beside me, his hands tucked into his pockets, shoulders slightly hunched as if the weight of his thoughts mirrored my own. I caught glimpses of his profile illuminated by the moonlight—strong jawline, furrowed brow, and the slight tension in his lips that hinted at his own inner conflict. I wanted to reach out, to reassure him that we were in this together, but instead, I remained quiet, each moment stretching between us like the miles of shoreline that lay ahead.

The air grew cooler, and I shivered, half from the drop in temperature and half from the electricity that still sparked in the aftermath of our kiss. Ethan turned to me, his gaze steady and searching. "You okay?" he asked, concern lacing his voice. I offered a small smile, hoping to mask the whirlwind inside me. "Yeah, just a little chilly."

He shrugged off his jacket, draping it over my shoulders with a casual ease that felt intimate, even sacred. The fabric smelled of his cologne, a blend of cedar and citrus, comforting yet invigorating. It felt like an embrace, a silent promise that whatever lay ahead, we wouldn't face it alone.

As we walked, the sound of water lapping against the shore provided a soothing backdrop, each wave a reminder of the ebb and flow of life—its rhythms unpredictable yet somehow reassuring. "I used to come here as a kid," Ethan shared, his voice breaking the spell of silence. "My parents would take me to watch the sunset, and I'd always pretend the clouds were made of candyfloss. I'd dream about what it would be like to float up there and just let go."

I chuckled softly, picturing a younger Ethan, wild-eyed and carefree, clutching a sticky cone of spun sugar. "Did you ever float away?" I teased, a playful lilt to my tone.

He laughed, the sound rich and genuine, breaking through the tension that had wrapped around us like ivy. "Not quite, but it felt good to imagine." There was a softness to his expression, a hint of nostalgia that made my heart swell.

In that moment, I realized how deeply I wanted to explore this connection, this burgeoning bond that had formed from our shared moments and whispered confessions. The path wound closer to the water, and as we reached the edge, I watched the moonlight dance upon the surface, casting silver ripples that seemed to mirror the fluttering of my heart.

"What about you?" he asked, his curiosity piquing. "What did you dream about as a kid?"

I hesitated, the question settling into the quiet corners of my mind. "I used to dream about being a writer," I admitted, the words spilling out like an unexpected confession. "I'd craft stories in my head, weaving worlds where anything was possible. But I never really thought I could make it happen."

"Why not?" Ethan's inquiry was gentle, his gaze steady.

"Fear, I guess," I replied, a wry smile playing at the corners of my lips. "Fear of failure, fear of judgment. It's easier to hide behind the safety of daydreams than to put yourself out there."

His eyes sparkled in the moonlight, a mixture of admiration and understanding. "You should never be afraid to share your stories. They're what make you, you."

The sincerity of his words wrapped around me like a soft embrace, stirring something deep within. "You really believe that?" I asked, a hint of vulnerability creeping into my voice.

"Absolutely," he affirmed, taking a step closer. "Everyone has a story worth telling. Yours is just waiting to be written."

I searched his eyes, looking for the truth behind his words. In that moment, I felt a shift within me, as if the weight of my insecurities began to lift, replaced by the warmth of possibility. Maybe this journey with Ethan wasn't just about navigating the tumultuous waters of our emotions; perhaps it was about discovering our own stories, together.

The air grew thick with anticipation as he leaned closer, the unspoken words hanging between us, pulsing with an energy I could feel in my bones. I felt the urge to close the distance, to bridge the gap between our fears and hopes with a simple act—a touch, a glance, a promise. And just as I was about to lean in, a commotion erupted from further down the path, a group of people laughing and shouting, their energy puncturing the bubble of intimacy we had created.

I stepped back instinctively, my cheeks flushing with embarrassment as reality came crashing back. Ethan chuckled softly, the moment broken but not lost. "Looks like we're not the only ones enjoying the night," he remarked, a playful twinkle in his eye.

As the laughter echoed around us, I realized that this was part of our story, too—unexpected interruptions and spontaneous moments woven together, creating a tapestry rich with experience. It was messy and beautiful, a reflection of life itself.

"Maybe we should join them," I suggested, a playful smile breaking through the remnants of tension.

"Are you sure?" he asked, his tone teasing yet genuine.

"Why not? Let's see what adventures await us."

With a shared laugh, we turned toward the noise, leaving the moonlit shoreline behind for a night filled with laughter and uncertainty, both exhilarating and terrifying. Together, we ventured into the heart of the evening, ready to embrace whatever twists and turns our paths would take.

The laughter and chatter of the group up ahead drew us in like moths to a flame, illuminating the otherwise serene backdrop of the lake. A small bonfire flickered, casting dancing shadows against the nearby trees. The warmth radiated not just from the flames but from the carefree spirits gathered around, their faces glowing in the orange light. As we approached, the air filled with the delicious aroma of roasting marshmallows and the unmistakable sound of someone strumming a guitar, its chords weaving through the night like an enchanting spell.

Ethan took my hand, the gesture both casual and electric, grounding me in the moment. His grip was firm, steady, offering reassurance amid the flurry of emotions that still swirled in my chest. We slipped into the circle of laughter, and I felt the weight of our earlier conversation fade, replaced by the infectious energy of youth and spontaneity. Faces turned toward us, smiles widening as we entered the sphere of camaraderie.

"Hey, you two! Join us!" a girl with vibrant blue hair called out, her laughter a melodic chime. I recognized her from college—Lila, a friend from the drama club whose antics were legendary. She waved us over, her infectious energy brightening the space. "We were just talking about the worst pickup lines we've ever heard. Got any good ones?"

Ethan laughed, a rich sound that filled the air, and for a moment, the remnants of our kiss hung forgotten in the background. I glanced at him, his eyes sparkling with mischief, and a sense of ease settled over me. This was how life was meant to be—full of spontaneity, laughter, and lightness.

"Well, how about the classic: 'Do you have a map? Because I just got lost in your eyes,'" he quipped, his voice dripping with playful sincerity.

Lila burst into laughter, and the group followed suit, their amusement reverberating through the night. I chuckled, the sound bubbling up from somewhere deep within me, the warmth of the fire casting a golden glow on the faces around us.

"I think I heard one that topped that," I chimed in, letting my competitive spirit rise to the surface. "How about, 'Are you a magician? Because whenever I look at you, everyone else disappears.'"

Ethan raised an eyebrow, his lips curling into a grin. "Not bad! You've got some skills," he replied, a teasing lilt to his voice.

The banter continued, each line more outrageous than the last, the atmosphere thickening with the intoxicating blend of laughter and shared stories. I watched as Ethan leaned back against a tree, his gaze flickering between the group and me, and I couldn't help but notice the ease with which he slipped into this environment. It was as if he was a jigsaw piece that had finally found its place, completing a picture I hadn't realized was incomplete until now.

As the night wore on, we shared our own stories—funny mishaps from college and wild adventures that had spun out of control. I spoke of the time I'd accidentally signed up for an advanced tango class instead of the beginner session, my feet moving in a frantic dance of embarrassment as I tried to keep up with the seasoned dancers. The group roared with laughter, and in that moment, I felt a wave of belonging wash over me, enveloping me like a warm hug.

In the midst of this vibrant exchange, I caught Ethan's eye, and the world around us faded into a soft blur. The laughter dimmed, the fire crackled, and time seemed to stretch as our unspoken connection hung heavily in the air. I could see a reflection of my own thoughts mirrored in his gaze, a recognition of the complexity we both carried. Yet, in this moment, it felt light, almost free, as if the chaos of the world beyond this circle had faded into a distant memory.

"Hey, how about we take this party to the beach?" Lila suggested suddenly, her eyes alight with mischief. "I hear the water is still warm enough for a midnight swim!"

A collective cheer erupted, and I felt a rush of excitement mixed with apprehension. The idea of plunging into the cool lake under a sky full of stars was undeniably tempting, yet a shiver of doubt danced along my spine. I looked over at Ethan, his expression a mixture of enthusiasm and a hint of caution.

"Are you in?" he asked, his voice low, inviting.

I took a breath, the exhilaration of the night urging me forward. "Let's do it," I said, surprising even myself with my conviction. The thrill of the moment overshadowed the fear, igniting a spark of spontaneity I hadn't indulged in for far too long.

We moved as a group, laughter echoing in the still night air as we dashed towards the beach, our footsteps soft against the sand. The moonlight danced on the water, illuminating the ripples that shimmered like diamonds scattered across a velvet cloth. The sensation of cool sand beneath my feet was exhilarating, and the sound of waves crashing against the shore infused my spirit with a sense of adventure.

With shouts and splashes, we bounded into the water, the initial shock of the cold water jolting through me, followed by laughter that erupted like fireworks. The world around us blurred; it was just us—young, reckless, and alive. Ethan splashed water in my direction, his playful grin infectious, and I retaliated with a shriek of laughter, the sound mingling with the chorus of our friends.

As I floated on my back, gazing up at the vast expanse of stars, I felt the weight of the world lift. Each star was a reminder of the countless possibilities that lay ahead, waiting to be explored. Ethan drifted beside me, the water cradling us both as we shared comfortable silence, the only sounds the gentle lapping of the waves and the occasional laughter from our friends.

"Isn't this incredible?" he asked, his voice a soft whisper above the water's embrace.

I turned my head slightly, catching the moonlight reflecting in his eyes. "It really is," I replied, my heart swelling with warmth. "It's perfect."

In that moment, I realized this was more than just a night of fun; it was a pivotal moment in our journey—a crossroads that beckoned us to dive deeper into the unknown.

"Can I tell you something?" Ethan's voice broke through the serenity, a hint of seriousness coloring his tone. I turned to him, curious and slightly apprehensive. "I know we're both navigating through a lot right now, but I really like being here with you. Like, really like it."

The vulnerability in his admission struck a chord within me, echoing the feelings I had been wrestling with since our kiss. "I feel the same," I confessed, my heart racing as I let the truth spill forth. "This—whatever this is—feels different, special."

He smiled, and in that smile, I saw a glimpse of the future—a tapestry woven from threads of laughter, shared dreams, and the uncharted territory we were eager to explore together.

As we floated in that calm embrace, surrounded by the symphony of laughter and the serenity of the lake, I understood that this was just the beginning. The waters of our lives would ebb and flow, but we were ready to navigate the currents, hand in hand, creating our own story in the light of the stars.

Milton Keynes UK
Ingram Content Group UK Ltd.
UKHW040257181024
449757UK00001B/92